Cover design by: GetCovers
Edited by: Melody Tyden

To The Love of My Life
Thank you for putting up with me
and for the cups of tea
Love you all the world

THE ALPHA'S HEIR

EMMA LEE-JOHNSON

CHAPTER ONE

Trials

*** Eva ***

It has been six weeks since I confirmed my husband was dead.

Six weeks of bliss with my fated mate and our little girl, living in the Packhouse of The Onyx River Pack, getting to know my new family and spending night after night wrapped in the strong embrace of the love of my life, Alpha Aiden Goldrick.

Then, this morning, Aiden gets called away because of a security breach at the border of his land and I concentrate on getting Summer ready for preschool so I can continue with my Luna training. However, my day is soon soured in an epic way.

My mother is the security breach. Although I told her I didn't want to speak to her or see her, she insists on forcing her presence on me anyway.

"You can't avoid me forever, Eva. I have nowhere else to go," she tells me in a calm fashion which is completely at odds with the hurt, humiliation and fury I feel towards her. My mother, my only parent growing up, betrayed me in a way no mother should ever betray her daughter.

"I just don't understand why this is my problem, Ms Duval. You made your bed- with my husband, might I add- so go lay on it."

My mother scowls at my retort. "Look, Eva, that was a long time ago. He's dead now and it's all over with."

I turn to Beta Preston as I stand to leave. "Ensure she is escorted off our land, please, Beta Preston." When I turn back to my mother, my voice is full of malice. "If you return here, I will have them kill you. Do you understand? I hate you for what you did, and I always will."

All our warriors bow in respect to me, but my mother refuses to back down. "Eva, please. Where will I go?"

My heart feels like she is pounding it with a hammer. Every single time something happens, she reverts to being a pained little girl and I am left to pick up the pieces, but not this time. This time there is no going back.

"You should have thought of that before. Did you ever think about what you were doing to me?" Of course she didn't, that would require her to not act like a victim, and that is a role Rose covets.

I leave the room before the tears burn my eyes. My own mother betrayed me, and I'm left desperate to know why? Why did she think so little of me that she would treat me so callously?

I could never ever imagine a circumstance where I would hurt my own daughter, Summer, in that way, degrading her and humiliating her and leaving her questioning her own self-worth. No matter how old she gets, I will never ever put my own selfish wants before my daughter's wellbeing. Aiden says it reflects my character; he says I am worth a million of Rose.

"It was hard for me, Eva; I was all alone raising you and Xavier promised to help us, but I should have known better than to trust the leader of a pack of dogs," she screams after me.

"Get rid of her now!" I shout as I flee back to my apartment.

Through my anger and disgust, I cry. I always thought my mother had been distant because of her husband, Claude. Now I know it was guilt and disdain for me. Out of everything that I have been through, this has cut the deepest.

I don't think I can ever forgive her, and I am both proud of myself for sticking to my principles and disgusted in myself for not being able to move past this. I hate what sort of a person that made me. I don't want to be hateful or full of resentment, but that is what has happened.

When I get back to the apartment, I climb onto our bed and cry until Aiden walks in. He doesn't say anything, he just sits next to me and opens his arms to me. After a few minutes, he finally speaks.

"Eva, I've had to put her in the cells. When Preston tried to remove her as you asked, she started ranting about telling the world about werewolves and how she would destroy us all. I think we need to speak to Xavier."

He's referring to my father, the man I hadn't known until a few weeks ago, the man who is desperate to be a part of my life and whose identity as a werewolf finally revealed my own hidden secrets: namely, that I am a werewolf too.

I have seen him on two occasions since the day I ran out on him. The first time, I asked a lot of difficult questions and became overwhelmed. The second visit went a little better and he spent time getting to know me and telling me about himself. I'm not at the stage where I want to publicly accept him or introduce him to Summer or anything, but I am open to getting to know him and seeing where that takes us.

"I will go and talk to her now, Aiden. I am so sorry. I don't want her staying here near me, but I will have to give her money to go away. She says she has nowhere to go." Aiden quickly pulls out cash, but I push his hand away. "No. This is my mess, I will pay her."

Aiden pushes the money back at me. "This is our mess, we will deal with it together. Now take it, there is more if you need it." I kiss him for being sweet and I thank him for supporting me.

"Thank you for loving me, Aidy, I had best go and sort her ladyship out before Preston gets a headache from her whining."

"I'm sorry to rush you, Shortie, but we have to be at the Chambers of Justice in just over an hour."

I forgot about our prior engagement. "Don't worry, I'll be ready."

Today is not about to get any easier.

*** Aiden ***

The past six weeks have been amazing, more than amazing. Eva and Summer living here with me has filled my life with joy. Of course, we have had stumbles in the road, like when I swore in front of Summer and she repeated it. Eva was ready to lynch me for that one. But I love the stumbles as much as the good times because they reinforce how much I would do to make my girl happy.

Eva has a lot to deal with and her mother arriving here unannounced like she is owed something really is salt in Eva's wounds. How did that despicable witch create a beauty like my Eva?

When Eva goes to the cells, I decide to bite the bullet and call Xavier to ask his advice. He is probably the best person to ask, seeing as Rose has been emotionally and financially blackmailing him for a quarter of a century.

Alpha Xavier, Eva's dad, is now my ally, but not so long ago we were heading for war over issues surrounding our mutual border. Some things were not worth fighting over, and if me fighting Xavier over a poxy piece of land would harm Eva, that was one of them.

Luckily for me, Xavier felt the same and so all border disputes are on hold for the time being. The priority is getting to know his daughter.

I dial Xavier's number and he answers within one ring. "Aiden? Is Eva okay?"

I smile at his concern. Although I feel possessive at times because she is mine now, I know his love for Eva is different to mine and she deserves that love too. I explain what is happening and when he growls, I am satisfied he understands.

"That fucking woman! Hasn't she done enough damage? What is the plan? I can come and collect her, she and I are long overdue for a chat about the shit she put my daughter through." I told Xavier everything that Eva had been through. I thought it best he understood her hurt and mistrust, and I hope it will help her in the long run.

I would rather Rose went with Xavier now, so she understands the implications of her threats and the ramifications for herself if she does any of the things she has threatened. Besides, Eva has made it clear she does not want to see her mother right now. Who knows, in time maybe she can forgive her, but right now her mere presence is causing my mate pain and so she must go.

"Yes, that will work. She is currently in my cells, and I have a prior engagement I must attend to, so if you come over later tonight, I will release her into your custody."

With no time to lose, I try to mindlink Eva. She is struggling with certain aspects of being a werewolf since she found out she is one, and mindlinking is something she finds tricky. She still hasn't been able to shift but she was able to mark me when I marked her, thus opening up the mindlink between us. However, Eva struggles to make the connection over a prolonged period or from further afield. She is getting better but it's taking a lot longer than either of us anticipated.

After trying and failing to connect to her, I give up and mindlink Preston instead, who tells me Eva is on her way back up to the apartment.

As I open the door for her, I notice her yawning. Come to think of it, she is tired a lot of late and she is looking a little pale. I hope I haven't been pushing her too far with trying to shift, teaching her self-defence and combat, and Luna training.

Once this hearing is out of the way, I will insist she takes some time out to rest. The last thing I want is her getting sick or feeling overstretched.

"Let me just freshen up and then we will make our way down to the Chambers of Justice for the hearing. I hope this is the end of this today, Aiden." I couldn't agree more but I can't give her any reassurances about that.

Holding her hand, we walk into the Chamber of Justice together and she shudders when she locks eyes with the man on trial.

"All rise. We are called today for the trial of former Gamma, Ellis Devine, who stands accused of the kidnap and deliberate endangerment of the Fated Mate of our Alpha, Aiden Goldrick. How does the defendant plead?"

All eyes return to the young man who stands defiantly in the enclosed dock with two guards and silver chains around his wrists.

"Not guilty."

*** Amber ***

Beta Preston and I have been called as witnesses for the trial of former Gamma Ellis. The trial was completely unnecessary. Both Eva and Aiden agree with the Elders if he makes an apology and accepts a demotion, plus completing a rehabilitation programme to educate him on appropriate behaviour, they would put the whole situation behind them, but Ellis is a stubborn little turd.

He continues to refute all claims that he endangered Eva and caused her harm. He maintains that the evidence of their bond proves he was right to take her for Aiden and that without his actions, they probably wouldn't be together. Aiden had to be physically restrained when he heard that.

Eva says she doesn't want it on her conscience if Ellis lost his throat or if he harmed someone else because he thought his actions were right. She is torn either way.

So here we are, at the Chambers of Justice and I can't help but feel like this is a practice run for my own trial.

"They will call you first, Preston, and once you have given your evidence you can stay in the room," the court clerk informs us.

My mate nods his head before making eye contact with me and through our mind link, he tries to reassure and soothe me.

I have to go back to the packhouse after my evidence, we've had to leave Delta Billy running things and he's already complaining.

His forehead touches mine and I tell him I understand. It should feel strange being this close and affectionate to Preston, but it feels completely natural. Since we finally succumbed to our mate bond and obvious love for each other, things between Preston and I have been amazing and that's even with the other things that blight our happiness.

Such as my own impending trial, for one. I try to block all thoughts of it out of my mind; I cannot think about that right now. I just need to concentrate on giving evidence today.

The shocking evidence we uncovered about my mother and father was also deeply upsetting. In fact, if it hadn't been for Preston, I don't know how I would have coped the past couple of months.

I feel bad that our Mating Ceremony is on hold, but it doesn't feel right to do it with a trial looming over us. I promise Preston we will do it as soon as I am a free she-wolf, and I pray to the Moon Goddess he won't have to wait too much longer.

The clerk calls Preston's name, and he stands and kisses me hard. "I love you; I will see you at home," he tells me before going into the Chambers.

While I wait for my turn, I think about my father and what happened when Aiden and I went to confront him a month ago.

~*~ *Flashback* ~*~

~~~ **One Month Earlier** ~~~

"If we want answers, we must confront him. He knows the truth and knows where she is, and we deserve to know too." The same argument between Aiden and I has been going on for the last couple of weeks. He wants to confront our father, whereas I want more evidence.

Aiden thinks I'm delaying because finding the truth scares me, as does the possibility of our mother rejecting me all over again. Maybe he is right, but I also know former Alpha John

Goldrick will have a cover story in place and so I want more evidence to confront him with.

Once Preston knows as much as we do, he takes us to speak to his father, who was our father's Beta. His behaviour and reaction just makes us all the more suspicious. However, I know he is bound by a loyalty to his former Alpha and without Aiden using his authority as the current Alpha, we can't force him to break his oath.

"Aiden, if we wait, we might find something solid to present to him so he cannot just fob us off." This is weird; it's usually Aiden advising caution to me. When did our roles reverse?

"We have waited over twenty years, Amber... twenty fucking years of thinking she fucked off and never spared us a backwards glance, twenty years of wondering why the fuck we weren't good enough. And he knew, he knew she had no choice and let us hurt like that, Amber... what sort of a sick bastard does a shitty thing like that to his own children?" I know from the amount of swearing he is doing that he is upset and angry and that is another reason why I have tried to delay the inevitable. It will come to blows. The subject is too emotive for them not to.

Maybe I can't stop the fallout that is coming, though, and it's becoming clear that the longer I make Aiden wait to confront our father, the angrier he is getting. He has as much right to answers as I do.

"Have you got a plan at least, Aidy?" He starts to pull off his jacket and gives me a serious stare.

"Of course I do. How about, 'Hey dad, remember us? Your children? Why the fuck did you lie about the reason our mother left us when we were pups?' I think that covers it, don't you, Amber?"

I shake my head and link Preston to tell him where we are going. I turn my back as my brother shifts into his impressive wolf form and wait for him to turn before shifting myself. Lizzie, my wolf, shakes out her fur and stretches before pressing off into a gentle run.

Our father, former Alpha John Goldrick, lives in the remote part of our lands with his chosen mate. For years, we have been anticipating they will be blessed with pups, but they have made no such announcement. It takes us about fifteen minutes to run there and once we arrive, we put on spare clothes kept in a hollowed-out tree trunk.

We walk in companionable silence for the last couple of minutes until our father's cottage comes into view. The chickens and vegetable patch in his garden demonstrate his attempt to be self-sufficient, but the idyllic image is marred by the shouting that comes from the cottage.

Our father's roar has always been loud and intimidating, but the thought of him shouting at his mate like that knocks me sick.

Aiden's eyes glaze over as he mindlinks our father. The front door of the cottage swings open and our father storms out as I try to imagine what Aiden said.

"You might be the Alpha, boy, but I am still your father and you do not show up at another man's house, uninvited and unexpected, and command him to stop shouting at his mate."

Our father looks a lot like Aiden: tall, with dark hair and pale skin. Father's hair is greying at the sides now and Aiden has green eyes like me and our mother, but apart from those differences, they look a lot like one another.

"Did you banish Mother?" Jeez, Aiden just jumps straight in there. In spite of my annoyance at my brother's lack of tact, I face my father and wait for him to answer.

My father's face goes from pale porcelain to beetroot red at lightning speed. "Why don't you ask her?" he snarls back at us.

"We would, but she left us, remember? And we haven't heard anything since we were pups, but we want to know if the rumours are true. Did she leave us or did you banish her?" The words are pouring out of me without restraint, like a dam bursting open. I know he is lying; I know he is trying to come up with another story.

"Amber, sweetheart, you, your brother, her mate, her pack, all of us weren't enough to keep her here. Why are you dragging all this up now? You have your mate, you can have a pup and make your own family, there is no need to be dragging all that stuff up now. Let's just move forward, okay?"

He turns to go back into the cottage when his mate comes to the door. Marissa is a little older than Aiden, maybe closer to 35 years old, and she has been my father's lover for a long time, probably close to fifteen years. They mated officially just after Aiden became Alpha and have lived out here for around six years.

"John, don't you dare run out on me again. We need to talk about this," Marissa shouts to my father. She obviously hasn't seen us yet, through her swollen, bloodshot eyes.

"GET BACK INSIDE NOW!" Father shouts and I cover my ears, just like I used to when I was a little girl. Aiden stands between me and our father.

"As your Alpha, I command you to stand down. Stop shouting and scaring your daughter and your mate." Marissa stops at the gate when she hears Aiden's voice, and I can see her trembling even from a distance. This is what our father does. He shouts and scares us until we relent or forget.

"No, Father. I can't just move forward. I want to know why I wasn't good enough for my mother to stay. I am going to find her and ask her. I am giving you a chance to tell me first, but I will not stop until I know. And if I find that she was banished, I will come and rip your throat out myself."

I walk away and Aiden follows behind me when our father calls out to us.

"I did banish her. I banished her because she took a second mate and chose him over us."

I run from him, refusing to acknowledge his revelation. Would she have visited if she hadn't been banished? Did she think of us? Did she ever write or reach out? Where is she?

~~~ *End of Flashback* ~~~

"Lieutenant Amber Goldrick, it's your turn to give evidence." The court clerk announces.

My legs shake as I stand and I wish I had kept my mind clear while I was waiting. Now, I feel overwhelmed with hurt, longing and sadness when I need to concentrate on what I am about to say.

Chin up. We will get through this, Red. I love you. Preston is mindlinking me as I enter the Chambers, lending me his strength in my time of need, as he always has done. What would I ever do without him?

*** **Salma** ***

I throw the stupid pink-and-white testing wand across the bathroom; my period is late, and I hoped it was because I was pregnant, but after 4 negative pregnancy tests, I think I can rule that out.

"Chula, what's up?" my husband Alejandro calls through the door and I groan in response. I hate letting him down. The overwhelming disappointment corrodes away not just at my hope but at my confidence too. What is wrong with me? Why am I not pregnant yet? "Salma? Please talk to me."

I unlock the bathroom door, but I don't open it. I go back to the other side of the bathroom to retrieve the offending testing wand and when I turn back around, my Ale is there with open arms. I just want to melt into his warm embrace, but I shake my head and show him the test so he knows why I am upset.

"Come here, it's okay, it's going to be okay, bebe. We just get to have a lot more practice, which can't be a bad thing." He winks at me, but I know he is as disappointed as I am.

"I thought this was it, I thought I was." I frown, deep in thought. My body is playing tricks on me, and I am unable to concentrate on anything else. All I want to think about is Ale and I being pregnant and having our own family.

My papa would have called it procrastination, but seeing as he is very much dead and still in my bad books, I don't think that it matters what he would call it. Ale says I am being unreasonable. I shouldn't keep my father in my bad books because he isn't here to defend himself. I therefore told him to shut up or he would get a place right next to my father.

We have moved permanently into Ale's apartment. Traditionally, as head of our Mafia firm, we would take Mami's house and she would stay with us or take a short holiday before moving to a smaller place. However, I am so angry with her and papa that I don't want to be anywhere near their house. It just reminds me that all I thought I had was a lie: there was no adoring, idyllic family. Just lies.

"I have to get dressed. I am due at Paloma Azul in half an hour." Paloma Azul is my nightclub, and the flagship club of our firm.

It is my pride and joy, and when papa started training Ale to take over instead of me, I threw myself into making it the best club around. My hard work paid off. Ale told me after my papa died that he was exceptionally proud of what I had achieved, but the rush of love I felt for my father now feels tainted by the secrets I have discovered since his death.

"I'll come with you; I have a couple of hours before I have to meet with my father."

I try to leave his embrace so I can get dressed, but he pulls me back to him.

"I thought you said we had half an hour?" he questions me as he kisses my neck, causing shivers of want and desire to stream throughout my body.

"Ale! No. I said I have to be there in half an hour!" I tell him in mock outrage, though I would always let him persuade me to be a little late. After all, what is the point of being the boss if you can't be late from time to time?

"So that's ten minutes to drive there, five minutes to get dressed and then fifteen minutes left to practise." I laugh as he picks me up and carries me back to our bed.

"You really think you can last fifteen minutes?" I tease him as he discards my silk nightdress and panties.

"When my wife is as beautiful and talented as you, no!" He trails his hand down from my shoulder and across my left breast and erect nipple, continually moving further to my belly button. He lingers over my tummy before slipping his hand lower again until his fingertips connect with my wet slit, which is already warm and damp with longing.

"I love you, Sal. I will love you until the end of time." He sinks two fingers into me, filling and stretching me, moving slowly and deliberately, touching places only he can reach. "You feel so good bebe, I bet you taste good too."

We will never be out of here in fifteen minutes. And right now, with Ale at my command, at my service, I don't really care what is going on outside of these four walls. All that matters is me, him and him fucking me with his fingers and his tongue.

Ale moves down my body and nestles between my open thighs, and in between fingering me, he darts his tongue over my folds and connects with my clit, extracting a sigh of contentment from me. When he adds his lips too, gently tugging and sucking on my most sensitive part, I moan in satisfaction. My Ale knows exactly what I want and what I like. He knows how to touch me to bring me to orgasm over and over and over again.

My body and mind edge closer to fulfilment, climbing higher and higher to oblivion. I crave the feeling of Ale inside me, his thick, hard cock splitting me wide open.

"I want you, Ale, I want you to screw me hard and slow. Please, Ale!" He shifts his weight and covers my body with his, and I can feel his hard cock pressed against my stomach, pinning me to the bed.

I wrap my legs around him, pulling him to me. "Now, I need you now, Ale! I just want you." I come as he finally pushes into me roughly, giving me exactly what I crave.

The tears that fall afterwards take me by surprise. Once they start, I can't seem to stop them. I am not pregnant, my papa was screwing around, he has a son who could challenge me for our firm, and he would have every right to. He had a secret mistress that my mother knew all about and I thought they had the perfect marriage. My life is a fucking mess.

Except for my marriage.

If nothing else, my union with Ale is the one true thing that has given my life meaning. It's the only thing I can depend on, he is the only one I can trust and sincerely know will have my back.

"Hey, come on mi amor, I'm not that bad at getting you off, am I?" Ale jokes soothingly as he holds me tight and keeps me safe.

"I'm sorry, Ale, everything just built up. I feel better now." I try to sit up, but he pulls me back to him. He strokes along my back as I lean against his sculpted body, and the stirrings of desire are already starting again.

"Don't run off, I want to talk about this. We know the first name of your papa's mistress. I think if we contact her and search for the name of her son, we could make contact within a few days." Listening to his wise words, I know he has my best interests at heart. "Then you can see for yourself if this man wants to challenge for his share of the firm and you can also decide if you want to have a relationship with him too."

I know he is right, but I fear reaching out to someone who could both enhance my life and destroy it.

"Ale, I need to find who poisoned my papa. I need to know why… I need to know if he knew what was coming. Looking back, it seems like he knew." He nods at me.

"Sal: about us trying for a baby. I want this as much as you, but I hate seeing you so upset about it. Do you still want this?"

It shocks me that he is even asking.

I look deep into his dark brown eyes and tell him the truth: "Alejandro, I have never wanted anything as much as I want this."

He smiles at me, that cheeky smile that makes me forget everything else.

"Right, get dressed then, you lazy mare, we have a club to

run, and we can't be lying in bed all day frolicking." He teases through his smirk. I smack him with a pillow as I jump up to get dressed and he playfully spanks me on my ass when I walk away.

When we arrive at Paloma Azul, there is a package waiting for me in my office. Ale goes to lift it so he can pass it to me, but I stop him in his tracks.

"Stop! We don't know who it is from, it could be a bomb for all we know."

His eyes widen with that realisation and he puts his hands up in the air.

"Chula, I wasn't even thinking but you're right, I'll have the Fernando twins to check it first." I give him my thanks while I check the CCTV recordings to see what they caught, but there isn't a lot to go on.

After a couple of hours, once Ale's associates check the box and give it the all-clear, I am finally able to open it.

It is full of photographs, ones of me as a child, my mother and father happy together, us all as a family. Then there are a few recent ones of Ale and me. The final one has red ink all over it, making it look like I have blood pouring from my eyes and neck. There is a single red circle in between Ale's eyes.

"What the fuck? Salma, these are outside our apartment, how the fuck did they get that close without us seeing them?" Ale starts to lose his composure, which is very rare for him.

I am not thinking about how close they got. My thoughts race with who they are and what the hell they want?

"Sal, we are going to have to move out for a while. We can go and stay with my parents. I think we need to locate this Dominga, and get a definite ID on your brother. This feels like a warning from him, a threat directly from him."

"If it is him, Ale, then this makes my life a whole lot easier. He is either on our side or he is our enemy…" I lift up the box. "…and if he is responsible for this, then he is most definitely our enemy. If he is responsible for this threat, brother or not, I will fucking kill him."

I go to my desk and take a box of ammunition from my drawer. I take one bullet and scratch onto it:

'Bastard Son Of J. Morales.'

CHAPTER TWO

Stranger

*** Preston ***

I walk into the Chamber and immediately see my Alpha and his mate sitting at the back. He gives me an encouraging nod and I wish I had thought of asking him to keep Amber company. I worry about her being alone with her thoughts, especially while waiting to give her evidence. She must be feeling so nervous.

After being called to the stand, I swear to give the truth on the Sacred Scriptures of the Moon Goddess, and then I give my account of the event.

Halfway through delivering my evidence, I notice Former Gamma Ellis shaking his head at me with a sneer splashed across his face, so I pause and address the panel.

"From the look on Former Gamma Ellis' face I would say he has an objection to something I have said, so I am going to pause while you question him about it."

I sit back and listen to what Ellis has taken exception to.

"He says that the human was injured but if she hadn't struggled, she wouldn't have bumped her head and the only reason I gagged her and chained her to the metal bars was because she was making a racket and trying to escape."

A growl escapes the Alpha and only his mate can calm him. I raise my eyebrows at Ellis, hoping he is starting to realise how much of an idiot he has been.

I provide the rest of my statement and answer the questions the panel has for me. Their last question puzzles me, and I really don't like its insinuation.

"Beta Preston, both you and Alpha Aiden objected to the appointment of Former Gamma Ellis in the first instance. Why is that?"

"We honestly thought the Elders were being overly sentimental in appointing him. His father had been the pack Gamma Wolf and died while still in that position. Ellis is a young wolf; I had no doubt about his ability to become a worthy and able Gamma in the future, when the pack was blessed with a Luna. However, at that moment in time, he was immature, undisciplined, and ill-prepared for the pressure and authority his position bestowed on him. For me, this was an accident waiting to happen and his actions only prove that we were right to have reservations."

As I am dismissed from the Chambers, Amber's pain and anxiety fill my chest, so I link her to reassure her before I leave, and her warm love flows through me as she thanks me. I love her so much and I cannot wait for her to get home tonight.

A great feeling of foreboding comes over me when I leave the Chamber to head back to the pack house. Though I take a look around, I don't see anything untoward, and in my distracted state, I almost knock over a woman who is standing nearby.

"I am so sorry, Miss. I didn't see you there." I apologise to her as my face turns crimson in embarrassment. I don't recognise her. She is medium-height, blonde and plain and probably a similar age to me.

"That's okay, Beta Preston. I was meaning to talk to you." She holds out a hand for me to shake and my hackles stand on end.

"Who are you? What pack are you from?" Our borders are closed and trespassers from certain packs face the death penalty. This woman has no right to be here and I mean to find out what she wants.

"My name is Nikki. Tell me, how is Amber coping with having to give evidence in the trial? She must be feeling the strain with her own trial being so close?" She raises her over-plucked eyebrows and Zack wants to take control. He begins pacing and growling in my head and I find it a tad distracting.

Stop it, Zack, I command in frustration.

"Why are you here?" I ask her. I don't know who she is, where she has come from or what she wants, but I want answers.

"I need to talk to you, Beta Preston. You see, I have the power to make Amber's court case disappear. It all depends on what you are willing to do to secure that."

I look at her in confusion. Who is she? How can she help Amber? Why does she want to help?

"How? And why would you do it?" I cannot help asking. I would do anything for the case to be dropped so Amber didn't have to worry about it anymore. The thought of my mate being sent to prison or being sentenced to death fills me with a hopelessness that nothing can shift. I want to help Amber.

"I can make certain evidence disappear so there will be nothing to pin her to the crime she is guilty of." There is something in that last sentence that creeps me out.

"Stop talking in riddles, woman, and spit out what it is you want." She starts to laugh, biting her bottom lip in a vain attempt to stop.

"Aiden, he's a boy. I would feel guilty for the rest of my life if I didn't try to reason with him to get him to understand why his actions affected me. They are going to sentence him to death and I do not want that on my conscience. Please, Alpha. Please let me talk to him."

She only has to look at me and call me Alpha and I crumble. "Okay, okay! But I will be with you. I do not want him to hurt you anymore than he already has, Eva." Goddess be damned, she is shaking her head at me.

"No, Aiden. He won't talk freely with you there. I need to do this alone." I let out a growl of frustration, I don't like this one bit.

"Compromise with me, Shortie. How about we meet halfway? I will wait outside with the door open so I can come to you fast if he starts anything." She contemplates her decision and reluctantly agrees.

I leave to arrange the meeting for her and return to find her and Amber whispering to each other. The relationship these two have built makes me so happy.

"Eva, we can go and talk to him now." My sister shakes her head incredulously and part of me agrees with her. Ellis had his chance and he blew it.

I hold her hand until we get to his holding cell, and I kiss her hands and tell her I will be right outside. She needs only to raise her voice or mindlink me. Roman howls and snaps unhappily. He doesn't think this is a good idea since he can't protect our mate from outside the room, but I need to let her do this for her own peace of mind.

As she walks into the room with the man who brought her harm, my heart rate accelerates and I know I will not know a moment's peace until I see her safe again.

*** **Eva** ***

Shock washes over Ellis' face as I walk into his room. I only realised how young he is when I saw him sitting in the Chambers.

In my mind, I have been so afraid of him and of what his actions have snowballed into, that he has become an almighty rabid werewolf, something sinister and cruel and evil.

However, now that he's in front of me, I can see he is just a young man who made a stupid mistake. A young man who needs a firm hand and more guidance.

I continue to look over at him, noticing how young and vulnerable he looks, and yes, I'll admit: my mothering instincts kick in. The situation remains the same as I have been too cowardly to confront him.

Until now.

Yes, he has been stupid and reckless, and he deserves punishment. However, for a young wolf like him, isn't losing his prominent position within his pack, in such a public way, enough punishment?

"Luna, you shouldn't be here, the Alpha won't like it," he tells me in rising agitation, anxiety evidently building within him.

"The Alpha knows I'm here, I asked to speak to you. Our Alpha is waiting just outside."

His eyes widen with concern, but he sits back down and offers me the other chair.

"I should have come and spoken to you sooner, Ellis, but I was afraid." He lifts his head so his eyes meet mine and I offer a small smile. The haunted look in his eyes tugs at my heart.

"I never wanted you to be afraid, Luna. I just wanted to give you to the Alpha so they could see I was worthy of my father's position." For a moment, I let that sentence sit between us.

"Ellis, I am a person, I am not something to own and to give. Surely you can see that now?" A light blush covers his cheeks, and he lowers his head. His light hair flops forward, making me think he needs a haircut. "You can't treat others like that, Ellis. How would you like it if I gave you to a stranger?"

He mumbles something inaudible, causing my temper to flare. This boy needs a firm hand.

"Do not mumble. If you are going to talk to me, look at me and speak up so I can hear you."

"I wouldn't like it. I am sorry, Luna. I didn't mean to hurt you, or your little girl."

Happy with his apology, I nod in acceptance.

"Thank you. I know you didn't mean to hurt me, Ellis. I just needed you to acknowledge that you did. That's how we know you have learned from this and can be assured that you will never do anything like this again. I don't want you to go to prison or lose your throat, but your Alpha cannot allow his wolves to run around acting as they please with no repercussions. What you did was stupid, Ellis, and as a Gamma wolf, you should have known better."

"Yes, Luna. I see that now. I was trying so hard to prove to Alpha Aiden and Beta Preston that I was ready to take on my father's job, but I can see now that they were right. I wasn't ready, I was too young and foolish. My father would be ashamed of me. I know my mother is." His shoulders slump as he takes his head into his hands.

His regret is evident now he understands why it was wrong to act the way he did. He looks like a lost little boy, not a defiant thug or a monstrous wolf I need to fear. Just a boy who made a stupid mistake. I cannot live knowing his imprisonment or loss of life is down to me.

"Change your plea. Stop this now, Ellis, accept responsibility and agree to complete the course and I will speak on your behalf. I will plead for leniency." I hope I am getting through to him. There is very little else I can do to convince him to do the right thing, not just for me and the pack, but for himself too.

"Your Luna has shown you bravery, compassion and understanding, Ellis. At least acknowledge what she is saying to you." I snap my head to the door to where Aiden stands. The light glowing around him makes him look like a god. His legs braced apart, his muscular and strong arms tensed but hanging by his side and his alluring green eyes full of determination. He doesn't look at me but at Ellis.

"Yes, Alpha, sorry, Alpha," Ellis responds immediately. "Luna, I think it may be too late, we are halfway through the trial."

Feeling panicky, I look desperately at my mate. Surely, he can do something? He is the Alpha of this pack after all. "This is what you want, Shortie? Will this make you happy?" Aiden asks me seriously.

I nod at him. "Yes, that is what I want. I am ready to put all this behind us and move on to the future, to our future, Aiden."

"Ellis, my recommendation to the board will be for you to be stripped of your position and for you to attend a compulsory rehabilitation course, on the basis that you change your plea to guilty, that you make a full public apology to your Luna and accept full responsibility for your actions. Do we have an agreement?" Ellis stands to take his Alpha's hand.

"Yes Alpha, I agree, I agree with your terms." They shake hands and Aiden turns to address me.

"Come on Shortie, we have a panel to persuade." He takes my hand and kisses it before pulling me from the room.

"Luna Eva. Thank you, thank you for trying to help me, and again, I am really sorry that I hurt you."

Having faced my fears, I feel better in myself. I just hope it is isnt too late to stop the trial now.

"Sweetheart, I am so proud of the way you handled that. You are becoming a great Luna to our pack." My face heats up at Aiden's compliment. The worry I had that he might see me as weak or over-sentimental for wanting to help Ellis has been needless, he has been nothing but understanding.

"I feel better for having talked it through with him. In fact, if you have a little time later, I'd like to try and shift again." He pushes me up against the wall, taking me by surprise. Desire ripples throughout my body for my mate and Lina purrs in delighted contentment when he kisses me hard, mating his tongue with mine. His hard body presses against mine and my blood burns as if it is on fire as it pumps through my veins, making me feel feverish with yearning for him.

"To be continued, my Luna. We have a mission to complete first,but goddess be damned, you get sexier and sexier by the minute." I laugh as I jog away from him and his teasing.

Aiden tells the panel he needs to speak to them, and I am so glad he is on my side and taking charge once again.

"Alpha Aiden, the panel is about to resume and complete the trial, can this wait?" Aiden shakes his head at them, and I admire his nerve and his tenacity. He is the ultimate leader.

Pride bubbles up in my tummy as he takes control. I still cannot believe he is all mine.

"It would please me and your Luna if you would hear us out. We do not wish to proceed with the trial. Former Gamma Ellis has agreed to change his plea, make a formal public apology and attend the rehabilitation course. He will, of course, be stripped of his status too."

The panel members all start to mutter between themselves but Aiden doesn't stop.

"There is no need to continue with the trial. However, if he steps out of line again, he is all yours."

The panel looks flustered as they ask for a few minutes' privacy so they may discuss the best course of action. Aiden scowls at them but I pull him from the Chamber and out into the lobby to await their decision.

If you shift, will you finally agree to a Mating Ceremony Eva? He is asking through mindlink because he doesn't want others to overhear. I love this man, I love him like I have never loved another man ever before… but a Mating Ceremony sounds very similar to a wedding and my last marriage still leaves a disgusting taste in my mouth.

One thing at a time, Alpha, one thing at a time.

*** **Xavier** ***

My son is still in my dungeon, but if I want my mate to forgive me, I will have to release him soon. She is still frosty towards me because of my secret child, but is more forgiving now she knows the child was conceived before we were mates.

I love my Lydia; she is a beautiful and strong woman, but forgiveness has never been a strong point of hers. I had always admired that trait in her until I was the one in need of forgiveness.

However, I am determined to learn my lesson from the mistakes I made with my daughter. I want Lydia to forgive and trust me and I therefore need to show her that I regret how I acted. So, as much as I want Lydia to forgive me, I need to do what is right, not what I want for my own means.

Junior is in shit up to his eyeballs this time and I still don't know the full extent of his involvement in the Mafia's business. All I know is he is involved enough that we are all in danger now. The Mafia always exact their revenge and Junior is a fool to think he could mess with them and not be in danger.

The boy is sheer arrogance personified. He told me that the Mafia would never know about his involvement because he and the woman he helped are in love. He is twenty-five years old and he still runs around like a hapless teenager, but this time, it's gone too far. This time he is in over his head, and he is bringing the rest of us down with him.

I march downstairs into the dungeons to where he is being housed. I can hear tapping coming from his holding cell and when I approach, he looks at me in feigned shock.

"Surely, Alpha Xavier Woodward hasn't come down into the dungeons to see his only legitimately born son! Well, I am honoured to finally be graced with your presence, father, and to what do I owe this pleasure?"

He clasps his hands together in mock glee and I want to turn right around and walk away from him. I want to wipe my hands clean of him and his sarcastic attitude.

"You haven't given a shit about me since you found that stupid bitch. You haven't bothered to check on me or see me. SIX FUCKING WEEKS YOU'VE LEFT ME TO ROT DOWN HERE."

"And I will leave you another six fucking weeks if you carry on acting like you are. Don't forget, son… I am your Alpha, and you will respect that." He sneers at me at first, but then it develops into a laugh, an unsettling laugh that curdles the contents of my stomach.

"Listen to me, old man. You are the one who has kept me in a cell because you are afraid of me. I ensured the most powerful don in this country was poisoned to death. ME! You carry on, old man, and I'll fucking poison you too and that fucking whore who thinks she is worthy of calling herself my sister."

A red mist descends on me. He might be my son, but he will not speak about my little girl like that. "I will rip your sorry pathetic body to pieces if you ever, ever speak about her like that again. She is my daughter, your sister. She is my Heir, not you."

My wolf, Ace, tries to take control, but Junior has already submitted. He cowers on the floor, trembling, and I step back from the bars.

"Don't ever forget who is in charge around here, son. I love you but if you continue to put the pack at risk and openly disrespect me, I will take your fucking throat myself."

Before I say or do something I will regret, I walk away from my son

*** **Alejandro** ***

After leaving Sal at Paloma Azul, I go to my father's office to meet him and my older brother Matteo to discuss Jose's death. I have a feeling my father will know about Jose's mistress, and I intend on pressing him for as much information as I can.

Laughter carries out from the office into the lobby and everything seems jovial, and I don't have to wait long to find out why. They both turn as I stride over, and my father greets me with the happy news.

"Ale, there you are! Matteo has some great news: Elena is pregnant, the family is growing again!" Instinctively, I plaster a massive smile on my face. I'm happy for my brother and his wife, but it's fresh off the back of the disappointment me and Sal suffered this morning.

For Salma's sake, I put a brave face on but I am full of disappointment that we aren't expecting yet. I spend my time reassuring Sal that it will happen and that it takes time, but deep down, I worry it's not going to happen for us. How can I say that to her? I need to be strong for her, and she needs something to focus on, a distraction to keep her positive. A part of being a man in the Mafia is being strong, and right now I need to suck it up, if not for myself, then for Sal.

"Congratulations, brother, I didn't know you were trying for a baby, but this is wonderful news… we should celebrate!" Although I try to keep my voice upbeat, I sound false even to my own ears.

"We weren't trying, Elena is livid," he tells me through his laughter. "She has cried non-stop about her figure being ruined and having to cancel our holiday. What can I say? I have super sperm."

My father claps him on the back as he laughs. "The Suarez family keeps growing, Lucia told your Mami she wants another baby soon too." Fuck, there is no escaping it, my siblings are spitting babies out left, right and centre and I want in on the action.

"When is the baby due, Matteo?"
He looks at me, baffled by my question. "I haven't a clue, Ale, you ask the weirdest questions!"

Inside I am screaming but I laugh with them, wanting to change the subject.

"Well, congratulations, I'm really happy for you. However, I am sorry, but I have to be a party pooper because I need to talk to you both. This was left at Paloma Azul a few hours ago." I place the box with the photographs on the table in front of my father. His face quickly changes from laughter to anger as he looks through them.

"Alejandro, this is your home. How did they get so close? Who the fuck is threatening us?" My father is up out of his chair and in an obvious rage. My brother takes the box and looks through it too.

"What does this mean, Papa? Who would want to harm Alejandro and Salma? Is this linked to what happened to Jose?" Matteo asked, but my father shakes his head.

"Salma thinks it's linked to her father's death. She believes her father's mistress might know something... or even Jose's bastard son."

It is evident from the looks on their faces who knows something and who doesn't.

"And from the look on your face, Papa, I can tell you know about this, don't you? You know why Jose wanted me to marry Salma and lead the firm and it wasn't just because she's a woman. He has a son that could challenge us, doesn't he? Jose's bastard son has a better claim to this firm than Sal and I do." My own indignation is growing. Why didn't they tell me in full so I knew what I would be getting into? Salma is at risk!

"We worried you wouldn't want to do it if you knew about the threat. Look, Jose loves his son, but he is illegitimate. Sal has trained for this her whole life. She was the right person and with you by her side, we didn't think anyone would pose much of an argument."

He pauses to take a sip of his water before continuing.

"Dominga has obviously not taken this as well as we thought she would. We can't rule her out of being responsible for poisoning Jose. I'm sure Jose would have mentioned that he wanted Salma to marry someone influential and Dominga would be an idiot to not realise why." My father trails off, deep in thought.

"So, what do we do? I do not want my Sal anywhere near the apartment, or Paloma Azul if I can help it. I will fucking murder anyone who hurts her."

Matteo and my father stand over me trying to calm me down. "Ale, Ale! Stop, Salma is family now. We will not let anyone harm her. You will both have to move in with your Mami and I. Salma will have to appoint a manager at the club until we can establish who dropped this box off and if there is still a threat."

My brother smiles at me, and I wonder why. "Little brother, I can see now that you love her, don't you? I did wonder if some of this was for show, but I was wrong. You are madly and deeply in love with her. It's not just about the Mafia or power."

With passion bursting from my chest, I smile back at my brother. "It's never been just about the Mafia. I wanted her from that moment I saw her sitting on the sofa with Lucia's baby in her arms. I fell in love with her when she tripped down the stairs and I caught her. It consumed me when she turned down her father's proposition. All I hoped for was her to give me a chance, and now she is mine and I will never let her go. No one will ever take her away or hurt her, not while I have air in my lungs."

"That settles it then. I don't know anything about Jose's son, but I have met Dominga a couple of times. I know what family she is from, and I can arrange a meeting between them and us and establish if Dominga is involved. Until then, you and Sal will stay with us," my father instructs me with a firm nod.

With both him and Matteo on my side, I know I have a better chance of helping Salma eradicate this threat. I won't let her down.

*** **Amber** ***

The trial has been postponed and I don't know why. After looking for Aiden and Eva, and not finding them, I make my way back to the pack house, alone, to find Preston.

When I gave my evidence earlier, a moment of pain twisted deep inside me. Even Lizzie felt it and we did not like it. Since then, I need my mate, I need his closeness, his embrace, his touch.

When I walk into our apartment, my gorgeous mate is sitting waiting for me. The room is dark except for the candles which flicker, giving out a soft, sensual light. Preston is sitting on a stool, and I can hardly contain my glee.

He's dressed up as a fireman. Vague memories of telling Preston about my ultimate fantasy come rolling back: for a buff and burly fireman to seduce me, and he has obviously gone behind my back to make my dreams come true.

"Lieutenant Amber Goldrick, I heard you had a fire that needs putting out." I giggle and cover my face.

"Oh, my Goddess! Preston! I can't believe you did this. I love it." He stands up and twirls for me. He is the finest specimen of a man I have ever seen. He has the jacket and trousers and even the suspenders holding them in place. Big black boots and a fireman's helmet complete the look, his toned abs stand out prominently and I want to run my tongue all over him.

"I thought I could give my girl a little treat after a hard day, so let me get out my hose and give you a dousing!" We both laugh at his joke, and it's enough to feel free, and light and loved. All thoughts of the horrible feeling I had earlier float away.

He sits me in the chair and seductively dances for me as he slowly strips off his clothing. I squeeze my legs together, craving the friction of my damp panties against my wet pussy. The heat rises within me as Preston rips the trousers off himself.

I can't take it anymore. His long and meaty dick stands to attention and I caress it slowly. My mate shudders as I do it. I love the silky, hot, and hard feel of him in my hand. When I see a tiny dew drop of precum on the tip of his head, I drop to my knees and slurp it all up, teasing him at first, just taking the tip of him in my mouth and then licking all the way down his shaft and back up again.

I keep repeating the motion, taking a bit more of him into my mouth until finally he is hitting the back of my throat. I cup his balls and he groans as he threads his fingers through my hair, holding me in place.

As I pleasure my man with my mouth and hands, I become his goddess and I've never felt as powerful. The act of making him feel amazing makes me feel invincible.

Preston fucks my mouth, groaning, and shouts, "Fuck, yes." With a final thrust and growl, he comes, ribbons of hot, pearlescent fluid shoot from him and onto my tongue, and I lick up every drop. He shudders and gasps with sheer pleasure and I love it. I *did* that.

"Red, I was supposed to be making you feel good, not the other way around." Climbing up on top of him so I can straddle him, I crave being close to him.

"It feels good for me to give you pleasure too. I love making you come. It makes me feel powerful. But now I need you, I am ready to explode all over you." He chuckles at my enthusiastic honesty.

"Oh, so you do need a fire putting out," he teases while slowly removing my top and bra. "I am going to stoke the fire first, Red. I'm going to cause an inferno right here inside you."

Overcome with need, I smash my mouth into his. My own need takes control. I love this man, I love him with every fibre of my being and I want to be doing this with him and only him for the rest of my life.

CHAPTER THREE

Sex on Fire

*** Preston ***

After spending a couple of hours worrying about what that crazy woman said, I see reason. Amber can fight the allegations. They say that widows can become crazy when they lose their mate. I am not going to hold much store in what that stupid woman threatened but first thing tomorrow I will go and let Aiden know what happened.

A great idea of how to bolster Amber comes to me. Last year, she made a request for us to try bondage. She likes to push our boundaries. However, since we have officially mated and marked each other, there has been a whole different level of intimacy between us. It is gentler, more loving, and tender, but I know she still likes all that kinky stuff too.

This time, I will initiate it. She dressed up as Wonder Woman for me one time and I loved it. I will dress up as a fireman for her and I am going to do all kinds of filthy stuff I have held back from doing with her. One time she did tell me that she found the fireman's uniform sexy and would love a fireman's lift. I just want her to slide down my pole!

My Red still likes to act like she is as tough as old boots, but I know her like no-one else does. This trial has really got to her and then her own trial is just around the corner. To top it off, she wants to connect with her mother, and so far she hasn't been able to locate her.

A good de-stress is just what my baby needs, and it is going to start with a strip tease from a horny fireman.

She loves the dress-up and role play. Although, at this moment in time I think I love it more than her. Not particularly the dressing up as such, but her reaction to it. The way she excitedly drops to her knees and deepthroats me makes me wonder what else would turn her on?

A seductive strip tease especially for her goes too far and she sucks my cock until I blow. Afterwards I pick her up, and carry her over my shoulder in a traditional fireman's lift to our bedroom. My desire to take my time and really work her up into a frenzy is at odds with my yearning to be balls deep inside her.

"Please, Preston, don't torture me anymore. Please!" She is begging, becoming wetter and wetter as she pleads for me to let her come. She likes being tortured, she likes to beg for it.

"Tell me how you want it, tell me what to do." She flips me over and straddles me, sliding down my cock just as I fantasised about.

"Frig me Preston, rub my clit until I come all over you," she demands and, Goddess be damned, my cock becomes even harder.

Her pussy is wet and warm against my hand, and Amber moans as I run my fingers over her sensitive clit . Amber grinds on me and I pinch her clit, extracting a squeal from her, a squeal of pain and delight all at the same time. Then I flick my fingertips lightly over the tip of her clit until I feel her wetness coat my hand, and she spasms as she throws her head back.

"Yes, yes, Preston. Yes, like that. Just. Like. That." She shouts as I thrust my hips up to meet her demands. As her climax takes over her body, I quicken my pace and I come again too, which causes little shockwaves to continue to ravage Amber's delicate little folds and clit.

Afterwards, I let her sleep. I wrap her up in a sheet while I get some food and drink for us. She'll be ravenous when she wakes in a little while.

The crazy widow interrupts my thoughts as soon as I'm away from my mate. I can't get any peace from her and her threats against my Red. First thing tomorrow morning, I need to talk to Aiden about this before I lose my mind.

The more I try to blank the crazy widow out, the more intrusive the thoughts become, until my heart is hammering away erratically and I am frantically searching for air to fill my lungs.

My terror increases for Amber; I can't lose her, not now. Not after everything we have been through and when we are just on the cusp of our own bliss.

There is so much I want from a long life with her. It starts with a Mating Ceremony and a human wedding. We both want a couple of pups and a family. No matter what, I only want it with Amber.

Amber will flip when I tell her everything the widow said to me, but I don't have any choice. Keeping this from her would almost certainly come back and bite me on my ass.

I climb back into bed with Amber after placing a bottle of water at her bedside. She is warm and snuggly, reminding me of a little cat.

I whisper against her beautiful head of red curls. "I love you, Amber Goldrick, and I would protect you with my life. I would give my life and happiness for yours. But first, I am going to fight tooth and nail for what is ours, for what I have been dreaming for all this time."

Filled with resolve to fight for what is mine, I plan my fight for Amber. My fight for us.

*** Aiden ***

Eva is a nervous wreck, and I am trying everything to get her to settle down but she is worrying about tomorrow now that the trial for Ellis has been postponed.

"I should have spoken to him earlier, Aiden. I am such a weakling. I hate being scared. I want to be brave and powerful," she says sadly.

No matter what I tell her, she will not accept that she isn't in the wrong and that she has gone above and beyond to help Ellis despite him being a stubborn little shit. Despite him being the one who hurt her.

"Eva, sweetheart, you have done everything you can. Please just... come here and sit with me." I open my arms to her but she continues to hesitate.

She's all wound up and filled with unnecessary guilt.

"Would you like me to call one of the Elders and ask to speak to them again on your behalf?" She shakes her head at me.

"Sorry, Aidy, I just hate feeling helpless." She sits on my lap without further instructions, making me smile. She has come a very long way in six weeks, my little Shortie. "I don't want them to kill him, I wouldn't be able to live with myself."

Well, I can't settle for that. "If they sentence him to death after he has changed his plea, accepted responsibility, apologised and agreed to complete the rehabilitation, then I will step in as Alpha and overrule them." She relaxes against my hand as I stroke circles on her back, holding back a groan of contentment when the mate bond tingles spark throughout my body.

"Thank you, Aiden. I know what he did was wrong, but jeez, he is only a young boy. I felt protective of him." I smile at her and her willingness to admit she has a tender heart.

"That's your Luna senses starting to kick in, Eva. Our pack members are like our children and it's our duty to protect them." She smiles at me and rests her head on my shoulder.

Summer is asleep in her bed, worn out from her day of fun and exploring, and the night is ours for now.

"We still need to discuss our Gamma situation, Eva. Did you give it some thought?"

She rolls her eyes at me and I raise my eyebrows at her. "Is it really necessary, Aidy? We have gotten this far without one."

I hold my laugh. What she doesn't know is that nearly every wolf under Beta Preston and Delta Billy has taken a turn guarding her and she has been completely oblivious.

"Every Luna needs a Gamma wolf, sweetheart; we have been over this. You could get pregnant at any time now and I need to know you are all safe if I am not here."

She is so resistant to the idea of a Gamma wolf. I had hoped we could put this all behind us and concentrate on her getting a Gamma, shifting and us having a Mating Ceremony and her officially becoming Luna. I am getting nowhere with any of the above.

"Okay, I will meet with the wolves you have suggested, but I want the final choice, Aiden. This person is going to be present for a lot of my life, so it best be someone nice." I nod and relent to her choosing, but internally I smile at her wanting someone 'nice'. I want someone ferocious, someone who will kill to protect her.

"The final choice will be yours; I promise. Thank you for agreeing to meet them." She kisses me softly on my lips before making her way down to her mark on my neck. She sucks and nips at it, flooding me with carnal need.

"Oh, I almost forgot!" She jumps off my lap taking away her sexy round ass and her teasing lips off my neck. "I would like to try and shift again."

Fuck. Me and Eva. In the woods. Naked. And I must concentrate on coaxing out her wolf when all I want to do is bury myself deep inside her.

*** Salma ***

I am being frog marched out of my own club by my husband. I tell him to stop, to wait, but Ale has a right bee in his bonnet.

"Salma. Please, mi amor, just listen to me just this once and I promise I will never ask anything of you ever again. I need to get you away from here. Now. We have to move now." I listen to him because my normally placid and calm Alejandro is worried about something.

Within four minutes, which is no exaggeration because I checked the CCTV afterwards, Ale had parked his car, marched into my club, convinced me to get out and drove us both away.

"Alejandro Suarez, you have two minutes to explain to me what the fuck is going on or I swear to fucking god, I will make earrings out of your bollocks." I squeeze his crotch as he drives, so he understands I will cause him pain.

"Fucking hell, Sal, we'll never get a baby if you chop my balls off, give me a minute." I move my hand; I do want a baby after all. "I am taking you to my parents' house, and my father is trying to arrange a meeting between us and the family Dominga belongs to. We have to be very careful, Sal. Whoever poisoned your papa has been able to get very close to us without detection. I am trying to protect you."

My first instinct is to attack. I want to attack Ale for insisting on protecting me. Do I look like a fair maiden? Do I need rescuing? Then I think of choking Dominga the stupid whore for starting all this. I could easily entwine my fingers around her throat and squeeze the life from her.

"Before you start ranting at me that you don't need protecting, Salma Morales, your papa probably thought the same thing and he's now dust in a box on your Mami's mantlepiece, so spare me the sexist remarks. I fucking love you and if any bastard wants to harm what is mine I will burn the fucker alive. Understand?"

Fuck! I have never been so turned on in my whole entire life!

"Pull over now!" I shout at him, and give him his due, he pulls into the layby we were about to pass. I quickly push the lever, moving his chair all the way back into a lying position and I straddle him. "That was so fucking hot, Ale!"

Crashing my juicy lips over his, my tongue darts into his mouth and passion quickly ignites and spreads throughout me. Ale growls in approval, his hands automatically skim over my tight skirt and search for the bottom of my blouse. He pulls it free from my waist band and lays his rough, warm hands on my back.

I moan into his mouth; I love the way he touches me. I love how his words get me aroused into a stupor even when they annoy me.

"No, stop, Sal. I need to get to my parents now. I am being deadly serious. Someone has been following us." He tells me as he springs my boobs out of my bra and pinches my left nipple, groaning as it puckers at him and his touch. "You are too goddamn sexy for your own good, woman!"

I laugh at him as I slide off him and sit back on the passenger seat, and he groans in displeasure. "You told me to stop Ale, make your mind up." He gives me a cheeky grin.

"Would you do anything I asked you to do, Chula? Only for me?" Yearning shoots directly to my core.

"All you have to do to find out is ask Alejandro... tell me, tell your wife what you want her to do." He sucks in air through his teeth.

"You are going to suck me off while I drive us to my parents' house." I lean over and unzip his trousers and help his thick cock escape.

"Drive, then. When you start to drive, I will polish you off." His pupils dilate, and there is a slight flush to his face. He wants to take control and so I will let him.

"Fuck, Sal," he says through gritted teeth as we hurtle along a country road. I have my head in his lap and his cock in my mouth. I look at him through my eyelashes and love that he is gripping the steering wheel like his life depends on it. Yes Ale, fuck Sal. That's what I want.

"Chula, stop, I don't want to come in your mouth." I can feel the power of his orgasm building, his cock goes even harder and the veins more prominent and the head is a deep purple now.

"Where then?" I ask him in mock innocence as I sit up and push my boobs together.

"You are driving me crazy, Chula. Just wait until later." Promises, promises, I think to myself as I sit back in my seat with my legs wide open. I pull my lace knickers to one side and stroke myself. The breeze against my sex, Ale looking so hot and bothered, and the thrill of doing this outside while Ale is driving made me wetter and more turned on by the second.

We come to another layby and Ale pulls in again. This time he lies my seat back until it's almost completely flat and climbs over on top of me. "I'm going to fuck you now, but when we get home it's all going to be about you."

He plunges into my depth, and I cry out at his invasion, both in pleasure and pain, but when I feel him backing off, I wrap my legs around him. I need him. I just need this.

"Don't stop, Ale, don't stop."

He grabs my face as he ploughs into me. "I am never going to stop, you are mine, and that will never ever stop."

I cling to him as I feel him unloading and I laugh as he grunts and groans. I feel alive, I feel loved.

"How the hell do you do that to me, Chula? I lost control!"

I just smile at him. We both know who is really in charge here.

*** **Eva** ***

We have an Omega named Mrs Moore who helps about the place and sits with Summer when Aiden and I are both needed. She is a lovely woman, a similar age to my own mother but a lot warmer and more trustworthy. Mrs Moore comes to watch Summer while Aiden takes me to the forest to try and shift again.

We approach and I already know the drill. We have tried this a couple of dozen times already, but I have struggled to visualise what it is to shift. I take my clothes off, but Aiden stops and laughs, catching me and holding me close.

"Do you remember the first few times I brought you here and you made me hold a towel up in case anyone could see you?" I blush when I realise anyone could be watching me right now, but I had forgotten.

"It seems like years ago, but it's been a little over six weeks since we moved in. I think you've made an exhibitionist out of me," I tell him through my shy grin.

"You must have always been one, Shortie, you just needed coaxing out of your shell, a bit like your wolf does now." Lina yelps in my head and I am still taken by surprise by it.

Come on, Lina, today is the day you get to have a run and mate with Roman. You want that, right?

She doesn't answer me but I am undeterred. I am desperate to see my own wolf form and for Aiden to reap the reward for all his patience and persistence.

"Right, Eva, remember what we talked about. Close your eyes, relax your shoulders and visualise Lina emerging. I'm here with you, baby."

I follow his instructions but Lina whimpers, she is frightened and it's too much for her. I reassure her that it's okay, but disappointment pools in my chest. I don't want to be disheartened, but I am. How can I officially become Luna without my wolf, how can Aiden and I complete the Mating Ceremony he has begged me for if I cannot shift? Why can't I shift?

"Eva, what if I shift first and Roman was here instead of me? Do you think Lina might like that better?" I shrug. I don't know anymore. Lina feels further away than ever, and I am starting to believe that I will never shift.

The cracking of Aiden's bones as he shifts brings me out of my useless pondering, and my heart leaps as Roman bounds over to me. I press my lips to the top of his head right between his ears in hope that Lina will want to do the same.

She purrs and chirrups when she smells Roman and that feels good. They are starting to connect through me as a vessel, but I hope I don't have to wait much longer to give Roman the mate he deserves.

Roman is such a sweetheart. Right now, he has surrounded me like a cloak, shielding my nakedness from the night air. He rubs the side of his face against my neck, sending tingles of delight throughout my body, and I use this opportunity to encourage Lina.

He has to make do with my body, what little use he has for it, until you emerge, Lina. He is so excited about finally meeting you, don't you want to meet him?

I wait for a minute for her reply. *Of course, I do, but if he really wants me and loves me, he will wait until I am ready. I am not ready to present myself yet. Please understand.*

I talk to Roman and tell him how much I have enjoyed spending time with him, but I ask for Aiden to come back now. Roman answers with a lick on my cheek and then I hear and see my mate shift back.

"What happened, Eva?" I cuddle into him, tears threatening to engulf me and, even though he is also naked, his embrace is warm and comforting.

"She told me she isn't ready yet. We have to wait." He kisses my head to reassure me, but if I am frustrated, surely, he is too.

"Then we will wait. I will wait forever. You and Lina are worth waiting for."

*** Melanie ***

The past few weeks have been hard, being alone and pregnant. However, seeing my sons more frequently has been a blessing and Ryan's parents, Mr and Mrs Jefferson, have kept in touch with me.

I think they are eager to meet their grandchild, the last gift Ryan left us. It's a girl. I had a scan just a few days ago to confirm it and I cried the whole night afterwards.

I always wanted a little girl. I want a little best friend and someone to share the more feminine things in life with. My sons are amazing, and they are very much loved and wanted, but there are only so many times I can talk about cars and trains and football.

Ryan left me scars and insecurities, he took the best years of my life and treated me appallingly. And yet, he might have also bestowed the best gift in the world on me too.

My ex-partner came by my home to collect our sons from their visit with me and he knew without me telling him that I was pregnant again. He has been supportive and for a moment, I thought I felt a spark between us, but he quickly backed off and confirmed he had met someone new and he was asking her to marry him.

I smiled and hugged him and told him I was happy for him. Disappointment is my only friend now, but I deserve to be alone. I broke up my family to be with Ryan and they moved on without me. I have to suck it up and accept that I fucked up.

I leave a couple of messages for Eva, asking her to call me back. I want to share with her that Summer will be getting a little half-sister, thanks to them both sharing Ryan as their biological father.

I hope Eva returns my call soon. Despite everything that went down between us, she is the only person who understands what Ryan was like and we have an unfortunate shared experience at the hands of someone who should have loved us. At this moment, she feels like my only friend.

Sitting on the floor of my spare bedroom, I am trying in vain to set up the baby's new crib but I am hopeless at DIY and my little girl would be anything but safe in the monstrosity I have made, even though I have followed the instructions to a tee. I just can't do this on my own.

I call Mr Jefferson, Ryan's father, who said he would help me out if I needed it, but his number just rings out too.

"I know I said it was just you and me, kid, but for the love of God, there must be someone out there I can talk to and lean on?" I shout to an empty room, all hope starting to fade, when, suddenly, my phone lights up.

Eva is calling. She is returning my call after all.

"Hi, sorry it's taken a while to get back to you, we had some issues to deal with, you know, with Aiden's business," she explains sheepishly, and although I don't know the ins and outs of Aiden's business, I know he must be very affluent and important from the way he carries himself, the cars he drives and the way he treats Eva and Summer.

"That's okay, I was just calling to check in on you and Summer and to let you both know that it's a girl." Her pause puts me off my stride. I think I should have handled this more tactfully. After all, the baby in question was conceived during Eva's marriage to Ryan. Her dead husband is my baby's father. "Eva, I've just realised how insensitive that was. I apologise. I just meant so we could tell Summer."

"No, that's okay. I was just a bit shocked. It makes it more real, I suppose. Congratulations, I am glad everything is going well." She's going to hang up, but I really need someone to talk to.

"Eva, I need a friend. I have no right to ask you after what I did to you, but I really, really need a friend. Is there any chance you could come for coffee one day or I could come and see you?"

"I'll try and come and see you soon. I will bring Summer. She will love feeling your bump and hopefully she will get to feel a few kicks too. It's important that our girls bond."

Eva says goodbye and I cry again when she does. I am making such a mess of things.

I give up on the crib, I will hire someone to come and build it for me. Right now, I need to work on building myself up, my little girl needs a strong mummy and in my current state, I am going to be as much use as a wet paper bag.

It's time to stop wallowing. It's time to pull up my big girl knickers and stop being a mess. I have a little girl on the way, and I need to show her what it means to be a strong, independent woman and to do that, I have to become one. No more crying over stupid things, no more guilt or feeling inadequate.

I deserve better and my baby definitely does too.

*** Aiden ***

Eva was upset after last night, and her phone call this morning also knocked her off her stride. I brought my exquisite mate here to live with me so I could look after her, and I am failing.

The next knock she must endure is the conclusion to Ellis' trial. She is a tightly wound bundle of nerves right now. I need to get her away from the pack house and the territory for a little while. It must be stifling her.

Preston tries to link me a few times, but I ask that he speaks to me later unless it's a matter of life and death. He grumbles at me, but I have the trial and my mate to deal with. Plus, our scouts are returning today and they have news about the last known location of my mother. When they called ahead, my bowels felt like they had turned to ice. Why am I so nervous? I just want answers. I just want the truth.

Our sunshine girl wakes up early this morning. She climbs up into our bed and giggles when I tickle her feet. I love that little girl with all my heart. She used to call me Teddy Bear, but over the past week or so it's begun to change, and of her own accord she started calling me Daddy Bear instead. I have never felt as honoured or as proud. I discussed it with Eva, because I didn't want her to be upset and I didn't want to do anything that would be disrespectful.

Eva's face lit up when I told her what Summer had called me and then quickly filled with concern. "Are you okay with that, Aiden, or do you want me to tell her to stop?"

I can't believe she's even asking me. "I love it, Eva, I just wanted to give you the heads up in case you didn't like it. You know I want to adopt her and raise her with our other pups. You know I love her."

"Ryan never let her, he never let her call him Dad or Daddy or anything. It always made me sad. She loves you like her daddy, and you do everything that a daddy should for his little girl. She obviously feels comfortable calling you it." Her eyes fill with tears, but she looks happy.

"Why are you crying, sweetheart?" I ask her as I hold her to me.

My girl is overcome with emotion following our conversation.

"You'll never know how much it means to me that Summer has you in her life. Thank you, Aiden, thank you for stepping up and loving her like you do." My sweet girl, I wouldn't have it any other way.

"She makes it so easy, Shortie. She is so incredibly cute and full of joy." She smiles now.

"That's why I named her Summer Joy. She was supposed to be born in the autumn, but she came early, and she is the joy in my life."

That was when we finally established that Summer is a werewolf too. She wasn't premature when she was born, Eva obviously had a werewolf pregnancy, which is shorter than a human one.

"Come on, sunshine girl, I will take you to the creche today while mummy finishes getting ready." Summer giggles in delight as I carry her on my shoulders. Eva quickly kisses her goodbye and tells me she will meet me in the foyer of the pack house in fifteen minutes.

I drop Summer off and go back to meet Eva. Together, we walk to the Chambers of Justice for, hopefully, the final time.

"You are quiet today, Shortie, is everything okay?" I know she's nervous, but she seems really subdued now.

"I'm just thinking, that's all. I'll be glad when this is over." She places her head against my chest and fills me with tingles and yearning and warmth and love. "How about you, Aiden? I know you've got a lot on your plate too. Don't keep it from me, I want to be here for you too."

"We'll talk about my worries after this bloody trial. I might have to leave the territory for a few days." Her shock-filled eyes meet mine. "We can talk properly later, right now we have to deal with this shit show." She gives me a thin smile as we are called into the Chambers.

The head of the panel stands. "We postponed this trial yesterday as the defendant, Ellis Devine, former Gamma, has decided to change his plea. Please rise."

Ellis stands up. "I, Ellis Devine, Former Gamma, wish to plead guilty to all charges." There is a collective gasp and talking in the gallery nearby before the head of the panel calls for order.

"Former Gamma Ellis, we will accept your guilty plea on the condition that you make a full apology to the future Luna and your Alpha for your actions. You will be required to go back to the position of Gamma-in-Training once you have completed a compulsory six-month rehabilitation course. If any of these conditions are not met, you will be ousted and declared a Rogue. Do you agree?"

Ellis holds his hand up to the Moon Goddess Scripture as he says, "I agree."

It's over. It's finally over. Eva, still holding my hand, tries to hug me and I laugh at her wrapping us up in knots.

"I am glad that's over with, although it's only two weeks until Amber's trial starts." I try to get Eva prepared for what is to come. Amber will be tried at the Silver Shore as a neutral territory to both of us, The Onyx River, and the complaining pack, The Moon Stone. Dread fills me every time I think of her trial.

We make our way back to my office and when I get there, Delta Billy informs me that one of the scout wolves has returned. He sends him to my office to give me my messages.

After observing the usual greetings, I ask him what he had discovered.

"Your mother was registered with a pack in Scotland. We did not get a confirmed sighting, but we believe she is now mated to a Scottish Alpha Laird.

CHAPTER FOUR

Answers

*** Amber ***

I am sitting facing my mate, my brother, and my brother's mate. Their mouths are moving but everything starts sounding distorted after they inform me they have a possible location for my mother.

She was in Scotland. Just a couple of hundred miles away. Until they said where she might be, it had been easy to imagine her as just vanished, nowhere. But now I knew where she had gone, I needed to go and see her.

I stand up mid-conversation. "Amber, sweetie, do you understand what Aiden is telling you?" Eva asks me soothingly.

I nod in reply. "I'm going to find her and demand some answers. Are you coming, Aiden?"

My brother hesitates and I am impatient to know why.

"Don't you want answers Aiden? I need to go and find her now and find out why... Why didn't she want me? Why didn't she want us?"

The tears stream down my face, and I hate that. I hate that I am showing weakness because of her. Preston stands but doesn't touch me; instead, he waits for my permission and right there in that moment I know I could never, ever live without him. I wouldn't want to.

Accepting his embrace, I allow the tears to engulf me, the hurt, the pain, the rejection flowing out through my tears like poison being extracted from my very soul.

"Of course, I want to go, Amber. I want the answers we both need to put this to rest. I can't just leave the pack, plus you have your trial in two weeks' time. Is now the right time?"

Of course, it's the right time. There may never be another time.

"Aiden, I am going with or without you. I might not get another chance." The pain that flashes in his eyes makes me regret my rash statement. My big brother, the big fierce Alpha, is worried about me. "Please come with me, Aidy, I need you." He nods his agreement and I run to my big brother and cuddle him in thanks.

This will potentially be my last jaunt as a free she-wolf, but I need these answers. The only fly in the ointment is Preston. My lovely Preston. I wanted to spend this time with him, I wanted to show him how much I loved, cared, and respected him in case it was the last chance I could freely give it all to him. I wanted to spend every day making love to him and memorising every inch of his body, his face, and his mind, so I could replay everything over and over if I was sentenced to imprisonment.

As I meet his hazel eyes, I know he is hurting. He is afraid this is the last chance for us to be together, but he also knows how much this means to me.

"Come back to me, Red, okay, just come back to me." The lump in my throat, formed of suppressed tears, threatens to choke me.

So, it is arranged. Aiden and I will leave the following day to travel to Scotland. Preston will run the pack and Eva will assist. Tonight, Eva has the opportunity to select a Gamma on a trial basis. If not, Aiden says he will appoint one.

I spend the whole night before I leave in Preston's arms. I want and need him to know how much I will miss him, how I wish we could spend forever like this.

I need to think about us, our little cocoon and the promise of what could be should I make it through this trial. I want to forget the world and lie with the love of my life. Maybe these moments will comfort me and keep me warm if I don't make it through.

Maybe that will be enough to keep Preston comforted and warm too.

*** **Eva** ***

I am bereft that Aiden is leaving but he assures me he will be back in two weeks' time because of Amber's trial. In the meantime, I must choose a temporary Gamma wolf to protect me and Summer should we need it. I have a vision of a glorified babysitter impatiently waiting around for me and my daughter to complete innocuous tasks in safe places. I have been resisting needing someone to 'protect' us, but I can see the worry and feel the anxiety in Aiden and I want to reassure him so he doesn't worry while he is away.

Aiden presents three candidates: all massively brutish men with bulging muscles and ferocious grimaces on their miserable faces. "I said I wanted someone nice," I spit at him through gritted teeth.

He grins and whispers back, "Looks can be deceiving, Shortie!" Which confirms to me he wi trying to tease me. Two can play that game.

"Yes, looks can be deceiving. After all, I thought you were hot and sweet and kind, but I see now you are a bad boy!" His eyes go wide as I nibble my bottom lip, and I notice his position shift. I hope his cock hardening makes him feel uncomfortable. That is his punishment for teasing me!

"Could you all introduce yourself to your future Luna and tell her a bit about yourself so she can make her decision?" The first guy steps forward. He looks really mean with a hook nose and sallow skin. His eyes remind me of little black beetles.

"My name is Cohen, I am 32 years old, mated, and my mother's father was a Gamma in another pack. I have been part of the Gamma guard since I left academy training." I give him a nod of acknowledgement.

The next man takes a step forward, and his teeth and gums threaten to jump out of his mouth. He would scare Summer. "Luna Eva, I am Craig. I have worked as a scout and investigator and as a Delta wolf. My mate rejected me, and I have no use or desire for a chosen one. I am dedicated to my work first and foremost. I am 29 years old, and I like to go fishing in my downtime." Yikes. He is scary. No, he will not do.

"Thank you, Craig," I say while giving Aiden the evil eye, I will give him an earful for that suggestion. Finally, the last man stands forward. He has sandy hair that softens his hard stare, and he gives me a little smile before starting to talk. My body physically relaxes as he speaks to me, his presence is calm and soothing.

"Hi future Luna, I am Max. I am the cousin of former Gamma Ellis. I just wanted to be upfront about that. I am 35, so I'm a bit older than these guys. I am unmated and I trained under my uncle for as long as I can remember, until his death a couple of years ago... I would be happy and honoured to be your temporary Gamma."

I give him a genuine smile. I think this could work.

"Thank you, gentleman, I will discuss this with your Alpha and allow him to make the final appointment." Excused, the three of them turn to leave. Max is the only one who bows to both me and Aiden, as is customary. The other two rush back and bow, but Max has already confidently walked away without bravado.

"I know you want someone nice, but I need someone competent and willing to defend you to the death, baby. These men are the best available." Aiden is trying to explain, but I have made my choice.

"I want Max, I like him and think I could trust him. I want him to be my Gamma."

Relief fills Aiden's face, his shoulders relax, and he looks a little younger and less stressed.

"You had me worried there, Eva, I thought you were going to refuse them all. I'm glad you found one you like... but tell me. Is it not weird that he is Ellis' cousin? I told him not to tell you that yet, but he said no."

I like him even more; he obviously respects Aiden, but he also has morals.

"I'm glad he told me. I suppose it could be weird, but if we were all judged by the actions of our relatives, we would all be screwed, right?" He raises his eyebrows and nods.

"Yes, I suppose you are right." His eyes glaze over for a little while and a couple of minutes later, Max walks back into the clearing.

"Alpha, you wanted me?" he addresses Aiden after bowing again to both of us.

"Future Luna Eva wants you to be her Gamma. This will be a temporary arrangement so she can test your connection and compatibility. Do you agree to shield her and our daughter, protect them from harm and give your life for theirs?"

"I do, Alpha." Max looks up to smile at me and I smile back. We are going to be good friends.

"By Alpha decree, I name you, Maximus Devine, acting Gamma to the Future Luna, Eva Smith-Jones, and I thank you for protecting her while I am away." They shake hands. "Report for duty at 8 am please, Max, and you will be required to take over the Gamma Guard and take an apartment on our floor."

Max smiles and agrees and walks off to put his affairs in order.

Once we are alone, Aiden lifts me up against his chest and I wind my arms and legs around his hard, hot body, unable to get close enough. My nipples stand on end, craving to be touched, to be tweaked and sucked by Aiden, and only Aiden.

"I am going to miss you so much while I am away, my love," he says to me as he kisses down my neck and nuzzles me. "I am going to miss sleeping in the same bed as you and waking up next to you every morning. I am going to miss our showers, our shift attempts, your lovely plump lips and beautifully fine body. I'm going to miss mating with you, miss making you come, and coming deep down inside you." My desire reaches a fever pitch with all Aiden's hot words.

"I already miss you, Aiden. I need you so badly." I can feel his hard arousal rubbing against my most private parts through the annoying restraint of our clothing.

"I need you too, baby, I need you so much." He carries me over to the shelter of an old oak tree. There is a blanket of leaves and grass covering the ground where he places me. As we gently and sweetly make love under the oak tree, under the stars, I pray to the Goddess I have recently learned about. *Goddess of the Moon, please guide my love to finding the secrets of his past so he may return to me.*

Aiden holds me like I am his most prized possession.

"I love you, Aidy, my big bad wolf".

He kisses my head, sending tingles throughout my body. "I love you more, Shortie."

*** **Preston** ***

As the car carrying Amber and Aiden to their destination leaves the territory, Zack howls in pain. I know she must go and get answers. I hope with all my being that she does get answers, since she deserves to have closure. I only wish I could have gone with her, or the trial wasn't looming over us, or we had more time. I just wish things were different.

With everything that happened, I didn't find a chance to tell them about the widow, Nikki, who approached me. To be honest, the more I thought about it, the more ludicrous it was. Surely, she really doesn't think I would reject Amber and take her as my chosen mate? I don't even know her!

There is still a really good chance that the trial will be thrown out because we were responding to our Alpha being taken hostage just a couple of nights after Junior had abducted him. So, in theory, unless Junior is tried too, Amber shouldn't face charges.

Despite my conviction, Nikki's words keep creeping into my thoughts. She implied she had the power to make this easier or harder on Amber, depending on how I cooperated. Was that real or was she trying to add some weight to her threat?

It doesn't matter. I will not be going to the border to meet her tonight. I will tell Aiden and Amber when they return and until then, I will train, look out for my Luna, and keep busy until my love returns to me, and I can take a full breath again.

I am glad that Eva has chosen a temporary Gamma to protect her and Summer. Max is a good man; he was the person I would have chosen off the bat. He was the wolf Aiden and I wanted as our Gamma when Ellis was appointed by the Elders. I know I can trust and rely on him to look after our Luna, which is one less worry on my mind.

What could go wrong?

Amber calls as they cross the Scottish Border. She and Aiden are already squabbling like teenagers. 'He drank my cola', 'she keeps playing bad music', 'his feet stink'. I am just waiting for the reports of hair pulling and friction burns to come and then I will know I have really been transported back in time.

I miss her terribly. Our apartment seems cold and bare without her in it. In a down moment, I wonder if this is how I will feel if Amber is sentenced to imprisonment? Am I destined to feel alone and lost forever?

After three days, I am patrolling the forest when Nikki appears from nowhere yet again.

"How did you get here? How did you know where I was?" I ask her, flummoxed. We seriously need to tighten the security on our borders.

A smirk curls her lip. "Hi, future mate, it's great to see you too. I was so disappointed that you stood me up the other night. It made me very, very angry." I can feel power rolling off her, but I cannot distinguish what it is.

"Who exactly are you? What are you?" I ask her exasperatedly, but she just laughs and shakes her head at me, and she closes the gap between us, stalking me like prey at her mercy.

"You can see a tiny fragment of my power and ability, Beta Preston, and you still resist the offer I gave you to save your mate." Fear starts to prickle up my neck and into my scalp.

"I love her. I don't want to leave her; I don't ever want to be apart from her." The facts pour out of me involuntarily, but I am not ashamed. I'm not embarrassed about the strength of my feelings for my mate, I am proud and loyal to our bond.

"I'm sure my mate didn't want to leave me either. It's not about what we want, this is about karma. I need to rebalance. I suppose I could just kill you and then we would be even, but that doesn't solve my issue of wanting a mate and a pup of my own."

She pauses to impress that point on me.

"I want vengeance and repayment. I want what is rightfully mine. You can give it to me and save your mate or you can both live with the consequences of Amber's actions." She seizes my wrists and holds me tightly to her ample chest.

"Stop, please. I don't want to. I love her, I love my mate." Before I can stop her, she starts to suck on Ambers mark on my neck, the mark I have had for less than two months after waiting seven years for it. I am filled with self-loathing and disgust as waves of pleasure and yearning course throughout my body. I close my eyes and I can see my Red. I can see her kissing my neck and rubbing her hands over my body.

"GET OFF ME," I bellow, my Beta voice and aura taking over and blasting her to the ground. It's unsettling and upsetting when my hardened cock starts to twitch like it has a life of its own. How the fuck did she do that?

"Preston, darling, I am just showing you how I can make you feel good. How I could pleasure you every night and every morning. I would give you the family you crave, the little boys to carry your legacy. I could give you it all. Just reject Amber, but first let me fuck you so the pain twists her up inside."

Her talking about my Red like that breaks whatever illusion she has tried to drag me under.

"Never. I will never, ever give her up. I don't fucking want you or your sons. You repulse me. I will rip your fucking throat out if I catch you on our lands again. Do you understand?"

She starts to walk away, undressing as she goes. Her dress slips off her body as she does so, revealing tanned, toned skin with curves in all the right places. She shouts over her shoulder at me.

"I understand the words that you are saying, my love, but I can feel the hesitation behind your conviction. You do want me, you can try to fight it, but you will do the right thing. I will see you in two nights. Same time, same place."

In a flash, she shifts and runs to the boundary.

I sit in shock for what feels like an eternity. I wish Amber or Aiden were here. I need their help. I don't know what to do anymore.

*** **Eva** ***

I finish baking cookies with Summer on the fourth day of Aiden being away.

"Where daddy bear gone?" she asks with wide eyes and her hands held out on either side. She constantly asks for her daddy bear.

"Remember, he had to go on a trip to see someone." She makes a dramatic "O" with her mouth and then shakes her head.

"Daddy bear come back?" She is frowning now and I'm not sure if she is asking if he is coming back or demanding that he comes back. The mix of her beautiful innocent brown curls, big blue eyes and dimples seem at odds with the fierce scowl she is trying to give me.

"Come here, sunshine." I scoop her up and sit down with her on my lap. "Do you miss your daddy bear?"

My lovely little girl nods her head. The frown is gone, but instead, her eyes fill with tears and her bottom lip quivers.

"Shall we call him?" I ask her and her face instantly brightens as I pull my phone from my pocket. I decide to video call him so Summer can see his face too. Aiden answers after two rings and my heart pounds and flutters when I see his handsome face looking back at me.

Summer seizes my phone and in between her babble, I decipher small parts of what she is telling him. "Mummy makes cookies, mummy looks sad. Daddy bear come back home, and we all be happy!"

Summer hands my phone back to me so I can hold it, while she shows Aiden her new jump, which is hilarious because her feet never leave the ground.

Aiden chuckles down the phone, laughter dances on his face and his eyes crinkle in the corner. Good grief, I have fallen hard for him. After assuring Summer he will be coming back home in ten sleeps, she runs off to play with her toys, leaving me alone to talk to my mate.

"She is really missing you; she had a wobbly lip and everything," I tell him, feeling timid talking like this over a video call. "I miss you too, just ten more sleeps."

"Ten more sleeps and I am never leaving the territory without you and our girl again. I miss you both so much." He looks back at me sheepishly. "We had to delay our travelling last night, Amber wasn't well. I don't know what was wrong with her but she was in agony. It was scary, and then it just passed. She's feeling better again now."

He tells me they have made contact with the pack his mother was registered in, but the pack has been elusive. Aiden and Amber have to get the agreement of every Alpha Laird to travel through their territory as the area they need to go to is in the remote highlands.

"Can I call you like this tonight? I'll make sure I have a room all of my own and we could... talk?" A thrill of desire curls and unfurls in my tummy. I nod my agreement, and we say our goodbyes, calling Summer back in so she doesn't miss it.

I wonder what Aiden has in store for me tonight. I have missed him and his touch so much that I cannot wait for our private call.

*** **Xavier** ***

My son is an idiot, and my mate is an even bigger one. She released him without my knowledge, and now the little toe rag is on the loose, causing all sorts of aggravation.

"What the fuck did you do, Lydia? You don't know what he has done, you don't know what he is capable of, and now you've put us all in more danger by setting him free. You've put Junior himself in danger because if the other mafia firm finds out about his involvement, he will be killed instantly."

My mate shakes with apparent nerves and awareness that our son, the light of her life, is a lying and manipulative piece of shit who would use anyone to get what he wants.

"Did he at least tell you where he was going before he knocked you out and locked you in here?" Shaking her head at me to indicate he did not, my heart jumps for her and the overwhelming want to comfort her pulls at me.

"I heard him on the phone talking to someone called Dom, but that's it. I was completely knocked out." Tears fall down my mate's cheeks and I swear to the Moon Goddess I will have Junior for this, for treating his mother like a fucking animal.

"Xavier, I'm sorry. I was trying to help our boy. I'm sorry." My primal need to calm my Lydia takes over.

"I need you to forgive me, we are so weak without each other. I need you back next to me, beside me. I did a terrible thing. I kept a secret because I was too cowardly to face the consequences. I lied to cover up, and I'm sorry. I am so sorry I lied, but I am not sorry I have a daughter. I love her, I have always loved her, and I think you would both like each other if you could move past this."

"No more lies. Promise me now, Xavier. I don't care how hard the truth is, I would rather be hurt by the truth than falsely protected by a lie." I kiss her so she stops talking. I have missed her so, so much. I will never have enough words to tell her how sorry I am. I will try to show her from now on.

"No more lies. I promise, Lydia. Can you forgive me?" She nods as she holds me close to her, with tears streaming down her face. "I love you and I miss you, my sweet. It's always been you. You've always been the one for me."

"What are we going to do about Junior? Can we protect him? How much trouble is he in, Xavier?"

I have promised no more lies and I intend on sticking to my word. "I don't know if we can protect him anymore, Lydia. This is so bad; I don't know how to protect him and the rest of us along with him. If I am honest, I don't think I want to protect him after what he has done.

He has killed a Spanish Mafia Don, a powerful one, and I would bet my bollocks they are already planning their revenge."

"Why did he do that? What did he have to gain by crossing the line and taking on the mafia?" My Lydia looks as perplexed when she questions me as I did when I first found out. It's only going to get worse, so I tell her everything I know.

"He said he did it for the woman he loves." Her eyes widen, a hint of joy evident as well as a pinch of confusion.

"Junior found his mate?" she asks with building excitement which quickly fades when I shake my head.

"No. She isn't his mate, my sweet. He has fallen for a woman who is most definitely not a werewolf and is certainly not his mate. She is part of a mafia family, though I'm not sure which one. And I am not sure why she wanted the don killed but I intend on finding out."

With a renewed togetherness, I know our challenge ahead will test our bond to the maximum, but whatever hurdles are to come will be easier to face with my mate by my side.

"First we need to find that little fucker. Let's send out the scouts and trackers, Xavier. Junior needs to be brought to heel. I will teach my son that he doesn't treat his mother like a piece of shit and get away with it." My Lydia is back, the fire is back in her eyes and I'm so glad she has forgiven me and is back, fighting at my side instead of against me.

"I missed you, sweet cheeks. I miss us being a team. Look, about Eva-" I begin, but she cuts me off before I can finish.

"One thing at a time, Xavier. I forgive you for lying, but this is still a lot for me to accept. I know she is your daughter... but she isn't mine. Maybe in time I can accept her as a part of your family, but right now, to me, she is just the product of your deceit against me. I don't want or need to talk about her or see her. I will not acknowledge her. It's up to you how you progress."

And just like that, the peace we had found in our relationship is shattered and this time, I don't think we will be able to glue it back together.

I don't blame Lydia for feeling this way, but Eva shouldn't ever have to apologise for her existence. She has been treated appallingly her whole life and I will not come into it now to heap more maltreatment on her. She deserves better. This was my transgression, not hers.

Reacting to the hurt in my eyes and face, she tries to reassure me. "I still love you, but I can't see her being a part of my life, that's all." Emptiness fills up inside me. She can feel it too, through our bond. The bond is starting to unravel and her eyes fill with tears in response. "What is happening? Xavier… I'm frightened, what is happening?"

I look into my sweet Lydia's eyes. "You know how it works, Lydia: the bond with our children will always be stronger than the mate bond. If you reject my daughter, you reject me too. She is a part of me, and she never asked for any of this. We have a full moon cycle before this completely severs us as a mated pair."

The dismay on her face makes it clear she didn't expect that, but it's clear to me now.

"I never wanted this to come between us, Lydia. Evangelina is my daughter and I am going to do everything in my power to make up for being a shitty father to her, because she deserves that at least. I hoped that you could accept her as part of my life, but by denying her very existence, you are rejecting her and her importance to me. The bond will not tolerate that. I love you, sweet cheeks and I am sorry I hurt you."

I walk away from my life mate with a hole in my heart. This

hurts, but I know I have to stay true to my vow of being a better father to my daughter. Above all, I want to stay true to that.

*** Amber ***

We enter the territory next to the place my mother was last registered and they strip us of our phones and devices. They take my knives and swords, which honestly makes me want to cry. They are suspicious of us.

We are given rooms in the pack-keep, which is seen as an honour, so I can't be too outraged. The clans up here seem nice. Fierce, hard and rugged, but they treat us with hospitality, and it is apparent they hold the Alpha Laird my mother was mated to in high esteem.

Their thick accents make them hard to understand, but after six days in the Highlands, I am starting to get used to it and don't need to ask so much for them to repeat what they are saying.

The Scottish clans are an infamous breed of werewolves. They maintain the old laws and systems; they have an Alpha who is also their monarch or Laird. They live in keeps, with moats and drawbridges. They settle arguments with a traditional fist fight and the rumours were true, they still wear kilts with nothing underneath. I am going to take one home to Preston.

The thing that sticks out most is that the whole clan is closed off to the human world. They are self-sufficient and private. They rely on the other clans and build their alliances accordingly. It is like a look back at the past.

I had a bout of tummy ache a couple of days ago and Aiden thought I was getting sick. The Alpha Laird hosting us had the healers see me almost immediately. He said it was because he didn't want a dead English werewolf to explain to his supreme council, but afterwards he told me he was relieved I was feeling better.

I worried about the illness I was experiencing. At first, I thought I could be with pup, but a pregnancy test quickly ruled that out. Then, as soon as it began, it ended, but Lizzie is feeling the lasting effects. She whimpers and cries for Zack and Preston a lot and I have already told Aiden I need to go home before the two weeks we allocated because I cannot bear to be away from Preston any longer.

Aiden has reverted to being my annoying older brother. He constantly fusses and is overprotective of me and the wandering eyes of the Scottish warriors are the bane of his day. I feel a lot like when we were children. A lot of the time, it was us against the world and Aiden was my rock when I needed something steady and my umbrella in the storm. He loved me when I felt unwanted and unloved by everyone else.

I haven't been able to talk to Preston for over twelve hours now and it's starting to get to me, and I know Aiden feels the same about Eva, in addition to worrying about life back home, and the pack, and a million other responsibilities. We are none the wiser about our mother despite it being five days since we left to find answers.

"Alpha Aiden and Lieutenant Amber, the Laird will see you now in the main hall."

This is it; we will officially ask to cross the border and find our mother. We will know once and for all if she is willing to talk to us. Aiden tries to prepare me in case she says no, but I don't think she will. I can feel her close by, I am sure of it, and I feel nothing but welcome here.

I hold Aiden's hand as we walk into the main hall, just like I used to when I was a little girl.

CHAPTER FIVE

Danger

*** Salma ***

It's claustrophobic being locked in like this. I hate having my freedom taken away; however, I have never seen my Alejandro like this. I have never seen him so wound up and consumed by worry and anger.

He is convinced someone is going to try and kill me. The Mafia do not fuck around. I should know, after all, and if I was aware of such a threat, I would have shot the bastard right between the eyes by now. My father was no pushover and yet he was poisoned to death.

Who is my brother? My mother refuses to cooperate with us and so we had to use Raul's contacts to find out which firm Dominga belongs to.

So far, we have found that she is part of the Serrano family. They are a very rich and powerful Mafia mob and we must tread carefully. I don't want an all-out turf war; I just want justice for my papa.

The Serrano Family are a more dominant mob than us because of their geographical position. They own most of London and that gives them a lot of power and extreme wealth to cover anything they may be lacking. They are not to be underestimated. Even with the Morales and Suarez families combined, the Serranos are still more powerful, with better connections and resources beyond our capabilities.

I am biding my time until Raul arranges for us to meet to discuss Dominga and the small matter of my father's murder.

My period finally starts and on top of being holed up for two days, I have to face my failure once again. My frustration and anger are ten-fold. Even Ale gives me a wide berth and I just want Eva, or papa or even Mami to hug me.

"You're stuck with me, Chula, so let me comfort you. Stop being so stubborn," Ale shouts at me after I push him away, but the truth is I'm scared. What if I can't give him a child? Will he begin to hate and resent me?

"Leave me alone, Ale, I'm sick of the sight of you." As the hurt flares in his eyes, I instantly regret being so nasty and harsh with him. "I'm sorry, I'm sorry. I don't mean it. I'm sad, Ale, and I hate that you're seeing me like this."

I don't resist when he pulls me to him. "If you just listen for a moment, I have brought you a present. Something I think will make you feel better, for a little while anyway. Salma, mi amor, don't hide away from me. I love you, warts and all."

"You cheeky bastard, I do not have warts! What did you buy me?" He's more than likely bought me chocolate or, more specifically, chocolate ice cream.

However, he shakes his head at me. "I didn't buy you anything. I caught it."

What the fuck is he talking about now? I wonder to myself. "What, like a fish or a rat?"

The look of amusement in his eyes makes my heart heal a little.

God above, this man takes my breath away.

"Yes, I suppose you could describe it as a rat, but why don't you let me show you? Bring your bag, you're going to need it." He's referring to my work bag, my bag of tricks, my bag full of instruments of pain and torture.

A thrill of excitement fills my tummy, and Ale knows it too, by the smile on his face.

"What did you catch for me?" I eagerly ask. What do I get to play with and take all my pent-up frustration and disappointment out on?

Ale leads me down to the basement. He covers my eyes for the last two steps with one hand and continues to guide me with the other.

When we reach the bottom of the stairs, he removes his hand from my eyes and whispers, "Surprise" at me. I blink several times to reclaim my sight. Then, I notice the middle-aged, plump and dowdy woman bound to a chair with a gag in her mouth.

Realisation floods over me. I have waited months to confront this bitch and now the time is here.

"Oh, Ale! Thank you, this is the best present ever." I kiss him passionately, allowing him closer than I have for the past two days, and he practically growls in satisfaction. "I'm definitely cutting her eyelids off though, as a special present to myself."

Ale chuckles a little. "Whatever makes mi bebe happy, you can do whatever you want with this piece of shit. She is all yours to torture before I chop her fucking head off." Ale's face darkens as he looks back over at his quarry. "Let me tell you a little bit about my best catch so far. She is implicated in the disappearance of at least seventeen children, all of them are little girls. They are thought to have been sex trafficked out of here. We got Summer back just in time because the same was probably planned for her too. Isn't that right, Carole?"

Through her gag, Carole Berkley is trying to shout. Tears fall involuntarily from her eyes, and she shakes her head and body side to side as she tries fruitlessly to escape.

The new information about the extent of her kidnapping and the reason behind it fuels me. This will be a full Mafia torture to the death. Crimes against small children are completely off the table, they are punishable by the worst means imaginable. The people who commit those crimes are the lowest scum on this earth.

As I approach her, Carole continues to try and shout. "Were you never told not to talk when your mouth is full?" I ask her sweetly, and Carole's eyes enlarge in realisation. She isn't getting out of this intact or alive. Justice has just caught up with her.

*** **Eva** ***

I can't contact Aiden and I'm worried about him. I ask my new Gamma Wolf, Max, to locate Preston so I can talk to him, but his guards come back empty-handed.

"He hasn't been to training and he hasn't been to the canteen. I'm just waiting for Gamma Guard Nyle to return from Preston's parents' place. Maybe he has gone there?" Uneasiness about it all nags my conscience, so I take the emergency key to Amber and Preston's apartment and command Gamma Max to stay and guard Summer.

"No, Luna. I will stand outside while you go in, but one of the other guards can stay and protect Summer." Max is very forward. It's easy to see why Aiden thought he would be the best suited for the job. However, right now I just want to smack him in the eye for being so stringent.

I scowl at him, and he smiles back at me. "What are you smiling at?" I ask him. "I thought we could be friends but you're too bossy."

He laughs and this time it reaches his eyes. "I'm not here to be your friend, Luna. I am here to protect you from harm." Well, there is no way to argue out of that one.

"Fine," I tell him as I kiss Summer and tell her to behave. He follows me as I leave my own apartment and walk down the corridor to Preston's and Amber's.

I knock lightly and wait but there is still no answer, so I turn the emergency key and the door springs open. "I will be right here if you need me, Luna, just shout to me." I nod to Max. He isn't a bad guy, he's just not as pliable as Aiden when it comes to getting what I want.

The apartment is in darkness despite it being daytime, and as I walk across the room to open the curtains, I fall over Preston, who is asleep on the floor. Unshaven, unwashed and dressed in dirty clothes, he stinks of stale drink and vomit.

"What the hell?" He shouts as I startle him awake. He pounces on me and pins me to the floor; I fear the look in his eyes, at least until he recognises me. "Eva? What are you doing scaring me like that?"

He quickly releases me and apologises. But all in all, the state of him, his clothes, the apartment, and the fact that he is so on edge confirms to me that something bad has happened.

"Have you heard something? Are Aiden and Amber, okay?" Preston looks at me with bloodshot eyes, straining to concentrate on me.

"…Evieeee! There you are, my new Luna, whatcha doing here?

Did you bring some brandy with you?" Preston slurs his words and as he tries to stand so he can bow to me he falls a couple of times before giving up completely. He is as pissed as a fart.

"Why are you drunk in the daytime, Preston? And where have you been? I've been trying to find you." My questions are fuelled by concern, but I stop my questioning when I hear him crying. His shoulders shake uncontrollably.

"I'm in shit, Eva, and I don't know what to do. All I know is I love Amber and I can't live without her, and I can't keep her safe. I'm fucked no matter what I do. Nikki will see to it no matter what decision I make."

In a confused state, I listen to him. I don't know who he is talking about or what they have to do with him and Amber, but Preston is like a brother to me now. I want to help him.

"I don't know what has happened, Preston, but I want to help you. Why don't you tell me what has been happening?" He takes a deep breath and nods.

I take his hands and help him stand up.

"Yes, I think I had better tell someone what has been happening and then maybe you can tell me what the hell I'm supposed to do. Let me get a shower and clean up first. I feel rank."

As he stumbles to the bathroom, I clear away the empty beer and liquor bottles and contemplate what it is Preston could have to say.

What could have possibly upset him so much?

*** Amber ***

We are given permission to cross the border but they keep our phones and weapons and we must travel the last part by horse.

The final leg of our journey is the most difficult and treacherous part of the whole trip. The rugged highlands of Scotland are some of the most breathtakingly beautiful and sinfully unpredictable and challenging terrain I have ever had to tackle.

It doesn't help that I feel awful. I am not sure if it's the distance between Preston and I, the lack of contact we've had or if I have a little bug. Whatever the cause, my stomach twists in knots. The further north we travel, the worse I seem to feel. I need my answers so I can go home to my mate.

Upon our arrival, Aiden and I walk into the main hall of the keep. The Alpha Laird is there, but there is no female. Where is my mother?

"Alpha Laird Rory, we have come here to reconnect with our mother-"

The Alpha Laird interrupts Aiden by coughing and raising his hand. His eyes never leave me. The expression on his face is unreadable.

"I know who you are and why you are here. Coral, your mother, was my fated mate and I feel like she has just walked into my hall again, just like she did all those years ago. You both have her eyes, but you look like her twin."

When he looks at me, it's with love and pain etched all over his face.

"I know you're here for answers, although I did expect you

both to come a long time ago. Your mother left you both memory boxes." She left them for us, I think to myself. Does that mean she's fucked off from here too? Has this been a wasted journey, a waste of the time I don't have?

"Why hasn't our mother received us? Surely she wanted to see us after all this time or is she sincerely that cold and unfeeling?" The contempt is apparent in Aiden's voice as he speaks, but it's Alpha Laird Rory's reaction to his words that captures my attention.

"You don't know, do you? I told John, I told him so he could tell you both because I wasn't in a fit state to travel."

"Tell us what?" My angry reply reverberates around the room. Has she taken another lover and moved again to pastures new? Where the hell is she?

"Aiden, Amber. Please join me at the table. We have a lot to discuss."

He directs us to an old stone table where there are already two boxes set out.

"I didn't realise. I thought you knew. I thought you were here to find out more about her. I told your father, but I am not surprised now, after everything he did, that he didn't tell you." As we sit, I get a better look at my mother's other mate. He's handsome, I'll give her that.

"Please, just tell us, Alpha Laird Rory. Where is our mother?"

"I'm so sorry, truly I am. She's dead. She died the year after she left you."

I've never had an outer body experience, but I have shifted and allowed Lizzie to have control and right now that's how I feel, except Lizzie doesn't have control either. Neither of us are in control.

My mother is dead. After all this time, she isn't even alive. She wasn't alive all this time. I thought she was rejecting me and evading me and ignoring me. All the times I cursed her for not loving me, or coming back for me or for not sending me a note, she was dead and gone.

My brother's voice penetrates my shocked haze. "Dead? How?" I can tell from his voice he is holding on to his emotions tightly. He sounds like he is straining to talk.

"Aidy." I can't keep the sob out of my voice as I reach out to my big brother, the only other person in the universe who understands the devastation I feel right now. Why?

"It's okay, Amber, I've got you," he assures me before turning back to the Alpha Laird. "How could you take another man's mate, take a woman away from her children, leave little pups with a no-good father and no bloody mother?"

"She wasn't your father's mate. She had one fated mate and that was me. She was nothing more than a plaything to your father. Sure, he made her Luna when she fell pregnant with you, Aiden, but she was never his to keep. Not that he wanted to keep her, he just didn't want anyone else to want her."

This is the first time Alpha Laird Rory has lost his composure in front of us and it stuns us into silence as he continues to tell us his tale.

"We found each other quite by accident. I was visiting the English Alphas as part of my training when a little redheaded pup ran past me heading for the riverbank and I caught her just before she jumped. Her mother was so relieved, and then the scent hit me. Her mother was my mate. I couldn't believe it. The mate of the Alpha I was visiting was my mate too. That was enough of a shock, and then I uncovered the truth."

He can't keep the bitterness out of his voice. "He didn't even mark her. She was nothing to him, and because she hadn't been claimed, our bond just grew and grew. I was prepared to go to war for your mother, but she wanted to keep things amicable. She wanted you to have both your parents and so we approached Alpha John and explained the situation."

Anger apparent in his expression, Rory doesn't stop. Maybe now that he's started, he can't stop. "He was furious at first, demanding to know if we had embarked on an affair, but I assured him that we hadn't, that I couldn't. To mess with the mate of an Alpha is punishable by death. But now I knew they weren't mates, fated or chosen, she was mine to claim."

Rory pauses to drink from a goblet before carrying on with his recollection. "We came to an agreement. Your mother and I could have shared custody of the two of you if we left quietly. That night, I received word that my father had been hurt in a hunting accident and I had to return immediately to my own territory."

His expression turns darker as he explains more. "Your mother obviously wanted to wait behind with you two, she wanted to have everything in place before she left the territory, so I left her behind thinking she would be safe with her pack. No-one knew she had found her mate and was leaving to be with him. We had no reason to suspect anything."

He pauses to look at us; I am visibly upset, and Aiden is shaking with pent-up anger. "I know this is a lot to take in but it's important that you know she loved you and being separated from you both killed her. Your father's wickedness killed her because if he couldn't have her, he didn't want anyone else to either."

Replacing the goblet on the table, he stands and walks to the open hearth before turning back to us. "By the time I had arrived at my territory and realised my father was fit and well, there had been no accident and it was all a ruse to get me away from your mother, I knew something bad was going to happen. I thought your father would have you all killed or that he would hide you away."

Tears fill his eyes. "I found my Coral broken on the road with just a thin dress on despite it raining heavily. He had banished her and told her if she ever returned, he would behead you both. He had mutilated her, thoroughly abused her and sent her on her way without so much as a coat."

I gasp in horror. How could that bastard do that?

"The bonds that tie us together are sacred. The bonds between a parent and their children are almost unbreakable. It is one of the most powerful phenomena known to our kind. The bond presides over all other bonds and… the only way I can explain is, if you ever see a fated mate couple reject each other, it is immensely painful and can destroy them. The broken bond between a parent and child acts like cancer, a disease, and slowly kills the parent."

I struggle to understand his lesson. There is so much to take in and I am still reeling from the fact that my mother is dead. "I accepted you both the moment I found out about you so that my bond with your mother was secure. I never had an issue accepting you because I knew you both had a claim on Onyx River, with you being John's heir, Aiden. I loved your mother and wanted her to be happy. Me accepting you both made her happy."

He's starting to reach an important point, I can feel it. I sit at the edge of my seat and Aiden leans forward too. "However, your father banishing her and breaking the bond between you was enough to kill your mother. I tried my best to save her, but I couldn't. My love and our bond would never have been enough to heal her broken heart and soul."

Alpha Laird Rory stops for a moment when his voice breaks

but quickly continues on. "She loved you both so, so much. You were everything to her. She would cry and talk about the times she had been cold towards you both because deep down she always knew John would use you to hurt her. She worried nonstop about who was caring for you both, who was loving you and if you would ever forgive her for not being strong enough to fight your father."

We all have tears in our eyes; this is not the outcome I expected or wanted. It was something I had never even contemplated. All this time, I thought she simply didn't love us and that we weren't good enough for her. However, tragically, us being torn away from her caused her heart to break and it killed her.

My father. Even up until a few days ago, he tried to blame her, he tried to cover up what he had done.

As soon as I have my knives back and we return to the Onyx River, I will allow Aiden to remove his throat before I chop his fucking head off and mount it on a big stick. He killed my mother. He murdered her.

I will make him pay.

"Where is she?" I want to pay my respects to the woman who carried and bore me. The woman who died because of her love and longing for us. I need to say goodbye and then I need to go home, so I get to my feet.

Rory rubs his hands over his face. The lines of grief are even more evident now and, out of reverence for his honesty, and for our mutual love of his mate, I cross the room to him and offer him a hug.

A little sob escapes him as he reciprocates and murmurs, "Goodness, you look so much like her, Amber, I feel like she's here with me." That comforts me somewhat, that a part of her is still alive within me.

Aiden approaches as well, offering his hand.

"Rory, I just want to apologise. I should never have accused you of taking her away. We didn't know. Our father has a lot to answer for. I want to assure you, as his son and Alpha, he will reap what he has sown. He will pay for this." I nod my agreement to my brother.

Time is up for former Alpha John Goldrick; karma is on its way in the form of his children.

*** Preston ***

No matter how hard I try, I cannot recall ever feeling so shitty in all my life. Even when I thought I was going to lose Amber when she struggled to commit, there had been hope that everything would work out. Now, it's like I've fallen into a black hole. Everything seems bleak and hopeless.

I have dreams that turn into nightmares. Amber is running in front of me, but no matter how fast I run or how hard I try, I can't reach her. I can feel the ends of her hair when I stretch out, but she remains elusive to me.

I wake covered in sweat with a scream stuck in my throat and my heart beating like an overactive drummer. Once or twice, I have woken up crying and I was powerless to stop my tears from falling. What am I going to do? What can I do?

It's like there is a large hole in my chest and Zack has even stopped howling all night long. When he was loud, I prayed for his silence, but now, I am frightened I may never hear him again.

I didn't make a conscious decision to drink, but once I begin to drink the whiskey, I find it easier to block everything out.

At one point, everything seems hilarious. I laugh maniacally at the most boring and unextraordinary of things.

When I pass the happy phase, I start to hurl in the toilet, all down my front and even in the lounge we have just finished decorating. I crash out on the floor and the next day I can't motivate myself to get up. I just want to curl up in a ball and die.

When the rest of the pack try to mindlink me, I block all attempts. I cannot deal with my own thoughts and feelings, never mind theirs too.

I even ignore the mindlink attempts my future Luna makes. I just want Amber, but I can't have her. Not now, and it is looking more certain that she won't be mine in the future either. My heart aches with loneliness and sadness.

Out of nowhere, I feel a kick in my side and sense someone is in my room. I think it must be Nikki! So I jump up with every intention of hurting her until I meet the eyes of my future Luna who, by this point, I have pinned by the throat.

"Eva! What are you doing scaring me like that?" I shout out, both relieved and infuriated that she isn't Nikki.

Finally, the dam bursts, and my worries pour out to Eva. Before I tell her everything, I need to freshen up and change my clothes. I look and feel rotten.

I have a shower and Eva cleans up the apartment a bit and makes a pot of tea when, suddenly, we are both overcome with sadness and pain. Eva is confused by what it means but I automatically know what the cause is; Amber is in pain, and Aiden too. We are feeling their emotions through our bonds. I frantically try to call my mate. I need to know she is okay.

"It's just going straight to voicemail. For fucks sake. I need to know if she is okay. I can't take it anymore!" I say, and the desperation and futility in my own voice claws at my heart. I am hurting more than ever now.

"Preston. Sit down. Please. Just sit down and talk to me. None of this is helpful to you or Amber. Tell me what is troubling you while we wait for Aiden to return your call."

"It's all such a mess. I don't even know where to start, Eva. It all began the day I gave evidence at Ellis' trial. The man Amber cut down from the Moon Stone pack... his widow came onto our lands and made me a proposition. She wants me to reject Amber and take her as my chosen mate."

Eva's mouth drops open in shock.

"She told me she has the influence to have Amber imprisoned for the rest of her life or even executed. In exchange for rejecting Amber and accepting Nikki as my chosen mate, Nikki will drop all charges against Amber. Amber would be safe and free."

From the look on her face, I can see she is at a loss for what to say in response to that. "Why didn't you tell us? Does Amber or Aiden know?" Eva is in shock at what I have told her. I can see the worry and concern in her eyes, and it forces tears to fall from my own.

"No one knows, you're the only one I've told. But, Eva, there is an even bigger issue to contend with too. I think she might be part witch or something because she was able to get onto our lands undetected. She was even able to locate me deep in the forest when I was patrolling."

My shoulders slump as the futility of it hits me again.

"I don't know how I can keep Amber safe anymore. I don't want anyone else, only her. It's always been her, and it always will be. But if I don't do as Nikki says, then she'll make sure Amber never sees the light of day again."

She pats my shoulder in an attempt at comforting me while she contemplates the information I have given her and what our next move should be.

When she stands up, my tiny Luna has a determined look in her eyes now. "I am going to be Luna of this pack and I need to start making decisions and working through problems. Therefore, Beta Preston, I think I need to pay my beloved Alpha father a visit. I have some important matters to discuss with him."

I nod my agreement to her, and she continues to tell me what her plan is. "Can you arrange that for me please and then we will have a better idea of what we are facing? But look, don't worry so much. You are not alone and as soon as Aiden and Amber return, we can all work on this together." I smile back at her, and even though she is much smaller than me, and a few years younger than me, in a way, I feel like she is the big sister and I'm her little brother who she's helping.

I miss Amber. The nights are unbearable. I can feel her heartache, her sorrow and her pain and the silence between us just increases my worries about where she is and if she is safe.

Then I torment myself some more by wondering and worrying about how long she will be safe once she returns home. I refuse to face a future with her, my mate, MINE. I have waited so long for her; I am not prepared to just give up on us.

I'd rather die than live the rest of my life without her.

With renewed purpose, I do my Luna's bidding and contact her father, Alpha Xavier, and arrange for Eva to visit him today. Alpha Xavier sounds elated that his daughter has requested to see him and offers to send an escort for her, but I explain that Eva wants to keep it low key and will be escorted by myself and her Gamma.

"I look forward to seeing her," he replies enthusiastically. I feel a smidge bad that the visit is not to get to know him but to address his pack members' threats against me. Not bad enough to correct his misunderstanding though.

Within an hour, Eva has settled her little girl, Summer, with Mrs Moore, and Max has left the rest of the Gamma Guard to protect her. Max asks Eva if she would like to drive, but she refuses, and I get a member of my Beta team to drive instead.

On the surface, Eva looks calm and poised, but both Max and I detect her nervousness. "Preston, remember, as soon as you spot that bloody woman you must mindlink me straight away," she reminds me for the third time.

"I will Luna, I promise," I assure her as I mindlink Max and ask him to help her calm down. Max talks to us both about little Summer chasing a squirrel yesterday.

"She was so cute, wasn't she, Eva, she would run all the way up to it and then squeal and giggle when it ran away again. She kept shouting, 'look mummy a squiggle'. It was the cutest thing I have ever seen".

Eva smiles in recollection and I quickly thank Max for distracting her. I think Max being Eva's Gamma Wolf is a perfect combination. They seem to get along very well together, and I feel assured about Max's ability to not only keep her safe but to tune into her feelings and support her when she needs it.

We are waved through border security; Alpha Xavier has prepared them for our visit.

The packhouse is around five minutes from the border and when we stop outside, Alpha Xavier is already there, ready to greet us.

"Eva, you look beautiful, welcome back to the Moon Stone territory." He walks over to his daughter and Eva's nervousness is unmistakable, she blushes and bites her lip.

"Thank you for allowing us to visit at short notice, father. There is a matter I need to discuss with you immediately."

As we walk into the pack house, my eyes meet Nikki's. *LUNA, THERE, NOW.*

Eva swoops like an avenging archangel and collars Nikki.

"And this is the topic of our discussion. Get in there now," Eva tells Nikki and we all listen to her.

For the first time, I realise Eva isn't just a werewolf, or a future Luna.

She is The Alpha's Heir.

CHAPTER SIX

The Red Mage

*** Alejandro ***

My Sal is feeling better about stuff now. She loved her little treat and took great pleasure in punishing that old hag before I chopped her head off and left our team to clean up. We are back to trying non-stop to get pregnant.

I am not complaining. Not one bit. She is a firecracker, she knows what she likes, and she is so giving. Satisfied is my usual condition and yet I constantly crave her too. I cannot get enough. I hope I never do.

Today, we are meeting with the Don of the Serrano family to get the information we need about Jose's mistress, Dominga, and I know Sal is as eager as me. Torturing Carole only served to whet her whistle. My Chula is after blood now.

Sal wants Dominga. She is adamant Dominga is the one who poisoned and murdered her papa, but I want her brother. He is all I think of, because Sal threatens his position and, therefore, she is his target. I will disembowel the fucker and make him eat his own innards for threatening the safety of my wife.

When Sal comes out of the bedroom, she looks stunning. Her dark hair is swept up, she wears a dark grey business suit, and she looks exactly like the bad-ass I know she is.

"I wanna fuck you senseless again, Chula, you look too goddamn hot to be going outside." She stares at me disapprovingly but ends up laughing.

"Calm down, big boy, you can have me as soon as we get back. Business first, and then pleasure all night long."

I don't even have to make her promise. If Sal says we are fucking all night long, we will. Even my father has commented and complained about the racket. I told him to shut it. We're trying for a baby.

Willy drives us into the city centre. He has taken over all our transport now and I really like that he is a surrogate father figure for my Sal. She trusts him implicitly and that is very important in our line of work.

Today, I have to be a diplomat. The mob we are about to meet are superior in muscle, money, and influence. However, there is a code of conduct amongst the Mafia; etiquette, if you will. Therefore, the head of the Serrano family has agreed to meet us without hesitation. As long as we remain respectful, this meeting should be pretty straight forward.

The only snag I can envision is if they refuse to give us information on Dominga or, even worse, if they accept she murdered Jose but refuse to hand her over… that is grounds for war. Hopefully, that will not happen.

"Are we both straight about what we are doing?" Sal asks me again. She taps her foot and chews the inside of her cheek, and I raise her hand to my lips and kiss it.

"We are straight. Don't worry, mi amor, we've got this."

We pull up outside a converted warehouse on the Thames. At one point, these buildings would have been ruins but now they are affluent and sought after.

The door is manned by heavies who frisk and search us, leaving Sal fuming when they take her Glock off her. I scowl at the man who takes my wife's plaything from her, but inside I'm laughing because if looks could kill, they'd all be buried. Sal seriously takes no prisoners. I never have to guess what is going on with her, because if she hasn't told me, her face, behaviour and mannerisms always will.

Tony Serrano is around fifty years old, he is fat and balding and has a massive bulbous nose with blackheads so big I bet flies could live in there. He is head of the Serrano Family and is a widely renowned and respected man.

I have only met him twice myself, but he welcomes us both as old friends. He sits back down behind his heavy oak desk and directs Sal and I to the seats on the other side.

Tony congratulates us both on our marriage and gives Sal his condolences for her papa passing away. When his minion returns with drinks for us all, he lights his cigar and asks us how he can help us.

"Tony, as you know, my papa was poisoned. We now know he was with a member of your family when he died. She was his mistress for many years. I would like to speak to her to establish her involvement. Out of respect to you and your family, I have approached you first, so you know what I want and why."

"Tell me who your father's mistress was and what evidence you have, please, Salma," Tony replies calmly. I have to give the man his due: he has heard us out and remained calm. The rumours about him are true.

"The evidence we have is that my father was with his mistress when he died, and they had been together for two days prior. She called my mother when she found my father had died and coerced her into covering up for them." Sal lays out all the evidence as she talks, the CCTV images, the bank statements and the pathology report.

"His mistress is called Dominga and she is the mother of his son too. We believe she killed my father to ensure her son gets the firm."

Tony sits back in his seat, contemplating what we've said before answering us.

"I know Dominga and, without knowing anything more, I would definitely agree she is capable of doing this. She has gone underground since we discovered her association with werewolves. You know we police and tolerate them. Well, she has shacked up with one, a young one at that." Chugging on his cigar which stinks like camel shit, he sits forward as he addresses us. "She refers to him as J.R. and we believe he is part of the Moon Stone Pack. The Alpha is called Xavier if you want to go and pay him a visit."

My blood runs cold as I look at Sal. This werewolf keeps coming up on our radar. However, this time, he will lose his throat if he has anything to do with Jose's death.

"Do you have any current whereabouts for her? Anything we can follow-up? And what about her son? I think he might be involved and I want to question him too." My voice trails off when I see a smirk forming on Tony's face.

"Alejandro, I promise you if Dominga is found by my men, I will call both you and your wife back up here to interrogate her. However, her son is off limits. I can assure you he had nothing to do with this."

The message is clear: he knows Jose's son. He knows and he is protecting him.

Salma picks up on it too. "How can you be sure? I want to talk to him, Tony, I want to ask him as I look him in the eye if he killed our papa. He had the motive and the opportunity." I put my hand on Sal's arm in an attempt to calm her.

Tony stands. "I personally assure you that your half-brother, Enrique, had nothing to do with this. However, I will take you to him right now, so you may ask him questions."

Finally, we are getting somewhere. We follow Tony out of his office into another room. The noises coming from inside sound familiar, like beeping.

"He prefers to be called Ricky. Be gentle." Tony opens the door and steps aside. Taking Sal's hand, we walk in confidently to confront the bastard son of Jose, my prime suspect for Jose's murder.

The room itself throws me off my stride. It's a games room. There is a large screen to the right and several games consoles below it. Directly in front of us is a corner suite with a hooded figure playing video games.

The thought that this fucker is sitting here casually playing video games while my wife has been breaking her heart about her papa infuriates me. I say his name aloud but in a calm fashion to capture his attention.

I am floored when he turns around. There is a similarity between him, Sal and Jose. They have similar colouring and features.

However, Ricky scowls at me. "You made me lose my game," he moans and at my side, Sal gasps in realisation that her brother, the one who threatened her position, who we stupidly thought was involved in her father's death and was plotting against us to take our firm away from us, is nothing more than a little boy.

"Oh my god, Ale, he's a child. He's a little boy," Sal exclaims, her shock and denial both evident.

"Hey lady, I'm not that little, I'm almost eight years old now,"

Ricky challenges in exasperation. "And who are you anyway? Where is Uncle Tony?"

Tony laughs from behind us. "It's okay, boy, I'm right here. You play your game for a little while longer. I need to finish talking to my guests."

Tony walks back out of the room and I go to follow but realise I will have to drag Sal, who is in deep shock at what she has discovered.

"Bye, then," Ricky shouts to us.

"Bye, Ricky," Sal squeaks out beside me.

Tony stands waiting for us and smirks. "Now will you accept why I know he wasn't involved? He's been with me for the past two months, since his mother abandoned him to be with her werewolf lover."

Jose's son has lost his papa and his mami ran off and left him. Jose will be turning in his grave. "We have to look after him, Sal, we have to protect him."

The shock turns to joy on Sal's face. "We will look after him. Ale, I have a little brother."

Some of the grief and loss and suspicion seems to melt away from her eyes and I fall more in love with my wife as she delights in hearing she is a big sister to a seven-year-old boy.

*** Aiden ***

Rory returns our phones; however, he doesn't return Amber's knives and she hisses at him. It's kind of cute. In another life, this man would have been our stepfather. The pain in his eyes shows me how much he loved my mother. He has been completely honest with us, even the painful truth of how our mother was cold and distant at times. I know I can trust him.

"We took your phones, but it was just as a formality. We are traditionalists here and we don't have any signal at all, so they wouldn't have worked anyway. You can have your knives when you leave, Amber. You could cut yourself on them."

Amber gasps in outrage, offended by Rory's insinuation, but Rory's face is full of laughter and mischief. "Your mother had a fiery temper too. It's the red hair." He tells us a couple of stories about her that make us laugh.

"We couldn't have a pup. I mean, she died within a year of leaving you both. Her heart was shattered. My wolf told me that your mother's wolf would not permit another pregnancy because the pain of losing her first two pups was too great to endure." That was insightful, I didn't know our wolves could intuit that deeply. I'll be giving Roman a whole range of new tasks once we get home.

Once Rory tells us about the situation with the phones, he gives us access to a landline. I rush to call Eva to check in on her and to tell her how much I love her and accept her and Summer. I want to make it official; I am going to ask to adopt Summer properly, so she is mine. I am desperate to hear her voice but there is no answer. In frustration, I call my own office and Delta Billy answers.

"Hey boss, Beta Preston and Gamma Max have escorted future Luna Eva to the Moon Stone to visit her father. They should be back soon." Geez, I have been away too long. Eva is now visiting her father. I want to support her with that and instead I'm on a merry chase in the Scottish highlands when my father could have saved us all this upset and told us years ago that our mother died.

I am going to kill him. That isn't a mere wish or threat. I am going to kill the fucking monster who destroyed our family.

"Tell her I rang, and I will call again when I can. There is no signal up here, but we are starting our journey back home tomorrow. I'm assuming everything is good with the pack?"

Billy assures me that everything is going well in my absence and wishes us a safe trip home. ,

The small box Rory said my mother had made for me is on my bed when I return to my room

Unsure of what I will find, I open it warily. I know Rory said my mother was banished with nothing, so I am intrigued by my mother's legacy to me. Inside, there is a scrapbook, a letter, a blanket, and a couple of small photographs.

The photographs are worn and faded, but it's one of a baby and on the back, is my name and then there is one of me, holding Amber just after she was born. I remember that photograph. I think I have the same print at home.

In the scrap book are drawings and little annotations. The day I was born, my first smile, my first steps, my first words. The nursery rhymes and lullabies she would sing to and with us. It is a labour of love, a masterpiece of her memories of us. A huge lump forms in my throat. I can't believe she is dead, and I won't get to see her or talk to her. I have been so bitter and resentful of her all this time.

I wish Eva was here, I need her. I need us and I desperately want us to be formally mated in front of our pack and I want to be a family with her. A family that I have yearned for. I wish my little mate was here so I could show her my soul and she could kiss away all the hurt. I would wrap her up in my strong arms and never let her go. I would never ever let her feel the way my mother did. Only a monster could do that.

The next day, as we make our way back home through the territories we came through on our way up here, both Amber and I are quiet. She also got a box, but her memory book is shorter than mine. She was just a babe in arms when our mother was banished and then died.

"Aiden, I am going to be executed or imprisoned for life anyway. I think I should be the one to kill Father so there is no comeback for you. All I ask is that I get to have one complete weekend with Preston when we return. And when I am gone, help him to move on. He deserves to be happy; I want him to be happy even if it can't be with me." She chokes on her last line.

I have just lost my mother; I cannot lose my sister too. "Amber, no. As Alpha, I have the authority to use appropriate punishment. He deserves to die for what he has done, and I will execute him after a fair trial so there are no repercussions. Do not give up, we are going to fight for your freedom and if they sentence you, I will get you out of the territory so you and Preston can flee before it comes to that."

She snuggles into me. Sometimes I forget she isn't a little girl anymore; she is a fully grown woman. But to me she will always be my little sister. Until Eva came into my life, Amber was the person I loved most in this world. She was everyone I cared about.

"I can't wait to talk to Preston properly, it feels like an age has passed since we last spoke. I miss him. I don't think I would have admitted that six months ago, Aidy, but I miss him so much."

I know how she feels. This journey home is going to be torture.

*** Xavier ***

My daughter walks into my pack house, all guns blazing. I honestly feel a bit scared of her. She has a temper that is slow to ignite, but hell hath no fury like Eva once you've provoked her too many times. She walks up to the recently widowed Nikki and grabs her by the scruff of her neck, and I swear Eva's eyes flash silver when she does it.

"Get in there, now. You and I are going to have words. Who the fuck do you think you are coming on to my land and threatening my pack members? You do realise you have messed up the whole trial to find the truth about your mate's death by intimidating a witness and trying to bribe him. Are you completely stupid?"

My daughter throws Nikki into the hall and walks in after. She has a commanding presence. Her short stature only amplifies how strong she is because she doesn't need brute strength to get what she wants; she commands respect.

She is my heir all right. I only wish her mate wasn't also an Alpha. My land and legacy will be swallowed up into his now. However, I know that is a small price to pay since my pack will be led by the best person and my lands will be safe in her hands. She already has a child who will be our Heir Apparent. Our legacy will live on.

"What is the meaning of this, Nikki? Have you been intimidating and bribing witnesses?" Nikki openly cries, and I am sympathetic because of the pain I feel from my own mate bond severing. She is very young to lose her mate, and before they had pups too. It is a shame for her, but we must abide by the law; they are there for a reason and she broke them.

"I miss him, and I wanted that *whore* to pay for what she did. She butchered him; he was severed all the way from his shoulder down to his groin. I wanted vengeance. I wanted her mate and his pup so it would hurt her like she hurt me."

Using my Alpha aura, I force her to submit. "That was why we informed the council when you made your complaint, so they could find the truth and deal out the punishment as appropriate. You made the complaint... that was what you wanted, and now you've ruined it all. You have no authority here or anywhere to condemn someone, or to decide what their punishment should be."

I look at my daughter, who seems to be calming down at least.

"I will inform the council straight away. And I am sorry on behalf of my pack member. I will ensure the council's punishment is served."

Eva nods back. "Thank you, Father. But first, I want to know how she got onto our land without detection and how she was to track him."

It's a good question, and I turn to look at the woman it concerns. Nikki has revealed her own secret now and she only has herself to blame.

*** Salma ***

My father's son, my brother, is a child. In my head, I pictured a beast of a man who was involved in the murder of our papa. However, he is a child and he's my little brother. He is so small with features uncannily like papa's that it is unreal. When Mami told me that Dominga was papa's only mistress for the last ten years, I assumed with time and age he had no need for a harem of lovers. I expected my brother to be a man, maybe a similar age as me, and my father had opted to keep his mother as his only mistress.

It's always been something I thought about: why didn't my parents have more children? Mafia families are usually huge. I wonder if mami couldn't have more. Maybe papa kept Dominga as his only mistress so she would give him another child? I guess I will never know. Not fully.

Tony said Ricky's mother abandoned him and ran off with a werewolf named JR. This werewolf and Dominga are now our prime suspects for my father's murder, and our number one objective is to find them. Although Mafia and Werewolf are not enemies as such, we certainly don't mix, so, it is intriguing to see how this happened and why.

I think it's time to visit my friend in her new home. Eva has been to visit me a few times, bringing Summer with her as well as an entourage of wolves that Aiden rightly insisted on sending 'just in case.' However, I think it's time to visit her and her mate and see if they can help me. Alpha Aiden will have extensive knowledge of his pack and the packs surrounding his. He might know someone called JR. He might be able to point me to my father's killer.

Tony names two other associates who may be able to give more insight into Dominga and her whereabouts. However, I want to hear his theory of why she would risk killing my father.

"She hated him, but she loved the power and status and having his son only increased that. The fact that she abandoned Ricky so quickly confirms to me that she had no real feeling for her son and he is a mere pawn in her game for power."

Tony stubs out his cigar before continuing.

"I believe Jose training you to take over and the rumours of your marriage to Mr Suarez to solidify that probably pushed her to act because she would lose her power and status if her son wasn't recognised as Jose's true heir."

He moves the paperweight on his desk, clearly deep in thought.

"She may have thought that killing your father would have killed your union too, thus weakening your claim to your firm. From what I heard, your father loved Dominga and he loved his son too, and I do believe he would have divulged all this to her."

Tony sits back and regards us both as a couple, raising both hands to include us both.

"It's common knowledge he handpicked Mr Suarez for you, Salma, and the fact that you resisted and fought against it is well known too and actually helped your take over. You are strong and we recognised that."

I smile and look at Ale, it seems like an eternity ago I was resisting being his wife.

"My oldest is a girl too, and you have forced me to acknowledge that a woman can lead successfully. Dominga may have had delusional thoughts that she could lead in her son's place until he came of age and received all his training. Maybe she saw herself as Donna Regent?"

Finally breaking eye contact, he looks for his cigar once again.

"Or maybe she found a new man to fuck and wanted an out? Maybe your papa's balls started to sag, or he couldn't get it up anymore. Maybe she didn't do it at all and we are barking up the wrong tree completely."

I smile at Tony; he is the first Don who continued to talk as he would if I was a man. He is also intelligently dissecting my problem for me, examining all the evidence we have so far in a clinical way. It is good to have an outside perspective that isn't tainted by emotion.

"What I do know is that our laws are clear and if she did kill your papa, I will execute her. Unless you want the honours, of course?"

I raise my eyebrows at him. Of course, I want the honours and I know he is teasing me. "Can I take my brother? I'm sure papa would want me to look after him and raise him, especially seeing as his mother has run off and left him." I hold my breath as he makes his decision.

Tony scrutinises me. "He's a good kid, Sal, would you harm him?"

Rage starts to bubble up in me… how fucking dare he ask me that? It infuriates me, but I realise he is trying to protect Ricky and I would have asked him the same thing if the scenario was the other way around.

"I am well aware of our laws, Tony; children are off limits, but I wouldn't harm him anyway. I want to be a big sister, the one I'm supposed to be. He is my kin, my last link to my papa."

A lump forms in my throat as I think of my papa, and his final gifts to me. They are priceless, better than any money could buy: My Alejandro and now my little brother, Ricky.

"I will look after him, protect him, train him and, when the time comes, he will have his rightful share of our empire. That is what is right and it's what papa would have wanted."

Tony addresses Alejandro. "Are you ready for this?"

My Ale smiles back at him. "Whatever she wants, I will give her anything… you know the score, Tony. She is my Queen. My Donna. Mi Amor." A shiver of desire runs right through me that seems to ping on my clit. I am going to fuck his brains out later.

"First, I think we should tell Ricky who you are and let him decide."

That sounds fair enough, but what will I do if he says he doesn't want to come with me?

*** Melanie ***

I am feeling increasingly isolated and alone. Am I going crazy? I'm not sure. Visions of Ryan keep intruding on my peace and it's terrifying me. While relaxing in the bath last night I opened my eyes and he was hanging in front of me, his face purple and eyes bulging. I can't carry on like this.

I am too frightened to sleep, and I am exhausted from the hypervigilance. I wish I had a friend I could turn to.

I seek out my midwife, Sheila. I tell her what is going on. She is keen for me to get some mental health support and finds me the phone number for the ante-natal psychiatric support team.

Sheila give me the details of support groups I could attend. All expectant mothers from all walks of life. I could go and make new friends in a similar phase of their lives, and we could support each other. It sounds perfect.

However, as with anything in my life, it is far from perfect. I attend the first support group later that evening. I walk in alone and everyone turns to look at me. The room falls silent. I am the only person without a partner. The perfect couples look me up and down and the imperfect ones seem happier that the scummy single mum has turned up, so they look more respectable in comparison.

At first, no one talks to me except the woman running the support group who offers me a drink before we both make awkward small talk about the weather and the latest political fiasco in the news.

We all sit in the support circle to introduce ourselves. There is the usual, "I am Tarquin, and this is my wife Audrey, and we are pregnant," as well as a few other stuck ups. When it is my turn, I stand.

"Hi, my name is Melanie, I am pregnant with my third child. My first daughter. I am happy to meet you all."

No one else is questioned, some people wave and say hi, but as I sit down, I am bombarded by questions.

"Where is the dad?"
"Aren't you scared?"
"Was it planned?"
"Will the dad be involved?"
"Who is your birthing partner?"

After a couple of minutes, I zone out, completely and utterly overwhelmed and feeling more alone than ever before.

My baby wasn't planned, and it is the product of me cheating with another woman's husband. I have no birthing partner and I am very fucking scared. Oh and the baby's dad will not be involved because he was a horrible bastard who told me he didn't want it and to get rid of it, and then went and killed himself by accident.

Can you imagine their faces if I said all that? I am shunned already; I would be burned at the stake if they knew my child was the bastard of a dead man who was married to another. That I am a whore and a homewrecker.

When the circle starts, I excuse myself, saying I need to pee. But in reality, I run to my car, drive home and decide I'm going to stay in the house until the baby's born.

Even the threat of Ryan's ghost won't keep me out.

*** Eva ***

Maintaining a civil manner is becoming increasingly hard. I am fuming that this Nikki has caused Preston all the upset and pain he has been in. He is not responsible for what happened, and Amber has submitted to the council and will accept their ruling. Nikki is completely and utterly out of order, and I am not standing for it.

As soon as Preston points her out, I grab her. She will not be getting away from me. I am here for an explanation. I want answers. What did she really think she would achieve? More importantly, how did she manage to avoid our border controls? I drag her by the scruff of her neck into my father's main pack hall and launch her onto her knees in the middle of the room.

"I am Evangelina Smith-Jones, future Luna of The Onyx River and Alpha Heir to Xavier Woodward. Submit to me now and explain yourself."

Lina is in my head now. She is in a rage that someone in our pack has been threatened and she is guiding me in my responses and reactions. I am struggling to maintain control over my wolf counterpart.

My father's look of shock quickly turns to pride when I frog march Nikki into his hall. I know finding Aiden has made me stronger, but I also feel strength growing inside me from being here in my father's lands too. It's as though the land recognises me and welcomes me home. My strength as a werewolf is amplified here, as my birthright.

From what I have seen, Junior is not around and it's a relief that he isn't here. He still creeps me out and although Aiden tried to relay what is happening between Junior and the father Junior and I share, I told him to stop. Not yet. I wasn't ready. I can barely believe I have a father; I'm struggling to accept that a loathsome leech is my half-brother.

I listen to what Nikki has to say for herself, looking at my father's reactions. I want to know what type of man he is: will he protect her blindly or will he throw her under the bus or will he lead impartially, taking both sides into account? The way my father handles this will colour my opinion of him. He doesn't know it yet, but he is on trial, and I am the judge and jury.

"How were you able to come onto my land without detection and how were you able to track Beta Preston?" Recognition flashes in my father's eyes. He knows how and if he refuses to tell me, I know what sort of man he is.

"My father was a Red-Mage. A jack-of-all-trades. My mother was a werewolf of the Moon Stone. Alpha Xavier promised to protect me and my identity and my abilities. You promised my mother on her deathbed you would look out for me. You promised!"

Lina growls inside me, she knows that we are close to the truth too. My teeth buzz with a new kind of energy and a peculiar feeling starts to descend on me.

"Nikki, I cannot protect you, you went against my express instructions and used the powers you have to manipulate and intimidate. I will have to inform the council." The power of an Alpha rolls off my father and a glimmer of pride glows inside me. He did the right thing. He is a good man after all. "The best you can hope for is that you apologise to my daughter and show some remorse for what you have done and get on your knees and beg for forgiveness for the wrongs you have committed against her and her pack."

The temperature in the room decreases, a chill settles in my bones and my teeth start to chatter.

"I should apologise? It seems Junior was correct; our Alpha

has grown weak since his little princess has returned." Nikki clenches her jaw and narrows her eyes. "That WHORE killed my mate. I will fucking destroy her, I will ensure every hope and dream she ever had rots in the soil under her feet. I will destroy every fucking werewolf who stands in front of her to protect her."

She stands, her hands balled into fists.

"I will not stop until I avenge my lover. I will not stop until she screams for death because of the agony I inflict on her sorry, pathetic life. He was my mate, my only family and she took it away from me, she took everything from me, and I will take everything from her and burn it to the ground."

Nikki spits as she rants, and a gust of mist and electricity flows in the air around her, giving her a mystical and otherworldly look.

"*You* could have had some semblance of a future with me, Beta Preston, if you had just submitted and done as I asked, but now you will *all* pay. Any pups born into your pack from this moment on will be subject to my curse. A curse to avenge my lost lover. Your pups will never find their mates, they will not feel the bond. This is the cost your mate will pay for killing mine. I place a curse upon every member of the Onyx River Pack and your offspring. May you all know what it truly is to be alone."

Lina growls and pounces and before I know what is happening, pain completely overwhelms me. My bones crack, snap, and transform. My back elongates and stoops, my arms become front paws and fur sprouts out from my forehead. As I shift into my wolf form, into Lina, Eva screams in agony and fear.

As the pain subsides, Lina howls and then pounces, attempting to attack Nikki. However, Nikki anticipates this and before Lina lands, Nikki throws something to the ground and a puff of red smoke fills the room. When it clears, Nikki is nowhere to be found.

The reaction of the others in the room is perplexing. They all look at me curiously and I start to feel paranoid. Have I shifted wrong? Am I a cat instead of a wolf? What if I can't shift back? I needn't have worried; my body transforms back and as I take my human form once more, a cloak is quickly placed around me.

"I shifted. I finally shifted!" I say, filled with excitement, but the look on their faces makes me reassess my joy. Why do they look at me like that? Maybe it's because Nikki escaped. "Where did she go? We can still catch her if we rush." Preston catches me as I scramble to my feet to go after her until my legs give way and I fall almost to the ground.

"Eva, take it easy, she's gone, we won't find her now. You need to rest... that was terrifying and intense." Preston looks at me with concern, but there is something more there. Is it fear? Or intrigue?

"I don't understand. Why do I need to rest? Did I do something wrong? Why are you all acting weird?" Panic rises within me. I have been concentrating so much on shifting and being able to complete the full mating ritual with Aiden, I never once thought there may be an issue once I actually did it.

"Luna. Eva. You did shift, but... you didn't become a wolf," Max, my Gamma tells me gently. In shock, I try to process what he is telling me. If I am not a werewolf... What did I transform into? Did I really become a cat or a dog?

My father kneels down in front of me and takes my hand in his. "Evangelina... You have a Dire Wolf."

What the hell is a Dire Wolf and why are they all acting like I am something that should be feared? Where did Nikki disappear to? What the hell is a Red-Mage?

I came here for answers and ended up with even more questions.

*** Aiden ***

An overpowering sense of foreboding fills me. Eva. Something is wrong with Eva. Roman challenges me for control, but I resist his arguments. I need to simply call and ask.

Amber rushes to me. "You felt that too, right? Something is wrong, Aidy. We need to head home. NOW."

If Amber felt it too, then this is bigger than Eva. This is Preston. This is the pack.

"Get our car now, we need to leave right away and we will not be stopping. We need to get home as soon as possible," I tell our guards who rush to do our bidding.

Both Amber and I keep trying for a signal on our phones so we can make contact with our mates. I alternate between feeling angry and then terrified.

The feeling doesn't leave us. It is a dark and heavy feeling of no hope that seems to drain the life out of us both.

As we hit the border between Scotland and England, our phones spring to life. It has been over six hours since the incident happened.

I call Eva straight away. *Please be safe, please be safe.* I am relieved when she answers, but when I hear how upset she is, anxiety floods me once more.

"Aiden, please come home. Please come back as soon as possible." As she cries down the phone, I try to work out what has happened.

"Lina is a Dire Wolf. I have a Dire Wolf."

Holy shit. Dire Wolves are extremely rare. They are huge, powerful beasts that are harder to control. How the hell has Eva ended up with one?

"Shortie, please calm down. Everything is going to be okay."

I say the words, but I am scared for my love. I am worried about the implications of her having a Dire Wolf instead of a regular wolf. They are so powerful that this could kill my little delicate mate.

I can't let that happen. I need to go home and protect what is mine.

CHAPTER SEVEN

A Dire Wolf

*** Xavier ***

When Eva shifts into her wolf form, I am terrified. Not for myself, but for my little girl. She is tiny, and Dire Wolves are distinctive for their herculean size. Her wolf form is at least four times the size of her human form. I reckon her wolf is around double the size of my own. The shift alone could kill her. I am finally part of her life and now it feels almost as if I am going to lose her all over again.

I send her back home with her Beta and Gamma. I insist on her wearing a silver bracelet to subdue her wolf so she wouldn't try to emerge again and to stop any further manifestations. Beta Preston assures me that he will have a full Beta and Gamma Guard to protect her, but I still feel uneasy about her going home without some of my wolves too, so I send half my Delta team with her. As the daughter of the Alpha, it is an honour for them to protect her and I know Aiden would appreciate the support. I have seen the way he looks at her, I know he loves her and will do anything to save her.

Eva looks shocked and tearful, and I want nothing more than to reassure my little girl, but I feel responsible. I have a little knowledge about Dire Wolves and how they come to be. I can only imagine what my girl has been through to manifest such a massive beast of a wolf. This could have been prevented if I had been the father she needed and deserved back then. Dire Wolves, to my limited knowledge, manifest when a werewolf isn't raised as a werewolf. When they do not exercise their wolves and allow the first shift in their teens, the repressed wolves feed off negative emotions and trauma. Eva must have suffered a great deal to have such a large dire wolf.

I have an old contact who used to work for the Werewolves Council. Elder Tabbatha is a werewolf Historical Researcher. I call her and ask her to come as soon as she possibly could. If anyone has answers, she does.

Elder Tabbatha is smart and funny with a keen and inquisitive mind. I have no doubt she will have information about Dire Wolves and how to treat them. I trust she will be discreet; people fear what they do not know, and I worry for my daughter's safety if this becomes common knowledge.

Reeling in shock and preoccupied with Eva, I completely forgot that Nikki has escaped. When I do remember, I send my Beta to inform the scouts and trackers and tell them to bring her directly to me, dead or alive.

Then I go down into the dungeon to question the piece of shit who raised my little girl with so much fear and pain in her life that she has managed to manifest a monster that is part of her.

Rose is a prisoner in my cells and has been since she made threats about exposing my world. Up until now, she refuses to talk to me, but today, I will choke the fucking words out of her.

"You can't keep me here forever, X." She has the audacity to shout at me through the bars. Who the fuck does she think she is? She hasn't spoken all this time and then she tries to goad me.

"No, I can't, but I might just chop your stinking, lying head off instead, Rose. I'm here about Evangelina. Something has happened and I need you to tell me why she would have been frightened or scared or depressed throughout her life. Help me with this. Help me to help our daughter and I'll let you go." Rose is a selfish, jealous woman, but on some level, she must have feelings for her child. I put my faith in humanity. Well, in Rose's humanity.

"I gave her an amazing life, X. I tried to give her everything, but she was always so moody and brooding. Every time I met someone who made me happy, she would kick up a stink about either having to move house or having to share a room. When I married Claude, she made up a story about him trying to touch her up. There was never any evidence and that made things very awkward between us all for a short time until she got married and moved out." She looks back down at her fingernails dismissively and Ace growls in my head, he wants to rip her throat out for not caring for our pup.

"That was the evidence. Her word, Rose. She told you and you should have believed her and protected her. I don't know what would have hurt more, the fact that he tried to touch her or you not doing anything when she confided in you." It's hard keeping the disgust out of my voice. I want her to know how repulsive I find her now, but I also need her to keep talking.

"I'm guessing you know what happened between her husband and me. I bet she couldn't wait to tell daddy."

I cannot believe the gall of this woman. She did wrong to Eva and she's the one acting as the victim. "I do know yes, but Eva has never spoken a word about it. Alpha Aiden told me what both you and Ryan confessed to her. Did this cause her harm?"

"I don't think she knew until I confessed, but from the short time I spent with Ryan and then the communications I had to have afterwards, I would say he didn't treat her very well. He called me from their honeymoon suite the night she lost her virginity to him and told me he had savaged her, and it was all my fault for refusing to sleep with him. He was brutal with her that night and the way she changed as a person, I would say he was brutal every night after that."

My heart is broken for my little girl. I don't know how she has endured all this. How has she been able to maintain such a sweet and caring disposition? My own wolf answers me: *Lina made her able. Lina would have protected her and taken the pain. And because our pup didn't shift, the build-up of pain caused Lina to grow.* Her wolf saved her. Her wolf took care of her when no-one else would or could.

"Alpha, your guest has just arrived at the border and will be here in about ten minutes," one of my guards informs me.

"We are not finished, Rose. Not by a long shot," I shout back to her as I climb the stairs back up to the ground floor. When I reach the hall, my mate peers out at me, sending slivers of sharp ice to penetrate my already battered heart.

"I heard there was a Dire Wolf here. Is it true? Was it your daughter?" I don't want her to ask about Evangelina if she is willing to break our bond over her being my daughter in the first place. I don't want her near me because I cannot stand the pain of losing her and potentially Eva too. It's all too much.

"Don't worry, Luna, your home is safe. My daughter has left and returned home. You have nothing to fear." I know I sound short with her, but I cannot keep up a pretence. I am in too much pain and turmoil to make a false front today. But as Lydia frowns at me, the worry is evident in her expression and I remember that none of this is her fault. I am being an ass. "I'm sorry for sounding short, I am extremely worried and the severing of our bond and the thought of my daughter dying is killing me inside.

Lydia rushes to me. "I don't want to lose you, Xavier, I don't want to lose us. I accept her, I will be her mother. We will help her excise her wolf so it can't kill her."

Excise her wolf? What is Lydia insinuating? How does she know this?

She explains without me having to ask. "I remember this happening to a wolf in my former pack. They killed the wolf so she didn't shift and was therefore safe. There were a lot of other things I can't remember but that's how Evangelina can live. You have to kill her wolf."

"She's right," my expert, Elder Tabbatha, shouts from the open doors. "We have to do it under an eclipsed moon and complete other rituals so that it works. It could kill her anyway. But she has to decide if she is willing to be wolf-less and try on the off-chance she doesn't die."

"Elder Tabbatha, please come in and take a seat. I need more information before we come to this conclusion. I will need to explain all of this to my daughter and to her mate, Alpha Aiden." Elder Tabbatha nods before entering the hall.

"It's been a long time since I've been here," she says as she looks around the hall. She had once belonged to this pack before meeting her mate and moving away. "I have other business here too, Alpha Xavier, regarding your son. There is talk of trouble with the Mafia because of him. What do you know about this?"

Oh, for fuck's sake, I need to sort one child out first before I move on to the other. "Let's talk about Eva first, that is more important." At least it is to me, but Elder Tabbatha shakes her head at me, and I look back at her in confusion.

"I'm sorry, Alpha Xavier, your daughter is just one person. What your son has done has endangered all werewolves in the territory. If the information we have received is correct, your son has gone rogue and killed a Spanish Mafia Don. This will bring a war. The council cannot and will not overlook it. I am here as your friend, but you should know the council has officials on their way right now to arrest you and the Luna."

My orders echo around the room in a roar. "Lock down the borders now and protect your Luna. I am going to fucking strangle that son of ours, Lydia!"

*** Preston ***

Eva insists that I take her directly to the cells. She is terrified and it shows. "I can't put you in a cell; you haven't done anything wrong and you're my Luna. Aiden would fucking kill me." But for such a tiny person, Eva's command is intimidating.

"You will lock me in this cell, Preston, you will lock me in and keep everyone safe from me until Aiden gets home and helps us find a solution. Do it now." I feel as low as a snake as I lock my little Luna in the cell. She should be resting in her room, being waited on, not waiting in a cold cell like a criminal. "Now I need you to organise help to make this place look nice and inviting. Summer will be home soon, and I don't want her to be scared when she sees me."

I quickly arrange for all Eva's stuff to be brought downstairs, leaving Gamma Max with her to ensure she isn't scared or feeling unsafe. I then call Aiden and tell him everything in detail. He promises to be home within a day and assures me I am right to do whatever Eva asks of me so she feels safe.

Later that evening, I visit my parents and speak to them about Eva and what happened. As I tell my mother, her eyes light up. "Do you know something about Dire Wolves, mum?" I ask her, leaning forward as my interest piques.

"When I was a teenager, just before I met your father, my mother was a pack healer and we had a woman with a Dire Wolf and I remember my mother saying, 'kill it with love'. She basically had to help the young woman heal from the pain that caused the manifestation in her wolf and as each issue was addressed, the wolf returned to its normal size and ability."

That sounds a lot nicer than some of the suggestions I have heard about excising her wolf, or simply killing the wolf. Those methods all run the risk of harming or killing Eva too, and I cannot and will not let that happen.

When I return to the packhouse and check on Eva, I am overcome with emotion as I spot her sleeping on the narrow bed inside the cell that is now kitted out with her pillows and duvet. Max had placed Summer's bed next to her mother's but outside the cell, so only the bars separate them. Eva and Summer sleep peacefully, clinging to each other's hands.

Gamma Max stands as I enter. He looks ready to sleep on his feet, so I tell him I will take the first watch and he can relieve me in four hours. He gratefully accepts.

As I sit guarding my Luna and her pup, I think about my mother's words and about all the things Aiden has confided in me about Eva. To heal all her trauma was no small undertaking, it could take months, years even but now she has her wolf and we know how loyal that wolf is to her human counterpart. I would feel awful killing that wolf. I have to convince both Eva and Aiden to try my mother's way. Lina deserves a chance; she did, after all, manifest into a Dire Wolf by protecting Eva.

Eva stirs in her sleep. "Preston, is that you? Go and get some sleep, I am perfectly fine here with my little girl." I shake my head no, and she smiles at me. "And you called me stubborn! When will Aiden be back?"

I watch her as she yawns again, her eyes already starting to close. "He'll be back just after lunchtime tomorrow. Try and get some sleep, Eva." As she slips into a deep sleep, I whisper my thanks to her. She really came through for me today and I will be eternally grateful to her for that.

I will do whatever it takes to support Eva the way she has supported me. I pledge my position as Beta to that.

*** **Eva** ***

I wake up in the cold cell and worry that Summer will feel the chill. However, when I look down I can see someone has kindly covered her in some pelts and she will sleep soundly for hours all snuggled like she is. She sighs in her sleep and I am thankful that she has taken all this disruption in her stride.

I, on the other hand, feel sick. Really sick, and I worry about all the shock and strain I have been under. As I heave over the toilet, sweat beads on my brow and my stomach churns. I worry about my little girl catching whatever I have because I have most definitely caught a bug.

No, you haven't. You know what this is, Eva. It's the first time Lina has spoken to me since her shift.

Lina! I missed you. Are you okay? I ask her quickly, forgetting what she is trying to inform me about.

I am scared, I knew I had manifested but that was frightening even for me. I had to manifest though, Eva, I couldn't let you wilt away. Not when it was in my power to help you. The human broke you down, but once I sent Summer to you, I didn't need to manifest as much because she gave you a reason to be strong and to carry on.

As I contemplate what Lina is telling me, I start to heave again. *You sent Summer to me?* Lina chuckles at me.

Yes, I sent Summer. The human wasn't worthy, but I allowed his seed to give us Summer because he was going to break your spirit. A child was the only way to teether you to this world until we met our mate. I couldn't stop our mate's seed even if I wanted to.

Her words sink in. *Lina... Am I?* She continues to chuckle away at me.

Yes, only just, that night in the forest before he left. We must keep the silver bangle on and not shift again. We have to protect our pup.

I'm having a baby. I'm having Aiden's baby. Love and hope and happiness rise from my chest to mingle with the terror and fright I have been feeling.

Don't worry, Lina. This is The Alpha's Heir. I will protect this little bundle with my life.

This complicates matters. I don't want to lose Lina, she is a part of me, and she protected me. Although I didn't know she was there, she has been the one constant throughout my life, and I have no doubt in my head that if she hadn't sent Summer when she did, I would be dead, either by Ryan's hand or my own. I owe Lina my life, and that means I owe it to her to find a way to save her.

For now, for both Lina and I, our collective priority is our pup, we have to do whatever is in our power to protect this pregnancy. This is Aiden's child and heir, this child is loved and wanted, and I will not jeopardise that for anything.

*** **Aiden** ***

The closer to home we get, the more restless I become. I just need to see Eva and make sure she is okay. Preston told me she had banished herself to the cells to keep Summer and the pack

123

safe and although I am raging my sweet little Shortie is in the cells, I am also overwhelmingly proud of her and the sacrifice she is making. She doesn't realise it, but she is nailing being a Luna.

Roman, on the other hand, is spitting mad. *Tell everyone else to get in the cells and let Shortie have the run of the packhouse.* He whines and sulks until I remind him that Eva wouldn't want that for everyone else.

As we reach the border of our lands, my bond with Eva feels stronger. I can feel her terror; however, there is also an overwhelming joy mixed in there too. I like to think that is because I am almost home and she is overjoyed about seeing me. That is until Roman laughs at my self-indulgent thoughts and starts howling in my head. *What's so funny?* But he doesn't tell me, he just continues to howl excitedly.

The whole pack comes to welcome me home and it takes too long to get down into the basement to the cells where my love is.

As I try to tune in to her emotions I realise she is no longer scared, she is filled with contentment. Now I am confused.

I race down to the cells and call out to her. "Eva, are you there?" She doesn't respond, so I enter the holding room. Eva is asleep in a rocking chair. She holds her tummy protectively in her sleep. I wonder if she is hurt.

"Aiden?" Her sleep-filled voice calls out to me and I open the cell to get close to her. By the time I have the lock open, she is up out of the chair. She jumps at me and cries when I hold her tight. "Thank God you're home. I missed you so much."

"So, what's all this? When I heard that my Luna had moved herself into the cells, I thought there had been some sort of mistake." She smiles at me before resting her head against my chest. "I missed you millions, Shortie. I missed you more than I could tell you. I have so much to tell you but first, I have a request to make of you."

I pull her over to her narrow bed.

"How are we both going to fit in that?" I wonder. "How did you fit on that?"

Her eyes sparkle in amusement. Goddess, I have missed that.

I look into her eyes as I hold both of her hands in mine. "I found out some stuff that really made things about our life together clear. I accept both you and Summer, and I want to be her daddy, properly and legally. I want to adopt her so we can be a proper family. I claim her as mine. I want to make it official as soon as possible."

Eva drops my hands and for a second, I am worried I have upset her until she thuds against me, pulling me tight into her arms. "Are you sure you are ready to be a daddy, Aiden?"

Is she kidding? I am delighted and honoured to be Summer's daddy. "I really think I am. I love her, Eva, she might not be my flesh and blood but she is my little girl."

She still hasn't said yes, and I haven't forgotten that, but I want this to be given freely and not coerced. "What about when we have a child together? Will you still love Summer and want to be her daddy then?"

I consider her question before I answer her. "Yes, I will always treat her as my own, and another child will not change that. They will all be our children." Roman howls in my head, he's acting very jovial for us to be home.

"Good. Good. We should do that soon then." We share a smile, but her eyes are twinkling. I had expected her to be a terrified wreck. But... My Eva is happy.

"What has you smiling so much?" I ask her when she continues to grin at me.

"I have dreamt of this moment since we mated. I have dreamt of the moment I got to give you this news. The last time I gave this news, I was completely shot down, but I know this time will be different."

My heart is pounding: this can only mean one thing. Eva is carrying my pup; I am sure that's what she means and as Roman continues to celebrate in my head, clearly already aware of our happy news, I wait with a grin. I wait so she can have her moment.

"Aiden, we're having a baby. A pup. Lina has just told me I am pregnant." Up until that moment, I had thought I would be happy that I was going to be a father and that Eva was expecting our child.

Happy doesn't come close to how I feel right now. Happy doesn't come anywhere near the elation and joy brewing inside me. For the first time in my life, I cry actual tears of joy as I thank my goddess for blessing me. I kiss my amazing mate who quite simply glows with her own happiness.

I thank her repeatedly and tell her how much I love her.

I try to take her to bed to show my appreciation until I realise we are still in the cells.

"You cannot stay in the cells, Evangelina. I won't fucking have it. You will live like a queen while you have my pup growing inside you, and no arguments."

When she looks at me with those beguiling blue eyes, I know I'm beat. Eva will do exactly what she wants, and I will help her and nothing I say, or command, will change that.

"I'll have the boys bring in a bigger bed."

*** **Amber** ***

I am emotionally and physically spent. The past ten days have drained me of every ounce of strength I had and the past 36 hours with Aiden have been a nightmare. We were both worried about our mates and the pack, as well as our confusion and heartache about our mother.

The whole pack comes out to welcome Aiden back home safely. He's never been away from home for this long before and the pack are in high spirits at his safe return.

I look about but I cannot see Preston. As the pack Beta Wolf, he should be here at the helm but, as I desperately search, panic fills me. Where is he?

Aiden slips off to find Eva and now the formality of welcoming the Alpha home is done, I continue to search out Preston. I need him. I need to breathe in his scent so it cleanses my soul of all the horrible events and revelations of the past ten days. Then I'm going to tell him off for not telling us sooner about the warped widow. I thought we had agreed we were in this together. I don't like him keeping things like this from me, but I am not such a hypocrite that I don't get it. I did the same, hiding my letters about the charges I would face. I wanted to protect him, and I didn't want to worry him. I guess he did the same for me.

As I look around, I become frantic to find him, but I am unable to see him anywhere. I am about to alert everyone that Preston is missing when, at last, I catch a glimpse of him. Dressed in his uniform with his head down, he reminds me of a naughty schoolboy. Goddess I love him! I run to him and call out his name. I don't miss the fact that his shoulders visibly relax, and the look of relief on his face evokes a small cry from me. This has really hurt my Preston. I know Nikki has lost her mate, but I want to slice her up for hurting mine.

To my own surprise, I jump into Preston's arms and once he recovers from the shock of my very forward public behaviour, he holds me tighter in his big, muscled arms, spinning me around and drinking in the sight of me, like a thirsty man looking at an obscure glass of water.

"Fucking hell, Amber, I have missed you so much. I couldn't see you and was dreading finding out that you had stayed somewhere else…" I stop his talking by kissing him, hard and urgent, so he knows exactly where this is leading. Instantly, he completely loses himself. Through our kiss, his excitement and anticipation builds and overflows. He carries me directly up to our room, where I find why he was late to the homecoming welcome.

Flowers cover every surface of our apartment, the lighting is low, and music is playing softly in the background. There are chocolates and wine and wine glasses on our little coffee table.

"Preston?" I give him a questioning look and my heart swells with love for him when he looks back at me bashfully. Even the tips of his ears glow red.

"I know we have a lot to talk about and work out, Red. I know I've fucked up. But right now, our time together is precious. Let me welcome you home, and tomorrow we will sort out the nastiness."

As the ache of missing him lessens in my heart and another ache grows between my legs instead, I give in to him. I have missed him immensely and right now I just want to be held by him and touched by him and to forget everything outside of our little world just for one night. I nod my agreement and his answering smile is enough to floor me. I can't wait for his body to merge with mine.

"Good, good girl. I've run you a bath, go and relax for a while."
I have no option but to obey him when he talks to me like that,
I'm like putty in his hands. He gives my ass a little tap on the
way past him and I try to absorb every sensation.

There are candles in the bathroom and rose petals in the water
with a generous mountain of fragrant bubbles too. A thick pile
of fluffy white bath towels are set near the side. I quickly strip
out of my travelling clothes and slide into the tub, groaning as
my bones melt against the divine hot water. Within minutes,
I am snoozing in the bath. I wake up when Preston comes in
with a drink for me.

"Thank you. Thank you for all this, my body feels like it's in a
cloud of bliss." I smile up at him, but his expression is intense,
and the pain is evident in his eyes. "Come on, get in with me." I
encourage him but he shakes his head.

"Just relax, Red. I want to look after you tonight. I want to care
for you and show you how much I love and adore you."

He's scaring me, it's like he is saying goodbye.

"Can I wash you please, Red?" He already has the body wash
and body mop in his hands, so I give another little nod. He
starts with my feet; the scratchy body mop tickles the soles
of my feet and causes me to laugh loudly. "Keep still!" Preston
chastises me mockingly, as he attempts to tickle me again.

He then cleans my lower legs, and as he edges closer to the
epicentre of my arousal, the junction between my thighs, my
excitement hits a fever pitch.

"Sit forward please, Red," he asks me all too soon and I groan
in frustration as I complete every action he commands of me.
When I lean forward, he scrubs my back in circular motions,
each stroke teasing my senses. He cleans all the way down
to the crack in my ass and then works his way back up my

sides. My skin puckers and my breathing hitches as he skims the sides of my boobs, and teases the underside of my breasts, barely missing where I crave his touch most. Lizzie growls in dissatisfaction when he moves away to my hands this time and then my forearms. The smirk on his face shows he knows exactly what he is doing, and he is enjoying making me squirm.

"Are you going to tease me all night, Preston? I swear to the Goddess, I will make you pay for this. It's been ten days and I need you!" He smiles at my whining.

"Okay, okay. You win, let's just wash your pussy and then we're done." My swollen clit practically jumps in anticipation. As Preston lathers his hands, I spread my knees as far as I can. His soapy hand strokes down my open slit causing me to whimper. "I've missed my pussy, ten days without it."

"Is that all you've missed?" It's my turn to tease him now.

He lifts me from the bath, causing water to slop all over the side and down his clothes. "You know I love your pussy, almost as much as I love your mouth, but I love you and I miss you, Red. Now get in that bed and spread your legs wide for me. It's time for my supper."

My core practically gushes at his words. "I want some supper too."

His eyes are black now, and I know I have awoken the beast from within. "In that case, I'm going to lie down and you're going to sit on my face so we can both have our supper at the same time."

My essence soaks the insides of my thighs at the thought of what he is suggesting. We haven't done a sixty-nine in a long time.

I lower myself onto his face and relish his first contact, a long, thick stroke along my inner lips from his rough tongue. As his wonderfully warm and skilled tongue explores my depths, I lean forward until I am eye level with Preston's impressively long and thick dick. He has a remarkable cock, and even more remarkable skills when it comes to using it too. His groan vibrates against my most sensitive part when I take the tip of his cock into my mouth. We both move in unison, flicking, licking, and sucking until I feel my impending climax.

I lean up slightly. "I'm ready to cum, Preston, but I want to ride your cock when I do."

He flips me around, so I am now face to face with him. I quickly straddle him and use my hand to guide his shaft up high inside me.

"Yes, Red. That's my girl, ride me." I move faster and with purpose as my climax builds again. Preston bites on one of my nipples and I shout his name as I fall off the cliff into a world of fulfilment.

In our haste, we forget to use protection. It's the first time Preston and I have fully mated without a barrier in the way, and I don't care. Every part of him is now mine, and this single act has fused our relationship to another level.

For the first time, I cry when I orgasm. I cry with relief at being back with Preston and I cry with the pain the past ten days has dealt us both.

My incredible, loyal and patient mate holds me while I weep and as I fall asleep in his arms, I know there is no better place than right here in his arms.

*** Salma ***

Walking back to the games room, nerves bubble up inside me. I hope Ricky isn't scared and I hope he doesn't shun me. He is a mini papa, my papa lives on through him.

Tony tries to reassure me. "He knows about you, Sal. He knows he has a big sister who doesn't know about him yet. He asks about you and says his papa told him about you." That confirms papa would definitely want me to take over Ricky's care. I steady myself; I can do this. He's my little brother, my family.

Ale opens the door for me, and my legs feel shaky as they carry me into the room. Ricky frowns in concentration with his tongue sticking out but he quickly smiles again when he sees we have returned.

"You came back, do you want to play? I'm going to have a go at Plants Vs Zombies now." He's trying to hand me a controller for his game and Ale nudges me forward.

"Is it okay if we have a little talk first, please, Ricky?" He looks up at me with big brown eyes and shrugs.

"Okay, but will someone please play a game with me after we've talked." Laughter stirs inside my chest; he's going to be a blast, this little brother of mine.

"Okay, you strike a hard bargain, but I'm sure one of us will play some games with you soon. Can I sit down?" Although he nods his head to say yes, a note of suspicion grows in his eyes. That will steer him well in the future as a Mafia boss.

I sit beside him, leaving a space between us but turning my body to face him in a way I hope seems open and friendly. "Ricky, my name is Salma. I'm- "

"You finally came! Papa said you would come." He launches

himself at me, hugging me tight and my eyes fill with tears of both joy and sadness. Why didn't we meet when papa was alive? He could have seen us together himself.

"I would've come sooner, but I only just found out about you Ricky." The wetness from his tears seeps through my jacket and onto my shirt.

"I thought you weren't going to come. I was getting kinda worried." I hug him tight to me. I did not know about this little boy an hour ago, but now that I do, I love him wholeheartedly and will protect him with my life. He is my flesh and blood.

"Well, I'm here now. Everything is going to be okay. Ricky, this is my husband Alejandro. Ale, this is my little brother, Enrique." Ricky looks up at Ale warily, but when Ale smiles and offers him a fist bump, Ricky grins at him as he bumps back. It's the cutest thing I've ever seen.

"You got married? Papa said he wanted you to get married but you were being a mule about it." I can't help but laugh, he obviously means I was being as stubborn as a mule or mule-headed. A wonderful, muddled recall straight from the mouths of babes.

"Ricky, my boy. Your sister wants to take you home with her. What do you think?" My little brother stands and struts over to the other Mafia boss.

"Uncle Tony, of course I'm going home with her, that's what papa said. Thank you for looking after me." And like a little Don in training, he holds out his tiny hand to Tony. Tony laughs loud and richly.

"It was my pleasure, boy. Now, remember we are allies, okay? Don't forget your lessons and listen to your sister." Ricky nods his agreement.

"Can I bring all my stuff? My computer and my clothes." As I assure him that he will have his possessions brought to him, Ale goes with Tony to make arrangements to get Ricky's stuff.

Left alone with my little brother is the ideal time to get to know him. He tells me all about his life, his games, his school, his friends. He tells me how sad he's been since papa died. "Mi mami, she just wanted to be with her boyfriend, and he didn't like me." My heart rate increases. This is an awful position to put him in, but Ricky could be a link between us and our papa's killer.

"Did you meet your mami's boyfriend? What was his name again? JR?" Ricky nods his head.

"I met him a couple of times. He was younger than mami and I don't think he liked kids," he tells me with a look of disgust on his face.

"We are staying with Ale's parents at the moment, but we'll soon be settled in our home. You will live with me, and I will look after you from now on. I promise." He jumps into my arms again, this little boy who, at the tender age of seven, has already lost so much, who just needs someone to love him, someone he can depend on.

I am more than ready to step up to the plate.

*** Junior ***

It never once crossed my mind that I would end up on the run, a rogue from my own pack. It has always been my destiny to become the next Moon Stone pack Alpha. My whole life has been spent training for it and then, bang from nowhere, my father produces this stupid little whore and declares her his Alpha heir and successor. Well, I don't fucking think so. I'm not going to simply step aside while some bastard of a human slut takes everything that is mine. I will snap her pretty little neck myself before I ever allow that to happen.

Nikki comes to seek me out and offer her support. I am now certain once word gets out that the rightful Alpha heir had been shunned by the old man for a usurper, a vile little creature raised as a human who knows nothing of our world and customs, nothing of our traditions, has no training and absolutely no understanding of what it meant to be a Moon Stone Werewolf, they will flock to me and declare me their Alpha because, for all intents and purposes, I am. As more of the pack pledges their allegiance to me, I will challenge my father for the right to take his place.

Nikki has interesting information about my father's bastard daughter. Apparently, she has a Dire Wolf. As soon as Nikki informs me, I report it to the Werewolf Council. That should keep everyone busy for a little while.

Dangerous beasts that threaten the exposure of our world and the safety of others are subject to the law, and by not declaring it to the council, my father, his bastard, and her mutt of a mate were all in violation of those laws.

By my calculations, the council will be dealing with the annoying issue of my father's illegitimate spawn. That does make me happy in some ways, but in other ways, it saddens me. I want to rip her throat out in front of my father to teach him a lesson. How dare he overlook me, his son and heir?

My plan is to get onto the Onyx River land, kill Eva and reclaim my position. Now, with Nikki joining my cause with her weird Red Mage power, I have found a way to get in.

"I'm sorry, Alpha. She is unreachable at the moment. I think she's in the cells at the Onyx River packhouse, we have to wait for her to come out into the open a bit." Well, that was better than I anticipated, I thought she may have exaggerated her tracking skills but it up

Nikki will be very useful to me in my quest for dominance over my werewolf pack, but this has caused tension between Dominga and I. Dominga is jealous that a young and attractive woman has made a pledge to help me. She also doesn't see the point in challenging my father if we are going after Jose's firm. However, our grasp on the Mafia is lessening by the day now that she has abandoned her brat.

I love Dominga but she is draining me. I have sacrificed a lot for her. My fated mate; the safety of my pack; my position as Alpha heir and my position in a pack. I am officially a rogue now, thanks to her impatience. The woman needs to calm down and let me do what I do best, which is dominate. I don't think I can take another day of her moaning and whining about Nikki coming on to me. If I want Nikki, I will fucking have her. As it goes, she's a bit of a strange one and she freaks me out, so I don't want to go there, but no matter how much I explain this to Dominga, she still obsesses about it, convincing herself that there is something going on between me and Nikki.

"Have there been any threats against the pack from the Mafia, Nikki?" She shakes her head, no, which does make me laugh. I poisoned a powerful Mafia Don, and got away with it. "I have informed the council about the bastard bitch's Dire Wolf. The officials should be crawling all over them by now. Hopefully, they'll execute her, which will weaken Alpha Aiden. Through his grief, he will leave Amber unsupported so you can get your justice. Do you want her dead or imprisoned?"

"I want to torture her, Alpha. I want to torture her until she begs me to kill her."

Maybe Nikki could be a match made in heaven for me after all! I've never felt as turned on by a woman's words as I do right now.

CHAPTER EIGHT

House Arrest

*** Xavier ***

Elder Tabbatha gives me enough warning that I manage to get protection in place for my mate before closeting us both into our chambers where we will stay until the whole territory is searched. I try to call Aiden and Eva to warn them but there is no answer.

The council officials turn up in their dozens, all looking for Junior and then questioning me regarding Evangelina. The allegation of a Dire Wolf is put to me as her father. I continue to deny any knowledge of a Dire Wolf, but I suspect the complaint about Eva has come from Nikki because of the vague information they have and the speed at which they respond.

Lydia and I stay in our quarters, we go about our regular daily tasks, and take our meals there. Slowly but surely, I feel my bond with Lydia stabilise. However, I don't want to push her, so I keep the conversation light and avoid talking about my daughter.

Lydia has other ideas though. In between her worried ramblings about our son, she asks me about my daughter. "She already has a child. You're a grandfather, Xavier!"

Wow. A grandfather. It is the first time I have thought about it that way. I am desperate to get to know Eva, and to be a part of her life, but I am also trying to respect her boundaries regarding her little girl.

There is so much I want to share, so much I want to tell Lydia, but I feel unable to because my joy comes from the same place as her feelings of betrayal. It is bittersweet and the person I love is the person I want to share it all with, but she is also the one person I can't open up to. I can't share it because I feel bad about lying to her.

"Let's talk about something else, Sweet Cheeks." Her crestfallen face shows me the degree of disappointment she is feeling.

"I am really trying here, X. I don't know what else I can do. You lied to me, remember? I don't want our bond to sever, and I don't want to lose you, so you either need to start sharing this and letting me in again or we cut our losses now." My Lydia is fighting for us, and my heart swells with pride that she is.

Without much thought of our current predicament and guests, I push Lydia up against the wall and smash my lips over hers. "MINE!" I shout at her. "You are mine, Lydia. I want to fight for us, but I need to know that I'm not hurting you by sharing my daughter with you.

Lydia is no pushover. With a flick of her wrist, she has me on my knees. "No, X. You are mine." She grabs me roughly by my chin. "I'm trying, X, because I know you are sorry for hurting me. Let me in or this won't work."

"My daughter, your stepdaughter, is called Eva. And yes, she has a child, so technically, I am a grandparent. And so are you if you accept them."

"A grandchild? Oh, X, you know I am ready for a grandchild." We touch foreheads. Lydia is overcome with emotion but also appears stunned. This may be our only chance now. Junior is in shit up to his eyeballs, so will either be dead or imprisoned by the time this all unfolds.

"I'm sorry I lied. I was wrong. Very wrong. I am trying to be a better man, the kind of man that you and Eva can be proud of." She nods before accepting my kiss. This time, the bond is not only completely healed, but also stronger, more resilient and robust. Together, we will overcome anything.

Eva is by no means a replacement, but a bond with her could help bring joy back to my mate's life. She always wanted more children and has looked forward to becoming a grandparent since we realised she wouldn't be able to have another pup. We all need a light in the dark and I have a feeling Eva and her child could be that to Lydia and me.

"Alpha Xavier. Oh, I'm sorry, I didn't mean to intrude." Elder Tabbatha is back. She whispers to us. "X, they are on their way to Onyx River to arrest your daughter. Alpha Aiden was spotted returning to his pack yesterday. He failed to notify the council this morning and now they have enough to arrest Eva."

"Are we under arrest?" Lydia asks, and Elder Tabbatha shakes her head. That's all Lydia needs to know. "Come on, X, we have to warn them. If we shift, we'll get there faster."

"Thanks, Tabs." She gives me a nod as I run after my mate so we can warn Eva that the council are on their way to arrest her.

I am happy to see when I arrive that Aiden has a full contingent of wolves protecting his packhouse. I present myself first and ask for clothes for my mate so she can shift too. Aiden comes to personally greet me.

"We don't have time. Nikki reported Eva for having a Dire Wolf. The council are on the way to arrest her." His roar of indignation pleases me. We will both stand shoulder to shoulder and protect her. No fucker is going to lay a finger on my daughter.

"Onyx Moon, It's time to defend. The council want to arrest your future Luna. They want to excise her wolf because it manifested to protect her. They want to do this while my pup, the heir to this pack, grows inside her. What do we think of that?"

Amongst the roars and growls of indignation is a splattering of cracks as warriors shift to protect their Luna. They have taken Eva into their hearts and will defend her to the death. There is also a celebration. This is obviously the first time news of Luna Eva's pregnancy has been revealed to them too.

"Eva's with pup?" I ask Aiden, and his face lights up when he nods. Amongst the chaos, happiness and hope charge through me. My little girl is going to have another pup and this time, I want to be involved. I want to be a grandfather and it would be wonderful to support Eva and Aiden as they expand their family.

"We found out just last night when I returned. Xavier, she has locked herself in the cells to protect everyone else. She's going to kill me that I have blurted it out at the first opportunity, she wanted to keep it private for now. How can we stop the council?"

They will not touch Eva. Right now, both Aiden and I would sacrifice ourselves to keep her safe and so would our packs. The council will have to listen to us.

"Send word to Alpha Martin, tell him I am calling in my allies, my daughter's life is in jeopardy. Lydia, get inside now."

Lydia nods and does as she is told. The last thing I need is to worry about her too.

"Luna Lydia, if you allow me, I will settle you in our guest room." Aiden's redheaded sister, the one who is facing charges for killing one of my pack members, graciously offers and Lydia lights up.

"Thank you, Amber, but could you take me to Evangelina? I think we need to become acquainted as fast as we can." As I expect, Amber looks for permission from her Alpha first, which he gives.

Lydia and Amber walk into the packhouse, and Amber returns a few minutes later, just as the council officials start arriving.

"I am Alpha Aiden Goldrick. You have not been invited onto my lands. State your business now or I will instruct my army to attack."

The gauntlet has been thrown down. I stand shoulder to shoulder with Alpha Aiden and will fight alongside him.

"I am Elder Esme. I am an Investigating Officer with the Control of Dangerous Beasts Bureau. I have been sent by the Werewolf Council in response to a complaint that has been made."

"What is the complaint?" Beta Preston asks bluntly.

Elder Esme shuffles her papers and pulls one out. "The complaint is that you failed to report a dangerous beast- "

She doesn't get to finish her sentence as Aiden growls and bares his teeth at the vermin that insultingly refers to his mate as a dangerous beast.

"Watch your mouth or you'll lose your throat, mutt," Aiden spits out at her. His pack members all growls and snarl, they are all wound tightly, ready to pounce on their prey. He has trained them well.

"The charges are that Evangelina, daughter of Xavier Woodward and fated mate of Aiden Goldrick, has a dangerous beast in the form of a manifested wolf. We are here to remove her from your pack. She will be imprisoned at the bureau until we have excised her wolf. If she survives, she will be free to return to you."

"She is going nowhere. My daughter is staying right here where she belongs with her mate," I tell them through gritted teeth. I want to rip their heads off.

"This will result in a war and trust me, Alpha Xavier, I have back-up arriving any moment now. Turn over the werewolf with the Dire Wolf and no-one else will be hurt."

"Never!"

The ground starts to rumble and tremble, and I am not sure if it will be our enemies or our allies. It doesn't matter either way: we will never hand Eva over without a fight and they refuse to leave without arresting her.

It looks like a war is the inevitable outcome.

*** Aiden ***

They've got to be kidding. The only way I'm going to let them take Eva is over my dead body. To my relief, Xavier's army and the thousands of his allies turn up just in time. Thousands of warriors have turned out to defend the honour of my little mate, and my heart swells with pride. The council will have a hard time overpowering us.

"My daughter is going nowhere, Esme. Now back the fuck off before you start a war. There is no need to spill blood here today. Evangelina is no threat to anyone, and we will ensure that her Dire Wolf is dealt with once she whelps her pup." Xavier takes the lead, and I am grateful, since I am close to losing all my restraint. I am terrified for my mate, our little girl and our teeny tiny pup growing inside her. I am powerless and without any control and I don't like it, not when it involves my family, the people I love and, most importantly, when it comes to Eva's safety.

"And how do you propose to keep the Onyx River Pack safe from your Luna? Dire Wolves are uncontrolled beasts." I start towards her; I've already fucking warned her that I would rip her throat out, but Amber and Preston pull me back.

"Don't you dare refer to my mate as an uncontrolled beast. Luna Eva will not be leaving our territory. At this moment in time, she is in our cells, where she will remain until her confinement is over. We will revisit the issue then."

"Who sent her to the cells?" Esme asks as she frowns at this new information. Her papers flap about as she attempts to record the information.

"She imprisoned herself when she realised her wolf had manifested. She wants to remain in the cells here at her own insistence. There is no threat to our kind, the problem is being dealt with," Beta Preston tells her.

"It's not just a matter of keeping her locked up, her wolf needs to be removed and destroyed so it can't hurt the werewolf community," Esme patronisingly tells Preston.

"Have you ever seen a Dire Wolf, Elder Esme? Do you have any knowledge of how they manifest and how to reverse it?" Preston demands of her.

"... Well, no, not personally. But I've read a couple of books and-" Preston cuts her off and I've never wanted to congratulate him more. He's always been far more astute and diplomatic than me, and it shows right now when I need him most.

"I have. I, therefore, have more hands-on experience of dealing with Dire Wolves than you do. I will personally seek a resolution to this issue for my Luna and friend. I believe I have found a way to reverse the manifestations without harming anyone, especially Eva and her Wolf."

Preston pauses to let this information sink in.

"By her own hand, my Luna sent herself to the cells because she wanted everyone else to be safe. She has been responsible and selfless and not one of us will allow you to move her. We have never felt safer than we are right now with Luna Eva looking after us all."

"This is most irregular." Elder Esme is flustered now, she shuffles her papers again like they will give her the answers.

"I'll tell you what is most irregular: sending a council official to detain a Dire Wolf when she's never even seen one. What was the council thinking?" Xavier is challenging the council now, and he has a point. If we have more experience and expertise at hand, why should they take her? "I propose that Luna Eva stays here in her self-administered containment, and we will consult all the healers we can with experience of dealing with a Dire Wolf."

Elder Esme has no option, not if she wants to avoid bloodshed. "I want to speak to Luna Eva, our officers will need to examine the suggested holding cell and she would be under house arrest. I will come back every Friday to meet with Eva and discuss any issues there may be." She paused. "Would that be to your satisfaction?"

She looks at us all, and obviously isn't waiting for an answer because she walks towards the packhouse so she can meet Eva.

As we approach the stairs to the cells, loud voices can clearly be heard and Gamma Max is trying to diffuse whatever the situation is and is failing miserably.

"Get out, I don't want you here. Please. Just leave."

"Eva, it's important to your father that we get along. I want to get to know you."

"Not right now, I'll tell father when I am ready. I already have a mother, a fat lot of good she is, and Summer doesn't need any more confusion right now."

"Come on now, ladies, there is no need for this to turn nasty."

"FUCK OFF!"

"Don't speak to him like that and don't swear in front of my daughter!"

"Guck ock…"

"Give me a couple of minutes first please," I apologetically ask Elder Esme. For fucks sake! I put out one fire and there is already another one simmering away.

The scene in the holding cell is exactly what it sounded like. Eva is in her cell, red-faced and pointing at Luna Lydia, who is in the holding area with Gamma Max, who is carrying Summer, and Summer is repeatedly chanting, "guck ock, guck ock."

"What's going on?" They all start talking at once until I shout again. "If you're going to keep arguing, can you leave? The council representative is here and wants to ensure the cell is secure. She needs to speak to Eva. I don't know what your disagreement is about, and quite frankly, I don't care. There is enough shit flying about- "

"Chit, chit!" My little girl shouts proudly. Eva glares at me, and if looks could kill, *I* would be dead and buried now.

"Please don't kill me. I'm sorry, I didn't mean to swear," I plead with Eva before she can say anything.

"We will discuss this later, Alpha. Luna Lydia, it was lovely to meet you, but I think it would be best if you returned to my father now. Max, could you please take Summer to Mrs Moore straight away? Sunshine, give Mummy and Daddy a kiss and be a good girl." It's heart-breaking watching Summer kiss her mummy through the bars of her cell. I kiss her too and ruffle the soft brown curls of the crown of her head. She giggles in response as she places a sticky wet kiss on my cheek and whispers, 'daddy bear,' to me.

After everyone leaves, Eva stares hard at me. "Are you determined to give her the mouth of a sailor? She's two years old and she now knows three swear words." I hold my hands up, the last thing I want is to upset Eva or Summer. I'm wound up like a coil, I'm stressed and on edge and I am worried sick, but Eva doesn't need to see that right now. She needs me to be strong and keep her safe. She needs me to stop swearing.

"Shortie, I'm so sorry. I will make more of an effort with my language. I don't know what happened. It just slipped out." She finally stands in front of me; the bars of her cage are the only things in our way.

"I know you're stressed out. It's hardly ideal, but her little mind is like a sponge, and she seems to sniff out swear words like a bloodhound." We stand toe to toe, if the bars weren't in the way, I would have her in my arms and half naked by now.

"I know, I'm really sorry, Eva. I have to tell you something else. I sort of blabbed about you being pregnant too." She actually growls at me. My little innocent, loving mate is growling at me.

"For fuck's sake, Aiden!" she shouts at me, but I capture her chin before she moves away. A flash of silver in her eyes tells me that Lina is close to the surface.

"Lina, thank you for allowing my pup to grow. I promise to do everything in my power to save you."

Eva's eyes widen in shock and surprise and when she smiles, I know Lina has persuaded her to forgive me. "Sweetheart, I'm so sorry. I'm not coping very well, am I? I need my Luna back by my side. The council is willing to place you under house arrest until our pup is born. Elder Esme needs to talk to you and then they want to examine the cell." I lean forward and place my lips next to hers. "Please forgive your idiotic mate, he might be stupid, but he loves you," I murmur to her.

"Of course, I forgive you, but next time we have a baby, I'm not telling you until we are through to the safe part. You can't hold your own piss." As I kiss her, all the familiar stirrings of desire wash over me, but Eva pulls away before it's even begun. "I think we have guests, Alpha."

I look around and, sure enough, Elder Esme, Amber and Preston are standing behind me, enjoying our show.

"Well, I can see you have no trouble controlling your wolf when provoked, Luna, and boy did your mate provoke you today. Everything seems to be under control. Luna Eva, I would like to arrange an appointment for next week and, so long as the cell meets the criteria of the council, your self-administered detention should suffice until your pup is safely born. Congratulations, by the way." Elder Esme rips off a piece of paper and asks Beta Preston to escort her back up so she can leave.

"Congratulations to both of you," Amber chokes out on a sob. At first I believe it to be tears of happiness on our behalf, until she speaks again. "I just wish I were going to be here to see it."

"Go and hug her," Eva instructs me with tears in her eyes too.

"Amber, don't worry, we are going to fight this, we won't let anyone hurt you, will we, Aidy?"

"No one will ever hurt you again, little sister, I give you my oath."

*** Alejandro ***

"We keep drawing a blank and until we talk to the werewolves, we won't get any further. We can now rule out Salma's brother. We know he is clean as a whistle." My brother crosses off 'Jose's Bastard' from our whiteboard. We are sitting around the large mahogany table in the conference room of my father's office. The air is thick with smoke and the table is littered with short crystal balloon glasses from which we have all imbibed too much brandy.

"I will approach the werewolves tomorrow. Salma has an in with the Alpha on a more personal level." My brother and cousin laugh at me, and make insinuations that Salma had a werewolf boyfriend before we married.

My fist connects with my cousin's temple, and I try to scramble over him to punch Matteo too, but he quickly dives under the table while he laughs at my attempts.

"Do not speak about my WIFE like that, you pair of assholes."

"ENOUGH! Will you lot pack it in? You're all fucking grown men, will you act like it? Senseless, the lot of you. Jose's murderer is still out there. If they can take him out, they can take us all. So, stop fighting amongst yourselves and think!" My father is not usually a man of many words. I hadn't realised until now how much his associate's death has affected him.

I sit back down in my seat and dump ice into a napkin, and

place it on my knuckles that are already swelling. "Dad, I'm sorry. You know this is important to me. It's my wife that is in direct danger here. I know the Alpha of the Onyx River pack because Sal's friend is now... shacked up with him. We worked together a couple of months back. He's sound, he can be discreet, and he'll have a way of finding any wolves in the Moon Stone pack that fits the description and have the initials JR. Sal wants to visit her friend anyway, and this will be the perfect opportunity to speak to him about it."

My father nods to me. "Thank you, Ale. You have really stepped up for your wife and your family. Matteo and Edouard could learn a thing or two from you. It's admirable that you wanted to defend your wife's honour, but let's remain focused on what is important here. We need to find that slut Dominga and this JR. That's all that is important, because until we have them, your wife and the whole family will always be in danger."

"I will report what I find tomorrow night. I'm going home to Sal." My father stands too; we are going to the same place, so we may as well share the ride.

Before we leave, my brother pulls me to one side. "Ale, we were just joking. I'm sorry, little brother. You know I respect Salma." I accept his apology. After all, I am embarrassed when I recall that I have also made fun of his wife in the past.

It is way past 2am when I finally climb into bed with Salma. She is already asleep in the stuffy bedroom at my parents' home. She is warm and snuggles into me as soon as I lay next to her. God above, how I love her. I kiss her head and within moments she runs her hands over my chest and down across my abs.

"Did you hit the gym?" she asks, her voice full of sleep.

"Yeah, I did," I reply as I pulled her closer to me. I turn her face to mine and kiss her. Our tongues dance as they explore one another. I grope her left breast through her pretty silk pyjamas which are grand purple and lavender in colour. Sal has the distinct smell of a woman. She always did. As I kiss her stiffened nipple through the silky material, I realise that it tastes like the woman who sleeps in it. It tastes like perfection.

Salma's lips kiss my chest, and she moves further down so she may wrap her tongue around my hardening cock. There is nothing more appealing than when Salma sucks on my cock with her beautiful mouth. Her lips are as red as ripened cherries, and as she sweeps her little pink tongue over my tip, I feel ready to explode. She grabs my balls and deepthroats me until I can no longer hold back, and I swear loudly as I cum in her mouth and down her throat.

I pull her back up to kiss her again and smile because her moans of protest are muffled as I kiss her even more. "Did you work out on this too?" she asks playfully as she strokes my now satisfied member.

"Oh no, he gets enough of a workout from you." I tell her with a smile. I pull her in tight to me and she kisses me again. While she's distracted, I lazily slip my hand down her body and find her pussy that is waiting for me to explore. It's already soaking and ready for me.

Lightly, I run my fingers up her slit and find her hard clit and graze the tip of my finger over it teasingly. Salma's back arches as she tries to push her pussy against my hand.

I press her back against the bed and trail sweet little kisses on every millimetre of her magnificent body. I reach her pussy and slowly glide my tongue up her soft wet lips, tantalisingly lingering on her clit. She wants more and pulls my head deeper into her pussy. With my hands on her hips, I rock her pussy up close to my mouth, creating a rhythm of pleasure for my girl.

My tongue greedily licks her lips until she starts to quiver. I spread her lips wider so I can brush her exposed clit with my thumb. Salma's moaning gets louder as her pussy thrashes up against my hungry mouth. When her thighs start to tense, I push my tongue deep into her. This is all my Sal needs to cum in my mouth, she is moaning and shaking as her pussy pulsates against my tongue.

"Oh shit, Ale!" she moans as her whole body shakes with her orgasm.

"That's it, Chula, cum in my mouth," I murmur against her glistening mound before peppering her engorged clit once more with random flicks of my rough tongue.

I watch her splinter apart once again, her warm juices flooding my mouth and sliding down my throat. I lick her pussy until she relaxes and gently suck her clit as her breathing calms. Her hand rests on the back of my head. When she is sufficiently relaxed, she pushes me away and sits up. I feel her climb over me and I raise my head to see what she is doing.

She kisses me as her hand wraps around my cock. Her lips kiss me, and it is as if she is tasting herself. The sensation makes me moan and I feel her body start to move on mine. I opened my eyes wider to see her naked body dance above me, her long dark hair cascading down her back.

I slowly move my hands up her thighs and over her hips, guiding her and then thrusting up deep inside her. I pull her down to meet my mouth. "I'm hungry again, Chula, let me eat your sweet pussy one more time." Her eyes darken with desire. "Come on, mi amor, make your husband happy and sit on my face."

As always, my Sal doesn't disappoint me. She lifts herself off my cock and I surprise her by turning her around. I help her lower herself onto my face and I take one long languid lick up her drenched slit and smile as she writhes in pleasure. I know she is getting close again. Her legs begin to stiffen and her jarring movements demand more from my mouth as she rubs her core roughly against my mouth and prickly day-old stubble.

She places one of her hands on her breast and starts to massage it herself, lingering over her erect nipple. She loves to pinch them, and I want to taste them.

I love to watch her as she plays with herself and so I flip her over, so she lands on her back again. I guide her other hand to her right breast and before I can get back to her to feast again, her body convulses and this time she moans long and hard.

What a fucking feeling.

When I look up at Sal, she is looking down at me with the most beautiful expression, her mouth open, her lips wet and swollen from my kisses, her cheeks flushed, her eyes half-lidded with desire and her full breasts heaving for air. I feel a response deep in my groin and I'm hard again. I'm fucking hard again, and I'm going to fuck her like she's never been fucked before.

"Get on your knees," I command her. She does so willingly. She has never resisted my orders.

I sit on the edge of the bed, my ass on my heels, my erect cock pointing to the ceiling, demanding to be inside of this beautiful woman. Salma looks down at me with a sexy look on her face, her eyes full of want.

"I want to watch you ride my cock," I tell her, my voice low and gruff with desire.

Now it is my turn to cum, I pull Salma up to kiss me again and I feel her slide her hand down my body, she grabs hold of my cock.

"I want to cum again but this time with you inside me," she moans against my lips.

"I am ready to come, Chula, so it's now or never," I say to her. She nods and accepts the challenge.

She straddles me and slides my cock inside her. She is tight and wet and it allows me to slide in easily. Salma puts her mouth to my ear and whispers in a hoarse voice, "I have been waiting for you all night, Ale. I've used my toys and made myself come twice before you got home. I thought of doing this with you as I played with myself."

I growl at her as my cock throbs as I imagine her getting off while thinking of me. I fuck her hard, her ass slapping on my thighs as I thrust into her. When her pussy is contracting around my shaft, squeezing my cock in her tight wet pussy, it pushes me over the edge. I groan as I come into her, copious amounts of red-hot cum. "Chula, that's so fucking hot, Bebe. What a welcome home that was!"

"I missed you so much Ale. I love you," she says to me as she falls against me.

"I love you too, Chula, I love you so fucking much." After the meeting last night, it brought home how much I stand to lose if I don't find Jose's killer. I can't lose her, not when I finally feel alive with her in my life.

I wake up to Salma lying on my chest, her hair sticking to her face and a large spot of drool on my shoulder. When I look at the clock, it's only 7am. As I look at my wife when she is unguarded and vulnerable, I realise how much I like this side of her, she is so peaceful. Badass Salma has my respect and admiration, but soft and vulnerable Sal completely captures my heart and will forever hold my loyalty. There is nothing I wouldn't do for this woman of mine.

"Morning, Ale," she croaks up at me and I kiss her on the head in response. "I have to take Ricky to meet his new tutor. No school until the threat is dealt with."

"How long is he with the tutor for, Chula?" I ask her. I think this is the perfect opportunity to speak to Alpha Aiden like I volunteered last night.

"About four hours, why?" She rubs her eyes as she starts to wake up, looking as cute as ever.

"I think we should go and visit Eva and Aiden."

CHAPTER
NINE

Secrecy and Plans

*** Junior ***

For the last two days, I've been stuck in this shitty hotel room with Dominga and Nikki and I am ready to explode in a rage. They have been fighting nonstop about anything and everything.

Dominga is insecure about our relationship. She hates that Nikki is younger and wilder and prettier. She despises that Nikki is willing to serve me, to help me get what I want and need, which is my bastard sister, Eva, dead.

Nikki has powers and abilities that Dominga couldn't even imagine, and to be honest, it is starting to bother me that Dominga is being so controlling and possessive over me. I have already killed her sugar daddy for her, when she asked me to. What else must I do to prove I am loyal to her?

Nikki means nothing to me, she is a stupid girl with a screw loose, but we have a common goal. We want to bring down the same people and she has abilities I don't possess. I need her, and she needs me. Dominga, however, just doesn't get it. Her neediness is sickening.

"You've got to get rid of that girl!" Dominga screams at me.

She looks maniacal, and it isn't attractive. In fact, she looks horrible with dark circles around her eyes and her face is blotchy with rage. I have never noticed before how much older she is, but I notice it now. She must be the same age as my mother. How can she give me an Heir to pass my mantel on to?

Nikki is throwing stuff around in the bathroom and I know she can hear Dominga's outburst. I roll my eyes and climb out of bed. Just what I need, not one hormonal woman but two of the fuckers.

"What girl?" I spit at Dominga, deliberately provoking her further. I am tired and bored of the two of them and their fighting. Two can play this game.

"Your little bitch, she is a dumb whore, and she can't help you! She is a liability; she has to go!" Dominga cries, and I throw my arms out in frustration.

"She has a better idea of what we are doing than you, Dom. You are being dramatic, you are paranoid! Go to sleep and stop worrying. She is not a threat to you, so stop being a jealous little bitch and try and get along with her."

I am growing tired of her and if she doesn't sort herself out, she will be out.

"I swear right now, Dom, stop this immediately or I will walk. I am getting tired of your shitty mood swings. If I wanted Nikki, I would take her. But I don't. Okay? It stops now or you can go, and I will find a bird who knows how to keep her mouth."

I am so tired, I don't even bother changing my clothes. Instead, I grab my phone, put my shoes on and walk out of the door, leaving the two thorns in my side to squabble without me.

I don't want to be around Dominga. I don't want to be around anyone, but especially Dom. I need to get away. I need some quiet time away from this wretched hotel for just a few minutes. I miss the open expanse of the Moon Stone Territory, I miss the forests, I miss my wolf, I miss my family, I miss my home and, most of all, I wish I had never started all this shit in the first place.

The static of energy between my fingers and in my ears mingles with the throbbing pain in my head. It's so bad I can hardly see. The lights in the lobby flicker and I can hear people laughing. I know I am losing control and I need to get away from these people.

Leaning against the cold walls of the hotel, the fear of being caught consumes me, making me feel sick. I shake my head, I need to find somewhere quiet. A place I can go alone to remember who I am. I need to remember that I am an Alpha Wolf, I am Xavier Woodward's son and heir whether he likes it or not.

When I return to the room, Dominga and Nikki sit next to each other. In another time and place, these two would probably be the best of friends, but not right now, not while Dom has her tail in a knot.

"We've come to an agreement. There is no point in waiting around. We strike this weekend and then we can all go our separate ways. Until then, Dominga and I will try to stay out of each other's way," Nikki explains to me.

They both obviously understand how close to the knife's edge I am. Dominga rolls her eyes and pouts at me. She thinks it makes her look cute, but I'm beyond that right now. However, Nikki is looking rather tempting. Her cheeks are flushed from exertion, and her breasts, full and firm, capture my attention. She could give me an heir. Nikki's sly smile knocks me off balance, she's done this on purpose, she's using her mage abilities so that I fancy her and it's working.

I nod to them both in agreement, "Okay, so this weekend we

will be hitting the Onyx River and, hopefully, put an end to this." I indicate the three of us. The sooner my father's bastard loses her throat and Nikki gets her revenge, the sooner I can shed these two lunatics.

*** **Preston** ***

My mother's presence is requested so she can relay everything she had told me about the treatment of Dire Wolves, and I therefore volunteer to get her. I try desperately to locate people who could help Lina reverse her manifestations. My plan is to get every healer here so we can plan the best treatment possible for my Luna. I have to help her, I owe her for standing up to Nikki on my behalf.

Amber is busy helping me with both locating the best healers and organising our defences should the council return and attempt to arrest Eva again. It is doubly important now that we protect her since she is carrying our future Alpha. Eva and her pup are the future of our pack.

The news of Eva's pregnancy didn't come as a massive shock. Aiden hasn't left her alone since he found her, and I knew he was looking forward to welcoming more pups as soon as possible.

Amber's reaction to the news is surprising, though. At first, she was full of joy for her brother, which quickly changed to her being upset that she might not get to meet her new niece or nephew. As I hold her in my arms afterwards, trying to soak up every bit of Amber that I can, she asks if we can play a game.

"What sort of game?" I ask her, full of curiosity. From the blush on her cheeks, I know she is embarrassed but I don't know why.

"We both close our eyes and tell each other what our future looks like in a perfect world, where there is no trial, no mad widow trying to seduce you and no pack expectations.

Simply whatever your heart desires." I agree straight away, even though I still don't understand her reason for acting embarrassed.

"Okay, you go first, Red." She closes her eyes and rests her head against my shoulder and tells me her heart's desires.

"We would have our mating ceremony and we could ask Aiden for a cottage like his. We would make love every night and simply enjoy each other for a short while. We would have a couple of pups, hopefully a boy and a girl and we would be a family..." She chokes on the last couple of words and tears fall spontaneously down her cheeks.

"Amber, we might still be able to have all that. You have just described my greatest heart's desire, to be a family with you."

"I didn't know what I wanted until it was too late, Preston, and now, I'm terrified. I'm petrified that I'll never get to have all those things with you. I'll never get to give you what your heart desires. If I don't win this trial, you are going to be punished too."

She cries and apologises for a solid hour. Nothing I say stops her from beating herself up over her failings. One thing is clear: Amber needs distraction or she's going to lose her mind. I therefore bring her onboard my mission to find how we reverse wolf manifestations.

As I approach the packhouse with my mother, Amber runs down the steps to me, her red hair flying out behind her.

"Preston, Preston! I've found something. For Lina to let go of the hurt, Eva has to confront the pain of the past that caused the manifestations. She has to confront everyone that has hurt her."

I look at my mother for confirmation and she nods, adding, "Your mate is right, son: 'kill it with love' was the mantra of the healers in my old pack. People hold on to the pain of the past to remind them of what could go wrong. We have to help the new Luna let go of what hurt her."

"How do we do that, exactly?" I am stumped, surely we can just tell her she has to let it go?

"Therapy, son, lots of talking therapy and confrontations. That's what will help the Luna out now. It would help if Eva would open up about who hurt her and why and we can then proceed with caution."

This is going to be a mammoth task!

*** **Eva** ***

Aiden has been preoccupied with whatever he found out while he was in Scotland. I want him to share these things with me, but he's so stubborn at times that it's infuriating. He tells me he wants me to relax and it's not important, but I do worry about it.

The cell is a whole lot comfier now. Aiden had our whole bedroom brought down into my cell, and Summer's belongings are now in the holding area. I am happier since I have my own bed back so I can sleep in Aiden's arms each and every night, but more importantly, I am ecstatic to finally have room dividers to give us some privacy when Summer is sleeping, and things heat up between me and my mate. I was so paranoid about her being there that I couldn't relax, but now it feels like she is at least in another room.

Not that sex has been a priority. Despite being apart for ten whole days, Aiden is treating me like a prized piece of fine china. No matter how much I reassure him, he worries if we have sex he will hurt me or the baby.

I'm not dissatisfied; far from it. I love oral. Every time he goes down on me, I wonder how I ever lived without it in my life. The rush of warmth and wetness to that area and the heady feeling of knowing he is tasting me and licking me is enough to make me dizzy with desire for his mouth. But I also like sex; well, sex with Aiden, at least.

He pushes me away for the fourth time and it crushes my confidence so much that I will not initiate it again. It is just too embarrassing, and I am quickly feeling like things are changing between us. I don't think I could take another rejection; I don't think I can do the single parent thing all over again either.

I need Aiden to open up and let me in, but right now his barriers are well and truly up and there is no way in. He is impenetrable, unreachable and it hurts so much.

I take solace in the fact that he seems to want to touch me, he just doesn't want to have sex, so maybe this is about him being cautious about the baby. All I know is Aiden went away and when he came back, something had shifted and I am starting to really worry it is his feelings for me.

Amber, on the other hand, has been firing on all cylinders, she is so busy I feel tired just watching and listening to her. I am sitting on the rocking chair contemplating what has been happening or, more importantly, not happening between Aiden and I when she bounces in, filled with energy. She stops when she sees me, her concern for me spreading over her face.

"A penny for your thoughts, Eva," she shouts over to me. I try to smile but it doesn't quite happen. "Oh, Eva, are you okay?" Amber's kindness hits me like a kick to the gut and the tears fill my eyes before I can stop them.

"What happened in Scotland, Amber? Aiden won't tell me; I know something is bothering him, but he won't talk about it, and I am worried about him. I'm worried about us." I know I have got to the crux of the problem when her facial expression changes from one of sympathy to another of guarded shame. Something happened, and I need to know what.

"I think you need to talk to Aiden about this, Eva. If and when he wants to share, it's his right to choose. He loves you, Eva, and you're carrying his child now. I know my brother and whatever is happening in his head does not affect and will never affect his devotion to you. I think you need a change of scenery and some fresh air, Luna; it sounds like you are getting cabin fever."

So, something did happen. Amber confirms there is something Aiden is keeping from me, and I simply have to respect that he will tell me if he wants me to know.

"I want to talk to you anyway, Eva. I need to get my affairs in order, and I believe you're the woman I can leave my final wishes with. Preston and Aiden will not allow me to talk about these things, but I need to get them off my chest. Therefore, as my Luna, I would like to tell you everything in case I am imprisoned or executed."

In the chaos of everything else that has been going on, I forgot Amber's trial is due to start in two days' time. I nod to her, and she sits on Summer's bed.

"I want you to promise to look after Aiden and be strong for him and keep him in line. Tell him how much I love him and admire him and remind him frequently he was the best big brother I could have ever wished for. Tell the baby stories about me and tell them I'm sorry I didn't get to meet them." Her eyes fill with pain and longing and mostly sadness.

"I will, Amber, you know I will."

"I'm not finished. Preston. I need you to help Preston through this. Help him mourn but then help him move on. Once I'm gone, I want him to find a new mate and be a daddy just like he's always wanted. I want him to find peace and some joy." The tears stream down her face, and I try to comfort her by putting my arms through the bars and holding her.

"I give you my oath as your Luna and as your sister-in-law. I will ensure your final wishes are fulfilled to the best of my ability if the worst-case scenario does happen. I also promise you, as your friend, that I will do everything in my power to clear your name."

Amber finally hugs me back but quickly pulls away. "I won't hurt the baby, will I?"

I roll my eyes at her. "Not you too. Aiden won't touch me in case he hurts the baby. I'm not the first woman to have a baby, you know. The baby is fine, it's very well hidden and protected, I promise you." She lifts her hand to touch my tummy, which is still flat. It's so early on that there is no outward change and yet her eyes still light up in amazement when her hand makes contact.

"Honey, I'm home!"

I don't know how long Aiden has been there, but my heart starts to pound in anticipation of his closeness. I miss him, I miss us, and I need him close to me.

"Aidy, talk to your mate. She misses you and it hurts her that you haven't opened up to her." My face reddens as Amber stalks out of the room shouting her instructions to her brother as she goes.

"You know I'm trying not to hurt her, I thought it would hurt her less to not tell her. I don't want Lina to manifest anymore. I am trying to protect her," Aiden shouts to his sister's back.

To our shock, she turns back around and shouts in reply. "It's hurting her that you are keeping this from her. Right now, she would rather be hurt by the truth than comforted by a lie, isn't that right, Eva?"

Aiden looks at me to see my reaction, and I nod before lowering my head. He has tried to protect me and now I feel like I have infringed on his right to privacy.

"It's okay, Aiden. I was worried you didn't want to tell me; I didn't realise you were trying to protect Lina and me. I wanted to support you, like you've supported me. But just tell me when you're ready and simply know that I'm here and I'll always be here if you need me."

"I'm going to find Preston, see you both later." The door slams and I am more aware than ever that Aiden keeps his distance from me. He hasn't opened my cell, and the distance between us feels like it grows and magnifies by the second.

"I found out a lot about my mother and father while I was away. I found things that I know would make you cry, and I just want to keep you safe."

I stay silent, not wanting to intrude on what he has to say. I don't want to discourage or encourage him. I want him to give me whatever he wants and just support him afterwards.

"My mother died. She died of a broken heart about a year after she was banished from here and from us, her children."

The gasp is out of my mouth before I can stop it. "Oh, Aiden. I'm so sorry."

"You, Summer and the baby are everything to me. I want to be the best mate, the best Alpha and, most importantly, the best father I can, because the thought of any of you suffering like my father allowed my mother to suffer breaks me apart inside."

He opens the lock to my cell and walks towards me.

"All I ever want is you, us and our family. I would do anything to protect that. I'm sorry you felt pushed away. That's the last thing I want. I'm sorry for being a dick."

"I'm sorry I'm a hormonal, needy mess, Aidy. I just want us to share everything. I don't want you to suffer alone, not when you have your family right here who love you."

I wait until he opens his arms for me, but he goes one better. At last, I feel loved and desired as Aiden sweeps me up in his arms and kisses me.

"I've missed you so much, Shortie. I'm sorry I got weirded out about hurting the baby. I spoke to the pack doctor who assured me that it was perfectly safe, and we could resume our usual activities." I bite my lip as my whole body fires up at his words. "Where's Summer and when is she due back?"

"She's with Mrs Moore and she won't be back for a couple of hours."

He picks me up and places me in the centre of our bed. "Good, that should be enough time for what I have planned."

My core gushes in sheer delight. Six months ago, I never would have thought I would be acting or feeling this way, both eager and yearning to feel the flesh of my mate pounding over and into mine. Now, it's my drug, my vice, and I will always be addicted to Aiden. I will always want more Aiden.

*** Aiden ***

When I finally returned home from Scotland, there was so much turmoil going through me that in my haste to protect Eva, I hurt her and made her question my feelings for her. Keeping a distance from her seemed the easiest way to protect her because I don't want to pile on to the emotional baggage she already has, especially now she is carrying our pup too. She has enough challenges to deal with, like her pregnancy, the fact that her wolf has manifested, and that she is currently under house arrest. No, I will not add to her worries. I will deal with this alone.

Every time I get close to Eva, I break out in a cold sweat. Terror runs through me at the thought of hurting her or our pup. A simmering anger bubbles sporadically inside me and at times I feel out of control, and it scares me. What if I lose control around her? She is so vulnerable sitting in her prison, so petite and gentle that it terrifies me. The last thing I want to do is hurt her or frighten her. So, I decide that not telling Eva what I found out about my mother and father was the best course of action. All I have to do is keep my distance until I deal with my father. This proves to be impossible.

Roman chastises me constantly. *You are an idiot, Human. Lies and secrets destroyed our childhood, you're letting history repeat itself. Tell our mate what happened.*

Although I have come home, I haven't truly come back to Eva. I am holding back because I am afraid the beast from within me will emerge and she won't love me anymore. For the first time in my life, I am doubting myself and who I truly am.

The anger seems to flare up without a moment's notice and the only thing that will ease it is my father's throat in my hands. However, I am a mate and a father myself now. I cannot do anything to jeopardise that, and I need to keep my fury in check until I can deliver justice to the man who caused the painful and lingering death of my mother.

I stand in the hallway outside Eva's cell and overhear her telling Amber how worried she is about us and I know from her voice that my actions have hurt her. I don't want that, that is what I want to prevent and yet, I hurt her anyway. I hiss at

Roman as he reminds me he told me so. I have to fix this. I must tell Eva why.

Amber leaves us alone, so I can open up to Eva as much as I can without falling apart or losing my composure. Her presence actually soothes me, and calms the rage that brews inside. It feels so good to finally be close to her, to bare my soul and still feel love and acceptance from her. Staying away from her is no longer an option.

My worries about hurting our pup were squashed by the pack healer. In fact, they encourage me to enjoy my mate because as the millions of other wolves would also testify, mating during pregnancy can be just as enjoyable. I just don't want to hurt them, her or our baby.

As I hold my fragile mate in my hands, I think I could hold her entire head in one of my hands. Her love soothes me, and I relax as Roman basks in the attention we get from our Eva. I am loved and accepted and that won't change because of my past, or my current anger.

As I kiss her neck, I smile to myself as Eva shivers from the sensations running through her body. "I've missed this, I've missed you. I'm sorry for pushing you away, baby."

She exhales and throws her head back, giving me better access to her sweet spot, the place where my mark sits. I suck it and she whimpers as our mate's bond connection fills her with pleasure.

Just as I begin undressing Eva, my phone rings. For a split second I consider answering, but both Roman and I need Eva. We've missed her. They can call back or leave a message. As soon as the ringing stops, it starts again.

"For fuck's sake!" I know it's no one from my pack. I told them all and Amber would have reminded them all to not disturb me. If this is Alpha Xavier, I will go to war with him. "Sorry Shortie, I have to check who it is." Eva's moan of frustration pleases me. I want her to want me, and she doesn't disappoint me with her obvious displeasure at having to wait again.

When I check the caller display, I answer. It's the Mafia, and as much as we are now on friendly terms with Sal and Ale, we are still answerable to their supervision of us as werewolves.

"Alpha Aiden, I hope you're well? Sal and I would like to visit you and Eva and I was hoping you would be free right now. It's a mix of social and business, unfortunately."

"Yes, of course. We are free now, when will you be here?" I am trying to estimate if we can fit in a quicky before they arrive.

"Actually, we are at your border now. If you give your patrol the nod, we should be with you in ten minutes." Well, there goes our mating time.

Quickly, I mindlink the border patrol and grant Sal and Ale access. "Sorry Shortie, rain check. We have guests arriving in a few minutes." She groans loudly this time and frowns at me.

"Couldn't you tell them to go away, Aidy? And then come back to bed. Just for an hour. I miss you." I smile down at her, she glows now she has my pup growing inside her and there is more feistiness in her attitude too. I really like it.

"You want me to phone Salma back and tell her to go away because my mate wants to fuck instead?" Her gasp in reply is so cute. It's more of a squeak. Despite being vocal and brazen with me, she is still shy around everyone else. Only I get the pleasure of seeing that side of her.

"Salma is on her way here?" She rushes about tidying things away and smoothing down her crumpled clothing and bedhead.

"Calm down, it's just Sal and Ale. It will be fine." However, I am also worried. How on earth am I going to explain to them why Eva is locked up? Sal will castrate me without even thinking about it, and Ale, who is known to be skilled at decapitation, will not lose a wink of sleep if he felt justified in taking my head. And let's face it, he may well do when he realises Eva is in a cell.

I link Amber and Preston and tell them the Mafia are on their way. They will ensure that all pack members are on their best behaviour for the duration of the Mafia's visit.

"I'll go and meet them at the door, Eva, and try to explain why you are in here so it's not such a shock." I pull her up to me, she smells so good and looks ever tastier. "I'll ask Amber to watch Summer tonight so we can pick this right back up." This causes a smile to curl her lips and I can hear her heart fluttering away. She wants this as much as me.

I meet Ale and Sal as they pull up with their driver. Ale shakes my hand, but Sal pulls me in for a hug. "Where's Eva?" she asks as she looks around in confusion when her friend doesn't greet her.

Inhaling deeply before I speak, I struggle to find the words to explain what has been happening in our lives since we last saw them. "We have so much to tell you both, and to be honest, I don't even know where to start."

Sal shows genuine concern for my mate, so I rush to reassure her.

"Eva's okay. Well, she's sort of okay, maybe she can explain better. You had best come in and speak to her."

I lead them down into the dungeon to where my love has made her new home and get the shock of my life when Salma slams the butt of her gun into my head when she sees Eva in the cell.

CHAPTER TEN

Kill it with Love

*** Alejandro ***

All hell breaks loose. Alpha Aiden hits the deck, unconscious, Salma has a gun in her hand and is shouting about her friend being imprisoned, and poor Eva is locked away in a cell. However, the more I take in the scene in front of me, the more I realise that something is amiss.

Eva is hysterical, she shouts to Aiden and rants at Sal for hurting him even as my wife continues to shout. "Get the wire cutters, Ale. They fucking locked her in. She is in a cage. Eva, why the fuck have they caged you?"

"SALMA! STOP! STOP RIGHT NOW. He didn't imprison me, I imprisoned myself. Ale, stop her, I'm dangerous. I could hurt you; I could hurt everyone."

We both stop as Eva's words leave Salma visibly and verbally stumped. Eva has never hurt a fly in her life. "How are you dangerous, Eva? Are you sick? Where's Summer?"

Aiden groans on the floor as he rouses.

"For fuck's sake, Sal, they're our friends! Try asking first before knocking him out." I help Aiden up off the floor, relieved that he isn't cut, and the bump that looked like a mini mountain is already starting to recede.

"As I was saying, we have so much to tell you both, and I don't know where to start, so I think I will let my girl tell you while I recover from getting my head pounded." He throws a look at Salma, resentful, and yet a bit wary too. He's a clever man, Alpha Aiden, and he is right to be wary. I would be too. Salma is overprotective of her best friend and right now she is livid at her current circumstances.

Eva fusses over Aiden, checking his temple and his eyes through her bars. I know from watching them interact with one another that this isn't a case of Aiden holding Eva against her will.

So why is his mate and Luna locked in a cell?

A very comfortable cell, I must admit, but a cell all the same.

"I think you owe him an apology, Sal," I tell my wife, who hisses me back into submission.

"No, she doesn't. It's okay. I'll give you that one, Sal, but only because I know you did it in outrage for Eva. I know you would do anything you felt necessary to look out for her and I'm actually happy she has a friend who would fight for her. We might need that in the future. Eva, please tell them what has been going on."

Eva explains everything to us. I am perplexed and lost at some points, especially when she starts to explain about Mages and Dire Wolves, the danger they pose and how she feels safer in the cell. Then came the tale of the Werewolf Council placing her under house arrest and, finally, how we can help reverse the manifestation of her wolf.

"Eva, just give me the list of everyone who has caused you harm, pain and upset and we'll go kill them now." My Sal is still feeling murderous and in her heightened state of vigilance, she is missing the subtleties. This isn't about eradicating people, this is about Eva facing her demons and putting them to rest.

"Chula, I think what Eva is telling us is that she has to tell people that they hurt her and why, so she can move on from it. She doesn't want them all dead, not yet." Eva gives me a small smile of thanks. "Just tell us if there is anything we can do, and we will help."

"So, you said this was a mix of business and pleasure. What's been happening in your life?" Aiden is back to the point and it's a relief to have his diplomacy.

"We need some information. Do you know a werewolf from the Moon Stone pack who goes by the initials J.R.?"

It is our turn to share, and this time I let Sal do the explaining. By the end of it, Eva and Aiden are as shocked as we were when she shared their tale.

"So, your father's mistress is in a relationship with a werewolf from the Moon Stone and you think he helped her to poison him? I mean we don't keep a full register of other packs, just the higher ranks. I don't recall a J.R. in them. Do you have anything else to go on?"

Sal hesitates but I don't know why until she explains it. "Ricky, my little brother, has met him and can identify him but he's only seven years old and I would rather he didn't have to. I want to protect him; he's been through enough. I don't want that information to leave this dungeon."

"No, we won't involve children," Eva assures her. "I will speak to my father; he will come and visit me if I ask him to. I won't say the reason behind me asking but I'm sure he can give me his pack register or something. Besides, he'll have to come soon and bring my mother so I can confront her."

Eva doesn't look happy at the prospect, and I can't say I blame her. She has a huge task ahead of her. What I don't understand is why the Werewolf Council has allowed her to stay in the pack and why she has a time frame for reversing her manifestations. It seems Sal has the same queries when she asks Eva why they didn't take her away and why she has six months to heal her wolf.

"Oh, yeah, that's our other news. I didn't want to say anything so early on, because we've only just found out. Aiden and I are having a baby." Happiness swirls with a sinking feeling right in the pit of my stomach. I feel Sal tense, only for a second, but I know from this tiny action that she is thrown by the news.

"Congratulations!" we both shout to them because we are genuinely happy for them and their happiness. However, another couple around us expecting just highlights that we aren't and the disappointment at being the only ones who aren't leaves me feeling sad. Sal and Eva hug and I shake Aiden's hand again.

He whispers to me when the girls are talking. "How long have you two been trying? I heard the change in both your heart rates." I explain to him it hasn't been that long, less than three months. "It'll be the stress stopping it. As soon as Sal can stop worrying about what happened to her father, it will happen."

I find comfort in Aiden's words, especially since he isn't bragging about getting the job done faster than me, or about being more of a man. Maybe if we can get Dominga and find this werewolf, both Sal and I could finally relax and enjoy being newly married and us getting pregnant will just happen.

When Sal comes back to me, I pull her close to me, not caring that we have an audience. They understand how it feels to be completely in love with an amazing person too. "Ale!" she whispers to me, but I kiss her quickly to silence her.

"Once this is all over, I want us to go on our honeymoon, Chula. Where would you like to go?"

She reels off a list: Bali, the Seychelles, St. Lucia. "But to be honest, I don't care as long as I'm with you, Ale."

She is becoming more open and loving with me in front of our friends, and that means the world to me. I don't want her to be shy about us. I want to shout from the rooftops that she's mine, but Sal has always been more reserved and formal until now. It feels amazing.

"What can we do to help, Eva? Is there anyone you need us to bring here to confront and talk to?" Sal asks her.

The most obvious choices are her mother and her ex-husband, but Ryan is dead and her mother is already being dealt with.

"I'm going to phone Melanie and invite her here. She wants Summer and her baby to bond, and I think confronting her about her affair with Ryan could be a start." She pauses for a moment, obviously still contemplating her next moves. "I would like to make contact with one person, I'm not sure if you still have contact with him, Sal. He didn't do anything wrong, but I only found out recently that he didn't, and I was hurt by what I thought were his actions. I just want to speak to him about what happened and draw a line under it. Can you get in touch with Luke? I'm hoping a phone call or a video call will suffice."

After sharing our troubles, we head back to get Ricky. We have a loose plan of action and friends to support us. What could go wrong?

*** Melanie ***

It is a surprise to hear from Eva. Her silence convinced me she had changed her mind about Summer bonding with my baby. Disappointment flowed through me at the prospect, but I knew I had to respect her decision. After all, she has been very gracious towards me despite everything I have done and if seeing me pregnant with her husband's child is too much, I completely understand and respect her decision.

The nightmares about Ryan continue to plague me and I continue to isolate myself in my home, not even leaving to get groceries, just surviving on what is in the cupboards or the small amounts of bread, milk, eggs, butter, and yoghurt that my milkman brings me. Fortunately for me, the milkman brings potatoes, fruit, and vegetables as well as fresh orange juice. There is no reason to leave, except for hospital appointments and now to visit Eva.

Eva explains to me that she is having therapy and that she needed to discuss some things with me so she could move on in life. She assures me she will still facilitate Summer being involved in my daughter's life.

I know I'm going to have to answer some tough questions from Eva. My cheeks flame in shame at the appalling way I treated her. With Ryan gone, my thoughts have become clearer, and I am riddled with guilt and embarrassment over my actions. As much as this is going to be hard and uncomfortable, I want to do this. Maybe giving Eva what she needs to move on will allow me to forgive myself and move on too.

Eva tells me that Aiden, her boyfriend, will come and drive me to her new home. So, the following day, I sit and wait for him and, despite waiting for what feels like three lifetimes, he rings my doorbell bang on time. When I open the door, Eva's boyfriend is there with a tall ginger woman.

"Hi, Melanie, I'm Aiden and this is my sister, Amber. Could we please come in and talk before we take you to Eva? There is something we would like to discuss with you."

I invite them into my home and sit uncomfortably, waiting for them to explain what they want to discuss with me.

"Something has happened in Eva's life, and she is under house arrest. When you come to see her, she will be in a cell but it is nothing for you to be worried about, nothing will happen to you or your p... child. You will be completely safe. Do you understand?" I nod that I did although I have a million questions about what they just told me.

"Good, so before we can grant you access, we need you to sign this Non-Disclosure Agreement." Shit, it sounds like Eva is in deep shit if I have to sign an NDA. I quickly sign the form and ask if we can go now. They seem satisfied with that.

The drive to Eva's new home takes about forty minutes and, although the car is luxurious and the drive is pleasant, I am eager to get out of the car and stretch my legs and breathe the fresh air into my lungs.

Saturday is my usual day I spend with my children. However, when I got the call off Eva, I quickly asked their dad to rearrange, which he agreed to. I will spend the day with my boys tomorrow instead. I never change my time with them, but this is important.

As we pull up outside the extremely large house, I cannot help but be in awe. "Eva lives here? It's huge."

"We have an apartment inside until the cottage is finished, but this all belongs to me and now it belongs to Eva too."

Before we go in, Aiden reminds me that Eva is under house arrest, but I don't need to be alarmed or scared.

They direct me down into what I presume to be a cellar, the air turns colder with each step I take. As I walk into the room where Eva is, I don't even see her. Instead, I come face to face with a massive man with the most beautiful eyes I have ever seen.

"MATE!" he spits at me through gritted teeth, and even though he is grimacing at me as he stares me down, I don't feel in danger or threatened. I have never felt safer.

"Max, stand down. Go back to your Luna. MAX! Snap out of it!"

I have no idea what is happening but the man who I now know is Max backs off away from me and sits on the other side of the bars to Eva, who I notice for the first time.

"Hi, Mel, this is Max… my… bodyguard. Max, this is Melanie." He gives me a short nod and looks away.

I try to break the ice; it feels so tense, and I have a feeling I'm the reason everyone is on edge. "So, Eva, what trouble have you been creating to land yourself in prison?"

When Eva smiles at my question, I almost feel the tension disappear.

*** Eva ***

Max is wound up tight, Melanie doesn't seem to realise what is happening and Aiden is trying to calm Max without coming across as strange to Melanie. "Call for Preston please, Aiden. I think Max could use a break."

Melanie doesn't seem to notice when Aiden's eyes glaze over, she only has eyes for Max and occasionally me. I wonder if she can feel the pull like I could with Aiden? I just hope Max handles this better than Aiden did to begin with.

"Thank you for coming, Mel, please make yourself comfortable and if there is anything you want or need, please let us know."

I pull out my notepad and consider the questions I have for her.

"I have some questions; I think you can answer some of them for me and that will help me to understand and accept what Ryan did so I can heal from his mistreatment. I just want to reassure you that I will only hold you accountable for your own actions, not anything he did, but any insight into why Ryan was so hateful would be appreciated."

She nodded to me. "I will be as honest as I can with the information I have. Please, ask away. I want to help you if I can."

With that assurance, I steady my nerves and start to confront the pain of my past.

*** **Junior** ***

With Nikki's mage power, we manage to make it onto the Onyx River territory without detection. It is still daytime, but I argue that the sun is our friend in this case, as we need to see who is about and where we are going.

Dominga is unwell this morning and we decide she should stay at the hotel for now, so she doesn't slow us down. She looks suspiciously between Nikki and I, her eyes narrowing into slits, but what can be done? She wants to be rid of Nikki, and I want to hurt my father's bastard. This has to be done.

When Nikki propositions me, I know Dominga has reason to be concerned. She waits until we are halfway to the Onyx River before she does.

"We could help each other, Junior, and I think we would make a good team," she starts off. "Dominga is old, she can't give you an heir, she's human and doesn't know anything about our kind. Can you imagine her as your Luna?"

Nikki has a valid point, but I don't tell her that these thoughts have been swimming around in my head since she joined our cause.

"I could, though." She doesn't add to that, she just leaves it hanging between us. The more I think about it, the more it makes sense, but how do I get rid of Dominga now? I am in so much shit with my father, my pack, and the Mafia now too.

"Dominga was right after all. You joined us because you wanted me?" I accuse her, although there is no malice in my voice, and I consider it to be gentle in approach.

"Oh no, I joined you so I could get revenge. I still want my revenge. But I also want a pup, a family and to belong somewhere. It was actually Dominga accusing us of it that gave me the idea." That does make sense. I have also thought of nothing other than what Nikki could give me in comparison.

"So, what exactly is it you want from me, Nikki?" I just want blunt, straight answers, no messing about. "You said you wanted to help me claim my rightful position and you wanted revenge... Tell me what else you want now."

"Make me your Luna, I will give you the pups you want and need to carry on your legacy. Imagine our pups, Junior, with your Alpha blood and my mage abilities. Our pups would be magnificent." I slam her up against the tree and she smiles back wickedly at me. "We could be good together, you and I,

Xavier Junior. All I'm saying is think about it. But be quick, I'm ready to have some fun. Are you?"

I'm rock hard solid for her, but niggling in the back of my mind is Dominga… I was madly in love with her not so long ago, but now I feel indifferent towards her. How did things change so dramatically?

Her hand begins to move back down my body, unable to leave me dissatisfied, and she grips my hardened cock as she does. "I know you want me too. Just think it over and maybe we could do something about this thick rod of yours. It must be bothering you."

I bet her body is smooth and toned, and still able to bear fruit. I want her; I admit it to myself. However, I'm not going to give in so easily. I want her to be grateful. I want her to beg.

"I will consider your proposal once my father's bastard is disposed of," I tell her firmly.

"If you say so, Alpha. Just let me go until you are ready." The challenge is there. I already have her pinned against the tree with my hands and my dick, which now throbs with need. She is willingly giving herself to me. All I have to do is accept.

Without further thought, I smash my lips over hers, just to test if we will be compatible, when suddenly I feel eyes on me. When I look around, no one is there. I'm just paranoid. However, the disruption means I am able to stop myself taking things further with Nikki for now.

We hide in a cluster of trees near the packhouse. Nikki tells me she can feel Eva inside and we try to hatch a plan to draw her out when something happens.

"That's Eva's daughter right there, Junior. Do you feel the connection?" I shake my head. The brat is nothing to me. "The woman with her is human. I don't know who she is. The wolf is

Gamma-ranked. This might be an opportunity to draw her out. If we take the little girl, Eva will surely come out of her hiding place."

I run towards the little girl to snatch her away before the decision is made. I didn't account for the Onyx River being prepared for an attack too.

*** **Eva** ***

It is tense in the cell. I want to speak to Melanie alone, but Aiden and Max won't leave, and now Amber and Preston are here too. It is embarrassing going over the more intimate details of my marriage and my husband's affair with Mel. It is torture doing it in front of a wider audience.

"You knew about Summer and me, so why didn't you stop it, Mel? That's what I find most hurtful. You knew he was married but you carried on seeing him." Melanie drops her head at first, but then she looks me in the eyes and speaks with conviction. She accepts full responsibility and apologises.

"Eva, I had known Ryan Jefferson all my life. I fell in love with him and really thought we would end up together, married with a little house and a white picket fence and for a long time, he led me on. He used me. I loved him, I gave him my virginity and he just discarded me."

She pauses while she gains her composure, and with her being pregnant, I want her to be comfortable.

"When he came back into my life a few years later, it felt like a second chance to be with him and this time he wanted me too. He lived with me, Eva, he came home to me every night and he told me that you two were separated and estranged but you were holding him to ransom with his money. I was stupid and needy. I didn't care about you and your little girl because I was finally getting Ryan back. I was selfish and wrong."

Summer returns from her afternoon with Mrs Moore, so I call our talk to a halt. I don't want Summer to see or hear this, and I need a break too. I speak to Lina, who tells me that finding out about Melanie came after the manifestations. Melanie didn't cause the manifestation in Lina, Ryan did and Melanie cannot and should not pay for Ryan's crimes.

"Thank you for your honesty. I need to take a break." Max offers to take Summer out for fresh air and when Melanie sees an opportunity to spend a little time with Summer, she asks if she can go too. I smile when Max shrugs indifferently. Despite his outward appearance, I know his wolf will be going crazy inside him.

When they leave, Aiden asks Amber and Preston to give us a moment too. He unlocks my cell, and the tears are falling before I can stop them. "Did it help, Shortie?" I shake my head no, because it didn't, it didn't help Lina. I don't know how to help her. What if I can't?

"She said Ryan's actions caused the manifestations, not Melanie's, but how can I confront Ryan when the fucker's dead?" He holds me in his warm embrace and strokes my head soothingly while I rant.

When there is a lull, he kisses me softly on the lips. "Eva, I have an idea. Maybe you don't have to confront Ryan? Maybe you need to remember everything he did, by talking about it or writing it down so you can address it and then heal from it."

I contemplate what he has suggested and I think that could work. We don't get to discuss it any further as the security alarms screech all over the pack house.

As Alpha, Aiden must be there, he quickly locks me back in the cell before running out to see what the breach is. "Aiden, get Summer. Check on Summer."

I'm alone in the cell and a sense of foreboding overcomes me. Something bad is about to happen. I can feel it. I need my little girl back in sight.

*** Melanie ***

When I am giving Eva the answers she asks for, I am embarrassed and feel wretched that she has to hear some of the stuff I am saying. Moreover, the fact that I had actually done those things in the first place made me feel even worse. I had no consideration for her based on the few details Ryan had given me. It just demonstrates to me how much I loathe myself, how little respect I have for myself to want to be with a man who treated his wife and child so shoddily.

Eva has a lot more grace and decorum than I do. She shows no outward reaction to my confessions, just as she promised. She is at least twice the woman I could ever dream of being.

I ask if I could play outside with Summer for a little while. I just want to talk to her about my baby, who will be her sister. She is so young she probably doesn't understand. The man with the lovely eyes comes with us and I wonder at the place I've been brought to that a little girl who isn't quite three years old needs a bodyguard.

Nevertheless, it is clear that Summer is comfortable and close with her bodyguard. "Up, Maxxi," she shouts to him, and he picks her up like she is a flower and places her on his shoulders, causing her to giggle. Summer is such a beautiful girl, so full of light and love. How on earth is Ryan Jefferson her father? I rub my tummy and pray that my daughter takes after her sister and not her father.

"So, you're carrying the child of the Luna's ex-husband?" Max asks. Shame and guilt trickles down my neck. I didn't have to wait long for the comments and judgements.

"This baby will be Summer's half sister because they share a father. However, this is *my* baby." I sound a lot surer of myself in comparison to how I feel. "Why do you call her 'The Luna'?"

"I didn't mean any offence. I was just curious." My cheeks flame again. I am jumping ahead of myself. "And I call her Luna because she is the boss now, well, the female boss. And she's too short to be called the female boss." He smiles quickly before his face becomes guarded again. I am confused by him, he seems indifferent and yet intrigued at the same time.

"Maxxi, down. And run," Summer shouts when we reach a piece of flat grass. As soon as Max places her feet on the floor, she imitates a wind-up toy, running as fast as her legs can carry her. We both laugh at her and her enthusiasm.

"She is such a sweet little girl," I say as I watch her roll about and giggle in the grass. Max nods his agreement; a smile almost reaches his eyes. But in the blink of an eye, the whole atmosphere changes.

Max grabs me by the shoulder, causing me to shriek. "Something is wrong, get to Summer now." I nod to him and run over to Summer; however, she thinks I'm playing and runs away from me, giggling and asking me to catch her.

Panic fills me, as I struggle to keep up with her. I turn back to Max and there is another guy there and a woman in the background. Max and the guy fight and shout and then the woman shoots something from a pipe in her mouth and it hits Max in the neck.

Max falls into a heap on the floor and the other man grins at me, as he sprints towards Summer.

I have never been athletic or sporty. I have never been particularly fast or fit, but as I see the menacing look in the man's eye, I know nothing good is planned for little Summer. I don't know how I do it, but it's almost as if I fly to Summer, who also senses the danger and runs to my open arms with fear and tears filling her eyes.

However, an unknown, unseeable force stops me. My hair follicles pop in my scalp with the pressure of being held back but I can't give up, the man is gaining on us.

I scream as I force my body forward. The man reaches for Summer, and I run headfirst into his side, knocking him off balance. I quickly push Summer behind my back, they will have to go through me to get to her.

And that is, unfortunately, what he does. The force of his weight hitting me is what I imagine being hit by a bulldozer feels like. I scream out in pain and when I open my eyes, Max's eyes meet mine. The woman who had been in the background is fleeing on foot and Max and the guy fist-fight.

I must pass out from the pain because I am sure Max transforms into a large dog. In my pain-filled haze, I hear snapping and cracking and growling.

When I finally wake up, I'm in a white room, surrounded by machines and lights and beeping. Max is asleep in the chair next to my bed, he needs a shave, but it looks cute. Why is he here and where is 'here'?

"Max?"

I try to wake him, but my voice is gravelly and croaky.

"Max!"

He jumps when he wakes up. "Melanie... Thank the goddess you're awake. You've been out of it for two days. I was so worried you were never going to wake back up."

"Where am I? What happened?" Flashes of my last memories

fill my mind; my hands quickly go to my tummy. "My baby?" I know from the look on his face he was dreading me asking.

"I'm so sorry, Melanie. Your injuries were too severe. Your baby didn't make it."

The room fades from my sight as I howl and scream in pain.

CHAPTER ELEVEN

Whudunnit

*** **Aiden** ***

The alarms ring out shrilly and I run from the dungeon. Preston briefs me as I undo my button-down shirt and kick off my shoes. "There's been a breach, undetected again. It's got to be Nikki, Alpha, and she's with Junior."

"Where is Max with Summer and Melanie?" As I say it, the distorted mindlink from Max makes my blood run cold. Junior is after my little girl and Max has been hit with something and is weakened.

I don't even take off the rest of my clothes, they shred as I shift and Roman takes over. I bound over to the patch of grass with Amber and Preston flanking me, and watch helplessly as Junior runs at Summer. He's too big and too uncontrolled. He will kill her without a doubt. Her tiny frame wouldn't stand a chance.

Roman howls as the scene plays out until an angel comes, her blonde hair blowing out, and spears the giant beast of a man who threatens the little girl in her care. We all stop in shock. Melanie saved Summer; her actions have without a doubt saved my little girl's life, but I am unable to stop him in time as he ploughs through Mel. Her scream of pain, her broken body and the copious amount of blood confirm this is serious.

Max shifts as he jumps through the air at Junior, and I don't stop him when he snaps his jaws at his throat. Max found out less than an hour ago that Melanie is his fated mate and now she lies lifeless on the floor, seriously injured at the very least, and all at the hands of Junior.

Max isn't successful in killing Junior, he is still weakened from what I presume is wolfsbane that was shot into his neck. Junior manages to escape, and he shifts and runs off too.

A woman flees on foot. I presume that it is Nikki, and send Billy and his team to track and capture them. I tell Preston and Amber through mindlink to sort Max out and get Melanie to the pack hospital as soon as possible while I return Summer to her mummy and explain what has happened.

Billy places Summer on my back. She's had a ride from Roman before and knows how to hold on as I run carefully back to the packhouse. Her tears run down Roman's fur and her little body trembles. I mindlink and ask for clothes to be brought to the door for me so I can shift and comfort my little girl properly.

An omega brings a dressing gown to the door for me so I can shift quickly. Once I'm dressed, I lift Summer so I can take her to the dungeon. It breaks my heart to hear her crying, and to feel the way her body shakes as she sobs for her mummy and daddy.

"I'm here, sunshine girl, your daddy is here. I've got you and I'll never let anyone ever hurt you ever again. I'm so sorry."

"AIDEN!" Eva shouts as she sees us. "Is she bleeding? There is blood on her feet." I shake my head at her and open the cell, allowing mother and daughter to cuddle and comfort each other properly.

"It's not her blood, she's pretty shook-up but she's not physically harmed." I explain to Eva. My voice shakes, and it is the first time I notice the lump of fear that hadn't moved from my throat since I saw Summer in danger.

"Whose blood is it, Aiden? And who harmed them?"

Summer physically relaxes in her mother's arms. No one can make it better like her mummy can and within moments she is asleep with her thumb in her mouth, a trait I haven't seen often from her.

"Aidy, what happened?" Eva's voice is firmer this time and after dragging my hands over my face and through my hair, I try to explain what I know.

When I finish explaining, Eva asks me to take Summer to her bed and lock her back in the cell. "I am so angry, Aiden. I want to rip Junior's throat out with my own bare hands. How dare he go after our daughter? How dare he come here, to her home and make her feel unsafe and frightened, how dare he try to harm a little girl who isn't even three years old yet." Her body shakes and I can see her losing control.

"Lina, please, calm down, if you emerge you will jeopardise the safety of our pup. Please calm down." Appealing to the wolf within is the only thing I can do, Eva cries as she breathes deeply and slowly.

"This is my fault for bringing her here, Aiden. If anything happens to her or her baby, I'll never forgive myself."

"Stop this now, Eva, this is not your fault. Melanie's own actions led her to be here today, and it was Junior that hurt her, not you. You need to think of our baby now too. This is not your fault."

She hiccoughs as she starts to calm down. "I want to call my father. This is war now and I want to know what side he is on, because if he supports Junior after what he has done, I want nothing to do with him. He must pick a side. I will be calling for Junior's throat for what he has caused today."

I agree with her, there is no grey area anymore, you're either with us or you're our enemy. I just hope her father doesn't break her heart by not choosing her once again.

Amber returns to the cells looking shook-up, even paler than usual. "How is she?" she nods towards the sleeping form of Summer.

"She's better now she's back with her mummy but it's frightened the life out of her. How are Max and Melanie?" Amber gives a quick shake of her head and looks pointedly at Eva.

"Just tell me. Is she seriously harmed, Amber?" Eva demands and my sister lowers her head.

"She's lost her baby. The doctor said it was the equivalent of being hit by a car doing ninety miles per hour. They are going to remove her spleen and give her a blood transfusion. Max sends his apologies, but he refuses to leave her side."

There is, of course, nothing for him to apologise for. He must support his mate now more than ever, even if they have only just met.

Eva asks for privacy while she calls her father, so I post one of Max's Gamma Guards to stand sentry while I go and debrief the pack and also make contact with the Werewolf Council to report a human harmed on my property. With Amber's trial about to start tomorrow, this is more fuel for them to burn us with.

Preston asks for a word in private and so we quickly go into my office. "Alpha, has Luna asked her father for the Moon Stone registry yet?" I shake my head; it was her plan to ask tonight when she called to ask him to bring her mother.

"No, but she is on the phone right now to demand he pick a side, her or her brother. Junior has just attempted to attack Xavier's granddaughter, which should surely have some weight. He cannot expect us to turn a blind eye to this."

"I think we need to talk to Xavier and establish something. It's been bugging me for a couple of days now. Junior is in shit, his own father had him in the dungeon, but we never found out what the trouble was." I wait for Preston to continue. "What if the answer has been under our noses? What if Xavier Junior is JR? Maybe we got the meaning wrong and it's not initials but an abbreviation of his name?"

Junior killing a powerful Mafia Don…. My first thought is why? Why would he do that? I have a feeling my new father-in-law could fill in some blanks, but it's whether or not he is willing to give his son up.

"Look Aiden, I don't have all the answers," Preston continues, "I might be barking up the wrong tree, but we know Nikki has gone rogue, and now she is with Junior. The last we heard of Junior, he was locked in the dungeons for causing his father aggravation. Also, Xavier told us that the Werewolf Council went to him to find Eva, but why did they stay there when a break-off team came here and saw for themselves that Eva was in our dungeon?"

Everything seems to fall in place. Beta Preston is an astute man and with everything that has been going on, maybe we have both been preoccupied, but he still got to a worthy conclusion before I did.

"I'll go back to Eva now and ask to speak to her father too."

I am too late when I get back down to Eva. The Gamma Guard is back inside keeping watch over her, which tells me her phone call is over.

Eva looks shocked and pale. "What's wrong, my love? You look like you've seen a ghost." I am becoming increasingly concerned about her and our pup and the strain this is taking on them both.

"Aiden, it's Junior. He's the werewolf Salma is after. He is the one causing all this shit. My father says he sides with us, and Junior is out of control. I'm taking him down, Aiden. He killed Jose; he has hurt Mel, causing her to miscarry. He tried to kill Summer and he'll try to kill me because I threaten his position as Alpha."

The rage and anger and panic she feels fills my chest too; Roman is baying for blood now.

"I need to let Salma and Alejandro know as soon as possible, Shortie; they'll want his head." She nods her agreement.

"They can have his head, but his throat is ours, Aiden. We can all have our vengeance."

My girl is back to looking in control, she looks fierce and strong. She knows who she is and what she has to do.

I've never felt prouder of her.

*** **Salma** ***

Life since Ale and I became a couple has been a series of ups and downs. I love him more than I could ever comprehend. Marrying him is the best thing that ever happened to me. However, the high of being in love was tainted with the lows of my papa dying, of finding he was poisoned and of his secret life and family. However, from that low, I also gained my little brother. The dry-humoured, silly little monster who is now my pride and joy had been a source of my sleepless nights until I realised he was just a young boy. He was no threat to me, quite the opposite. He has completely stolen my heart and warmed it with his love and fun and innocence.

The truth about my father's death continues to elude me and with each passing day that goes by without answers, our standing within the Mafia wanes. We are losing respect. I need to take action and bring the culprit to justice and soon or the vultures will come to take what is mine.

Ricky has settled into the Suarez house with me and Ale, but I crave getting back to our own space and settling into our own groove as a family. Ale got me a load of realtor details with properties we could have. Now that we are Ricky's legal guardians, we will need a bigger permanent base and my mother still refuses to move out of our family home or share it with "Jose's bastard", as she put it. She has become increasingly bitter since I got custody of Ricky and resents that I have put his needs above hers. I want to swing for her for being such a selfish, uncaring bitch. Ricky is a child. Papa's child. His place is with me now.

No matter how I look at the limited evidence we do have, I still come up with nothing. No leads, no iota of an idea of where Dominga is hiding or the werewolf she is in cahoots with. I am beginning to believe that we may never get answers, and that means I will never get justice for my papa.

I am watching Ale interact with Ricky as they play a building game on his PlayStation. Ale is amazing; he hasn't been resentful or even offered a word of complaint about our new-found responsibilities. He embraces them and excels at being a guardian and it cements in my mind that I want a family. I want to give Ale a child more than anything in the world.

My phone rings and the caller display shows me it is Eva. "Hey, how are you?" I ask absentmindedly as I watch my boys playing their game.

"Sal? Sal, I need you to come to me as soon as possible. I have the information you need." My heartbeat pounds in my ears, and the ground shifts momentarily. "Sal, did you hear me? Come to the Onyx River now, bring Ale, we need to plan, and we need to do it fast."

"Who is it?" I need to know. I want to know. Who killed my papa?

"Its Junior, the fucking idiot I share a father with. It's him, Sal. The Werewolf Council is also after him, so we need to move fast. If they get there before us, we will not get our chance to pay him back."

"Ok, I'll be there soon."

I hang up and try to take a deep breath but my body doesn't feel like it belongs to me. My legs feel weak and like they are made of jelly and my head is spinning with overwhelming thoughts and emotions.

"Salma, Salma. What happened, did you faint?" How silly. I have never fainted in my life, my constitution would never allow it. I am a Morales; I am a Mafia Princess. Salma Morales does not faint!

And yet here I am, on the floor, sprawled out like a fallen bird as Ale crouches over me, checking my head and eyes with worry and concern etched all over his face. He strokes the side of my face which throbs, I must have banged it on the way down. "You're going to have one heck of a shiner, Chula. Your eye is already starting to blacken."

Ale lifts me from the floor with ease and my body continues to shake and sweat. "Are you getting sick, bebe?" he murmurs to me gently and tenderly and I shake my head at him in reply.

"Ale, that was Eva, she's found out who JR is. We have to go back to the Onyx River now." I jump out of his arms, and cringe when I am still unsteady on my feet. I take out my iPad and upload a picture of Junior Woodward from social media. "Let me just do a check. Ricky, do you know this man?"

My little brother pauses his game and looks over at the picture I am showing him. "Yes. That's my mum's boyfriend. That's JR." With that settled, he immediately returns to his game.

Ale takes the iPad too and looks at the photograph. "Junior Woodward? Eva's half-brother?" I nod to him, still not trusting my voice. "Do you want to stay here with Ricky, and I will sort this out once and for all?"

I clamber up off the couch. "NO! No way, Alejandro. I am coming with you." He smiles at me, and I realise he pressed the right button to spring me out of my spiral of panic.

"Hurry up and stop fainting then, we can ask my mother and father to watch Ricky for us and be out of here in twenty minutes."

He kisses me hard, pulling my head to him roughly. "Eurgh, get a room. You two are so gross," Ricky shouts at us while pretending to vomit.

"Just wait until he's older and in love, I'll get him back." Ale whispers against my ear while suppressing a laugh.

We quickly change our clothes and get our bag of goodies together. I tell Ricky I will be back soon and to keep his phone turned on so I can contact him.

As we leave the Suarez family home, I can't help thinking this might all be over really soon. Justice is finally going to be served.

*** **Xavier** ***

The cat is out of the bag, as the saying goes. As soon as Eva mentions what has been happening at Onyx River, everything else pours out of my mouth. I have no intention of lying to my daughter, she is the innocent party in this, and I will not be responsible for her being hurt once again. Besides, Junior has attacked a pup, my grandpup to be exact. I want him punished for that. No, *I* want to punish him for it.

Lydia is starting to realise that our son is unlikely to make it out of this alive. I wish I could make this better for her, but Junior is a grown man. By the time I was his age, I was running this pack single-handed. I had been in a fair few scrapes and battles; I had suffered defeat and tasted victory. I took every lesson. My son just doesn't. He takes every slight as a personal dig, and now he has made a grave for himself, and the way he is going, he may as well hand them the axe to chop off his head too. As much as someone is going to kill him for what he has done, I concur that Junior has been instrumental in his own downfall.

That doesn't make it any easier for his mother, the woman who grew him from a seed in her own tummy, who almost lost her life carrying him and birthing him. The mother who raised this little boy and had so many hopes and dreams for the future for him. My heart is sore for her, and for us. But Junior has crossed boundaries he should never cross and now he has werewolves, the council, and the Mafia after him. That's before we even get to the point of him attempting to hurt or kidnap Eva's little pup and seriously injuring a human, causing her to miscarry.

Junior has made his choices and now he has to pay the price for those choices, but so will we as his parents. I have a daughter now and that gives me a reason to carry on. Lydia doesn't and I worry if she is strong enough to overcome the loss of her child. Despite what Junior has done, my Lydia doesn't deserve the heartache she will undoubtedly suffer if he is executed.

I want her to be a part of my daughter's life so she has something to live for. I know it's not the same, but having grandchildren to look forward to might just be what makes the difference.

Lydia has been so upset since we returned home yesterday.

"I messed up so badly, X, I scared the little girl and Eva seemed so mad at me." I remind her of what she was like when Junior was little, and she smiles. "Yeah, I suppose us she-wolves are overprotective of our young. I want to try to get to know her. I'm just scared she'll reject me. After all, I am not flesh and blood to her."

The Council are still swarming my lands and the seriousness of the situation is starting to filter through to the pack.

Everyone now knows Junior has killed a powerful Spanish Don and that his firm wants revenge. Several members of the pack have voiced their concerns and have also questioned my ability to continue leading. I need to discuss the succession with Eva and Aiden as soon as possible, but so much is happening right now that I haven't found the right opportunity. Eva is my heir, and I believe that is the reason why she was able to shift when she came onto my land. The land recognises her as the future of this pack. However, right now, Eva is in no position to lead. She has many admirable qualities, but she has no Alpha or leadership training and she is currently locked in her own cell as a potential danger to herself and others because of her Dire Wolf.

I have to face facts: Eva isn't going to leave her mate to come and lead here. Therefore, I need to extend my olive branch to Alpha Aiden and ask that we merge our packs. That way, he will become Alpha over both packs and Eva will be his Luna should things not work out as I would want.

I also need to reach out to the Mafia and hope they won't take my head too, although with the prospect of losing my son, my mate and my pack, maybe death will be a welcome reprieve.

*** **Amber** ***

It doesn't matter what is going on at home, I still have my trial to attend. Aiden is beside himself with worry and responsibility and Preston looks ready to kill the next person who looks at him funny. I tell them I can go by myself and to just stay at home and deal with Junior, the Mafia, and the council, but they won't hear it.

"You are not going to your trial without us, Amber. No way." After making his position clear, he turns to my brother. "I'll go with her, but if they start looking like they aren't going to let her go, we are going rogue, right Red?" Preston is on edge, and it is making me on edge. I don't have the energy to fight him today. I don't want to fight him. I want to climb back into bed and pretend this isn't happening.

"Aidy, you have to go with them, Summer, and I will be fine in here. Mrs Moore will look after her and the Gamma Guards are still patrolling and reporting for duty. You have to be there. I want you to go." Eva is demanding he go, but I know Aiden feels torn.

"What if Junior comes back? What if you need me and I'm not here?" he agonises and I sympathise wholeheartedly.

"Would you feel better if I asked my father to come here, just in case?" Eva looks pained at the thought of asking her father for more help, but since Xavier isn't due to give evidence until tomorrow, there is no reason why he couldn't help out. He will know Junior's weak points without a doubt.

"Would you, Shortie? For me? I'd feel a bit better knowing another Alpha who also loves you was here to protect you." And although I can see her reluctance, she does it because she knows it'll give Aiden some reassurance. I love that my brother finally found his mate, and that it is Eva. They are perfect and it makes going to this trial more bearable knowing Aiden will be cared for regardless.

Eva asks us to give her privacy while she speaks to her father and Aiden pulls me and Preston to his office again. "Before we get in there, you both know the plan, right? You know where the passports and fake IDs, clothes and money are all stashed?"

We've been over this plan several times. Aiden has made all the arrangements so that if it looks like the trial is not going to fall my way, Preston and I can leave the country, get as far away from here as possible and never look back. It is a last resort. I hope it doesn't come to that.

"We know, Alpha, don't worry, no one is going to touch my girl. I promise you I'll get her out of here if needs be."

Aiden nods his appreciation before he turns to me. "And you: have you stashed your knives and swords? Use them as needed, but don't draw attention to yourself. I love you, kid." It's been years since I've heard my big brother call me kid, and my throat stings as I gulp back the tears.

The guard on duty mindlinks Aiden to tell him Eva wants him and so we return to her cell.

"My father will be here with Luna Lydia in about forty minutes, Aidy. I'll be well looked after. Summer is going to meet her grandparents." I notice how my brother's eyes soften, how his shoulders relax, and it confirms he will be fine here with Eva if Preston and I have to leave.

Once Alpha Xavier arrives, we leave to head to the Silver Shore Territory where my trial will take place. It doesn't take long, around half an hour to get there, but it feels like every minute stretches out for an hour. I both cannot wait to get this over and done with and also want this journey to stretch out even longer, so I don't have to face my fate.

There is a commotion as we arrive, and my legal representative ushers us into a side chamber. "Ms Goldrick, you are going to be offered a plea deal. If you plead guilty to the lesser charge of Unlawful Killing this morning, the trial will be stopped and you will be sentenced this afternoon. You'll probably receive less than ten years imprisonment, but you'll be out in seven for good behaviour."

"No. No way. Don't even consider it, Amber. You used reasonable force. No deal," Aiden shouts as he agitatedly paces.

"Aidy..." I start to protest before Preston's cool, calm voice stops me.

"Why are they offering her a plea deal?" Preston asks. "Remember you are representing Amber here, not them, and you need to be advising the best route to take. So, answer me... why? Why now?"

The legal representative sits down and quietly invites us to sit too by gesturing to the remaining seats. "Look, I'm not meant to say anything. My boss will kill me if I mess this case up. It's been so high profile; this could destroy my career and the company I work for. The main complainant hasn't showed up and is now facing charges relating to witness intimidation. Her Alpha has also withdrawn his support of her complaint and has given additional evidence that supports your defence."

"What does that mean for me? Will there still be a trial?" I am impatient to know. This is my life after all and right now I am so out of control.

"This case has come so far and cost so much money that they will want to proceed if you don't accept a plea. Would you like my advice now?" I nod, I don't know what to do anymore, Aiden and Preston look ready to kill and I just need this to be over.

"Please, tell us what you advise and why," Preston pleads in the background. The desperation in his voice claws at my heart.

"They want something to show this hasn't been for nothing. If you want to avoid a trial, give them a plea back, but instead of prison time, offer community time. Tell them you will plead guilty to the lesser charge 'Inappropriate use of an offensive weapon', but tell them you refute all other charges and see if they accept that with a punishment that is more acceptable. If not, then you are looking at a full trial."

I think the way forward is clear. I only hope my mate and brother will agree too.

*** **Preston** ***

Call me biassed, and I don't care if you do but I do not see what my Red has done wrong. And I therefore do not see why she should plead guilty and be punished. It's stupid. They should have Junior and Nikki in here for what they've caused too.

"What do you think, Preston?" Amber asks me, and before I have a chance to be diplomatic, all my uncensored thoughts tumble out.

"It's all bollocks. It's all political bollocks. So, basically, even though she hasn't done anything wrong, they want to convict someone, so they don't look stupid and in the absence of Junior and Nikki, she has to take the fall?" My face is red with fury, I am full of nervous energy and so I stand to relieve some of the tension. My body trembles and I know I am seconds from losing control.

Amber gets up and walks to me and gently places her hand on my cheek. I look back at her, stunned. Amber is not a featherlight-stroking type of person, she doesn't calmly react. What on earth is going on? Needless to say, she has distracted me enough that I can't remember what I am shouting about. "I want to offer the lesser plea deal for a start, if they refuse or continue to insist on prison time, we'll go to trial. What do you say, Mate?" She looks for my agreement, and when she flashes her bright green eyes at me, I am helpless to do anything but what she wants.

I gulp and nod at her, and I don't miss Aiden's smirk at her display. She has just played me, and it worked. God damn it! "Thank you for supporting my decision, Preston," she murmurs sweetly at me when the legal rep leaves us all and Aiden goes to get some coffee and to obviously call Eva and check in with her and Summer.

"I would do anything to take you home tonight, Red. I just didn't like that someone had to take the blame and, in the absence of anyone else, you're in the firing line. No one treats my girl like that."

"I don't want you to be ashamed of me, Preston, but I'm just tired of fighting, I want to go home with you and live the life I thought I might have lost." My heart flutters as my hopes rise. Does that mean what I think it means? Can we have our mating ceremony and start a family?

Hey, calm down, boy. Let's not get ahead of ourselves. I still might get a custodial sentence. I thank her for saying it through mindlink, knowing it would have stung more in the moment if she had said it out loud.

Sorry, I can't help it. I have wanted this for the longest time and it is close enough that I can touch it. But you're right. One step at a time. We kiss and only stop when Aiden returns.

"Sorry, I didn't mean to interrupt." Aiden never apologises for this stuff. He normally tells me to get off his sister. I wonder what has rattled him.

"Are you okay, Aiden?" I ask him, slightly concerned.

He nods and then frowns. "I just had the weirdest conversation with my mate. Apparently, we need to have a talk with her father when I return home tonight. I wish everyone would fuck off and leave us alone. I want one day of peace with my mate. It's been nothing but drama since we met. I'm going to be grey by the time the baby comes."

Despite the glumness of the situation, the uncertainty of the future, we all end up laughing at Aiden's expense. What's the point in living if it's without a bit of fun and laughter? No matter what is happening in your life today, find something that brings you joy. It's those little moments that carry us through the tough times.

CHAPTER TWELVE

Let Me Love You

*** Melanie ***

My body doesn't feel like it belongs to me anymore. In between the surgeries I had and the pain killers and numbness, I just feel like a sack of meat that is tortured by my thoughts and feelings. I wish for oblivion. I wish for drugs so powerful I won't feel anything. But if anything, I feel more pain. I don't think there will ever be a moment in my life when I will be free from pain. Not now.

Max, who is Eva's bodyguard, hasn't left my room since I was brought here. I have told him a couple of times that he can leave but he just ignores me. I know there is something strange about this place and the people here too, but I cannot be bothered to find out what it is right now.

When the doctor comes to check on me during his rounds, he mostly speaks to Max and the small parts I do catch don't make any sense to me.

I hate the looks of pity and sympathy that are invariably sent my way. I think I preferred it when they all looked at me in disgust for being the woman carrying Eva's ex-husband's baby.

I would take a million of those hateful and judgemental looks right now. I would take every insult and insinuation if it meant I could have my baby back. As soon as my thoughts turn to my baby, I try to block them out. If I don't think about it, then it can't hurt me. If I don't think about it, then for a couple more days I can simply pretend nothing has happened and everything remains unchanged.

"Melanie, would you like a drink?" Max's voice steals my attention. He has such a lovely voice. It sounds smooth and soothing. His whole demeanour is cool and calming. I am bound to be well enough to be discharged soon and then I will return home on my own, but for now, it is nice to think this man actually cares for my welfare.

"No. Thanks," I reply and his eyes flash with annoyance and concern. I try to turn but my tummy is still sore from the surgery and the angry puckered cut that is held together rather gruesomely with thick black stitches itches and pulles, constantly reminding me that I have been relieved of my spleen.

"Melanie, you need to eat and drink so you heal." His voice caresses me in a way I don't deserve. I don't deserve sympathy or understanding.

"I'm okay. Max, why are you still here? Surely Eva and Summer need you. You can go, you know. I'm a big girl." He looks back at me, hurt, and as he grits his mouth together, I notice a little tick along his strong jawline. He is really controlling himself.

"I've told you. I'm here because I want to be here. With you." He spits the last two words out. I want to be weak and just accept this man's kindness, but who is he to me really? Why would I waste my time getting attached to another man? Nothing but trouble comes from me being attached to the opposite sex and, therefore, I need to keep reminding myself that no matter how much I could use a friend like Max, he isn't going to stay around.

He isn't mine to keep, and I have no intention of infringing on another of Eva's relationships, even if it is completely platonic between them.

Eva. She called me, and I ignored the call. Max tries to relay her messages, but it just hurts too much. I finally started to feel like I could belong in a small corner in someone's world. The concern she showed me and her willingness to allow Summer to bond with me had given me some of my self-respect back. I want to be a better person and being friends with Eva seemed to ignite that.

Now, the purpose behind it all is gone. I have no reason to encroach any further into this woman's life. It's like I am losing part of my family as well as my baby.

I can't stop the silent tears that fall when I think of my baby. She was everything I was holding on for, my chance to redeem myself and make something of my shitshow of a life. She was so precious and now she is gone.

When he sees the tears that fall noiselessly, Max stops nagging me about having a drink and holds me. He holds my hand and strokes my head and although most of the words he whispers to me don't make any sense, my broken heart seems to glow from the inside out from the tenderness he shows me. No-one has ever cared for me like this. And yet, this stranger, this huge, handsome man, gives it so freely to me, a person he doesn't even know.

"It's okay, I've got you. It's going to be okay, but you must take care of yourself, Melanie. You have to eat and heal and become strong again. You have to fight."

I think of my sons, my beautiful little boys, and I know he is right. I am just so heart broken right now, so filled with loss and anger and guilt and confusion. I ask WHY? Why me, why my baby? But deep in my heart, I know the answer. This must be my punishment. This is my penance for wrecking a home. This is the price I have to pay for the despicable things I did to Eva and Summer.

"Why do you care, Max? What does it matter to you?`` My voice is whisper-soft, so he knows there is genuine curiosity and no malice in my questions.

"What do you remember? From the attack?" I try to think of that day. Was it three or four days ago now? But as soon as I try, my heart rate quickens, and my tummy turns in genuine terror. I can't do it. I can't think of that day, not now. "Shhh, okay, don't think about that just yet. You're safe here with me now. I won't let anyone hurt you ever again."

His answer puzzles me. I find comfort in the fact that he seems to want to be close to me, but his statement makes little sense. As soon as I am discharged from hospital, I will return to my desperate life, and he will go back to being Eva's bodyguard. How can he stop anyone hurting me ever again?

"I know you don't feel it like I do, but you're my other half Melanie. You are my soul mate. I felt it when you came into Eva's cell and the bond between us grows every moment we are together. I want to be with you. I want to get to know you, and for you to get to know me. I want us to be a family."

Yes. So, Max is a crazy person. He smiles sheepishly at me after making his declaration. In another lifetime, I would have melted under his stare, but I'm too old, bloodied and scarred by my past for that now.

"Have you completely lost the plot, Max? You don't even know me! Besides, the reason I'm here in the first place should have you running for the hills if you have any sense at all."

A flash of shame and anger flares in his eyes. He's such a complex man. I have no idea why my words would cause that reaction in him. "You are here in this hospital bed because you were attacked, and I failed to keep you safe. I let you down. It will never happen again."

Well, now he's really gone and done it. The tears aren't silent or graceful. Max wipes my tears away with his large, calloused hands, and with the reassuring look he gives me, I completely unravel emotionally. Once my tears are completely spent for the time being, I rest my head on his shoulder, hiccoughing and sniffing like a child.

"I didn't mean why I was in the hospital... I meant why I was here visiting Eva. Doesn't it bother you what I've done?" From the way Max is treating me, I can tell he is an amazing man; a gentle giant and it would be so easy to fall in love with him. But I know the person I am, I am an accumulation of my past transgressions, and he deserves so much better than me. I don't deserve a happy ending. I don't deserve anyone's kindness. I got what I deserved. I know many others will feel the same about my current position too.

"No. It doesn't. I mean, it did, but your past is your past. I'm talking about our present and future. I know it will take time, and I can be patient. But you are mine and I have every intention of keeping it that way." I should be offended that he called me his, but somehow it feels good that, despite my black soul, someone as good as Max can see a bit of light or potential in me.

"I don't know what all this means, Max. I know something strange is going on around here and I hope you can tell me what that is when you trust me enough. But right now, I think my pain medication is giving me hallucinations. I think I need another nap."

"Sure, you do, honey. You have a sleep and I'll be right here waiting for you." He pulls his chair closer to my bed and I am once again astounded that he wants to stay.

Max Devine is rewriting everything I thought I knew about men. Is he someone I can rely on? What if *he* is the rainbow at the end of the stormiest and hardest experience of my life? Do things like that really happen to people like *me*? I don't know. All I do know is that right now, I need an anchor to hold me still and Max has more than stepped up to the plate. *Maybe* my story doesn't end here. *Maybe* the future is still unwritten.

*** Max ***

People keep telling me to go home and rest, but they don't understand. Nothing about the small apartment where my belongings are temporarily housed is home. Home is right here, right here with my fated mate. Besides, my wolf, Ray, will never allow her out of our sight. Not now, after waiting 35 years to find the other half of my soul and then her almost dying within an hour of meeting her.

I'm still having trouble believing that I have a mate. The hope of finding my own mate faded many years ago. As with most things, it seemed I wasn't quite good enough to be blessed with a mate, just as I hadn't been good enough to take over the Gamma position when my uncle died. I therefore embraced the bachelor life.

As soon as Melanie set foot on our territory that day, Ray was on edge, already sensing something was afoot. When my Alpha entered the dungeon, my stomach lurched as Ray shouted in my head *MATE. MATE.* My face reddened when I realised I had said it out loud too. The overwhelming scent of honey and the sight of the blonde-haired beauty took me completely by surprise. Surely this couldn't be the Melanie that had an affair with the Luna's ex-husband?

As she confessed her transgressions to my Luna and made apologies for her conduct, I wanted to dig this Ryan up from his grave and fucking kill him. How dare he treat her like that? It is bad enough that my Luna is hurt because of his actions. Now my mate is not only carrying the emotional scars of his treatment, but she is answering for his crimes against others too.

What had either of them seen in that scumbag? It smarted that my mate was carrying another man's pup, but it didn't matter. As she so eloquently put it: that was her baby, not some dead man's.

I accepted both her and her children in my mind because I want her, every part of her. I intend on claiming her. I just didn't know how much information she had about us and our world.

The thought of Junior Woodward's throat in my mouth intrudes my sleep, which is already broken from sleeping in a chair next to Melanie's bed. I have only left the room to use her en-suite to shower when my friends and family bring clean clothes and towels for me. I don't want to go too far since she may need me, and I would do anything and everything for her. From now on, she will be worshipped.

Her whimpers break me out of my pondering. She cries a lot in her sleep, and my heart aches for her and for what she has lost. Ray reminds me we can now give her our pup instead, but my human side knows it's not as simple as that. She will have to grieve and heal. She will have to accept us. She will have to want to move on from this horrific event and what it cost her.

I gently wipe away the tears that rest on her cheek. Her pale skin is soft and cool, and the warm vibrations of the mate bond course through me, filling me with longing and desire. She is mine. At long last, I have my mate.

My Alpha comes to visit and congratulates me on meeting my mate. "It's a small world really, isn't it, Max? How is she doing? Eva is doing her nut worrying about her, so I promised to pop in and check up on you both."

I thank him for his consideration and officially resign from the temporary Gamma position.

At least I try to, but the Alpha won't accept it. "Just take your time, Max, there is no rush. Eva's not going anywhere for at least the next six months, and she trusts you and will want to keep you.

I smile at him. "I'm going with Melanie and if she doesn't want to stay here, I will go with her." He gives me his blessing either way and tells me I will always have a home at the Onyx River. The Gamma position is mine until my future with Melanie is sorted.

"Hopefully, you can persuade her to come and live here with us, but I understand your predicament completely. When I first met Eva and still thought she was human, the pack were not happy about her being my mate and, therefore, their future Luna. I told her if they didn't accept her, I would relinquish my position and move to a human town to be with her instead, and I meant every word."

"What are the chances of Melanie having a secret Alpha father too?" Alpha Aiden actually laughs at that question. "What can I tell her about our world, Alpha? How can I tell her what I am, what we are?" I had run through several scenarios in my head where I explained to Melanie that I was a werewolf, but they all sounded way too cheesy and unrealistic.

"Just take things slowly, she's been through a massive ordeal. Don't be too fast to put labels on things just yet. Time is what she needs, time and care."

I thank him for his counsel and send him home with my best wishes for our Luna.

Melanie seems to sleep a lot, but the pack healers reassure me that this is normal for a human who is healing. When she wakes, after I told her she is mine, she gives me a tiny smile. "You're still here," she says in surprise.

"I'm real, Melanie and I'm not going to just vanish. Can I get you anything?" I want to look after her, but she refuses when I ask. When I see the nurses giving her a bed bath, I am full of envy and want to rip out their throats. *MINE.* Ray growls in my head, but I know we have to be cautious and patient.

"I really want to get a shower, but they say no to me because my stitches will get wet." I kiss her hand, just a small peck, and her eyes widen in alarm at the short, innocent contact between us.

"Leave it with me, Honey." If Melanie wants a shower, I will get her a shower.

Twenty minutes later, I am wheeling her to the shower room. "Melanie, I will have to stay in case you feel faint or fall but I will give you privacy, okay?" She gives me a stiff nod of consent and starts to undress before I can turn around.

"Look, I have to be realistic, and we have to be adults about this. This body, this battered and scarred body, is just flesh. It's flesh that needs cleaning, and I need you to help me clean it." She makes it sound so simple and yet Ray is already chirruping in my head at the thought of seeing and touching Melanie.

Moon Goddess, why do you torture me? What did I ever do to you?

I help her with her nightgown and socks and before I assist her so she can stand, I run the shower so it is warm for her. "Place your hands around my neck," I tell her. She is fronting this out, but her vulnerability is evident in her expression. "Place your feet on the ground. Good, now I'm going to straighten up really slowly and help you to stand."

As I stand and straighten, Melanie's body follows mine. Her breasts press against my chest. "I need you to unfasten my…" She indicates around her back. My hands shake as I slide them down her back to the clasp on her bra. I undo it in one motion, though I don't know how I managed that, as my hands tremble like mad. "Thank you. Now I need to take off the rest of my clothes. I'm sorry, Max."

As a sweat breaks out on my forehead, my eyes flash open. "Why are you saying sorry?"

She keeps her head lowered. Her body starts to tremble too. I wonder if she is cold.

"I have to take off the rest of my underwear. It's not something you want to see right now." She is obviously embarrassed about the bleeding and the pads she is wearing, but I couldn't give a shit about it. It doesn't bother me.

"Don't worry, Honey, let's just get you cleaned up and feeling better." I hold her up as she uncovers the rest of her body and I help her to step into the shower cubicle. As the warm jets of water hit her body, she moans in pleasure. This is going to take a lot more control than I initially thought. After standing for a minute or two, she starts to tire, so I get the shower chair and when she sits down, I shampoo her hair.

I've never shampooed someone else's hair before. My own hair is short and easy to manage. Melanie's hair is long and looks like spun gold. As I lather her hair she closes her eyes and exhales when I massage her head. I rinse off her hair, careful to not get suds in her eyes.

Once she has finished washing everywhere, I shut off the shower and cover her with a pile of thick, white, fluffy towels. I carry her back to the bench to dry off and dress. Before I place her down, she touches my face; her light blue eyes are deep and mesmerising.

"Thank you, Max. I don't think anyone has ever done anything like this for me before." My heart fills with affection for my fragile human mate.

"I want to look after you like this forever, Honey. I just need you to let me love you." Her eyes widen and I'm shocked when she drops her head to my shoulder and cries.

"I want to. God, how I want to let you. But what if you change your mind? I am barely holding on as it is." She's scared to let me in in case I leave like everyone else. She has never been anyone's priority. Well, from now on, she will be my number one. The be all and end all of my life.

"Eventually, you'll realise that I am never going to leave. Maybe not right away, but in twenty years' time when we start to grow old together, maybe then you'll know I'm a keeper. Until then, let's just take it one day at a time, an hour at a time if you have to."

She nods her agreement to my plan and a tiny amount of the pressure in my chest eases. She is showing me what her needs are and now it's my turn to show her how I can more than meet those needs.

*** **Eva** ***

Even though I have been stuck in this cell, life continues to hurtle on at an alarming pace. I hate that Aiden is being stretched so thin and there is very little I can do to support him.

When my father and his mate arrive to keep me company, Aiden, Amber and Preston leave for the trial in the Silver Shore territory.

Luna Lydia stands in the doorway, she seems timid and shy, which is a total contrast from the other day when she marched in here introducing herself to Summer as her new Granny. I was angry and startled when she did it because I hadn't even introduced my father to Summer yet. I don't want Lydia to feel uncomfortable and if she is willing to accept Summer and me, then I am happy to do that, but I need to do it at a more gradual pace.

"Thank you for inviting us both here today, Evangelina, it's such a pleasure to meet your little girl." I smile at my father. So far, he has done everything by the book for me. He is trying to be honest and open with me and though we have had several things that could impact on our wobbly foundation, instead he keeps steadying the ship.

"Summer, come here, sweetheart. This is your grandad. This is mummy's daddy." My little girl looks confused between me and my dad. "Do you want to say hi?"

She frowns and shakes her head. "Where my daddy bear gone?" Oh geez, she must think I'm trying to replace Aiden.

"Your daddy had to go out and he'll be back later for story time. This is my daddy." Summer looks between me and my dad with wide eyes and then giggles. "And this is your granny." I reach out to Luna Lydia and, with an expression full of shock that quickly transforms into joy, she comes and joins us.

"Thank you, Eva. With everything going on, this is just what we needed." My father's gratitude melts my heart a little more. I want to be close to him and I want Summer and the new baby to have grandparents.

I hold out my arms through my bars and my dad finally comes and gives me a hug. My eyes fill with tears when he does. We have missed so much time. I don't want to miss any more time.

"Thank you for coming and sitting with me, Dad. And you too, Luna Lydia. Thank you both for everything." They both look choked up at my words, but I mean it.

We play games and talk. The Omegas bring drinks and food and Luna Lydia insists on me calling her mother or granny for Summer's sake.

Summer settles for a nap and we sit and talk quietly when she does. "How is your human friend doing now?" my father asks solemnly. I know he, like me, feels responsible for what happened to Melanie.

"She lost her baby, and she had to have some pretty serious surgery. She is still in the clinic. Max stayed with her. He found out just before she was attacked that she is his mate."

Both of them seem to pale under the significance of Melanie's injuries. "I'd like to visit her on your behalf if that is okay, Eva. I could take her some books or magazines, fresh pyjamas and flowers, fruit... whatever she may need." Lydia's kindness is heart-warming. I think we could become friends and it would be nice to have a mother figure.

Contentment fills me like I've never known. My father is finally part of my life, and his wife didn't reject me, she wants to be part of this blended patchwork of a family that is flourishing in front of my very eyes. I feel slightly uncomfortable for a passing moment and Lina purrs loudly in my head as sensations very similar to an elastic band twang inside me.

Eva... it's happening. Bonding with father has reversed some of the manifestations. The hurt of him not being in our lives is healed by their acceptance of us and Summer.

"Why are you grinning?" my father asks as he grins too.

I hug him again, "Lina said that our bonding is healing some of the manifestations. I'm so happy that we are all becoming a family. I've craved this all my life." I reach out to Lydia too and the three of us hug each other, with only the bars of my cell in the way.

"I'm so happy too. I have always loved you, darling. I wish I hadn't been such a coward. Eva, there is something we both need to talk to you and Aiden about. I wish we had more time, but we don't and it's important that we sort this out as soon as possible."

I have been expecting this, especially now that the Werewolf Council will have to punish Junior, and that's before the Mafia and Aiden get a hold of him for what he has done.

"I will tell Aiden when he calls, and we can sit down and talk then." They both smile, their relief obvious that their request would at least be heard by us.

"Did John go to court today to support Amber?" My father asks me when the conversation starts to dry up. No one else knows that Aiden and Amber's father has been hiding since their return from Scotland. There will be plenty of questions today as to why he isn't there supporting his daughter.

"Aiden didn't say. I still haven't met his father and I'm not sure I want to after what Aiden has been through."

Lydia writes out a list of things I may need for Summer and myself and the baby growing inside me. She also promises to come back and visit Melanie on my behalf. "Would you mind if I started knitting for the baby, Eva? I have the patterns for blankets, cardigans, booties and hats."

Shyly, I admit that I would love her to do that. When my dad notices my timidity, he cuddles me and tells me to let them help, that it is their pleasure.

"Thank you. You don't know how good it is to have your support. Apart from my friend, Salma, there was no one to help when I was having Summer. I have so much support now." Every word is true, I am blessed with love and support and I am so thankful for it.

There have been some really shitty times in my life, but the good times far outweigh the bad and now, with my family around me, supporting me and loving me, I can only see blue skies ahead.

*** **Amber** ***

The wait is killing me. I just want this over and done with. Preston and Aiden are both driving me wild with their pacing and impatient growling and complaining.

The legal representative returns and instructs me to sit down at the small table, which I do. We sit facing each other.

"The Council has considered your counter plea. While this is a lot less than they would have liked, they are willing to accept a guilty plea to the lesser charge of 'Inappropriate use of an offensive weapon'. However, there will be several stipulations to your sentence."

For a moment, I don't fully understand, my hearing seems muffled like my ears are filled with cotton wool. The rep's mouth moves but nothing makes sense.

It's only when Preston and Aiden surround me with massive smiles, whooping and cheering that I realise that it's good news. I don't know what the sentence is... did she tell me?

The burden of the past couple of months has completely and

utterly drained me, and although I am relieved, I am also exhausted and overwrought. "I'm not going to prison?" I ask, bewildered.

"No, sis. Didn't you hear? You got a suspended sentence. You need to stay out of trouble for three years or they can recall you and you must attend a course. But other than that, you are free, you're free!" The stress of the past couple of months seems to have piled on top of my brother too. Although he is restraining himself, it is clear to see that he is emotional and when I jump up to hug him and my mate, he finally lets it all out. "I was so worried we were going to lose you, sis. It's been driving me crazy, feeling so out of control and not being able to do anything more to help you."

My big brother, the big soft wolf, holds back tears of relief. "Did father come, Aidy? Will you find out if he is here?" He looks away from me, and I already know the answer. "He didn't come, did he? The son of a bitch. Well, now the trial is dealt with…" The insinuation is clear; we have already agreed on our plan of action if I was acquitted and Aiden latches onto that thought.

"Now we can go and deal with the vicious little bastard," he says, and I nod at him in agreement before returning to my mate's arms and holding him tight to me.

"Aiden, there is one more thing. Can Preston and I have our Mating Ceremony this weekend, please? I don't want to wait any longer now that the trial is done. Preston has waited long enough." I look into the passionate gaze of my mate as my brother instructs me to organise it. With excitement bubbling in my tummy, and an overwhelming ache building right between my legs, I can do nothing but nod my enthusiastic response to Preston's mindlink.

Come on Red, let's go home and celebrate. Just you and me and our bed.

I am a free woman and I get to spend the rest of my days exactly how I want. I can think of nothing better than Preston's suggestion for now and for always.

*** **Junior** ***

I watch from our hidden cave as my mother and father cross our border to the Onyx River. Those traitorous pieces of shit. Especially her, that useless, unworthy whore. I'm glad I hit her to escape the dungeon. She deserves it.

Nikki and I have been trapped here since the attack. Luckily, she has been able to place repellent charms, so we haven't been found. The battery on my phone is dead, so I have no way of contacting Dominga. At times I really miss her and then at others she fades from my mind like she never even existed.

In the lulls, we get so bored that we fuck to pass the time and, I'm not going to lie, it feels amazing. Nikki is a passionate and demanding lover, but she is also very skilled in the art of love making too. She is completely draining my balls and, with a lack of condoms available, even if I could be bothered to use them, her wish for a pup will soon be fulfilled: of that, I have no doubt.

I know the officials from the Council are looking for me, but my blood runs cold when I see the Mafia princess, the one I had been following and whose father I poisoned for Dominga. I am in far deeper trouble than I ever anticipated.

Has Dominga sold me out when I didn't return like I said I would? I will kill her if she has. However, my father's bastard, Eva, she is at the top of my list. This is definitely something to do with her.

Eva must have found out what I did and is now telling the Mafia so they can get rid of me, leaving the path clear for her to take my Alpha position at the Moon Stone. Well, if I can't have it, no one can. Her throat will be mine too.

We'll see who's laughing then.

CHAPTER THIRTEEN

Missing

*** Salma ***

"When we move to our house, you can have your bedroom any way you want it. I want you to know that it is as much as your home as it is mine and Ale's." Ricky is worrying me. He is withdrawn and I don't know how to make it better for him. Why the fuck didn't papa or Dominga leave an instruction manual? I am out of my depth and I'm not ashamed to admit it. I don't know the first thing about an eight-year-old boy and what his needs are. I keep looking about for an adult to help, but it's me… I'm the adult and it's up to me to look after Ricky. That has to start with finding out what is wrong with him and how I can fix it, so he is happy again.

"Can I have my PlayStation?" he asks earnestly, and although I want to smile, I try not to. His PlayStation is his pride and joy, his comfort blanket and best friend all in one.

"Yes, of course you can. All your stuff will come with you because that'll be our home forever." The fleeting look of sadness is there and gone within milliseconds, so fast that I almost miss it. "Ricky, you do want to live with me, don't you?" The expression on his face changes so fast and my heart

225

pounds when big fat tears fall down his cheeks.

"But you're looking for my mami, and you're going to send me back to live with her." He wails and I curse myself for not being more careful in front of him.

"Ricky, Ricky. I promise you. Listen to me, I promise you on papa's grave that if you never want to see her again, you don't have to. I am looking for your mami. I need to ask her some questions, but I will never ever let her take you away from me if you don't want to go with her. I want you to stay here with me, forever. Both Ale and I want that. Okay?"

I pull him onto my lap and cuddle him close to me. "What about when you get your own kid?" he mumbles. Bless his tender heart, he has been worrying a lot about this.

"Ale and I do want a baby, but that would make you Uncle Ricky… Tío Ricky. I need you here to help me and to help Ale too. This is our family now, Ricky: me, you, Ale, and any babies that come along too. I love you, Hermanito (little brother) and your place is here with me, and it always will be."

"Just don't send me back to live with her, please. It makes me scared." I wonder why my little brother is so scared. I know his mother abandoned him but the way he shakes with fear has me riled; no child should ever live in fear.

"Will you tell me why?" I look at him as he lowers his eyes. I wish he would open up to me, but this boy has trust issues, and it makes me want his mother's head even more. What the fuck has she done to my little brother?

"She goes out and leaves me for a long time. And sometimes I get scared and sometimes it's cold and there is no food. I don't want to go back to her, Sal, I want to stay with you and Ale." My little brother can front out in front of the best of them. He already has papa's poker face and in a couple of years he'll have his nerves of steel too. I will ensure he does. However, the little boy in front of me is in desperate need of nurturing and loving. He's been neglected and hurt and hasn't felt safe. I will make it my life's work as his big sister to ensure he grows to know what it means to love and be loved and, most importantly, to belong.

Once Ricky settles down and is happily playing on FIFA, I call Ale, who is out meeting with Tony Serrano. "Is there any news?" I asked him impatiently.

"Chula, I was just about to call you, get your bag ready. Tell my mother and father to watch Ricky. I have Dominga cornered and will bring her to you as soon as I can."

As Ale delivers his news, I watch Ricky innocently playing and a pang of guilt jabs at me, forcing me to take notice. I want to do what is right, but what if killing Dominga hurts Ricky? Dominga did kill our papa after all, but she is still Ricky's mami when all is said and done.

It seems I developed a conscience and ethics and morality when I got a little boy to love, and I have never been so conflicted in my whole entire life.

*** **Preston** ***

My anger at Amber's conviction is short-lived. Yes, the system is all fucked up but... Amber is free. We are free to move on with our lives. We are having our Mating Ceremony at long last, and tonight is the beginning of forever for us.

We hold hands as we walk back to our room. After the uncertainty of the day, I just want to get her back home where she belongs, right here with me.

I want to spend all night making love to her, I want her all to myself just for tonight. I tell her what I want to happen and her lips curl in a knowing smile.

"What are you planning to do to me, Preston?" she asks in feigned innocence as she quickly discards her jacket and shoes.

Unclipping her red hair, I let the wild curls flow freely down her back. "You look good enough to eat, baby," I murmur against her cheek. I can't resist the urge to devour her soft lips and nibble gently on her lower one. Amber has the most delicious lips I've ever tasted. I will never get enough of her.

I kiss her more and more until she is breathless, all the while removing both of our clothes. I stop only briefly to look at her when she is just in her bra and panties, the black lace covering my prizes from my view. I take great pleasure in removing them slowly, causing her to whimper in response.

We kiss again after she pulls my shirt over my head, giving up on the buttons completely. I then work my way down her neck, biting my mark on her neck before lowering her to the centre of our bed.

Amber's skin is warm and supple, and it feels like silk under my palms and fingers. Her ample breasts feel soft and full in my rough hands. Her thighs are toned and smooth, and the sweetness at the junction is simply divine.

Her skin is warm, but it's not soft. She's toned and muscular, showing she is strong and healthy. She has a hint of freckles on her nose, they are cute as fuck.

I lick her body in a very slow and deliberate fashion. I lick every inch of her body returning repeatedly to her breasts. I nibble on those sexy, round globes, paying particular attention to the rosy peaks, and I kiss them and suck them until she is writhing beneath me. "Please, Preston, I need you inside me, now," she moans. She grinds against me, craving the friction against her wet pussy and swollen clit, but I want to tease her some more before I finally impale my hard cock inside her.

Amber moans and whimpers when I move lower, finding her entrance with my fingers and her clit with my tongue. She continues to grind as I eat her. I take my time to really work her up into a frenzy.

Within a few minutes, her thighs are wet and slick with her juices and her breathing quickens. Her moans are throaty and soft. "Preston. Now, please," she begs again.

Looking upon my Red, my beauty, this really does feel like the beginning of the future for us. "Condom?" I ask her because we are still to discuss what our plans will be, but she knows where I am. I want a family; I don't want to prevent that any longer.

Zack howls in joy in my head when she refuses the condom. "No more condoms, Preston, we both want this, right?"

I can only nod at her, overwhelmed with love and longing for both her and the promise of the future. It is ours, at long last it can all be ours.

My cock is throbbing, I need her so badly. I need her desperately like I need the air I breathe.

I enter her slowly. "Oh, yeah," Amber moans. "Fuck, you are so good. Don't stop, Preston. It feels so much better like this, I can really feel you." She is so tight and hot; her pussy is the best place to be. I want to pound in and out of her hard and fast, but I also want this to last. I want to make this pleasure last for as long as possible; forever, in fact. I am thrusting deep and slowly, and she is meeting me with every single thrust. I love the feel of her velvety folds, her tight and wanting hole that both accepts me and constricts me, sending overwhelming sensations throughout my entire body. A single thrust has me groaning with pleasure as I tingle from my temples right down to my toes from the unencumbered connection with my mate.

She is slick with her juices, and she squeezes my cock inside her, and every time it gets better and better. I don't know if I can last much longer. It feels far too good. Her body continually writhes against mine, she wants more from me, wanting all of me, but I keep a slow and easy pace. I know she won't take long to come, and I am right.

"I'm coming, Preston. Fuck, I can't stop." She moans loudly and groans as I quicken my pace, stroking her deep inside with each thrust. Her body shakes and quivers against mine, she is coming hard and I am about to explode too. I can't hold on any longer.

I thrust into her one last time. "Fuck, Amber." She is a sight to see, her hair is all messy around her head, her breasts are bouncing with each thrust, and she makes the most beautiful moans I have ever heard. She is impossibly beautiful and I am so lucky to have her. She is mine and I want to shout it from the treetops.

I tilt my head back and groan as I release deep inside of her. "I love you, Amber. You're my whole world."

She smiles lovingly back at me. "I love you, too."

I will never tire of this.

The following morning, Aiden mindlinks us both. *I know you will want to plan your Mating Ceremony, but I want to go and confront father. It's time to lay all our demons to rest.*

Amber nods to me. "He's right, Preston. I want everything dealt with before we take our vows. It's time for father to face the consequences of his cruel behaviour."

She is resigned and fierce and ready to deal with the past.

It is with the greatest pride, I think: That's my girl!

*** Aiden ***

Relief continually washes over me. Amber is safe and now I can go after my father and once I deal with him, I can fully focus on Eva, Summer, and the new baby. I can concentrate on the future.

Even though going home means going to sleep in the dungeon, I am eager to get back to my mate. We've yet to have a moment's peace since my return from Scotland. I am going crazy with need for her and yet our little girl will be asleep in the bed next to us and so there is little chance of anything more than a kiss and a cuddle. But that is okay. That will suffice until I can have some quality time with Eva. Just being near her completes my world. It is the greatest privilege to sleep beside her and hold her all through the night.

Amber and Preston practically run to their apartment as soon as we arrive back onto our territory and not so long-ago, Preston would have had two black eyes from me for even thinking about my sister. However, Amber has grown over these past couple of months. She radiates happiness and contentment now that the court case is over and I can't help smiling when I see how happy they are together.

As Alpha, it is my responsibility to ensure the well-being of all my pack members and so I stop by the hospital before I return home. I want to check in with Max, he has had a shocking few days. The surprise of finding his mate, who is human and pregnant, and then watching her as she almost lost her life protecting my little girl caused him plenty of upset and distress. However, since Melanie has regained consciousness and the healers confirm she will make a full recovery, Max appears calmer and less anxious.

When he tried to resign from the Gamma position, my heart fell into my boots. Eva has already told me she wants to keep Max and give him the Gamma position permanently. I will literally do anything to keep him here. Eva has plans for where he and Melanie can live and how we can slowly explain to Melanie that we are werewolves.

The nurses show me straight to Melanie's private side room, but I don't go in when I realise I would be interrupting a tender moment between them. I watch them through the window in the door and smile when Max fluffs up Melanie's pillow and helps her to sit upright in bed. He places a chaste kiss on her forehead before sitting down beside her and helping her with her crossword. I catch the fleeing looks of admiration from Melanie and the gaze of adulation plastered all over Max's face.

As much as I want to talk to Max, I will not interrupt this precious moment between him and his mate. The first steps are the most important in building up trust and respect with your respective mate. I know because I have only just gone through this phase myself. Eva held back as much as she could but the bonds and attraction between us were insurmountable and being able to trust me is what helped move us to the next level. I hope Max is as fortunate as I have been.

Eva will be delighted to know that Max and Melanie are bonding. She feels extremely guilty for bringing Melanie here in the first place and that Melanie was protecting Summer when she was hurt. To top it off, it is Eva's half-brother who carried out the attack. Eva blames herself but I know, and everyone else knows, this is all Junior Woodward's doing.

I had forgotten that Alpha Xavier and Luna Lydia were still here with Eva and waiting to talk to me and I groan internally when I see them. I just want five minutes alone with Eva, just a few minutes to truly connect with her. I greet them cordially. I'm not ungrateful since they are here looking out for what is mine and I owe them, but I just want a little time, just me and Eva and Summer, of course.

"Daddy!" My heart swells with pride when I hear my little girl. She runs to me and I lift her up when she reaches me. "Daddy come back."

"Of course, I came back. My girls are here, I had to come back." She is such a sweet, easy-going pup, she giggles after planting a wet kiss on my cheek and then squirms to get back down again. I place her back down on her feet and watch in wonder as she zooms off to her next activity.

Eva waits for me by the bars of her cell. The scent of her arousal hits me full force as soon as I see her and my own desire threatens to overwhelm me too. God, I miss us so much.

Regardless of the audience, I pull her to me through the bars and kiss her passionately. "I've missed you so much, Shortie. Goddess, I hate seeing you in this fucking cell." I tell her once I push slightly away from her.

"Aiden, some of the manifestations have healed!" she tells me excitedly. Relief exudes from her, and I just want to scoop her up and entwine my body with hers. I want to share everything and never be far away from her.

"Tell me everything, but first I think your father wants to talk to us both."

Xavier looks at me sheepishly. "The thing is, son; we need to secure the future of The Moon Stone Pack. We now know that, at the very least, Junior will be imprisoned. I think the Mafia will ensure he loses his head for what he has done."

Although both Eva and I had expected this talk, we weren't expecting it so soon. Now is not the right time for Eva to take her rightful place. She hasn't had any training.

I expect him to ask Eva to start Alpha training and as much as I don't want her to go away, I want to support her. She doesn't feel competent or confident right now, and she is under house arrest for the Goddess' sake!

"Junior has put us all in peril. My leadership will be called into question for not keeping my own son in line. If I don't step down soon, they will strip me. I cannot have that. This is my pack, and Woodwards have been the Alphas of the Moon Stone for centuries."

If I was in his position, I would feel the same. The pack will be taken over by a stranger as directed by the Werewolf Council.

"Evangelina is my successor, but given her current predicament and the fact that she cannot leave her cell for the time being, we need to make alternative plans." This is what I wasn't expecting.

"What do you mean?" I ask. Eva smiles meekly back at me and, although she looks more relaxed, I can sense her nervousness.

"My father would like to merge the Moon Stone Pack with another pack. I might be an Alpha Wolf, but I've had no training, I have no skills and I cannot lead from my prison cell. I have enough to deal with right now. I have told my father I cannot become the Alpha of the Moon Stone, but I know someone who can." I keep quiet while they continue with their explanation.

She continues to grin at me with a small smile on her face. "Who? You don't know any other wolves, do you?" She raises her eyebrows, giving me a clue, but she cannot mean what she is saying. The packs would never go for it. Roman, sensing what is being suggested, growls in my head. He is not happy about us having to share our lands, they belong to us.

"My request is that you merge the Moon Stone and the Onyx

River and be Alpha over both packs. My daughter will, of course, be your Luna. Part of my conditions is that Summer is named the rightful heir of the Moon Stone while your child with Eva, is named the heir of the Onyx River."

"What do you think, Aidy? Will you do it?"

*** Alejandro ***

We need to find Dominga and Junior, but I haven't found anything of value. I trace them to a hotel, but they abandoned their room a few days ago without paying the bill. The more I look, the further away they seem from my reach.

I go incognito. Alone and under the cover of darkness, I search for the piece of shit that neglected a little boy, killed her lover and is now threatening the safety and well-being of my wife. I know Salma wants to be here and doing this too, but it is too dangerous, and Ricky needs her right now. So, I go alone, knowing I am less likely to attract attention this way. I am less likely to set tongues wagging about my whereabouts and intentions too.

Word filters through that Serrano cars are coming and going at an old, abandoned warehouse along the docks. I decide it is worth checking it out. Maybe Dominga has heard about it too and will go looking for allies. I stake out the place for four hours and I consider calling it a night when all the people I have been watching drive away. The sun rises, and my cover will be blown if anyone looks too closely.

My car is parked a couple of miles away, so as not to draw any attention to my presence. Having come the rest of the way on foot, I now begrudgingly start the long, cold walk back when another car catches my eye. Having seen that licence plate not so long ago, I recognise it immediately. It is Tony Serrano, driving himself all alone to an abandoned warehouse.

Something feels off. I'm not sure what is happening, but a Spanish Mafia Don coming out to an old, abandoned warehouse at the crack of dawn on his own is unusual and therefore exceedingly interesting to me. From my hiding place, I watch Tony, and I begin to regret my decision when he simply sits in his car for six hours, talking occasionally on his phone and smoking.

I am cold, hungry, and bored. I consider approaching Tony and asking him to drive me to my car, that's how desperate I am starting to feel.

Before I can, though, I see Dominga, acting like the Queen of Sheba, the very woman I've been searching for. She pulls up in an old Mercedes and she flashes the headlights at Tony's car. After getting out of her car, she walks towards the warehouse and Tony follows her once she disappears inside.

Sal rings me and I tell her to get ready, I will be bringing Dominga to her. I am sure of it. Tony must have had contact with her, and he is getting information for us. I am so sure about it, I don't think twice when I slip into the warehouse and creep up to where the raised voices echo around. I take my gun, which is loaded and fitted with a silencer, and creep closer.

"You weren't supposed to fall in love with the fucking mutt though, were you? And now you've completely blown your cover. You were meant to trick the dog into doing the dirty work and haul your ass out of there. Now you have half of fucking England looking for you and your lover boy and believe me, you'll both lose your heads over this."

"I just need a couple of hundred grand and a passport. Come on, Tony, you owe me. I did this for you. You wanted the Morales and Suarez turf and it's all there, ready for you to take.

It's not my fault you lost your bottle."

"The way I see it, Dominga, Salma and Alejandro believe you and your fucking puppy are responsible. They have no reason to suspect me, not when I looked after your little boy and helped them reunite with him. They trust me. I owe you nothing."

"YOU FUCKING BASTARD, TONY! YOU PROMISED ME! HALF A MILLION IF I WORKED WITH YOU. IF I AM GOING DOWN, I'LL TAKE YOU WITH ME, I PROMISE THAT NOW." A cold laugh reverberates off the walls, and a woman's cry of distress follows.

"And who is going to believe an old whore like you, Dom? They have all the evidence they want and need that puts you and the wolf at the scene of the crime… they have some half-hashed motive that they've made fit into what they want to believe. I am in the clear and you are well and truly fucked. Go on girl… tell me… who is going to believe you?"

I don't know what possesses me. Is it his arrogance or my own? Is it finding out the truth and knowing we have made all the square pieces fit into a round hole? Or is it just plain anger and carelessness? I'm not sure, but for some unknown reason, I step out of the shadows and shout, "I believe her."

I'm not sure what happens next. Is it a scream or the click of the gun? Either way, the whole place turns dark and cold. Tony Serrano has revealed his hand, and I have inadvertently revealed mine too. It cost a life… but whose? Who is lying dead in an old, unused warehouse?

*** **Eva** ***

Aiden looks back at us all and it is evident from the expression on his face that he didn't expect this, and we have shocked him.

"Aidy, say something. Please." I plead with him because I am afraid I've overstepped the mark. I am under no illusion of the size of this task, but I have every faith in Aiden and his ability as the Alpha. I know he is the best Alpha for the job, the only possible candidate worthy of the position.

"Eva, you're not always going to be in a cell. You said yourself that the manifestations are starting to reverse. Once we merge the packs, it will be impossible to make you the Alpha. You would have to challenge me."

A thrill of desire ran through me, as an image of Aiden and I play-fighting intrudes into my thoughts.

Really, Shortie? In front of your dad? I always knew you were filthy. Thank God he mindlinks, the shame!

Well, obviously, they don't need to be present, I tease him back, knowing it would arouse him in the same way I am.

"This is a lot to take in. I am honoured that you consider me a worthy candidate. I will think about this, and I will obviously need to consult my Elders Council and the rest of my pack. And my mate too." My father shakes my mate's hand and Luna Lydia pulls him into an embrace and whispers thank you to him.

"We'll take Summer for her dinner while you two talk things through." Lydia takes her new granddaughter's hand and encourages my father out of the dungeon.

"I know what you're doing, Lydia, I'm not that stupid," I hear my father mutter to Lydia, and I blush at Lydia's response.

"Lighten up, X, what's he going to do? Impregnate her again? That was some serious sexual tension that needs to be addressed. They'll both be able to think clearly later. You know it and I know it. Come on, let's go and get some food."

"She is very wise, your new step-mother. I have thought of nothing but us since I left for Scotland. It's been too long, Eva; I fucking crave you. I need you." My very core floods at his words as he unlocks my cell. Aiden's eyes glaze over and a couple of seconds later he tells me we will not be disturbed.

"I miss us too. I've never felt so frustrated, Aiden." He has a gleam in his eye as he lifts me up. I wrap my legs around his waist and my arms around his neck as we finally kiss unrestricted.

"You smell delicious, baby; you're so fucking sexy. I don't think this is going to take long! And I can't have my Luna sitting in a cell all sexually frustrated now, can I?" I giggle at him; I don't think it will take me long to reach my climax either. Aiden's mere presence ignites all my desire for him and, for us, my yearning overflows. In a matter of seconds, we have each other's clothes off and I straddle him and his length as he sits on the edge of our bed.

"Don't make me wait so long next time, Alpha," I tell him as I grab his long, thick cock and slide down his full length, moaning involuntarily as he stretches and fills me.

"Fuck! I forgot how good you feel," Aiden says in a hard-edged voice. "You're so wet and tight, it feels amazing." And he feels amazing too as he strokes the heat within me repeatedly, bringing me closer and closer to oblivion.

I grind against him, trying to find the friction that my clit craves while Aiden explores the rest of my body. My boobs are already feeling heavier and fuller, and I think he likes that. He sucks one nipple excitedly while palming the other and I throw my head back in ecstasy.

His hands are rough against my skin, and I can think of no better feeling. My excitement continues to build as he grabs my hips, guiding me as I ride him. "Eva, slow down or I'm going to come." His hand dips lower, finally connecting with my clit, pressing and swirling it about with the pad of his fingers and the beginning of my orgasm completely consumes me. My heart rate increases and so does the rhythm I set. I am frantic, needy and wanting.

"Then come with me," I instruct him as my whole body convulses in pleasure. His groans mingle with my breathy pants. Wave after wave of pleasure and fulfilment crash over me. I am thankful that Aiden continued to thrust up deep inside me, hitting the very spot I need him to as I come in unison with him.

The comedown is quick. I don't want to be caught in a compromising position by my father and there are a few things I want to discuss with Aiden before they return.

"Come back here, I've missed you and you're already putting your clothes back on. They're in the way!" Aiden paws at me, kissing any exposed skin he can. The sparks of our bond ignite once again across my skin, giving me shivers and tingles that only increases my hunger for him.

"Stop it, they'll be back any minute, and I still need to talk to you." I chastise him as I kiss him back, wanting very much to continue with our interlude.

"I don't care, they can leave or watch, I haven't finished with you yet." I love it when Aiden is like this, when it is just us and we can express ourselves. The world may be turning, but right now, the only people who exist and matter are him and me.

"Aidy…" I have to talk to him, as much as I want to slip away in our little bubble, we have to talk. He continues to nuzzle me. "Aiden!"

"Okay, Eva. What is it? I'm not going to get anywhere until you talk to me, so tell me what is bothering you so I can have my wicked way with you one more time before anyone comes back."

"I don't want to be an Alpha. I don't know how to be one. I am unlikely to become a competent one because of the short amount of time we have. However, I felt the power of being in the Moon Stone. I think that is why I was able to shift. It's like the land was calling me home. I don't want it to go to some random stranger if they strip my father. By rights, that is Summer's legacy now." He listens to me attentively without interrupting.

"So, you want me to take on both packs? Eva, sweetheart, do you realise how hard this is going to be? This will be one massive pack to lead. There will be plenty of resistance too."

"I've almost finished my Luna training and that is something I sincerely believe I can do well. We both knew this was going to happen in some way or form. This way, you'll be the Alpha and I'll be your Luna. I won't have to go away to do Alpha training. We won't have to run two separate packs." To me, it makes logical sense, but I understand the magnitude of the task to Aiden.

"I will still have to consult the Elders and the rest of the pack, but if you truly believe this is the best way forward, you know I'll support you. I just wanted to ensure that you understand the implications and the size of the task we would be taking on. This isn't going to be easy." Relief washes over me in waves. I can conquer the world with Aiden's support, nothing is impossible with him cheering me on from the sides.

"Thank you, Aiden. This is what I think is best."

I don't resist when he pulls my clothes off me again. "Now come on, Shortie. You said one more time if I listened." I don't deny him; it would be fruitless to do so. I'm already aching for him to be inside me.

We have a lot of time to make up.

*** Salma ***

I am frantic with worry. I spoke to Ale over eight hours ago and he said to get ready, and now he's nowhere to be found. I have no idea where he is and if he is safe. The phone he called me from is a burner and so I cannot trace him. He is alone, so there's no one else I can contact either.

A feeling of dread threatens to take over me entirely and so I had to tell Raul and Penelope what is happening. Within an hour, a search party is assembled to locate Alejandro. Pain and weakness like I have never known fills every inch of my body.

"Salma, you need to wait here with Ricky in case he comes back. Elena will wait with you. Don't worry, we will find him." I don't doubt that they will. It is whether they find him dead or alive that concerns me. I can't lose him. I can't live without him.

Elena and I have not had the opportunity to spend time together and I don't know her very well despite us being sisters-in-law. She is a typical new-age Mafia wife. She stays at home, away from the action and looks pretty. With her dyed blonde hair and designer clothes, she resembles someone from a high-end glossy magazine. Beautiful, well groomed, and flawless. As for what is under that polished exterior, I am still to determine. I just hope she isn't an airhead, or this night is about to turn excruciating.

"Don't worry, Salma. Alejandro is strong and can handle himself. I'm sure he's just got side-tracked. Matteo and Raul won't give up until they find him." I notice how she absent-mindedly rubs her tummy and feel a pang of longing. Ale told me she is expecting.

"Thank you. I'm just going to call my friend. I won't be long." I need to talk to Eva. I need my mami. In the absence of Ale, I need someone to tell me he is okay.

"Sal. I know we are practically strangers, but we can help each other here. I know what you are feeling, because it could be me at any time too. We need to trust one another and start building that support network that Penelope had with your mami. That's the only way we are going to get through this with our sanity intact." I sit back down and begrudgingly accept that she is right. Elena knows more about being a Mafia wife than I do because I was raised to be a Donna.

The gender difference expectation keeps creeping into the recess of my mind, making me question if I am cut out to lead after all. The first sign of trouble and I have fallen apart without Ale. Would he fall apart if the roles were reversed? I don't think he would. He is calm, cool, collected and calculating. I think he would take all this in his stride.

Well, I wouldn't know because he isn't fucking here. So, where the fuck is he? What keeps Alejandro away from me and away from home? I can't help the worry and concerns I have because, deep down, I know there is nothing in this world that would keep him from returning to me. Something really bad must have happened.

CHAPTER FOURTEEN

Justice

*** Amber ***

We run to my father's house the following morning. Preston comes with us and insists on the Beta Guards being on stand-by in case we need assistance.

"I'm not taking any chances, Red. I need you to be safe," he tells me as he caresses my back and ass.

Aiden is fired up and ready to confront the beast who sentenced our mother to the most painfully excruciating death ever, the selfish man who allowed us to think that she was alive and deliberately ignoring us. My blood bubbles in unspent rage. I will extract answers today. I will do whatever needs to be done to get the truth today.

When we arrive at his cottage, Marissa, his mate, is sitting outside the garden on a large boulder. She weeps and shivers, so after I shift back into my human form and quickly re-dress in my clothes, I approach her.

"Why are you crying, Marissa? Is there anything I can do?" I ask her. Her head darts up quickly at the sound of my voice.

"Amber? What are you doing here? Your father won't be happy." She quickly wipes her tears away and plasters a serene expression on her face, but it is futile. The evidence of her upset is still plain to see.

"Aiden and I need to talk to him, but first, I want to know what has upset you. Why isn't your mate here trying to make it better?"

Her eyes fill with fresh tears and the sobs that wrack her body breaks my heart. This is a desperately unhappy woman, and I know in my gut that this is my father's doing.

"I'm not pregnant again and John blames me, but my wolf tells me everything his wolf says. She tells me it's John's fault. This is his punishment from his wolf." As Lizzie laughs and rolls about in my head, I try my best to comfort my stepmother.

I sit beside her and drape my arm around her shoulders and allow her to cry all over me. While I comfort her, Aiden and Preston approach the cottage. Despite summoning our father, he did not come out.

"Get out here now!" Aiden roars from outside his door. From my position, I can see the anger displayed physically on his body. He is tense and tightly wound, and his fury causes the back of his neck to turn red.

Our father is unable to refuse a direct order from his Alpha and begrudgingly opens his door and steps outside.

"What do you want? Who do you think you are, summoning me in my own home? You've got some nerve, boy."

I don't often see my brother taking full advantage of his Alpha position, but today, Aiden shows no mercy, just like our father showed our mother no mercy. He is taking no prisoners; he exudes power and my pride in him swells inside me.

"Bow to your Alpha, you insolent old fool," Aiden spits out at him through gritted teeth. "I'm not a boy, I am a full-grown Alpha werewolf, it would do you well to remember that. And don't ever question why I am here. I say jump, you ask how high. I am your Alpha, understand? Now BOW."

My father bows to his Alpha, falling to his knees, and exposing his neck. His body does it involuntarily, without question. When he straightens up, the venom is clear to see in his eyes. He has nothing but hatred and resentment towards us.

"You allowed us to believe that our mother abandoned us. You caused us pain. Tell me why I shouldn't take your throat, right here, right now." As Aiden starts talking, Marissa walks towards him until I pull her back.

"Don't get involved, Marissa. We need to confront him." Despite my words, she shakes her head at me as she pulls away from my grasp.

"I'm already involved, don't you see? John, tell them everything or I will. Tell them now." I can't comprehend how Marissa knows and yet we don't. Didn't we deserve to know what happened to our mother?

"Go inside, Marissa. I want to talk to my children." My father's voice is fierce and, despite her shaking, Marissa stands up to him and defiantly refuses.

"No. You ruined Coral's life and now you're ruining mine. I used to love you and admire you, but now I can see you for what you are. A bully. A pathetic, controlling and insecure bully." Marissa turns to Aiden and continues to talk. "Your father has been blaming me for not getting pregnant, he says he can obviously conceive because he has you two. But his wolf told mine that he is punishing John for hurting his mate and children. He will never be blessed with another child because of the appalling way he treated the mother of his pups."

My father pounces on her before we can stop him, clawing and screeching at his mate as she wails in agony. The snap of her neck echoes around the woods surrounding the little quaint cottage. Aiden shifts and pins our father to the wall, but it is too late. Marissa is dead. Her beautiful face is unrecognisable because of the welts and scratches her mate inflicted on her. The person who was supposed to love her and protect her has destroyed her.

"You fucking bastard. How could you? She was so sweet. And young. How could you treat her like that? What is wrong with you?" I scream at the top of my voice; the horrific scene is burned into my memory for all eternity.

I have seen many things in my life. However, when my father's face starts to contort and change, I freak out. "Preston, what's happening to him?" I ask him, repulsed by what I am witnessing. Preston doesn't answer though, he doesn't have the answer.

However, my father's wolf answers instead. "You need to kill him. Kill him now, and me too. He is evil, he has always been evil. I made him transfer the position of Alpha. I threatened to kill us if he didn't." I can visibly see my father fighting against his wolf, but his wolf has taken advantage of him being weakened by the death of his mate.

"He refused to tell you even when we could see how hurt you were, thinking sweet Coral didn't love you. The truth is, she wasn't allowed. He smothered her but wouldn't mark her and when her true mate came, he punished her."

His own wolf has turned against him. He must have caused his wolf unknown pain for him to willingly sacrifice himself in this way.

"I, Alpha Aiden Goldrick, find you, John Goldrick, guilty of causing the unnecessary death of Coral White, guilty of causing mental and emotional damage to your children, Aiden and Amber, and guilty of the unlawful killing of your chosen mate, Marissa Goldrick. I sentence you to death." He rips out our father's throat so fast that his body remains upright a couple of seconds after his heart stops before slumping in a pile on the dirt floor.

"Aiden, are you okay?" I ask him softly. He is in a trance-like state and doesn't move. "Come on Aiden, let's go home, this is over now. Let's get back to your girls." The mention of his girls wakes him up and gives him the incentive he needs to move.

"I'm sorry you had to witness that; I didn't want you to have to see that. I can't believe he killed Marissa, the selfish fucker." I find it hard to believe too and yet I saw him do it with my own eyes.

Preston organises for Marissa's body to be taken to the mortuary, ready for her send-off. She will have a pyre and be sent off to the Promised Land in dignity. Our father, on the other hand, will not. Aiden digs his grave himself and plonks him without any grace.

"Do you want to say anything, Amber?" he asks me with a spade in his hands, ready to refill our father's final resting place.

"Yes. Yes, I do. Rot in hell." I spit into his grave before walking away. I will not waste another minute on that man. He killed my mother and completely ruined my childhood and any esteem I had in myself by allowing me to believe I wasn't wanted, I was abandoned, and I was unlovable. I almost threw away my mate and our bond based on those beliefs. He never once showed any remorse or regret for what he did. The way he treated Marissa today demonstrated that he was evil to the core. He was rotten and the world is better off without him.

I wait at the edge of the property for my brother and embrace him when he reaches me. "Come on Amber, let's go home. It's time to let go of the past and start living for the now and the future. That is what our mother would have wanted."

The past has already robbed us of too much. It is time to look forward, and now, I have so much to look forward to.

*** **Salma** ***

Ale had been missing for fifteen hours when his father and brother return to me. "There was no sign of him anywhere, Salma. We're going to have to call in some reinforcements." Raul tries to cajole me but, if anything, it unsettles me even more.

"I can't just sit around and wait for him to be found. Please watch Ricky for me. I'm going to find my husband." I call Willy and within half an hour, he has my usual team assembled.

"Ale has been missing for almost sixteen hours now. We know how precious this time is. We have to find him and find him fast. I need you to go above and beyond. I need you to help me find him. You boys have never let me down. If anyone can find him, it's you lot."

Karl raises his hand. "Mrs Morales, there were rumours of activity at the docks. I think we should check it out." A shiver of dread runs throughout me as I give my agreement to his plan. That seems like the sort of place you could have someone cornered, but why hasn't he come home? Am I going to find my Ale alive and well or has Dominga snuffed his life out too? I am nauseated at the thought.

Matteo asks if he can come too. "I won't be able to settle, Salma. He's my little brother and I need to know what has happened." I am thankful for his support. At this moment in time, we both have a common goal, we both love Alejandro and want him home safely.

The drive through the city to the docks doesn't take long. It is late at night now and the roads are mostly deserted.

As we pull into the docks, my stomach turns when I realise the magnitude of the task ahead of us. There are a million and one places Ale could be here. I don't let it stop me. I put my gun in my belt and carry a second one in my hand. "We need to split up and do this systematically. In twos, everyone, and if you see anything suspicious, call for me straight away."

We search into the night. "Where are you, Ale? Come on, I need you. Don't do this to me," I mutter continually under my breath. I will never give up. I know Ale would never give up on me.

"Salma. You need to get some rest. You need to stay strong for Ale and for Ricky now too." Willy has become a father figure to me, and I know he means well, but I can't just stop. Not now.

"Just one more hour. I feel like we are getting close to something, Willy." He nods but I can see the concern lining his face.

We carry on searching and decide to check out the warehouses. Around twenty minutes later, I hear one of my team shouting out to me. They have found something. My heart pounds in my chest as I make my way through the dilapidated building. If it is Ale, they would have said they had found Ale. Except if he is dead. Then they wouldn't tell me they would show me. Have they found Ale? And if not, *what* have they found that would be of interest to me?

Dominga.

They found Dominga's dead body. A single gunshot wound right between the eyes has more than likely granted her a fast and instant death. There is a trickle of blood running down her face but that is it. She could be sleeping if you cover the hole in her forehead. All I can think is at least I don't have to kill her now. I can continue to look my little brother in the eye.

That's one problem solved but another question still begs for an answer: where the fuck is Ale?

"Mrs Morales, there is something else too." My heart somersaults. Please don't be Ale. Please don't be dead. However, less than 100 feet away from Dominga's body is a decapitated body.

I moan as I fall to my knees. I know from looking at the body, I know.

It isn't my Ale.

Relief and horror washes over me. "ALE! Where are you?" I scream out; the bank of pent-up emotion bursts within me and I can't hold it in any longer.

Willy and Matteo run to me. "Shhh. Sal, Shhh. Do you hear that?"

I listen out to hear what they can: a thudding. "ALE!" I shout again as I search frantically for him, following the hollow tapping that seems to quicken every time I shout.

"Fucking hell, Chula. What took you so long?" The scratchy whisper, hardly even audible, makes me fall to my knees.

"Ale! Oh my god! Oh my god." The boys swarm around us and quickly pull Ale out from behind the crates and debris. He is in a bad way.

"Whose body is that, Ale?" I hear Matteo ask his brother.

"It's Tony Serrano, he was behind it all, Sal. He wanted our firms and got Dominga to help him take out your papa. His firm is now mine because I took his head."

I gag as Ale rolls Tony Serrano's head out from beside him. "He shot Dominga and me at the same time. She died instantly, but he got mc in the leg. I think I passed out after I killed him."

Not long after that, Ale passes out again. We can't take him to the hospital because it would attract the attention of the police, so I do the only thing I can think of. I contact the only person with the power and resources to help us.

I call Alpha Aiden Goldrick and beg him to save my husband's life.

*** **Eva** ***

I ask Mrs Moore to take Summer for a little while when Aiden returns home from his father's. I can tell from the blood and dirt on him that something terrible has happened. I just want to offer him the same level of love and support that he has always given me.

He shakes and shivers as he stands in front of me. My big strong Alpha is hurting, and he needs me. I need to be strong for him now like he has always been strong for me. I start the shower until it is really hot just as he likes it, and I remove his dirty clothes.

Once he is down to his pants, I take him by the hand and direct him to the shower. I wash away the dirt and the blood and stench of desperation. It's only when I rinse him off that I notice his eyes are full of unshed tears. Despite being fully dressed, I step into the shower with him and hold him close to me as he releases all his pain and anger.

At first, Aiden tries to pull away. He tries to stop his tears, but I hold his face in my hands. "Let it out. You saw what holding onto pain did to me and Lina, so let go of it, Aiden. Share it with me because I am sharing mine with you too. Then we can both be free of our demons and can move on to the future together."

His salty tears fall between us, he kisses me as he cries, and when his need becomes too much, I give my body to him to provide any comfort and support he needs. He rips my clothes from me with urgency and lifts me so I can wrap my legs around his waist. The exquisite feeling of Aiden's hard cock filling me and pushing into me repeatedly has me panting with my own need.

"Eva. I love you. Please, can we have our Mating Ceremony?" I chant yes to his request; I chant it over and over as my own orgasm erupts and consumes me. I clench him deep inside me and, with a groan of satisfaction, he shudders and stills inside me. His cock continues to twitch as his red-hot come coats my inner walls. "You said yes."

I look into the deep, mesmerising green eyes of my mate; the tears are spent but there is still longing there in them. "I did. I wasn't sure about the ceremony. I thought it was like a marriage, but nothing between us is anything like what was between Ryan and me. I feared tainting what we have and it turning like my marriage did, but I know with certainty now. I love you, Aiden Goldrick, and you are the love of my life. I want to spend forever with you, loving you, supporting you and sharing everything with you. So, my answer is yes. I want our Mating Ceremony too."

Excitement and joy flows through our mate bond as Aiden kisses me passionately. His cock is still inside me and starts to harden yet again and we slowly make love this time, taking our time and really enjoying each other. Aiden angles his thrusts so he is hitting my G-spot with every stroke. He keeps me upright with one arm and with his other hand he caresses my clit. My body shakes and trembles as I edge towards a second climax, and I cling to his strong shoulders as my body submits to the delight only my mate brings.

"You're fucking perfect, Eva. You're my perfect mate. My perfect lover. My perfect Luna and I love you and want the world to know." He thrusts deeper and harder than ever before, there is an urgency in him that I have never seen before.

"I love you too, Alpha. I love you with all my heart and cannot wait to declare it to the world." He growls as he finally comes inside me again. I wrap my arms around his neck and rest my head up against his chest.

"I don't know how you do it, but I feel a lot better now. Thank you." He gives me a quick peck before helping me down and this time he cleans me. "I didn't hurt you, did I? I know I was a bit rougher that last time."

I drag my lips across his, "It was all amazing. It felt so good, Aiden, and it was what you needed. You needed to be close to me. I am more than satisfied and happy."

As we dress in the cell, stealing kisses in between, reluctantly pulling our clean clothes on, Aiden's phone starts ringing. "Ah, fuck it, I'm not answering. It's late and I just want to snuggle with my girl."

However, it rings again, and again, and then my phone starts ringing too.

"Who the fuck is ringing us?" Aiden asks as he crosses the room to get his phone. "Oh. It's Salma, something must have happened."

My initial thought is that she has found Junior. "Sal? What's up?"

"Ale's been shot, he's in a bad way and I can't take him to the hospital. Please ask Aiden if his healers will treat him." I start to shake as I tell Aiden what has happened.

Aiden takes the phone from me. "Where are you?" Her answer is inaudible to me. "Where has he been shot? And by what? How long ago? Bring him straight here, now, I'll clear it with Border Control and brief the healers straight away."

Aiden mindlinks Border Control and the Healers and I try to put the rest of his clothes on him.

"I'll send Sal to sit with you. Ale's is in a really bad way from what she said. She'll need her friend."

"I'll be right here, go and save our friend." I kiss him goodbye before he locks the cell and it's not the first time I have felt helpless by being held inside here.

Sal comes down into the dungeon to wait about an hour later. She shakes with nerves and exhaustion, and I do everything I can to comfort her, but the only thing that could make this better is Ale being okay. Summer returns from Mrs Moore's care and she hugs Sal and sings nursery rhymes to her and settles her in a way I never could. The pure adoration my daughter has for her Auntie Sally is so beautiful to see.

Summer settles on her bed and Sal sits and strokes her head. "She's so precious, Eva. She is such a beautiful soul."

I couldn't agree more. I know she is my daughter and, therefore, I love her no matter what, but she is so caring and fun. She has a soul as sincere as an angel.

"I forgot to tell you: I got Luke's number for you. I told him that you just wanted to talk, and he said that was fine." She writes down the number and passes it to me. "I hope this helps you both so you can move on. Ryan did a job on the two of you."

I take the number and as soon as Ale is safe, I will call Luke and finally clear the air between us.

After a couple of hours, there is a knock at the door, and it's a surprise to see Max. "The Alpha told us what happened, and Melanie wanted to come and sit with you both if that's okay, Luna?"

"Of course, Max, bring her in." Max smiles at our easy

acceptance of his mate and I am thankful that Melanie has been mated to a kind and gentle and understanding wolf like him,

Max returns up the steps and carries Melanie back down. "Hi", she greets us meekly, but I haven't had a chance to thank her yet or to tell her how sorry I am for her loss, so I stand at the bars with my hands outstretched waiting for Max to bring her to me.

"It's great to see you up and about, Mel. I hadn't had a chance to say thank you to you for what you did. You saved my little girl's life, and I will be thankful until the day I die for what you did." I embrace her, the woman I once thought of as my foe, my biggest enemy, but now consider my daughter's saviour. "I'm so sorry about your baby, Mel. Aiden has people looking for Junior and we will get justice for you and your baby. I promise you that."

"Thank you, Eva, and to both of you for letting me come and sit with you. Go on, Max, leave us be. Come back later for me, okay?" I can't help but smile when Max kisses her against her temple and Melanie blushes in reaction. They are falling for each other and fast. That's how it is for werewolves. When you know, you know.

"I know you've probably got a million questions about Max and me but I just need to pass this message to Salma first." She lifts a white envelope from her pocket and hands it to Sal.

Sal reads it and lets out a sigh. "Thank God. They've got the bullet out and have cut out the corruption, now they have to sew him up and hope for the best." She starts to cry with relief. "The stupid idiot has me weeping with relief. I'm going to kill him when he's out of surgery!"

We laugh along with her, her joy evident at Ale being safe. "So, tell us and you and Max, he seems to be smitten with you, Mel?"

Melanie blushes again. "I've never met anyone like him, he's just so... I mean I like him, but you probably think this is too fast and that I'm just jumping from one man to another. But Max is different. This is... special."

I can see myself a few months ago when Aiden came into my life. I couldn't comprehend how strong my feelings were for him after such a short period of time. "Mel, that's how I felt about Aiden. When you know, you know. And no one would begrudge you a bit of happiness. Max is a good man, and he will take care of you."

"This is the first time he has left my side since the accident. I know I've been high on pain relief, but he is so amazing. Last night though, I think he was trying to make me laugh. He told me he was a werewolf!" Salma and I look quickly at each other and then look down, and the smile falls from Melanie's face. "Wait, you know something. Oh my God, is it true? Is Aiden one too?" She looks shocked but not repulsed or disgusted, so I nod slowly to her.

"Yep, Max and Aiden are werewolves. And I'm one too," I whisper as I lower my head.

"Really? Was he telling the truth? So, is it true then about the mate's bond and everything?"

I nod to her but to my dismay, she starts to cry. "Mel? It's okay, Max isn't dangerous or anything, he won't hurt you, I promise." Melanie takes her hands from her face and looks up at me and I realise she is smiling.

"He's mine and I am his... He wants us to be together, he wants us to be a family. I can't believe it!"

Having found the love of my life in a similar way, I understand how lucky she is feeling right now. The Moon Goddess has honestly blessed us all.

*** **Preston** ***

After taking Marissa's body to the morgue, I inform her sister of her death and explain what happened. Her sister looks like she expected this, and my blood runs cold as a result .

"It wasn't a healthy relationship. He used to beat her and abuse her. I'm not surprised it ended like this, but at least she is free from him now. Tell the Alpha I thank him for being so swift with his justice. I will speak to him tomorrow at the pyre."

When I return home, Amber is already in bed. Her vibrant red hair is still wet from the shower. "Are you sleeping?" I whisper to her, and she shakes her head at me in response.

I strip out of my clothes and shower quickly and then climb into bed with my love and hold her close to me. "I'm right here if you need me. I'll always be right here."

"Preston, I just want to concentrate on the future now. This is over, he's gone, and he'll never take up any more time and space from my life." I kiss her forehead; her words have never made me happier.

"We have so much to look forward to Amber, starting with our Mating Ceremony this weekend. We have our whole lives to plan. What do you want to do first?"

She looks at me with wonder, looking younger and carefree now. The strain of the past and her trial had put years on her and now it is gone, she is a young woman with the world at her feet once more.

"Can we have a holiday soon? Just you and me?" I laugh at the sparkle in her eyes. We won't be able to leave just yet, not while Junior and Nikki are still out there and while the Luna is still under home arrest, but hopefully soon I can give my love everything her heart desires.

"Once Eva is allowed out of the cell, we will, but right now, Aiden needs us both." In the back of my mind, I hope that Amber will be carrying our pup by then.

She pushes back against me. "I love you, Preston, I can't wait for the weekend to tell everyone else too." I kiss her goodnight.

"I love you too, Red. I always have and I always will." Within minutes, she is sleeping and once she hits a deep sleep, I crawl out of bed and continue to make more arrangements for our ceremony this weekend. I want this to be spectacular. I want Amber to know how much she means to me.

I contact my mother who confirms she has arranged all the flowers and food. My father will meet me in the morning to go to the tailor's and he has the rings I commissioned.

I will be meeting with the Pack Shaman tomorrow morning to confirm our vows and to take instructions from him.

I am so busy overseeing all the little details that it takes me a while to realise that the room is cold. A movement outside catches my attention, and with a start, I realize that in the shrubs just outside my window are two people.

When I open the window, Nikki's scent, mixed with someone else's, quickly travels in. How the fuck has she got on our lands again? I mindlink Aiden and Billy but as soon as I open the window, Nikki hears me and runs away, but not before she shouts a reminder.

"Your pups will be cursed. Remember that. You will never be free and happy. Amber will pay for what she did. You will all pay for what she did." I shake with both anger and realisation. In the whirl of everything else happening, I had forgotten about the curse Nikki placed on my future pups with Amber. It was right after Eva confronted her and we found she had a dire wolf. How could I have been so reckless and forgetful?

By the time the trackers get around to their hiding spot, there is no sign of Nikki or Junior. I wake Amber and tell her I am going to Aiden; I need to talk to them both about what happened, and about the curse.

"What curse, Preston? You never said anything about a curse." She sounds perplexed as she wipes the sleep from her eyes.

As I explain to Amber the curse that Nikki had placed on our pups, her hand goes to her tummy, and I have never felt so guilty. "Preston, our pup could be growing inside me right now. Why didn't you tell me?"

It's a valid question: why didn't I? I can only surmise that with everything else that happened, I had simply forgotten. Had I really taken it seriously? No, maybe I hadn't, but I did sincerely push it to the back of my mind when Eva transformed into a ferocious Dire Wolf.

"I'm sorry. I didn't remember until she just shouted through the window, reminding me." Amber sits with her head in her hands. "Red, please talk to me, tell me what to do. I am so sorry."

"How do you break a curse? Did she say what the conditions were, Preston? Did she say what the get-out clause was?!" I rack my brains trying to remember what she said. I don't remember any conditions.

In the end, I shake my head at her. "I don't remember, Amber, I'm sorry. She cursed us, Eva transformed and scared the shit out of us all and Nikki ran away while we were all distracted. I don't remember anything else she said. I just remember her saying that she placed a curse on all pups that come from our union."

I thought that Aiden was answering my earlier mindlink when

he sent a message to meet him in the packhouse lobby. I take Amber's hand and we rush down to meet our Alpha.

However, such is life in our little quiet pack at the moment, another incident has happened with the Mafia, and Aiden had actually called to brief me as the pack Beta.

"So Dominga is dead? Well, that explains why Junior is now in cahoots with Nikki."

Amber punches me in the arm. "Really, Preston? Have you forgotten again already? Nikki placed a curse on our future pups, Aiden, and there is a possibility I could already be pregnant." I cringe at the last line and I tense in anticipation. Just as I thought, Aiden smacks me across the other shoulder.

"You got her pregnant while there was a curse on you both? What the fuck is wrong with you, Preston? You are supposed to be the clever, level-headed one. I wish everyone would FUCK OFF!"

I can see that Aiden is being pushed to the edge. It has been a challenging time for him since he met his mate. I get it.

"Look, I'm sorry. I fucked up. You go and deal with Alejandro and the Mafia, and Amber and I will wake the Elders and get advice from them. We'll speak to you tomorrow."

Aiden pulls his sister back to him. "No more shifting in case you are carrying, Amber. That's my little niece or nephew in there. Let us all look after you now."

I am hopeful that Aiden can persuade Amber to take a step back, but she pushes her brother. "Piss off, will you, I might not be, and it's only been a couple of days. I'm not disabled if I have a pup, it's not an illness. Goddess, you two are imbeciles." Aiden and I grin at each other; there is the strong and sassy Amber we both know.

We alert the Elders and wait for them to join us in the

conference room. While we wait, I tease Amber about what Aiden said.

"No more shifting, and we might insist on bedrest for you, Red. You will be carrying valuable cargo." Her eyes flash in annoyance until a little glimmer of mischief kicks in too.

"I'll have you waiting on me hand and foot, *fluff my pillows, rub my feet, peel my grapes.* I will have you whipped." She giggles as she teases me back.

"I would do all those things and more, Amber. I would do anything for you, for us and for our future pups. I promise that." Our foreheads touch as we think of the promise of the future, despite the curse and the threat it poses. Our own child, mine and Amber's, would simply be out-of-this-world phenomenal. It would be the best thing to ever, ever happen to me.

"What is the meaning of this, Beta Preston? Do you realise it's 4.50am? This had better be important." Elder Joshua is always so grumpy, getting him up out of bed in the middle of the night only adds to his irritability.

I explain to the Elders, who grumble and whine about missing their beds and being cold. "So, this Nikki, her father, was a Red-Mage?" Elder Joshua asks. "What exactly were the words she used, Beta Preston?"

I close my eyes and try my best to remember.

"She said Amber was a whore and had killed her mate, and now she is going to destroy her and every other werewolf who tries to protect her. She'll never stop until she avenges her lover. She said that Amber took everything from her, and now she is going to take everything from her and burn it to the ground and she won't stop until Amber screams for death."

Amber shudders at the side of me, but I haven't finished yet. As soon as I remember the beginning of Nikki's rant, the rest just blooms in front of me.

"Then she cursed us, she said *'you could have had some semblance of a future with me, Beta Preston, if you had just submitted and done as I asked, but now you will also pay. Any pups that come from your union will be subjected to my curse. A curse to avenge my lost lover. Your pups will never find theirs, they will not feel the bond of the mate. All pups born into your pack from now on will be subject to my curse. This is the cost your mate will pay for killing mine. I place a curse upon you all and your offspring. May you know what it is to be alone'.*"

My eyes go wide as I realise what I've just said.

"Holy shit, she didn't just curse Amber and me. She cursed us all."

The Elders look equally concerned. "Then there is nothing else for her: this Red-Mage must die as soon as possible. The Alpha's Heir is in jeopardy too. To stop a Red-Mage curse, you need to kill the host and take their heart. The heart must then be burned to ash. The ash then needs to be kept with the Alpha."

Simple as that, then. We need to trap the Red-Mage and kill her before she causes any more damage.

CHAPTER FIFTEEN

A Legacy

*** Junior ***

Nikki is crazy. She is as mad as a box of frogs and I am stuck with her, with nowhere else to go. We have been trapped for days now and apart from shifting and eating rabbits and salmon when I could catch it, I take no other real sustenance. It is affecting my strength, my decisions, and my ability to resist the wily little minx who insists on riding my cock at least four times a day. In my weak state, I can't resist her attempts to plant my pup inside her. I'm sure Dominga will understand. After all, it isn't my fault that I am so horny. I am an Alpha Wolf. My overwhelming desire is to please, seek pleasure and reproduce. It's a primal need and Dominga cannot fulfil my needs right now.

I consider making contact with my mother for help, but my father would have poisoned her against me by now. My father favours his bastard, I bet, the shifty shithouse. I have to get out of the Onyx River territory. Nikki is taking unnecessary risks and I am not running the threat of being caught so she can taunt her prey.

My only hope now is to get back to Dominga. She still has the power to get me out of this shit. She always used to say that we could move abroad once this is all over and we can live our lives out on the beach if we wish to. What can I do about Nikki, though? If she is carrying my pup, I want it. That means keeping Nikki alive long enough to birth a healthy pup. I don't think Dominga is going to be happy about that, especially if Nikki continues to flirt and demand my cock inside her. But Dominga can't give me a pup, she's too old, so I need this. It may be my only chance.

"We need to get back to Dominga. She can't know about us." Nikki scowls at me, unhappy with my command. I grab her by the face and laugh when she squeals. "Is that going to be a fucking problem? Did you see what I did to that human? I will do the same to you, you fucking little bitch, if you don't do what I say. We need to get off werewolf territory and get back to Dominga, she can get us money and get us out of the country until our pup is born."

The mention of our pup is enough to persuade her. "So, what do we tell her if I am pregnant?" I tread carefully here. She might be beneath my station, but I have witnessed first-hand how crazy she is.

"By the time we find out if you are with pup, we will have discarded her anyway, so it won't matter. We just need to keep up appearances until we get out of the country and get some money and then we will dump her. Right now, you aren't officially pregnant and, therefore, Dominga doesn't need to know that you might be."

There is a part of me that is completely disgusted by Nikki. She is so needy, so desperate for love and affection, I could really be anyone just as long as she was getting her pup. But then there is a small part of me that feels a connection with her. I can relate to her and although her state of mind is a concern when it comes to my pup's genetics, she really is quite adorable in her own way.

When we arrive back at our hide-out, Nikki drops to her knees and pulls my cock out. "I will get us to Dominga, and I will keep quiet about us if you give me your oath. Tell me I'm your Luna. Make me your Luna, mark me, fuck me, and give me your pups. Promise me, Junior."

She finally shuts up. My cock is already hard, jumping slightly when she wraps her tongue around the tip. She suckles it and then licks all the way down my shaft. I've never felt anything so exquisite before. She tenderly cups my balls as she licks all the way back up to the purpled-headed tip of my cock. "Fuck, yeah!" I shout as I use both hands to push her head and mouth to take my full-length in. However, Nikki resists me.

She wipes her mouth with the back of her hand. "Oh, no. First you promise and then I will suck you like you've never been sucked before." She holds up two fingers and replicates what she means on them. She moans loader as she sucks hard past all the knuckles on her nimble fingers and then she slurps all the way down. My cock is burning with need now, it strains for release, begging for Nikki's mouth or her pussy.

"Suck me, come on Nikki, don't make my balls turn blue. I can't give you a pup that way." She shakes her head at me, refusing me.

"No, promise me, Junior. Promise me and it's all yours, every hole, every position in every way. Make me your Luna, say the words and your cock will be rewarded. Every part of you will get my rewards. SAY IT. Promise to make me yours."

I can't take the torment any longer. "I promise. I am going to make you my Luna. I am giving you my pups. Now, fucking suck me!" She deepthroats me for a couple of minutes before I blow my thick hot cum down her throat.

Throwing Nikki down onto the floor of the cave, I pull her

leggings and panties from her. "It's my turn to eat, open your legs, let me see your tight little pussy." She spreads her legs wide for me, showing me her moist pink slit and tight hole. She isn't as groomed now as when we started out, our circumstances have prevented it. "Do you want to come, Nikki? Do you want me to munch on you until you scream my name again?"

"Yes, eat me, do it now." She pants and moans as I crawl between her legs, craving me. My skills must be unparalleled. "Come on, Alpha, don't make me wait, your Luna needs you."

I stop just a couple of centimetres from her pubic bone. "Promise me. Promise me you'll keep our secret from Dominga, and you'll be on your best behaviour until we are out of the country and safe. Promise me or I'll bite your little clit right off and you'll never feel pleasure again." She struggles beneath me, scared I will take away her pleasure button, and just to tease her I lick all the way down from her clit to her asshole, gently and suggestively. Nikki bucks her hips trying to absorb more of my superior touch. "Oh no, not until you make your oath. Come on, it'll be practice for your Luna Ceremony… that's what you want, right?"

"I promise, I promise. I won't tell her. Just fucking lick me properly, Junior. I need it now." I continue to tease her with featherlight strokes of my tongue against her most sensitive parts, before gripping her clit between my teeth. I don't break the skin, but I pull the area gently from her and look into her fear-filled eyes. I'm showing her what I could do if she defies me. I release her clit with a slight pop and then lick her, I lap at her and smash my lips at her swollen clit until she is writhing in pleasure again. "I'm gonna come, I… I." Her lusty moan fills the cave as she comes.

I move between her thighs and plant myself firmly inside her and she clenches me with her hot and wet walls as I do. I am rough, but from her squeals and moans I can tell she likes it. Why wouldn't she? She flips me over so I'm on my back and she's on top, her lithe frame grinds against me. "Look at me, Alpha. Look at your Luna as she rides you." My eyes meet hers and I am overwhelmed with affection for her.

"Yes. My Luna, ride me, fuck me. Make me yours." Then unexpectedly, as my cock is pumping my muck inside her, she leans down to my neck and marks me.

"Mine!" My wolf is furious, but I have to remember that I commanded that she make me hers. "You're mine now and always, Junior. Now make me yours too."

I bite down hard on her neck, over her past lover's mark, ensuring mine is larger so it covers his. The bond between us, although not fated, is strong and complex. I am disgusted when I realise I would do anything to protect her, my chosen mate. I would do anything to ensure her safety and happiness. She looks at me, filled with pride and knowing. She knew I would feel this way, she knows because she has already had a mate and felt the bond.

As much as I want to destroy the little bitch for stitching me up, I also want to kiss her soundly for being so clever and conniving.

"I know what you did. Now you'll never use your power against me again or I'll destroy us both. Understand, *mate*?"

She smiles sinisterly and sweetly at me before kissing me. "I understand, Alpha. Now come on, let's go and find your old whore so we can get out of this hole." Despite myself, pride in my mate, pride for her power and determination fills me.

"I could really fall for you, Nikki. We could build something strong and powerful with us working together as one." I thought she would appreciate my flowery words, but she looks back at me with confused panic and alarm.

"Let's not forget that this is a union of convenience, Junior. This is fun and if we both get pups from it, that's even better, especially if they have your Alpha lineage and my Red-Mage powers. But that's it, Junior. Don't blur the lines."

What the fuck does that mean? She has been incessantly badgering me to make her mine for the past few weeks and now she tells me it's a union of convenience. She really *has* lost the plot.

"Whatever you say, *Luna*."

*** Melanie ***

Sitting here with Eva and Salma, I almost feel like we have been friends for years. I am one of the girls, and they accept and value me. I can't remember a time when I felt so normal. They listen to me and confide in me too and I could get used to being friends with them. I hope that is a possibility.

I sincerely thought Max was joking last night when he told me he needed to talk to me about something serious. "Melanie, I need to tell you something about me, and then hopefully the rest will make sense to you. I'm a werewolf. And that means I can feel a bond between us that tells me that we are fated to be together."

Bursting into laughter, I truly think this is a funny story to make me laugh. "You're crazy, Max, with your stories and funny sayings. You've really kept my spirits up."

I didn't take a bit of notice of what he said, but when I relay the story to Eva and Sal and see their reactions, I know there is some truth in it. The realisation that Max means everything he's told me overwhelms me, causing joy to burst in my chest. We are meant to be together, the mates bond is a real thing, everything he told me is true.

I can't wait to talk to him about it later. For now, I wipe my tears away and share my happiness with my friends. This has been bittersweet. I am heartbroken that I lost my baby and I don't think I will ever get over that. But the promise of someone destined for me, someone as lovely, kind, and sexy as Max, well, that makes moving forward and looking to the future a little easier.

Eva tells me why she is in the cell and it sounds really scary. I ask her about Summer and they believe she is a werewolf too. It's a surprise that Ryan never knew, but it makes sense when she explains that she didn't know either until recently.

"So, Melanie, has Max told you what he wants in the future?" My face fills with heat now that I know he won't change his mind and that he is being deadly serious about wanting me to move here with him and us being a family. He even said there would be room for my boys whenever they want to visit or stay too.

"He asked me to move in with him, he said he would ask for a bigger accommodation for us so my boys can come and stay too. But I told him I would have to talk to you about it first. I don't want to infringe and if me being here causes you pain then I will tell him no." I look at them both to gauge their reaction. It was one thing to invite me to sit with them. It is a whole other thing to live in close proximity to me and be involved in everyday life with each other.

"Are you kidding me, Mel? I've been setting up an appropriate place for you both to live. The past is the past, no one is perfect. I am so happy to be welcoming you as a member of my pack, as my Gamma's mate and as my friend. You deserve to find some bliss now too. Be happy, Mel." My eyes fill up with tears again as I take it all in. I have a mate, a pack and friends as well as two healthy sons and a promising future. Yes, times have been hard, but everything led me on the path to Max.

"What are the next steps in your therapy, Eva?" Salma inquires. Salma is able to relax now that she knows her husband should be safe. The next steps of Eva's therapy are also of interest to me. Now that Eva knows I'm not part of her therapy, what is the next step for her and her recovery?

"I am going to phone Luke in a little while. Aiden and I are working through my issues with Ryan and tomorrow my mother is coming so I can confront her too. Hopefully, I will be out of the cell soon and then Aiden and I can have our Mating Ceremony." I have no idea what that means but this is something I can talk to Max about now.

The thought of having someone as considerate and loving as Max to share my life with fills me with warm love and longing. When he walks back into the cell, my tummy somersaults. His hair is wet, but his clothes are dry. "Is it raining?" I ask him, but he shakes his head at me.

"Did you let Ray out for a run?" Eva asks him and he looks at me quickly before grinning and nodding. "Don't worry, we've explained everything to Melanie. She believes you now. Don't you, Mel?" I nod my head at him, shyly.

"Come on then, Honey, you should get back to the hospital and get some rest. Mrs Morales, I can take you over to see your husband now too, if you want. He's in recovery."

I hug Eva goodnight and whisper my thanks to her that she has been able to forgive me and welcome me into her pack. She wishes me goodnight.

"Max, you and Melanie should come and have a look at the available apartments once she has recovered."

Max smiles at her and then at me. "Yes, Luna, thank you," he says as he takes me by the hand.

"Who's Ray?" I ask, I think I know but I want him to tell me and introduce me.

"He's my wolf, or the wolf side of me. I'll introduce you sometime, he is very eager to meet you." Butterflies swirl about my tummy when he looks at me. He mesmerises me. How can someone as decent as Max like someone like me?

Salma surprises me by hugging me farewell too. "Thanks for keeping me company tonight, Melanie. I won't forget this."

Max and I wait outside the clinic. It's cold because it is the dead of night, but the fresh air feels fantastic after being cooped up inside since my accident.

"You believe me now, then?" he asks. Looking into his eyes, I nod. "And about the mate bond and how I feel about you."

He steps closer to me. "Max..." He pushes my hair back behind my ear and cups my cheeks with his warm, calloused hands. I could just melt into his embrace, leave my past behind and start afresh with Max, but the thought is so enticing, it scares me. "I just need time. I think I do want this, but everything is happening all so fast and unexpectedly. I'm scared of messing it up."

He gives me a short, soft nod of the head to show he understands. "That's okay, we have all the time... but I want to kiss you, Honey. Can you spare me one kiss for now?"

My breath catches in my throat as I slowly nod. Max smiles at my response before he pulls me closer to him. His body is hot and hard against mine, and when he runs his hands up my neck to my face, my body reacts almost instantly. He leans down and kisses me, but it's not the soft and sweet kiss that I expect. This is a hot and demanding kiss, a carnal kiss. This is the sexiest kiss I have ever experienced. A little moan escapes from me, a sound I didn't even know I was capable of.

He pulls away from me all too soon and I want to sulk like a child. "Does that make you want more, Honey?" In the past I would have been coy, I would have pretended to not want anything, but I want to be completely honest with Max.

I nod to him and to my delight, he kisses me again. This time I match him, stroking his tongue back with my own and holding him closer to me by wrapping my arms around his neck. He nibbles and tugs on my bottom lips before pulling away once again.

"I'm just asking for a chance to show you how good we could be together. For an opportunity to show you how I could treat you like a goddess. So I can give you a snapshot of how a life with me would be. What the prospect of us becoming one and of how hot and fulfilling it would be for both of us. I want it all with you Melanie. Don't forget it, because I won't. Not after that kiss."

I continue to stare at him wide-eyed.

"One more kiss?" he asks me and I nod more eagerly this time. This kiss, I savour. I thread my fingers through his hair and don't object when he slips his hands down my body and grabs my ass.

A cough interrupts us, and I jump away from Max like he's on fire.

"Alpha, I'm sorry, did you need me?"

Aiden stands there with a grin on his face. It's so embarrassing that he caught us, I'm sure the capillaries in my face are bursting with shame.

"No, Gamma Max, you're okay, the nurse is getting worried about your mate. I assured her she is perfectly fine with you. It's good to see you both… getting along so well. Your Luna will be very pleased too."

I groan at Max when Aiden leaves. "That was so embarrassing. We aren't teenagers, Max, we can't go around acting like we are."

Max laughs at me and my objections. "Honey, honestly that was nothing, not by werewolf standards." Even though I chastise him for kissing me in public, I am forlorn when he doesn't kiss me again. Max is full of surprises and his ability to kiss me into a stupor is probably the biggest and most welcome. If he could send my mind to mush with just his kisses... What else could he do?

Thoughts of Max's intimate abilities and what werewolf standards are run incessantly through my mind until I finally fall asleep after sunrise.

*** Eva ***

I settle in bed while I wait for Aiden. He should be on his way back to me now, and he is bound to be exhausted. Werewolves have excellent recovery abilities and don't need to sleep as much as humans, but this has been a very busy time for my mate. I hope he is able to rest.

Aiden walks in and greets me with a massive smile. "Why are you so happy?" I ask. I thought he would be tired and grumpy and in need of TLC, but the man standing in front of me looks positively ecstatic.

"Hello, my gorgeous girl. What's not to be happy about? My sister is free, my father is gone. Our friend is making a good recovery. I've just caught our Gamma and his mate kissing the face off each other and now I'm here with the love of my life spread out in my bed." I smile back at him until my cheeks hurt. If Max and Melanie are kissing, there is a good chance he won't leave the pack to be with her. Perhaps they will stay after all!

"Do you think Max will be staying, then?" I ask him tentatively.

He nods as he removes his clothes, "I reckon he's already planning on Melanie moving here with us, seeing as he mindlinked me as I walked away to request a bigger apartment." Aiden is now down to his pants again and he strides over to the bed. "I told you Max would win her over."

I sit up to hug him. I am fond of Max and don't like the thought of having to find yet another Gamma. "You did, but I like to have something to worry about." He chuckles in response and leans down to kiss me.

"You have too many clothes on," he complains as he pulls my chemise over my head. "I want to see and feel your beautiful body." My body is already reacting to him, his touch, his scent, his words, his proximity. Everything about Aiden turns me on.

I don't resist. Sparks erupt across my skin from where he touches me and we make love once again. This time it is sweet and slow and tender. He takes me from behind as we lie on our sides, his hands have free access to every part of me. He cups my breasts, plucking my nipples and rolling them between his fingertips. I moan and arch against him, begging for more, more and more. His hand then trails down to between my legs. He quickly and expertly finds my sensitive nub and gives me the pressure I need to find fulfilment.

"You're so wet, baby," he whispers against my ear as all the sensations combine to push me further and further to the brink. "Go on Eva, my love, come for me."

He thrusts deeper, faster, and more deliberately, all the while keeping up his assault on my clit. He places hot, wet kisses along my neck that cause my skin to goosepimple. The feeling hits full pitch and my legs quake as the rest of my body splinters apart. "That's it, that's it my girl, come for me. You look so beautiful and powerful when you come." With a final thrust, Aiden comes too.

Once we have cleaned up and properly got ready for bed, we discuss the day, all the things that have been happening and about our day ahead tomorrow. "Are you ready to see your mother tomorrow? Both your father and I will be here, but I'm concerned about the toll it will take on you and on our pup."

I am concerned too, but I have to do this. I want to do this, and I think I have an ideal way to test the pain and how much I could cope with. "I've been worried about it too, and so, I thought I could tell you about my wedding night, about how Ryan treated me that night. I could tell you why it hurts me to think about it, even now. I will be addressing the pain and also testing out how far I can push before it becomes too much. Do you think you could cope with that tonight too, Aiden? I know it's been a long day for you, so if you want to do this another time, that's okay."

He considers my request before he answers. "Are you sure you're ready for this, Eva?" I nod to him in confirmation. I need to do this before I lose my nerve.

We sit on the floor, I sit in between Aiden's outstretched legs with my back to his chest, he wraps his strong, muscular arms around me, protecting me. "I feared becoming like my mother. I didn't want to go through marriage and divorce like hot meals. So, when Ryan proposed, I almost said no. But he knew how to pull on my heart strings and I ended up saying yes. We married at the registry office with our witnesses. I wore a simple white dress, and my mother gave me a posy of white roses. She told me there was no other colour for me because I was so pure."

I pause to take a sip of water, and to give myself a chance to keep a hold of my composure.

"I knew there was something not right almost as soon as we married. I felt like he was angry with me, or like I had done something wrong. He got drunk and when we got to the bridal suite I changed into my lacy underwear, ready to lose my virginity to my husband, but he couldn't do it. He was too drunk, and he started to hurl abuse at me, telling me it was my fault. He said I was cold and frigid. I went to bed and cried myself to sleep."

Aiden rubs my upper arms, and I appreciate the gesture of support as I get to the most difficult part.

"I woke up in the dead of night. The room was pitch black, but I could smell Ryan; well, the alcohol on him, at least. He ripped my nightgown from me, completely ripped it to shreds, and then he tied my hair around his hand, gripping it tightly. And without any warning… he climbed on top of me and took my virginity. He hurt me, and afterwards, he told me I was a woman now. He told me I would get better at it and that this was what first times were like for everyone." By the time I finish, my face is wet with my silent tears. Aiden has stiffened and remains silent behind me. "For a long time, I thought that's what sex was. And the worse it got, the more I didn't want to do it, and the more he would call me names for being frigid and cold. Aiden, say something, please."

I can't stop the tears. For years, I have held onto the pain and humiliation, and look at how it continues to hurt me. I need him to say something so I know he doesn't see me differently now that he knows this, that he can still love me, even the broken and weak side of me.

"You are the bravest, strongest and most amazing person I have ever met, Eva. I mean that. How did you get through all that and still remain so sweet and kind?" His strong embrace, his words of praise and comfort gives me the strength to finally confront my fears and pain.

"I was a real-life person, a young woman, and he treated me worse than a dog. I've always felt there was something wrong with me, that I was silly to expect or want more. I considered myself foolish for thinking he would have been gentle and considerate of me. It's only when I met you that I realised that this was the proper way a man treats his partner. It wasn't me who was asking for too much, it was Ryan and his warped thinking that were the problem."

I finish talking and I am suddenly overwhelmed by the snaps and twangs of elastic breaking inside me. It's more painful than the first time, but I'm stronger now too. Sometimes, we don't know how strong we are until it's put to the test. I wouldn't be here today if it hadn't been for my strength, and for my wolf, my amazing voice within, always guiding me and helping me.

I cry out in pain as more of the manifestation is healed. This time, Lina howls as I cry, both of us needing physical release from the emotional trauma.

Afterwards, Aiden lifts me up on his lap and holds me tightly to his chest. "I'm sorry you went through all that, Eva. He was wrong to treat you that way and I hope now you can see it was never you. There is no rhyme or reason with people like Ryan. I don't want there to be. The day we start relating to scum like him is the day we're all lost."

His love and support means everything to me. We get back into bed together and my wolfmate strokes my tummy as I fall asleep.

"I used to visualise having a few sons when I thought of the future and my own pups. However, I hope this little one is another girl. I'd like that."

"Summer would have that best friend we talked about. I don't mind either way. I just hope I'm able to come out of the cell by the time he or she makes an appearance."

"If it is a girl, I'd like to call her Coral, after my mother. Would that be okay?" I smile at his sweet gesture.

"Coral... I like that, Coral Goldrick. Future Female Alpha of the Onyx River Pack."

When I fall asleep, I dream of two little girls playing together. Our little girls.

CHAPTER
SIXTEEN

Try

*** Xavier ***

For many years, my worst fear was Lydia finding out about Rose and Evangelina. I would wake in the middle of the night soaked to the bone with sweat; the sheen of a guilty man. Pangs of anxiety would assault me from nowhere as I wondered: would today be the day she found out? What would she do once she did find out?

Then there was the guilt I felt about my daughter, for not being present in her life. At first, the temporary reprieve worked. I provided financially for her, and quite well too. It was enough to justify to myself for a little while that she wanted for nothing and would have the best of everything. But deep down, I knew that Rose was there for the money, and the guilt and shame of leaving my little girl with that selfish money-grabber would devour my soul. I hated myself for being a callous coward.

Today is my chance to somewhat redeem myself. My mate not only knows about my daughter, but they are bonding too. Lydia and I as a team helped to heal some of Lina's manifestations. Today, by bringing Rose to her, I hope to help her face her pain and reverse the rest of the damage.

Rose and Lydia look each other up and down in disgust. "So, this must be the mongrel you turned your back on your daughter for?" Rose tuts and shakes her head, but my Lydia stares her down and hisses at her.

"One more word and I'll slit your fucking throat from ear to ear. I'm the Luna here and what I say goes. You are alive only by my grace and that is only because I love Eva and Summer and would never want to harm them. If you don't cooperate today, I will ruin you. Have no doubt in your mind, I despise you for what you've done to that girl. You are a disgrace. So, don't you dare look down your nose at my mate for walking away when you have deliberately hurt her."

Rose pales under the intense hatred of my mate and her vehement promise to dole out punishment for any lack of cooperation. I am proud and grateful to have a strong and principled mate. Lydia has always been a perfect mate and the greatest Luna. I must remind her of how much I appreciate that.

"That was hot as fuck, sweet cheeks. Just wait until later when I ask for an encore." Even though I murmur it, she still blushes.

"Xavier Woodward! Watch your mouth," she whispers back to me whilst smiling. She almost looks carefree though she is far from it. She has walked the carpet in the bedroom threadbare with her pacing at night, worrying about our son and the consequences of his actions. But Lydia is the consummate actress, she appears serene and full of grace, just as any Luna should.

We arrive at the Onyx River Packhouse, and Beta Preston meets us and takes us down to the dungeons and into Eva's cell. "Well, he's made it nicer in here for Eva compared to what you have made me stay in," Rose complains. "Your place is a hell hole."

I smile at her before I answer. "Eva is the Luna here; her pack would do anything to serve her and protect her. You are in my cells for your crimes against her. You're lucky that you're still alive. Now shut up and stop moaning. We've brought you here for a reason, and it's not for you to air your dissatisfaction with your accommodation."

Rose looks like she is about to object and argue again when our daughter's voice reaches us both.

"Hello, Mother." Eva's voice is devoid of emotion. It is measured and controlled, and my pride in her doubles. She is starting to become the person she was always meant to be: a strong Alpha Heir and a gracious Luna.

"Oh, Eva! I've been worried sick about you. Where is little Summer?" Rose's tone completely changes; gone is her venom and in its place is a saccharine sweet tone.

"Why?" My daughter asks one simple question: why? And it has her mother stumped.

"Why what, sweetheart?" she asks back with her artificial simper, and her look of feigned interest and concern sickens me. How could I have left this monster to raise my child?

"Why are you worried about me?" Eva asks her simply as she raises her eyebrows in question and laces her fingers together. Rose looks about the cell, her eyes bulge as she shiftily looks around the space.

"I'm your mother, of course I worry about you. I always have and I always will." Rose puffs her chest out, but none of us are impressed with her posturing.

"Take a seat, Ms Duvall," Aiden says to his mother-in-law as he points to a wooden seat that faces Eva, who is still behind bars.

"Actually, I am going back to my maiden name now that Claude is divorcing me." She places her hand on Aiden's arm and he pushes her away as though her touch scolds him.

"I don't care what you call yourself. Don't ever touch me." I don't miss my daughter's mouth twitching. That one gesture secures Aiden's place in her heart, if there was ever any doubt. His look of genuine disgust is the icing on the cake.

"Did you worry about me when your husband tried to touch me? Did you worry about me when you sucked off my husband and whatever else you got up to? Did you worry about me when I became a shell of my former self at Ryan's hands? Did you worry about me as you stole thousands of pounds from me while me and my daughter lived on the breadline? Did you worry about me when I went into premature labour and birthed my child all alone?" Eva stops and takes a deep breath. "Do I need to continue?"

Rose scowls at Eva and it makes her look older than ever. The lines on her normally beautiful face reflect the ugliness that bubbles away below the surface. "Why do you always have to be such a drama queen, Eva? You insist on being the centre of attention, constantly making up stories to draw everyone's sympathy to you, continually creating or exaggerating. You are a grown woman now, Eva. You must stop this."

"Did I make it up when I told you that Claude tried to touch me and that he made me feel gross and uncomfortable with his sleazy ways? You didn't care what he did to me so long as he didn't leave you. I got out and away from his wandering hands, but I jumped out of the fire and into the frying pan. Why didn't you believe me?"

"I did believe you, Evangelina, but you made a mountain out of a molehill. Men like to touch women. It's no big deal."

I growl from deep down in my chest. "Only if the women are of age and give their consent to touching, Rose. What the fuck is wrong with you?" Ace's voice comes through. It's lower and more menacing than mine and when Rose cringes away, Ace chirupps in satisfaction .

"You let your husband touch me. Your own daughter. Can you not see how twisted that is?" Rose doesn't answer. Eva's body begins to tremble and her eyes flash silver. Aiden notices too. "Answer me." Rose falls off the chair and onto the floor in submission to Eva's power. I would be proud, but my daughter is starting to lose control.

"Aiden," I warn him, and he gives his nod of agreement and talks to Eva as we planned.

"Shortie, have a little sip of water, remember what we are trying to protect here." Eva accepts the drink and gulps. Her eyes are returning to blue, and her body stops shaking as her mate coaxes her to calm down.

"I have two questions. Just two questions, Rose. Answer them truthfully and you can leave. Did you ever truly want and love me or was I just a cash cow to you?" Eva blinks away the tears.

"There are no repercussions for my honest answers?" Rose asks, and Eva shakes her head at her. "Then I will tell you. No. I didn't want to keep you. By the time I found out I was pregnant, it was too late to get rid of you and then, when you were born, I placed you up for adoption, but your father begged me not to give you up. He told me he would contribute financially if I provided a home for you. It seemed as good a job as any."

Rose continues to sit, unaffected by her cold admission, but we all shudder at how anyone could be so unfeeling. Eva's tears stream silently down her face, but she hasn't made a sound since she asked her first question.

"Thank you for your honesty. And finally: Ryan... How could

you? You are my mother; how could you do that to me? Did you love him? How long did it continue for? Did you know how he was treating me?" My little girl has done so well to hold on to her composure, but the hurt, the humiliation and the pain are taking its toll. Her body is practically vibrating, we need to end this as soon as Rose gives her answer.

"Well, it's simple biology, Eva, I did it because I wanted to. Ryan was young and handsome and very sexually frustrated. I kept him satisfied for you so he didn't go looking elsewhere. No, I didn't love him. What was the next part?" My hackles raise as Rose looks indifferently at her nails. However, Aiden answers her, saving me from having to.

"How long did it continue for, and did you know how Ryan was treating her?" he spits out at her, while Rose rolls her eyes in bored defiance.

"It started the day after you introduced him to me and continued throughout your marriage, although it was just blow jobs and it was mostly because he blackmailed me. And yes, of course, I knew how he was treating you. He took great delight in telling me everything that happened between you both. He threatened to be rough with you on your wedding night if I didn't sleep with him too. Then he called me the next day and told me he destroyed you and laughed as he did."

"GET OUT! Get her out! And stay out, stay away from me. You are a monster and I do not want you in my life, Rose. You are poisonous."

Beta Preston and Lydia grab Rose and drag her out as Eva loses control. She howls in agony as her body convulses. "Xavier, I need you to help me, we're going to lose her. I can't lose her," Aiden shouts to me. His voice is full of pain and panic.

Eva's howls turn to blood-curdling screams, the walls start to tremble, and cracks run through them, debris falls all around us and dust puffs out angrily. A massive crack opens up in the floor right where Eva is violently shaking on the floor.

I've only just got my daughter back in my life and terror and overwhelming pain fills me as I contemplate the fact that I'm about to lose her all over again.

*** **Aiden** ***

Excruciating pain travels throughout my whole body. I didn't tell Eva last night, but when she was reliving her memory of her wedding night, I felt every ounce of pain along with her. As her body writhes in agony on the cell floor, Roman howls inside me, a haunting howl that scares me... what is happening to me and my wolf?

When Eva starts to convulse, I lose my composure. I am going to lose her. I am going to lose the love of my life and our pup too, because I can't save her from the hurt she had to endure while waiting for me.

I get down on my knees next to her. "Eva, baby, please! Please come back to me. She didn't love you, but I do, we all do. You have so many people here who love and respect you and want to help you through this." Her movements slow but the screaming doesn't and neither does the pain destroying my own body. "Eva, don't let this beat you. You've got to try, for you, for me, for Summer and for our pup. You have to try for your dad, stepmom, your friends and your pack. We all love you."

"Mum and Dad. I need Mum and Dad," she tells me in between sobs of anguish. I don't understand. She's just told Rose to leave and now she wants her back?

"Xavier, she needs you and Mum. She's asking for mum and dad." Xavier's eyes glaze over, then he enters the cell and holds

Eva, cradling her head.

"Daddy's here. I'm never going to leave. I love you with all my heart and your mum will be here soon too. We both love you the whole world and more, Evangelina, don't ever forget that. I am so proud of you and how you have conducted yourself throughout this whole ordeal. I admire you so much for accepting my mate as your mother figure."

Lydia! Now it makes sense. Eva told me that Lydia insisted she call her Mum and that's who she needs now. She needs a proper mother's love.

Lydia dashes into the cell. "I'm here, X. What can I do to help?" Xavier instructs her to hold Eva's hands and talk to her. Slowly but surely, Eva's screams turn to cries of grief and anguish.

"Oh, my sweet girl. Don't worry, Mum's here now. Mum and Dad are here, and we'll always be here to love and support you and our grandpups. Let it all out."

Lydia grasps one of Eva's hands and strokes her face with the other hand. She makes soothing noises at my mate that comfort her and reassure her.

I feel completely redundant. I don't know what else to do to help, but my concern for Eva and our pup still weighs heavy on me. I can feel every bit of pain her body is having to endure, and I don't know how much more it can take.

I mindlink directly to Lina. *Please, Lina, let us help. We love you. We love our pup. I'm beyond worried about Eva, her body cannot cope with it anymore.*

Roman. I need Roman. I need my mate, Lina's shaky voice tells me.

I shift straight away, unable to comprehend how the hell I'm meant to help my mate in wolf form. As soon as I give

Roman control, he wraps his body around Eva's and almost immediately Eva starts to calm down. Her body becomes balmy, covered in a sweaty sheen, but her screams stop. Every so often, Roman bursts out into the grief-filled howling that is inside me, and I notice that Eva is emitting the same sound. That is Lina. Lina is using Eva's body to express her pain.

Roman links words of comfort to Lina and I am so proud of him. He instinctively knows what his mate needs and gives it to her. His easy acceptance of both Eva and Lina and his willingness to endure whatever pain he had to in order to help them are a credit to him and him alone.

I realise that I have wanted to limit the pain that Eva must feel, but the only way to heal is to walk through it and then let it go. I hate the thought of her being in pain, but that is the only way. She must face it and, therefore, we will face it together. From now on, I will ensure we always do. She will never have to do anything alone anymore. She will know nothing but love and acceptance from this moment until her last. No one will ever mistreat her again; I will skin them alive if they even try.

Aiden, Lina is almost back to being an ordinary werewolf. The manifestations are mostly reversed now that the pain of the past is addressed. Eva needs to rest now to protect our pup. This has been hard on both of them. We need to keep looking after them. Roman is clear about what must happen, but I can tell from his strained tone that he still has concerns about them.

I shift back to my human form and pull on some clothes before I lift Eva up in my arms. She resembles a limp rag doll. She still whimpers as she sleeps, and her tears cling like dewdrops on her eyelashes.

"Where are you moving her to, son? Is she going to be okay?" Xavier has remained with us throughout the whole ordeal, and I had been so focused on helping Eva and Lina that I forgot to include him in the progression I could see and feel through my bond.

"Sorry, Xavier, I keep forgetting that I need to tell you what's happening too. Lina says the manifestations have mostly reversed but Eva needs to rest and be looked after for a while. I am taking her home. The cells are no longer safe with all those cracks, and I want her to be waited on, hand and foot for the remainder of her confinement. She isn't out of the woods yet, but with some tender loving care and pampering, I am sure she'll be feeling better soon. I really thought I was about to lose her."

Xavier gives me a pat on the shoulder and back. "She's strong, Aiden, stronger than any of us. Probably the strongest She-Wolf I've ever met."

I smile because I completely agree. Eva is the strongest person I have ever met.

When I reach our apartment, Eva stirs and whimpers. "Aidy? Where are we? Tell Roman I am sorry, I am so sorry for causing him so much pain." I shush her.

"It's fine, Roman wanted to help and now we know we can get through anything together. Come on, let's get in bed and snuggle our sunshine girl. This has been the hardest time of our lives. It's time for us to relax and let the healing do its job.

"Thank you, Aiden. Thank you for loving me."

I will love her with every inch of my capacity until the end of time. She is my mate, my love and the inspiration in my life. I have never felt prouder that she is mine.

*** **Salma** ***

I march into that hospital room. Now that I know Alejandro is safe, I am ready to give him a bollocking for almost getting himself killed.

"Chula! You are a sight for sore eyes," Ale says to me through half-opened eyes, obviously thinking I will be happy and relieved to see him.

"Don't you Chula me, Alejandro Suarez! How dare you nearly get yourself fucking killed? If anyone is going to kill you… it'll be me. Understand? I swear to God you've taken years off my life with that stunt. Don't make me knock some sense into you, because I will."

He looks pale and tired and although he gives me a small smile, it's far from his usual one, and the fight evaporates from me. I love him and I'm glad he is safe, but goodness, he is paying for my next hairdresser's appointment. My hair will be full of grey after all the worrying I've done over him.

"I understand, mi amour. I am an inconsiderate bastard and I promise, next time I will hand you the gun. But right now, I need you to help me make a claim on the Serrano firm. We own their asses now, that's the least I'm owed for the fucking run around Tony gave us and for the mess he has made of my leg." He winces as he tries to move, and I hold him down to stop him from moving again.

"Just lie down and relax, Ale, everything is taken care of. I do have to leave you for a little while now, but you can use this time to contemplate how many different ways I will torture you if you ever do this again. And you can rest and sleep too." I kiss him gently on the head, the effects of the pain relief make him drowsy, and his eyes struggle to stay open. "I love you, Alejandro, I'll be back soon."

"Are you ready, Mrs Morales?" I shake my head at Willy.

"Not yet, Willy, I have one more person I want on this mission. It might take me a while to persuade them though." I smile at my hidden joke that no one else will get yet.

While I brought Ale here to get treatment right away, Raul, Matteo and Penelope secured the Serrano Firm for us. Everything is ours. Ale is now a Don in his own right, and I am so proud of him. Dominga is dead, and although I don't relish the task of telling my little brother that she is dead, I am relieved that my adoption of him will be straightforward and uncontested.

The true icing on the cake, though, is that Junior has been spotted looking around for Dominga and he has another female with him. He is still sniffing around Serrano property, unable to find his lover.

My plan is to go and take him out once and for all, but first, I need a sparring partner. I can think of no one better.

I walk through the packhouse and knock on the door. Beta Preston opens the door and looks at me in confusion when he does. "Hi, I know it's late or is it early? I didn't even know what time it was anymore. Is Amber awake? We're going on a mission."

*** Junior ***

Dominga is on the missing list and panic rises fast within me. Where the fuck is she? After searching the hotel we stayed at and finding all our belongings gone without a trace, I have no option but to go and find her. I have to try her home, her club, her Don's address. Anywhere she may be.

"Junior, let's just forget about Dominga. If we go back home, the pack will follow you. Your dad is getting old and soft and if you challenge him, you'll win, and then we can be The Luna and Alpha of the Moon Stone."

Her ravings and ramblings are really starting to grate right down my nerves. She doesn't seem to realise that we will be detained on sight and both of us will lose our throats. We are in too deep with everything now, but Nikki is deranged, or stupid. Maybe she is both. Even if I could depend on the pack to protect me from the Mafia, they will never stand for my attempt to kidnap a small child or for seriously injuring a human. If Dominga is not here to help me, I know I am screwed. I will have to go rogue and hide.

"I am not going to challenge my father. Now, will you stop your nagging and help me find her. She is our last hope." I speak to her slowly like she is having trouble comprehending what I am saying, but if anything, this angers her into more rants.

"What is your obsession with her, Junior? She is older than your mother and her face is like a leather chamois. She must be good in the sack because she has you obsessed with her." Nikki's jealousy is starting to show and the cracks in her mental state are becoming large gorges. I can't remember the last time she ate or had more than a twenty-minute nap.

"Will you leave off about her? She has the money and power to get us away from here with our throats intact. That's what you want, right? To live long enough to have your pup?" I raise my voice and instantly regret it, so again, I use the possibility of a pup to my advantage. It's all she is concerned about. I walk towards Dominga's neighbourhood when Nikki shouts out to me from the dark and malodorous alleyway we have been hiding in.

"I will feel it if you fuck her. And if you fuck her... I will harm both of you. Do not betray me, Junior. You are mine now."

Has she seriously lost her marbles? "You threaten me again, bitch, and I'll solve both our problems by ripping your throat out. Is that what you want? There will be no pups then. So, get off my back and concentrate on finding Dominga." I growl at her, and she submits with a whimper.

"Yes, mate," she spits out at me between her teeth, trying once again to rile and defy me. I grab her by her long hair.

"Don't 'yes, mate' me. If Dominga hears you saying that, she'll know. Is that what you want? We need her to get away from the council and the Mafia. Do you realise how much shit we are in? We'll lose our throats, Nikki."

Nikki laughs manically at me. "Take a look around. She's not here. Don't you get it? She's probably gone abroad to safety without you, and you are running around like a little puppy trying to find her. What is it going to take for you to get the hint?" My palm stings from slapping her soundly across her face, it shocks me as much as it shocks her.

"She won't have left. You need to calm down. You're the one who said this was a business arrangement. So, stop being jealous and bratty and fucking find her."

I push her away from me, but the hair on the back of my neck stands on end. Is that Nikki's doing?

It's not me, I feel it too. She mindlinks me and I nod to show I understand as I look around.

I search the area and find no one and nothing out of the ordinary, but obviously quarrelling with Nikki attracted attention. "I'm sorry. I won't fuck her, but we do need her, Nikki. How else am I going to get you and our pup out of here?" Brute force isn't working. I think Nikki actually likes it, but appealing to her maternal side seems to work.

"I'm sorry, Junior. I can't find her. She must be dead." Before I know what is happening, she leans in and kisses me. My wolf growls in appreciation, but I still have enough sense to know this is dangerous. My mind and thoughts are everywhere. She can't be dead. We are meant to be in this together. How am I going to get to safety now?

"Nikki! Stop it. Don't say shit like that, concentrate on finding her." I push her against the wall and my hand wraps around her neck. She is not the mate I want. She isn't even fated for me. I want Dominga. And this little whore is going to prevent that and tortures me by telling me that my true love is dead? I press against her neck. "I gave you a chance, Nikki. I gave you a chance to be my mate and carry my pups, but you are completely insane. I don't want you. I want Dominga. Are you going to cooperate?" She nods at me with tears in her eyes.

I loosen my grip. I do want and need my heir and I am pretty certain she will be carrying a pup by now. In my moment of distraction, she manages to claw down my face with her dirty talons.

"I'd love to cooperate, but I can't feel her or sense her. She's not here, Junior. We are wasting our time. So, we go rogue on our own or you challenge your father for the Moon Stone. Stop being a big wuss and make a decision."

"SHE IS NOT DEAD!" She can't be. We had so many plans, and I need her to bail me out of the shit. I finally snap. "I'll tell you who is dead though: you. You and the fucking pup inside you because I don't want you. You're a useless whore and I don't want your tainted pup. Goodbye, Nikki".

This time I have made up my mind. I am not dragging this crazy, dumb-ass woman along with me. Pup or no pup, I cannot bear another moment in her presence. I choke the life out of her and, although she resists me, I am too strong for her.

"Get your stinking hands off her, mutt." Before I can turn around, something hits me across the head. I have no option but to let go of Nikki's throat as I fall unconscious on the floor.

*** Salma ***

At long last, I have my father's murderer in my sights. The red mist doesn't descend on me. I have never been clearer about what I want and how I intend on doing it. When I see him assaulting who I now know to be his mate, I smile internally. I have absolutely no remorse, no qualms, and no hesitation about killing Junior Woodward. He is a disease.

"Get your stinking hands off her, mutt," Amber shouts at him and I lift my Glock and whack him full force across the head.

As he falls to the ground at an odd angle, he mutters, "Oh, fuck!" to himself.

"Are you okay? Let me take a look at your neck?" Amber picks the woman up off the floor, but the woman doesn't appear happy with the situation.

"Get off me. I don't need *your* help," she shouts abrasively at Amber.

"She's just saved your life, don't speak to her like that." I stand between Amber and the beaten rag of a woman who screeches and flails at my friend.

"I wouldn't even be here with that big idiot if it wasn't for her. I would be at home with my mate and his pup inside me instead of the pup of a man who disgusts me. You took away my future. You took away my life." She crumples in my arms and sobs and my eyes fill with tears of compassion.

"I am so sorry for what I did, Nikki," Amber says. "I am sorry that my actions destroyed your future. I cannot tell you how sorry I am that my actions resulted in you losing everything. I was trying to rescue my brother. Junior had already attacked him once and then Aiden was taken again, and I panicked. I regret killing your mate and if I could turn back time, I would."

I watch in shock as Amber Goldrick pours her heart out and apologises for her action. However, the biggest revelation is Nikki's reaction to Amber's apology.

As her shoulders slump in defeat, Nikki ages in front of my eyes. "I'm so tired of hating you, and of pining for my mate and what should have been our family. It was everything I ever wanted in life, and I was burning with hatred for you for taking that away. But now you're here in front of me and I can see you're not a monster. I can see you are just a werewolf who made a mistake. I've made enough of them myself."

The silent tears that stain her face never cease and her eyes burn with sincerity as Nikki pleads for her life and for that of her unborn child.

"Please don't kill me... I think I am carrying Junior's pup. It's really early but I want this child so much. It's all I've ever wanted. I promise I'll behave, I'll be on my best behaviour. Please, I am begging you: don't kill me or my baby."

"You have to reverse your curse, Nikki. You have cursed all the pups that will be born in my pack. If you don't agree to reverse the curse, they will kill you. I will stand and fight for you and your baby if you promise to reverse the curse." Nikki nods her agreement to Amber but adds that if she is pregnant, she would only be able to do the reversal once her baby is born.

Outwardly, I roll my eyes as Amber holds her hand out to Nikki, clearly offering her an olive branch, but deep down, I am happy that they both manage to find a positive resolution despite the ugliness of the whole situation.

There will be no such resolution for Junior. I call my back-up and send Amber back with her prisoner.

"Sal, are you sure you'll be okay here? I can come straight back." However, I know all about Amber's suspended sentence and now that she has settled things with Nikki, I want her as far away from here as possible.

"I'll be fine. I am finally going to get vengeance for my papa. Check in on Ale for me please." As we embrace, Amber discreetly passes me a sheathed double-ended dagger I had been admiring earlier.

"Just in case," she whispers to me. Yes, just in case.

CHAPTER SEVENTEEN

The Fighter

*** Eva ***

Waking up in my own bed in my own room with Summer and Aiden makes up for the fact that my whole body aches and pulses. It's like an electric current is charging through all my nerve endings. Yesterday was a lot harder than anything else I have had to endure so far. Although I knew hearing Rose's confessions would be difficult, I had been naïve in thinking that she may be remorseful for everything she had done.

Even though my body is in pain, I feel lighter and at peace with what has happened. It isn't nice, it certainly isn't pretty, but the truth is a healer and I'm sure once the physical toll eases, I will be ready to move away from that part of my life.

Lina has been incredibly quiet since last night. She cried for Roman, and he didn't let us down. The way he nuzzled me, comforted me, and accepted every part of both Lina and I was overwhelming. I am eager to have Lina and Roman finally meet and mate too. But first, I have a little one to grow in my tummy. I whisper to my tiny bump that's hardly even visible yet, though I know my baby is growing strong inside me. I stroke my tummy, hoping that my baby knows how loved and wanted they are.

"How are you doing in there, my little pup? Mummy is so sorry if you felt any pain yesterday. Hopefully, that's the worst of it all over and done with. We are all looking forward to meeting you and for you to join our family. I love you, little one, please hold on tight in there."

Tears sting my eyes; I love Summer and my new baby so much that I cannot comprehend how my own mother could feel the way she does about me. I could never ever treat my children that way. I would never conduct myself in such a lowly manner. A part of my healing has been the realisation that Rose is damaged. This all stemmed from her actions, and I can move on now, safe in the knowledge that no matter what I did, even if I had managed to be the most perfect daughter in the world, Rose would still have behaved the same because that's who she is.

It is a relief that I will never have to see her again. I can't have her in my life, not when I have a daughter who will be learning what it is to be a strong, principled woman from me.

"Hey, baby, you're awake." I turn towards Aiden's voice. He looks exhausted too, still absolutely gorgeous but tired and wary. His black hair flops down and the urge to run my fingers through it overcomes me.

"I am, but you should try and get more sleep, you look tired." He leans up and kisses me on my head as I reply to him. "I need to go to the toilet and find a hot water bottle or something. My whole body aches."

Aiden will not hear of it. He tells me to go to the toilet while he organises everything and, sure enough, once I pee and freshen up, I return to the bedroom and Aiden has summoned hot water bottles, hot tea, aspirin, and a couple of bottles of massage oil.

"Don't worry," he reassures me. "These oils are recommended

by the doctor herself for expectant mothers. I know you are probably too sore and tired right now, but I'd love to give you a massage later." My heart fills with joy. It's been the crappiest time, but with Aiden by my side, I know we can weather any storm. We are solid and the future is bright for us.

"I love you." It's a sweet and simple statement but it's true, and there was nothing more romantic than honesty.

"I love you too, and now you're out of your cell, you have my mark and you're carrying my pup… when are you going to make a happy and honest man out of me?" I am eager to make us official too.

"Soon, really soon. I promise." As the warmth from the hot water bottles seeps through my skin and deep into my bones, my eyelids start to droop again. But before I fall asleep, there is one more thing I must do. "Could you pass me the phone please, Aiden? I need to make one last call so I can move on to the present and future with you."

Aiden passes the phone to me and looks at me with concern. "Don't overdo it," he warns me.

"I won't, this shouldn't take more than a couple of minutes." I tap my phone and pull up Luke's phone number. I take a deep breath and puff out my chest before dialling. It rings twice before he answers. "Hi, is that Luke? It's Eva Smith-Jones."

*** Junior ***

Groaning as I wake up in a cold, dark and damp room, I find I am completely naked and all four of my limbs are bound with rope, which stretches and pulls them tightly. My mouth is gagged.

I hear the men call for someone. "Mrs Morales, he's waking up." My bowels turn to ice water. The Mafia have caught me. I am surely about to be tortured to my eventual death and, despite my posturing, I am terrified of what Salma Morales is capable of.

"It's nice of you to finally join us, Junior." I try to plead with her, but the gag prevents me so all that echoes around the stark room is my muffled moans. "Shhh. You're going to listen while I talk." Her cold and controlled demeanour scares me more than if she were to shout and threaten me.

She stands in front of my naked body with her hands behind her back and looks me up and down.

"I must say I can see why Dominga was attracted to you. You have a decent body, and your cock is thick and long... did you know how to use it?"

Under her hard stare, my cock seems to shrivel and invert.

She smiles as she looks away for a moment. "Karl here thought we should cut your dick off and make you eat it." Another man laughs in the background. "After all, you took away something that was precious and sacred to me, and the saying is an eye for an eye, isn't it?"

I shake my head and moan continually at her as much as I can through the gag. Not my cock! Anything but my cock, for fucks sake. Tears begin to sting my eyes. I'm in all this shit and it's way over my head.

"Oh, don't worry, I ruled that one out. It's not final enough and a bit too messy for my liking." With her arms still behind her back she paces in front of me. "Now Willy thought you might have loved Dominga, and your new mate was right. Dominga is dead, her body is on a slab in my private mortuary, so we thought we could have baked her into a pie for you. A nice, big, juicy Dominga pie. What do you think? Do you fancy a bit of that?"

I shake my head furiously at her, no. No, NO, NO! I don't want to eat Dominga. Pain twists in my gut. I can't believe Dominga is dead, she can't be. I don't want to believe it.

"Oh, yes. She's dead, and to prove that I only tell the truth, I brought you something to confirm it." She nods her head, and two burly men walk into the room, pushing a serving trolley between them. They lift the large silver dome cover from the top of the trolley and Dominga's bloody head sits there.

Bile rushes up from my stomach, burning my throat, but the gag prevents its exit and so, I have to choke it back down.

"I usually pull every fingernail and toenail out on the people who slight me. I once even pulled someone's teeth, but I'm not going near your mouth after you just puked up. My other favourite thing to do is to cut off people's eyelids and then they have no option but to watch as I end the world they live in. That would be appropriate, seeing as you ended the world I lived in when you killed my papa."

I cry out, and my knees buckle. The thought of losing my eyelids is grotesque. I need to talk this out with Salma, but she won't let me talk. Panic and fear fill my entire being. There is no way out. I am overwhelmed with terror and Salma's self-controlled, cool as a cucumber façade is frightening the living daylights out of me.

"I could have granted you a quick death, a bullet right between the eyes just like that backstabbing whore, but you don't deserve the dignity and swiftness of relief that would give you."

Right now, I would give anything for a quick death. I don't want to plead for my life. I just want this to end soon. I can't take much more.

"I could have given you a drawn-out death. Scaphism… I've

always wanted to do it but it's so messy and time-consuming. Hung-drawn-and-quartered... I didn't want so many people being able to take credit for killing you. I want that pleasure all for myself."

A small grin spreads across her face at that anecdote, marking one of the only times she has shown any emotion in front of me.

"The newest torture I've found is the Spanish Donkey... you'd love it. It's a large triangular shape that your victim sits on like they are riding a horse or a donkey. But it has razor sharp edges, you would have your legs tied up and they would slowly be pulled, forcing your body to completely split in half."

Her eyes light up and I thrash my body about as hard as I can to try and escape. I don't want to be slowly split in half. I'm crying and trying to plead. It's all futile as there is no escape for me now.

"You killed my papa. And now I want you to know that I am going to kill you, but I am going to do this my way. I am the Donna here now, and men like you have been oppressing women like me for years. Telling us we aren't good enough, or we aren't able, or that you are superior. Forcing us into marriages because we are told we cannot do it because the Mafia is a man's world, and I am just a girl."

The hair stands up at the back of my neck and my skin puckers into goose pimples. I get the overwhelming urge to defecate, so great is the fear building inside me.

"Well, look at this girl. Look at me. It's my turn to conquer the world and I am going to start with you."

*** **Amber** ***

This is not the outcome I have been anticipating. The more I discovered about Nikki, the more convinced I had become that I am going to rip her throat out. She went after MY mate. She tried to hurt me through the sacred bond I have with Preston. She promised to destroy me. She made this personal against me. And I get it. I truly get it. I killed her mate.

Everything changes the moment I see her pleading desperately for her unborn child's safety, as Junior, the fucking big bully, pins her to the wall by her throat. She is just as broken and fucked up as I am, except I have my family, and most importantly, I still have my mate and the promise of our pups to come. She has nothing left.

I am not a cold-blooded killer. I didn't kill her mate in a premeditated or targeted attack. There hasn't been a day and night when I haven't thought about the man whose life I snuffed out when I responded to what I thought was the second abduction of my brother and Alpha. The weight of my sword as it connected with the junction between his neck and shoulder still wakes me during the night. The sight of his open body will haunt me until my dying day.

So, as this broken, bedraggled woman accuses me of destroying her life, I do the right thing. I hold my hands up and apologise, because ultimately, I did. I didn't intend on doing it, I didn't set out with that objective, but nevertheless, that is what had happened. I killed her mate and her hopes and dreams with him.

I don't expect her to accept my apology. If I am being truthful, I wouldn't. I probably would kill her on sight if our roles were reversed. But she does accept it and my own guilt and discomfort ease when she does.

I'm not completely naïve. I know what Nikki is capable of and so to prevent her escaping, I cuff her to me and give her the same serum she injected into Gamma Max. It is only a tiny dose, but it is enough to subdue her wolf and mage powers until I get her back to the Onyx Moon and hand her over to my brother and Alpha Xavier.

We travel in silence for a short distance before Nikki turns to me, concern lining her face. "Is that woman going to kill Junior?" Without much thought, I give a short nod to her question, and she loses all control. "Let me out! I have to help him. I can save him; I don't want him to die. Not again."

Her gut-wrenching screams fill the car, and it takes all my might to hold her down as she thrashes against me, the car door, and the seats. I panic when I hear my arm snap. It'll heal fast enough but it will make holding Nikki a bit more tiresome.

"It's too late. Nikki, stop. It's already too late. The Mafia have him and he's done some serious shit, including killing a powerful Spanish Don and critically injuring a human, causing her to miscarry her baby. He made threats against his sister and tried to hurt her daughter. He's got no chance of surviving tonight, Nikki. I'm sorry, but you seriously cannot want to be mistreated by him for the rest of your life?"

Her shoulders shake as she inconsolably sobs into my chest. "You should have just killed me. I don't think I can survive another dead mate. I can't go through that pain again."

Onyx River can be seen in the near distance, so I periodically try to mindlink Preston to get back up to help me, hoping we are close enough for me to reach him, but there is no reply. I know he is helping Aiden and Eva today with Eva's mother and therapy, but I thought he would be finished by now.

I try Aiden but he blocks me. *Not now, Amber. Try Billy.*

So, I mindlink Delta Billy, who arranges a Delta contingent to meet the car. "Be gentle with her, she might be pregnant. Can you get Alpha Xavier and Luna Lydia here, please? I need to discuss something with them. Tell them we will be in the hospital."

We enter the hospital and the first person I see is Gamma Max. "What the fuck is she doing here?" he growls at me.

"She's my prisoner and she has been assaulted and needs to be seen. We'll stay on this side. Go back to your mate, Gamma." I try to use my authority as Lieutenant, but Max's anger overrides me. He is riled and his back is up.

"I'm not happy about this, Lieutenant. I don't want her here. Make sure she stays away from my mate."

He walks away, leaving me under no illusions of how hard my task will be to get them to spare Nikki's life, a life she now no longer wants. For fucks sake.

Nikki continually whimpers and cries, and her thin and emaciated body trembles. By the time Alpha Xavier and Luna Lydia arrive, she is talking manically and incoherently to herself too.

"Lieutenant Amber, please call the Council and tell them she is here. She isn't our problem anymore," Alpha Xavier instructs me.

"I'm afraid it's not as simple as that. Please, sit down and I'll tell you everything I know." And so, I explain to them how Nikki and Junior had mated and marked each other, that the Mafia had caught their son and that Nikki is highly likely to be carrying his pup.

By the end of my telling, Luna Lydia looks ashen and has to sit down and Alpha Xavier holds his hand in his hands. "My son isn't coming home, is he?" Uncomfortably, I confirm that Junior is as good as dead now.

"Is all this true, Nikki? Did you and Junior mate and mark each other? Could you be pregnant with his pup?" Through her nonsensical ramblings, she confirms what I have told the Woodwards.

"I know this is a difficult time for you, but if she is pregnant, that is your grandpup." Lydia processes the thought before Xavier has a chance to absorb the information.

"X, this is our grandpup. X, say something please." They look at each other as they mindlink and I shift awkwardly like a voyeur in their private moment.

"I would like for Nikki to have a scan to confirm there is indeed a pup. We will decide from there what will happen," Alpha Xavier requests and so, I quickly locate the nurses and tell them this is urgent, and they quickly arrange the staff and equipment.

Twenty minutes later, I sit at the side of Nikki, and I am stunned into silence when the nurse confirms not only is Nikki pregnant, but she is also expecting twins.

Nikki smiled at the grainy black and white image on the screen. "My family," she whispers gently as she reaches out at the screen. For the first time since she arrived here, she appears settled and rational.

The calm doesn't last very long. Alpha Xavier promises to keep Nikki safe until her twins are delivered and then she will come to us to reverse her curse. Before we can complete a blood promise, Nikki begins screaming. A high pitched, blood-curdling howl of pain, something I have never heard before.

Nikki writhes in agony, clutching her chest. Perspiration beads her forehead before eventually drenching her whole body. She howls like a wild animal and the sound echoes all around the hospital, attracting the attention of other patients and staff.

Lydia cries too, obviously realising this is the pain of the bond breaking. Nikki feels everything her mate is. When the emptiness and pain of the broken bond hit, it leaves her a shell of a person. She rocks back and forth, her eyes large, glassy, vacant orbs. Nikki's mind has completely broken. She lies on the hospital bed, catatonic. The only sign of life is her occasional whimpers of pain.

Junior must be dead.

*** **Salma** ***

Patience is not a virtue I am blessed with, but today I can wait. I will wait until that piece of shit wakes up before I kill him. I have visualised this moment many times since I found out Junior Woodward is responsible for killing my papa.

We bring him to the docks and to the same warehouse his lover died in. I inject him with wolfsbane, which eradicates any risk his wolf poses and stops his superhuman abilities such as speed, strength, and fast healing. We are now evenly matched and that makes me feel even more powerful.

I have fantasised about slowly torturing him until he squeals like a pig for his mami. I dream of a nice clean gunshot to his head. None of them seem appropriate and it takes a while to figure out that it doesn't matter how he dies. It won't bring my papa back. My heart will remain broken for him. It shattered my heart into a million pieces that he took my papa away in such a way. I don't think my heart will ever feel whole again without him, but taking vengeance for him will allow me to move on in the knowledge that I made the culprit pay.

So, after I mind fuck him a little bit, I get down to business. I want to get back to Ale. I want my ice-cream.

I walk towards him with my hands behind my back, relishing the small, childish whimpers that emit from him. "Well, look how times change. You are here at my mercy, and I am the Donna of the biggest firm in Britain. My papa's legacy lives on, whereas yours ends right here, right now."

His unclear protests continue to echo about the room.

"Carry on interrupting me and I will draw this out, Junior. You attempted to hurt Summer. You seriously hurt my friend, causing her the unimaginable pain of losing her baby. You have threatened my best friend, your own sister. All of these things are the reason why I want to hurt and humiliate you."

I stop in front of him and look him dead in the eyes, the same eyes as my best friend, and my heart twists in pain.

"You broke my heart when you killed my papa. Now, I'm going to take yours." From my belt, behind my back, I take out the dagger gifted to me by Amber and plunge it into Junior's chest right up to the hilt. Warm blood covers my hand as I twist the dagger and drag it down, separating his breastbone.

The life drains from him, but I am not finished. I pull the offending dagger out of his chest, passing it to one of my men. Then I force my hand into Junior's chest, clutching on to his heart and yank it out of his body. Junior makes a horrible gurgling noise before dropping dead on the spot. I throw his heart on the floor and stomp on it and confidently walk away from him.

"Can you guys clean this up, please? I'm going back to see Alejandro so I can share my ice-cream with him."

*** Aiden ***

Eva dials the number for the boy she was supposed to go on a date with all of those years ago. A twinge of jealousy flares inside me but I quickly dispel it. Eva is mine, her heart belongs to me. This is nothing more than her settling the past for our collective future.

I wink at her, noticing her nerves and wanting to reassure her.

"Hello, is that Luke? Hi, it's Eva. Thank you for taking my call."

I put a thumb up to her and she returns it with a small smile on her face. She will shout for me if she needs me. I return briefly to my Alpha duties that have been neglected for far too long, but I can still hear Eva's conversation.

"I wanted to call you because I found out recently that... that it was you who asked me on a date and not Ryan. He told me that you had set us up, I got a text from you and everything saying you thought we would be great together."

I can hear her making agreeing noises back to the inaudible voice coming from the phone.

"Yes, I know. Why didn't you tell me? I did? I mean, well yeah, I suppose. I got Summer from it, and she is one of the best things to ever happen to me. No, I'm sorry too. I hope you're happy, Luke. Yes, I have, I'm really, really happy, and incredibly lucky. Aiden... he's amazing and we're expecting a baby. All the best to you too, Luke. Bye."

A warm feeling spread throughout my chest. I pop my head back into the living room and watch my girl as she watches television and laughs at the terrible jokes. "Are you feeling better, Shortie?"

Her eyes regard me with the remnants of her smile still there. "The best. I am finally free." Those little words set my heart alight. Eva's pain used to restrict us. I didn't realise how much it weighed on her, and therefore us, until it was gone. My girl had been similar to a fish stuck on a fishing line. Her therapy has allowed her to be thrown back into the sea, free to swim and live and, most importantly, love again.

"Good. Now we concentrate on your pregnancy and our Mating Ceremony and on us." My cock stiffens in reaction to the scent of her arousal which fills the room. Summer is still asleep in our bed, and I have been summoned to the hospital by my sister, and whatever happened overnight does not sound pleasant. I have also had an irate Max asking me if Melanie could continue to recuperate in the packhouse instead of the hospital. I have no idea what the issue is, but sooner or later, I am going to flip out if things do not start to calm down and fast. No one can accuse us of having a boring start to our relationship, that's for sure!

"Lina is very happy and content. She has to wait until after our pup is born but she is finally ready to reveal herself to Roman so they can mate and mark each other too. His support last night sealed it for her, she adores him as much as I do now."

Too right she does, I'm a catch! Watch out, human, they'll both be fighting for me. Roman, the cheeky scoundrel laughs as I grumble.

Eva sits looking at me, biting her bottom lip, with a hint of a grin. "You know we love you too, Alpha. I cannot resist you." Where has my little shy and timid mate gone? The strong and fierce warrior in front of me, with her teasing and flirting, is the same girl I fell in love with, but now she has shown me the strength she always had inside her. She isn't strengthened by the suffering; she endured because she is strong. She always had that strength within her.

I sweep her up and kiss her, I want nothing more than a week in bed with my precious love, but her tummy rumbles and then Summer runs in. "To be continued," I tell her and her eyes flash as she moans a little, clenching involuntarily as she does. I love the way she reacts to me. Every touch is exquisite and leaves me craving more and I know she feels the same.

"Mummy! Daddy!" Our little girl shouts to us, bounding into Eva's arms. I know it's been hard for them to be separated by bars. All they had was each other for such a long time. It's good to see them able to hug one another without a barrier in the way.

"What would you like to do on your first day of freedom?" I am hoping I get to tease her some more but from the expression on her face, I can tell she already has some ideas.

"I need to get both Summer and I something nice to wear for Amber and Preston's Mating Ceremony and I was hoping we could stop by the hospital to visit Melanie and Alejandro." A pink blush covers her cheeks as she looks down timidly. Goddess above, she is so fucking hot! "I also hoped with you being the Alpha and all, you could arrange for us to have a scan so we can check that everything is okay with the baby?"

I pull her back to me, kissing her on the temple. "Whatever my Luna wants, my Luna will surely have. I will call them straight away. I can't wait to see our little pup." I am such a lucky man. I can hardly believe this is my life.

While Eva calls the seamstress and the hairdresser, I mindlink Max. He is already moving Melanie's stuff to his apartment. *She is not staying in that hospital while that creature is there, Alpha. I'm sorry, but no. My mate's mental health is more important, and this could knock her right back.*

I am perplexed. Is he referring to Alejandro? *Mr Suarez is there as my esteemed guest; you will mind your tongue and show him the respect his station commands, Gamma.*

I physically feel Max's confusion. *Alpha, I wasn't talking about Mr Suarez, I was talking about the Mage that has been screeching like a banshee all night long. Nikki is in your hospital right now. And after her involvement in Melanie's accident, I cannot keep her here. I don't want to.*

Nikki is in my hospital? Am I hearing this right? I quickly organise help for Max to move Melanie into his apartment, while also hoping Max has cleared this with Melanie.

I then call the hospital manager. First, I arrange for Eva to be assessed and scanned, and then I enquire about Nikki.

"She was brought in last night by Lieutenant Amber. She's dying, Alpha."

I need to talk to Amber, and I growl in frustration. There is never a settled moment. Not even just a little five minutes to exhale and bask in the last triumph before something else starts up. It's only going to increase now that I have agreed to be Alpha over the Moon Stone too.

It's a surprise to find Alpha Xavier and Luna Lydia are at my hospital when I arrive. Is there any fucker not in my hospital right now?

I need to get my ducks in line. My duties have been neglected for long enough. I need to take back control and be the Alpha I was born to be and, with my new Luna at my side, nothing will tear me down.

*** Xavier ***

My son is dead and although he was difficult and idiotic, my heart is destroyed thinking of the little boy I helped learn to ride a bike and of the young man I encouraged through his first shift. The tiny baby I cradled in my arms moments after he entered the world.

There is no doubt in my mind that he is dead. His new mate's suffering confirms what we suspect and, despite the trouble she has caused, I am devastated that she is having to endure another bond breaking because of the untimely death of her mate, especially now she is carrying his pups.

Twins. The last set of twins born into my family were my younger sisters. The only thing that seems to be keeping my

Lydia going at the moment is the thought of Junior's pups, the future generation. She wants to move Nikki in with us so we can help her raise the babies, but Nikki has not coped with the breaking of the second mate bond in such a short period of time. The healers say she is dying and not even the promise of her babies can save her. Her heart and soul are irreparably damaged, and Nikki is already starting to fade.

"We can try to keep her comfortable and alive until her babies are born, but there are no guarantees she'll make it to a viable gestation." Despite the doctor's warning, we have to try. These little pups are all we have left of our son, and they now represent our hope for the future. I don't know if Lydia will survive without this.

"I know now isn't a good time, but we need to keep her under guard, she won't be able to break her curse on our pack until after she's had her babies. By then, it might be too late and we would have to complete the only other ritual that would break the curse." Amber squirms uncomfortably as she explains. I know she doesn't like having to discuss this as Nikki slowly and painfully fades from this life.

I decide to request a meeting with Aiden and my daughter to discuss all our findings and to finally combine the packs. I can't do this anymore. My heart can't take much more of it.

Luckily, Aiden has finally been briefed on what has been going on while he has been caring for my daughter and is ready to get the ball moving as soon as possible.

By the end of this week, I hope to relinquish my position and concentrate on rebuilding some sort of ordinary world for me, my mate and hopefully the grandpups that will come to us.

CHAPTER EIGHTEEN

Looking Forward

*** **Amber** ***

Aiden summons me, telling me I better have a good fucking reason for bringing Nikki to our hospital. I quickly mindlink Preston to back me up that I had to bring her here. Aiden might not see it that way, but I had to!

Preston laughs at me through our mindlink. *You are not scared of your brother. I've watched you two fight and you've pinned him plenty of times but if you need me, I'm all yours.* A few months ago, I would have told Preston I wasn't scared of Aiden and that I would fight him if he shouted at me, but I'm okay with admitting now that I want my mate's support.

Unless you want me sporting black eyes for our Mating Ceremony tomorrow, get your sexy ass over here now! Now I know I'm pushing my luck because Aiden would never physically hurt me, and even if he did my eyes would be healed within an hour, but I want my mate.

Preston, as always, comes to my rescue. "Why is he pissed with you?" I realise just in time that Preston is likely to be pissed with me too for bringing Nikki here.

"Actually, you can go on home. I can handle Aiden, don't worry about it. I'll be home later," I bluster at him as I push him away.

Preston grabs my arms to stop me, "What's going on, Red? That was a quick 180 turn."

Before I can gently explain about Nikki, I hear Gamma Max behind me. "Beta Preston, can I have a word, please? I am not happy about your mate bringing that monstrosity into the hospital while my mate is still recovering."

Preston glares at me. *You didn't! Tell me you didn't bring Nikki the nut job back here, Amber.* I avoid his eyes, knowing I will see hurt and disappointment there.

"Please try to understand. I felt bad for killing her mate, worse than bad. She's going crazy with grief because of me, Preston. I can only guess how much pain she is in. I nearly lost you and I thought the pain was going to kill me." I chance a look at him and the passion burning in his eyes. "I know you all think I'm this hard-nosed ice queen, but she was heartbroken, Preston. I couldn't leave her like that."

Preston's weight crushes me against the wall, he pins my hands above my head and kisses me hard, and his hot breath sends shivers down my spine. In the background, I hear Gamma Max swearing under his breath as he walks away. "I don't think you are a hard-nosed ice queen. I know you are a fiery, bad-ass warrior with a heart of pure gold, no matter how much you tried to hide it. You are mine."

His pride warms my heart. "All yours, Preston." As we kiss again, I forget where we are and don't resist when Preston palms my breasts and pushes his hard erection into my tummy.

"Will you two get a room!" My brother's voice echoes throughout the hospital corridor. "Amber, why the fuck have you brought Nikki here?" He demands answers off me as he pushes Preston away from my embrace.

I explain everything to my brother and mate and even Gamma Max comes for a listen.

"So, she's pregnant and has lost a second mate and they're not sure she will survive it. When I heard she was pregnant, I knew I couldn't hurt her, and she wouldn't be able to break the curse while she is carrying. After she accepted my apology, I brought her here. She's just messed up like me." The three men stand staring at me, Preston winks at me and Max gives me a small nod and pats me on the shoulder.

"You did the right thing, Amber, I'm proud of you. I think we can all agree that we all would do irrational things if someone harmed our mates. I think you handled the whole situation perfectly." My heart swells at the pride in Aiden's voice. I did the right thing. I have always been a bit of a rebel, pushing the boundaries and flouting the stereotypes. Now, I am being me, just me and I am incredibly proud of how far I have come.

"Max, move Melanie to your apartment. You are right it's not fair for her to see Nikki here after what happened." Aiden and Max smile at each other.

"Maybe this will make persuading her to stay easier!" Max comments with a smirk, and for a moment, we all join his merriment.

"We have to get ready for our ceremony run-through. Do you need us here while you talk to Alpha Xavier, or will Eva be coming with you, Aiden?"

"Eva will want to discuss all this with her father, I'm sure, and I have a small matter of accepting his pack to sort out too. but you two go on. You've waited a long time for this." I bow to my Alpha but give my big brother a hug.

I need to go and prepare for tomorrow; I cannot wait to officially be joined with Preston now.

"Come on, Red, my parents are waiting for us." I take Preston's hand and happily walk away to plan our special day.

*** Max ***

Alpha Aiden and I stand and watch as Beta Preston takes his mate by the hand, and they walk away in their own little love bubble. "I can't believe he finally cracked her; she was a stubborn one, Alpha. I'm not sure I could have waited all that time."

My Alpha smiles at me. "I don't think we appreciated how hard it was for Preston until we found our own mates." I nod in agreement. It is killing me waiting for Melanie to catch up to the same place that I am at and it has not been that long for us. Preston waited years. I appreciate him in a whole new light now and I am happy that my friend is finally going to get his happy-ever-after.

"Are you two waiting for me? Sorry, Summer wanted to finish her drawing for Melanie to bring to her." My Luna walks down the corridor towards us with her little girl who is clasping onto her hand while waving a drawing in the other.

"No, you are just in time, a quick visit with Melanie, peek in on Alejandro who is insisting on going home today and then we have a meeting with your father." She gives a small nod and looks at Summer.

"I can watch her. I've missed my little charge." I wink at Summer, and she giggles as she runs towards the side room where Melanie is.

"No, she's going to be spending the day with Mrs Moore. They are helping with the catering. Isn't that right, Summer?" The little girl nods to her mum. "But don't worry, Gamma Max, you'll be getting lots of duties as soon as you are ready to return to my service."

That means a lot to me. After the accident, I couldn't help but analyse my own conduct. Had I been distracted or preoccupied by finding my mate? Should I have noticed faster that something was wrong? Could I have protected them both better? Everyone assured me afterwards that I did everything I could, but to have my Luna confirm she wants me back protecting her and her daughter gives me the peace of mind that nothing else could.

When we enter the room, my mate is sitting up in bed. She is starting to get a bit of colour back in her face. As soon as I see her, I want her. I want her so badly that my body aches, especially my heart.

I watch from the doorway as Melanie interacts with little Summer and a warm contentment fires up inside me. This could be a glimpse at my future. Me, my mate, and a little pup. I didn't realise how much I desired that, how primal that need was. Maybe it wasn't until now, until Melanie.

Eva hugs her friend and shows that she has a bag full of essentials for her. As they settle and talk, the Alpha and I take the little one for a walk to get some drinks.

"How is your mate now, Max?" I look at my Alpha, and I know I could talk to him about anything, and it would be kept between us.

"She's doing a lot better. She talked to her children and her body is slowly healing. We're getting to know each other. She's pretty incredible, to be honest." Aiden smiles at me knowingly. "She let me kiss her, I think she's starting to like me back."

"Yeah I saw you kissing her, Gamma, remember." I laugh as my face turns crimson. I had been so caught up in the moment that everything else around us ceased to exist.

"I want more, I want everything with her, but she's been through hell and back, so I know I have to bide my time and be patient. I stopped looking for my mate years ago. I cannot believe she's finally here."

"Before I met Eva, I used to think of my potential mate as someone who worked for me. They would have my pups and raise them. But as for anything else, I could never picture it. Maybe that was because I never saw my father with my mother. When Eva came into my life, my whole world changed, she became the centre of it. She wasn't just an addition to my life: she is the be all, end all and absolutely everything to me. I guess you know what I mean now?"

His words ring true to me now as my mate is also the centre of my world. I'm finding it hard to remember a time before her. "Yes, I know exactly what you mean. How do I win her over? I don't just mean how do I get her into bed… I want that too of course. But how do I get her to be mine?"

Aiden thinks over my question before he answers. "You know what Eva went through with her ex-husband? And you know that he was also Melanie's lover and if she suffered anything like Eva did at his hands then she is going to need to see that you will treat her better." He pauses before carrying on. "I tried to show Eva what life with me could be like. I agreed to dating, didn't rush her to bed and basically spent the time listening to her and getting to know her."

I nod and thank him for his counsel.

"There is no rush, Max, make sure your mate knows that. After all, you aren't going anywhere."

After my talk with Aiden, I know exactly what to do to win Melanie's heart, and how to secure our future together. There are no shortcuts; this is too important for there to be a quick fix. But as he rightly pointed out, I have all the time in the world. No matter how long it takes, I'll be right here trying to win her heart.

When the Alpha and Luna go to visit their other friend, I sit at the side of Melanie's bed. "I'm taking you home to care for you there. Is that okay, Honey?" She nods to me. Her eyes are like orbs, startled and unbelieving. "I want to show you what a future with me could look like. I want to show you how I will look after you, love you and build a life with you. I want you to know that this is real, and it's for always and there is nothing I won't do to make you happy."

"Max, this is so quick. I want to let you in, you've already shown me what a kind and gentle man you are. I want to try. I want you too." I kiss her, I let her have the sweet, gentle kisses this time and after a couple of minutes my hands and face are wet from her tears.

"Don't cry. I promise, I won't let anyone hurt you. I am going to cherish you and worship you because you are my Goddess now. You are everything to me."

"I just need to be sure this is right. I have made such a mess up of my life so far. I don't want to mess this up too. So, yes I'll come and stay at your home, but I still need time. Can you live with that, Max?"

I am actually looking forward to the chase.

*** **Alejandro** ***

My leg burns and itches to the point that amputation starts to seem like the better option. "Ale, stop bloody itching it, you are going to tear the stitches." I groan in frustration as my wife chastises me.

I'm stuck in a tiny hospital bed in a room that smells like

cleaning fluids. I want to go home and get in my own bed with my wife. Just the thought of being with Salma in bed is like a tonic. That would help me recover faster.

"Once Eva and Aiden have come to see us, I will arrange for us to go home. I want to go home too. I need to decompress and I want my ice-cream."

The change in Salma is refreshing to see. Now that her father's death has been avenged, the anger that had been burning a hole through her has receded. She is the Salma I fell for from afar, the badass, acid-tongued princess who wears her heart on her sleeve and she is all mine. The grief is still there but the bitterness and annoyance isn't as prominent anymore.

"Do you think you'll be able to come back tomorrow for the Mating Ceremony?" I know Salma is really looking forward to witnessing the ceremony but I'm not sure if it's a good idea.

I hate disappointing Sal, but I don't want to fabricate anything either. "Chula, I feel like a bag of shite. Let's head home and if I feel better in the morning, I'll bring you back for the ceremony."

"Hello, peg leg!" Eva comes into the room with Aiden and Summer and her teasing greeting makes me laugh.

"Hello, Wolf girl, have you been in any dungeons lately?" She laughs at my quick reply, and I smile when Summer looks at me with concern.

"Ale got sick?" she asks Sal with tears forming in her eyes.

"Oh no, sunshine girl. Silly Ale hurt his leg, but the doctor fixed it and it will be all better soon, won't it, Ale?" I nod my head to the curious little girl who eyes my sore leg.

"Sally kiss it better," Summer commands. She points between Sal and my leg until Sal gets down and kisses my leg gently. Summer claps her hands gleefully. "All better now."

Salma's kisses could make me better, I am sure of it… she might have to kiss other parts of my body too, just in case.

"Thank you both for allowing Ale to be treated so fast and for saving his leg and his life. We won't forget this."

It's the first time Salma has spoken about how bad things could have gotten. I now feel awful for making her worry so much. I owe her a massive apology and I have some serious making up to do.

"Our private ambulance will be here soon, and our doctor can take over Ale's care from here, but we both cannot tell you how grateful we are and will always be. Thank you."

Our transport arrives and Aiden, Eva and little Summer wave us off from the door of the hospital. I wave back, happy in the knowledge that I am going home.

"Chula, listen, I'm sorry. I didn't realise how worried you were. I won't do anything like that ever again, I promise."

She kisses me hard, pushing me back. "Shhh. The Donna wants to please her Don… You can make it up to me by lying back and enjoying this."

Who am I to refuse my Donna? My Salma opens my pants and my cock bursts out. Standing proud and loud, ready for her. "Sal, fuck, that feels good!" She strokes me firmly along my hard shaft, and with her free hand, she cups my sensitive balls.

"You were very naughty, Don Alejandro Suarez. You almost left me here with no husband. No child. Nothing. All I could think of is every wasted opportunity I had to do exactly what I wanted but I never did. It taught me that life is too short. I want to ride you right here, right now." Her hand is moving faster now, up and down over my length that strains for more.

I drag her forward towards me. "Spread your legs now," I

demand, and with a smile she slowly slides her legs apart, giving me free access to her wet core. I quickly push her panties to the side, find her clit and wait for her sweet little moan that tells me she likes how I am touching her. When I hear it, I release a tiny bit of precum in excitement.

"I need to ride you, Ale, I need you inside me while I grind on top of you." She climbs up onto my bed and straddles me. As my hard dick probes her wet entrance, she pants with her raw need. We both groan loudly as she slides down my cock. The friction between us is immense, it takes all my control not to blow as I feel her stroking my length deep inside her as she writhes on top of me.

"Fuck! Slow down Sal or I'm going to blow," I warn her, trying desperately to hold onto whatever remnants of control I have left.

"Yes, Ale. Yes, don't stop." I continue to flick her clit as she grinds on me and within seconds she falls apart in my arms as she finds fulfilment. I let myself lose control too and thrust up one last time as I explode deep inside my love. "If you ever nearly die again, Alejandro, I will fucking kill you. Do you understand?"

"I understand," I groan out at her, still pouring myself inside her. "I promise you, Donna, I promise I will never ever do anything without consulting you first. I love you, Chula."

She rests against my chest, still joined to me. "I love you too, Alejandro, more than I could ever tell you. Now, let's go home."

*** **Eva** ***

After waving off Salma and Alejandro, Mrs Moore comes to collect Summer so we can go and speak to my father and stepmother. They are sitting in the side room with Nikki, who is rigid and pale in the bed between them.

I go directly to my stepmother and hug her and express my sorrow at her loss. I didn't know or like my half-brother, but I know she will be devastated as his mother and that is all that matters right now. She has supported me so much in the short time I have known her. I want to support her and my dad now.

"Oh, Eva, thank you so much for coming to see us." Ever the gracious host and faultless Luna, Lydia greets us as I hug her.

"I am so sorry for your loss. If there is anything we can do, please tell us." I know it's just the obligatory thing people say but I don't know what to do to help them, so if I offer my services and support, they know I am willing to do anything to aid them through this.

I go to my father and hug him too. "I'm so sorry, Dad." He kisses my forehead as he blinks back tears.

"Nikki here is carrying twin pups, they are Junior's. They mated and marked each other while they were on the run. When he... he... passed, her fragile mind was broken. The healers say she is dying and all we can do is hold on to see if she can get the pups to a viable stage. We want to raise the pups. Whether Nikki survives or not, they are our family." I smile at the massive, bulky man who is a gentle soul really.

"Of course, Alpha Xavier, you will have our full support with that. We both hope you can get the pups to a viable stage and can raise them in lieu of their biological parents. They are lucky to have you." Aiden pauses and I know it's because of the subject matter. He's worried about being insensitive, but this needs to be addressed. "What we are concerned about is that Nikki agreed to break the curse she placed on my pack before Junior died. If she is not able to because of her pregnancy, and now because she is dying, I need to request her heart if she doesn't survive. This affects mine and Eva's baby too, your grandpup. You know this is needed although I appreciate it is in poor taste. However, I have to secure the future of my pup and pack too."

My father stands and I wince slightly at the two Alphas standing face-to-face. "Son, I want to transfer the pack today. I don't want to be Alpha anymore. Whatever you command once you become the Alpha of the Moon Stone too, we will do. I have no objections to your request. I know what needs to be done."

My father holds his hand out to my mate and they shake hands on not only what happens with Nikki, but about the future of the pack too.

"So, you still want Summer to be named as the Alpha Heir?" I ask my father. I don't know if having Junior's pups changes things for them.

"Yes, of course I do. She is your eldest child; you are my eldest child, and she is also my eldest grandchild. The land recognises you and it will recognise Summer too."

I thank them both and agree to go to the Moon Stone for the Handing Over ceremony and Alpha Anointment.

"We want to move Nikki to our facilities as soon as the healers say it is safe. Until she delivers the pups and breaks the curse, she will be under full guard. Is that okay with you both?" Lydia asks. I nod to my stepmother, and we smile at each other.

We say our goodbyes and tell them we will see them this evening. Hopefully, Nikki will be moved by then too.

"Shortie, there is something I want to show you before we go back home." Aiden covers my eyes with his big hands, the tingles from our bond work their way throughout my body. He guides me down the path. "It's not 100% ready yet, it needs your finishing touches but we should be settled in by the time the new baby arrives.

My heart skips as I realise what he is showing me. He lifts his hands and, for the first time in a long time, I see our cottage. The roof is repaired, the windows and doors have been replaced, the garden has been planted and there is a ribbon wrapped around the front door.

"Want to see inside?" he asks me, and it warms my heart that he is nervous of showing me. This must mean a great deal to Aiden.

"Of course, I do. This is our forever home, Aiden. Thank you for doing this, I love you so much, Alpha." His eyes flash black in desire before he takes my hand again.

"I love you too, my Luna."

*** Preston ***

The day is finally here. I wear my suit and smartly polished shoes. My hair is slicked back, and I've even had a wash. My parents tell me I scrub up well. I hope I make them proud today as I make my commitment to Amber and to our future.

Our pack Shaman and the Elders all take part in the ritual that bonds me and Amber together for all eternity in the light of the Moon Goddess. We've already mated and marked each other, but now our wolves get to seal their commitment to each other too.

Amber mindlinked me about an hour ago in a bit of a tizz. *Your mama is curling my hair and is clipping little pink flowers in it, Preston. It's a good job I love you or I would be scarpering right now. I'm a warrior, for fuck's sake.* Although I laugh, I am also relieved that the two most important women in my life are getting along. Even though Amber is grumbling about the hair situation, I also know that deep down she is happy to have my mum's help and support today and for the future too.

"Are you nervous?" my Alpha and future brother-in-law asks me and, in all honesty, I'm not. I don't have a smidge of doubt about my love for Amber. My only regret is not doing this a very long time ago.

"No, not even a tiny bit. I have wanted this for the longest time. I am beyond excited. I cannot wait to make my declaration." Aiden smiles as he pats me on the back.

"I couldn't have asked for a better mate for my little sister. I wish you both all the luck and happiness in the world. Look after her, Beta, like you've always wanted to." We embrace as friends. Friends who have been through hell and back together and are both here living to tell the tale and both within reach of our happy-ever-after.

"I will, you know I will." Aiden's eyes glaze over, and he tells me Amber is ready. My parents join me on stage and Aiden leaves to collect Amber.

"We are both mighty proud of you, son." My father, the tough-talking, formidable former-Beta, has tears in his eyes as he finally watches me claim my mate.

"She looks gorgeous, Preston, an absolute stunner." I'm about to tell my mum that Amber is always gorgeous, but when she steps into the ceremony room linking arms with her brother, my breath catches in my throat.

Amber walks towards me, tall and lithe. Her skin sparkles and her red hair is curled and cascades down her back. Her eyes are bright and clear, her face is flawless. She is wearing a white and gold floor-length gown, she looks otherworldly, like an ethereal goddess sent for me to worship. A lump forms in my throat as she slowly makes her way to the stage. I am in disbelief that this is finally happening.

Aiden whispers to Amber and she nods to him, and he holds

her hand as they climb the steps together. As she approaches me, my heartbeat accelerates. This is it; she is going to be mine and I am hers. Aiden places his sister's hand in mine.

"I wish you both good health and fortune for your lives together. May the Moon Goddess bless you both and this union."

Amber's hand trembles in mine. This woman has taken on men twice her size, has battled and brawled with the best of them and yet she is shaking right in front of me.

Nervous, Red? I mindlink while looking into her eyes.

Just a little bit. Don't let me fall over, will you? The whole audience, my parents, our Alpha all disappear. It's just me and my mate, and the Shaman who conducts the ceremony.

I will never let you fall. I will always be there to catch you and support you. I love you, I tell her honestly.

She stares, mesmerised, into my eyes. *I love you too.*

As we finish reciting our vows and make our blood promise, the pack cheers and applauds us. I am overjoyed when I feel the binds that tie us together strengthening and tightening. I kiss my mate to the chagrin of our congregation, and I am astonished when I see the tears of joy streaking her face. "I'm sorry I made you wait so long, Preston."

"You are worth the wait. Thank you for finally making an honest man out of me, Red."

Later, we will shift so our wolves can finally mate and mark each other, and our bond will be solidified then. But for now, we go and celebrate with our friends and family. At last, she is mine.

*** Aiden ***

Eva is a blubbering mess by the end of Amber and Preston's ceremony. I laugh at her as she blames her tears on her hormones. I cannot help but kiss her on her temple as she wipes away her happy tears. "Oh, Aiden, I can't wait to have our Mating Ceremony now. That was incredible. It was so touching and beautiful and meaningful."

It has been my hope that once Eva saw a ceremony, she would be more willing to make that commitment to me, and it looks like my plan is working. "As soon as our pup is born, and you can shift, we'll have ours too. We could do your Luna Ceremony before then, though." I have no qualms about naming Eva my Luna before our official mating ceremony. Yesterday, her father named me Alpha of the Moon Stone in her stead. This pack is officially half hers now.

My lovely little mate is bubbling over with excitement. Now that all her manifestations are healing, Eva has been able to move forward. She is able to feel happiness, and plan for a fulfilling future. Her contentment becomes my joy. Her pleasure is mine. I've never been as happy as I am right now, and Eva is the catalyst for that. She has become my everything.

We take the short walk to the stage to congratulate the happy couple, but on our way we see Max and Melanie. I am extremely proud of my pack for the way they have welcomed Max's mate and taken her under their wing. It would have been hard for any other human to infiltrate my pack. I remember bringing Eva home when we still didn't know she was a werewolf and the reception she got was frosty at best. The news had spread quickly that Melanie was injured protecting Summer, and the pack had instantly become indignant on her and Max's behalf.

Melanie has been adopted by the pack because bravery and loyalty speak volumes to us. We always look after and protect our own, and Melanie is one of us now.

"Don't they look happy and cute together?" Eva whispers to me, and I agree with her, because they look extremely happy with one another and like a couple that had been together for years, not just a couple of weeks. Summer runs to give her auntie Mel a cuddle before returning to us asking for an "up" from me.

To the side of the room are Salma and Alejandro. Sal has also brought her little brother Ricky, who chats away animatedly to Ale.

Despite having had life-saving surgery on his leg, Ale is walking with just a cane and his gait is hardly affected at all. He is obviously stronger and a faster healer than most other humans, or maybe his nurse has something to do with his fast recovery? Whatever has made the difference, it is good to see them both up and about. They actually look like a proper little family now with little Ricky in the mix too.

Once we have congratulated Amber and Preston, we will go to Sal and Ale so they don't feel alone in a room full of werewolves.

We reach Amber and Preston and I hug them both. "Congratulations, I am so proud of you both."

Eva kisses them both on the cheek. "It was such a beautiful service. I cried all the way through." They laugh along with my mate, but I know they are touched by her honest affection.

We each take a drink. I take a flute of champagne, but Eva and Summer have to settle on orange juice and we join Sal and Ale as we make a toast to the mated couple.

"Mine!" I hear from a voice that has no business making a claim on anyone. "Mine!"

"She's been listening to you too much, Aiden!" Eva admonishes me. "She's going around thinking she can claim anyone and everyone she wants." I laugh as I scoop up my little girl.

"Hey, who are you claiming, Sunshine Girl?" She giggles as I tickle her, but when I stop, she points right at Ricky, Sal's younger brother, and repeats her claim.

"Mine!" Her voice is so steady and sure that I don't know what to say in response. It does make me wonder, though, what will happen in the future? Is this Summer feeling a pull? Could Ricky really be her mate? I make a mental note to ask Preston if he felt anything for Amber before the bond presented itself.

I stand up as Alpha and call for everyone's attention before making the first toast. "To Beta Preston and Lieutenant Amber, I wish you both a long, happy, healthy, fertile, and wealthy union that stands the test of time. To true love."

I kiss Eva, my true love, and thank her for being mine. In a short period of time, she has gone from being an abused married human to a powerful Alpha Heir and now to the future Luna, who is blessing me with my own Alpha Heir too.

When I used to picture the future, I never saw myself as a happily mated man with a family. I had to meet the love of life first. The Moon Goddess above knows my Eva was well worth the wait.

EPILOGUE

~~~ Three Months Later ~~~

*** Melanie ***

Today is Eva's baby shower and I have been helping with the preparations. The place looks beautiful with pink, white and rose-gold decorations all around. We are having a traditional English afternoon tea party in the gardens and the weather is perfect for it. Plenty of people are attending and Eva is glowing.

"Thank you all so much for coming to help me celebrate, it won't be long until this little madam is joining us too." I smile at my friend and Luna as she rubs her tummy, she has a perfectly oval little bump and a pang of longing rushes up inside me.

I moved here three months ago to be with Max but little has happened between us since then. We have kissed and we share a bed and a home together, but that is as far as it goes and I am starting to believe he has changed his mind about me. Sometimes, he can be really short with me, and he seems so grumpy now when he has always appeared so patient and understanding before.

I think I need to bite the bullet and ask him outright if he has gone off me. I want to take things further, I want to commit to him, I want to have sex... I want to have his children, but if anything, Max couldn't care less.

Eva comes and sits at the table with me, Amber and Sal. "How is my little niece doing in there?" Amber asks Eva.

"She's using my bladder as a trampoline. I don't remember Summer being this active." Amber laughs at her sister-in-law.

"What did you expect? This time the pup you're carrying has two Alpha werewolf parents. Of course, she's strong and active... Aren't you, Coral?" Amber talks to Eva's bump affectionately. "I can't wait to start trying, too."

"I'm so sick in the morning I can't seem to get anything done. When does the sickness pass, Eva? I can't do this for another seven months." Salma's usual tan complexion has a green hue to it at the moment. She recently discovered she is also expecting.

"I wasn't really sick, I had a bit of nausea but I think it should pass soon, Sal. Just hold on in there, it'll be worth it." The normally glamorous and gorgeous Salma is looking tired and worn out since finding out she is going to be a mother soon.

"Well, I am so jealous of you both. I want to be pregnant too." Amber looks wistfully at her own flat tummy.

"You two will be next, I promise," Eva assures us with authority. I would feel comforted by that, but for me to get pregnant I would have to have sex with Max and Max hasn't so much as touched me for weeks now.

"I know Preston is right, it's the responsible thing to do to wait until the curse is broken before trying, but it's all I have thought about since our Mating Ceremony."

"Are you waiting for the curse to break too, Mel?" Salma asks me directly and my face heats up with embarrassment.

"Not intentionally, no. I don't think Max is interested in me in that way anymore." It stings my pride when Amber bursts into laughter.

"You are kidding, right? Melanie! He is head over heels in love with you. I'm sure if you told him you are ready to try for a baby, he would be delighted by all the extra mating."

"We haven't mated. We haven't done more than kiss. I think he's gone off me. I'm scared to talk to him about it because… I'm in love with him, I want to be with him, and I love living here. What if he doesn't want me anymore?" There is stunned silence around the table. When I lift my head to look at them, the three of them look back at me in shock.

"Melanie, this is a big miscommunication. I know for a fact that Max wants you. I can smell it whenever he sees you or is near you. He is crazy about you. He might be just about the dumbest wolf on the block for not realising you feel this way, but sometimes we have to take the wolf by the tail. Tell him. At least then you'll know either way."

"Besides, if he's stupid enough to turn you down, the pack will kick him out and keep you instead." I laugh at Eva's interjection.

Before long, the men return to the baby shower and, despite my reservations about his feelings for me, Max stands behind me and places his hands on my shoulders and whispers. "You look beautiful, Honey, did you have a good time?"

I nod to him. "Yes, it was lovely. I'm tired now though, can we go home please?" We say our goodbyes and Max takes my hand as we walk back to the packhouse.

As soon as we approach our apartment, Max becomes rigid again. "Actually, I need to go and work out so I'll just drop you in here and see you tonight." He attempts to place a chaste kiss on my cheek, but I pull away.

"Please, come in, I need to talk to you." If he didn't look so comical, I would be offended, but Max... the big overgrown Gamma werewolf who is around double my size, is looking for a way out, his eyes fill with panic. Why is he so afraid of being alone with me?

"I do have to train. I have to keep strong to protect my Luna," he reiterates as he backs up away from me.

"I think I should move back to my house. You obviously can't stand to be in the same room as me. I don't know what changed but... I can't do this."

I run into the apartment and shut the door behind me before bursting into tears. My little bubble has popped and now I must move back home and the man I thought cared for me is just letting me walk away.

"Like fuck you're leaving me!"

I didn't hear him come in, but I hear him now. Max is furious! He stands in the doorway with a scowl that would frighten the devil himself. I pull out the suitcase from under our bed and start pulling my clothes from the wardrobe.

"Why are you leaving me? What did I do? Tell me and I will fix it." I don't reply because I think it's too late, he's only here offering to fix stuff because I've made a scene.

"It's okay, Max, I get it. You don't want me any longer. You can't even bear to be in the same room as me for long. I had hoped that I was wrong, and that you could feel for me the way I feel for you, but I guess I was wrong."

"Melanie, I don't have a clue what is going on. Have I done something wrong? I don't want you to leave. I never want you to leave me." Why does he have to confuse me so much? First, he can't stand to be near me and now, he's begging me to stay.

"I hardly see you, you're always running away from me and I want to start moving things along between us, but if anything, we've never been so far apart." Tears threaten to engulf me once again, but I stand my ground. Having lived with werewolves for the past three months, I have learned that if you want something you have to grab it and I want Max. I want Max to want me.

"What do you mean... move things along?" I groan and cover my face; he's going to make me explain in-depth. I don't know if he really is that dense or if he likes to watch me squirm.

"Become a proper couple Max, you know, sexually. You say you want a pup, but how are we going to achieve that if we hardly even kiss?" I front it out as much as I can, but then I lower my crimson face. I have never felt so embarrassed.

"Are you ready to mate? Is that what you're telling me?" Yep. He is definitely dense. I can't front this any longer. I let down my walls and look him in the eyes.

"Yes. I love you, Max. I'm in love with you and I want the future you painted for me when I moved here. But you've been so distant, I hardly see you and when you're here... you're not here, not mentally anyway. So, if you've changed your mind, that's okay but you need to let me know so I'm not sitting here day after day hoping and wishing for something that isn't going to happen."

"You love me?" I nod to him. There's no point in denying it, it must be obvious to everyone else apart from Max that I have fallen in an epic way for him. "And you're ready to take things to the next stage?" I nod again.

A massive smile covers his face as he strides towards me.

"Then what the fuck are we waiting for?"

I frown at him, but he takes my face in his hands and kisses me, he scrapes his teeth over my bottom lip and slips his tongue in, deepening our kiss. A fire ignites inside me, one I thought had long been extinguished, and I squeal a little as Max lifts me and carries me to the bed.

"I have been distant. I have tried to keep a distance between us because I want you so badly, but I needed to be patient. I needed to give you time to be ready. I have been in love with you since the moment we met. I will love you until my dying breath." He lifts the hem of my dress all the way up and over my head, leaving me standing in my bra and panties. "Fuck! You are stunning!"

I leap into his arms, returning his kisses. I frantically unbutton his shirt while he kicks off his shoes and unbuttons his pants. We embrace again, our bodies intertwining and I moan as I enjoy the feel of his skin against mine. "I wake up in the night while you are sleeping and have to take a cold shower because I need you, I want you, I want to be inside you, I want to become one entity with you and I want to please you until all you can remember is me, and the feel of me.

I unclasp my bra and let it fall away and in less than a second Max is cupping my breasts. My nipples harden under his touch and he groans before licking each of them in turn. I whimper in response. It feels so good and yet I want more, more of Max all over my body.

I run my hands down his body. I have seen him naked a couple of times and I know he has an incredible body and a cock that matches his physique. I have fantasised about how he will fill me up as he presses into me, reaching places that have never been reached before. I skim my hand over the bulge in his underwear and he groans loudly when I do. "Word of warning, it's been a while and I have been dreaming about us for months."

I smile back at him. A few short minutes ago, I thought he was happy I was going to walk away from him, and now I find he was dreaming of being with me too.

He slips his hands between my legs and touches me expertly. I have never been with a man who was both talented and giving in the bedroom. Most were just wham, bam and thank you ma'am. I think that is about to change.

I moan as he grazes his fingertips on my clit, rubbing my gathering wetness over it. I pull down his underwear and as I fall to my knees to take him in my mouth, he pulls me up to him, pulling off my panties as he does. "Not today. Today, all I want is you, I want to feel you. I want us. I wanna hear you shout my name as I make you cum over and over and over."

I clench my legs together, whimpering with need and desire. Max applies a small amount of pressure to my clit and my body climbs higher to oblivion. I've never cum as fast as I might today. "Wrap your legs around me, Honey." He is on top of me, his manhood pressed against my core. "Shit, I just remembered. Condoms. Do you have any?" I shake my head.

"I don't want a condom, Max. We both know what we want." He nods his agreement as he lines up with my entrance.

"Melanie, sweetheart, I love you. I have wanted this for so long. I want this forever." He pushes into me, filling and stretching me just as I knew he would before he stops inside me. "I'm not going to last long, you feel too good!" I giggle a little, and he laughs with me.

Max moves his hand back down between us, he pounds away inside me, edging me closer and closer to fulfilment, the added pressure to my clit is all I need, and I shout his name as I cum just like he asked me to.

"Fuck, yeah! Cum for me," he shouts and then groans as he cums too.

"Was that what you meant by moving forward?" Max asks me afterwards as I bask in the glow of our lovemaking.

"That was just the first step, Max. I want so much more with you."

"Good, now we can talk about our Mating Ceremony."

*** Xavier ***

I have a lot of pent-up anger and grief and my mate tells me I have to do something about it. So, I do. There are some old scores to settle and the first one takes me to the South of France, to the home of my daughter's ex-stepfather.

"Claude Duvall?" I ask as a tall, greying man answers the door. He nods to me, frowning in confusion at the English man who had turned up out of nowhere. "Good. This is for touching what you shouldn't."

I dislocate both of his shoulders before breaking both of his wrists while he screams in agony. "And this is for looking where you shouldn't too." I flip him over and jab a pen into each of his eyes. "My daughter is Eva. You made her feel unsafe. You looked at her and touched her. Now I'm going to cut your cock off. And if you tell a soul who did it I will come back and cut your throat too."

"Please no, don't do this. Not my cock!"

The fact that I am avenging my daughter makes this all worthwhile. It gives me an outlet for my grief and maybe now I can look forward to the birth of my grandchildren without the grief and guilt that consumed me at the moment.

Claude screeches and squirms in agony as I enforce the toll on him for messing with me and mine.

~~~ Six Months Later ~~~

*** **Eva** ***

I hold the two little girls in my arms, my nieces. Lydia called them Hope and Serenity because their mother, Nikki, died as they were pulled into the world. They are tiny. My own little girl, Coral, was born around the same time and is double their size. My heart fills with pride when I think of our little girl: big, bright green eyes like her daddy and chestnut hair like me. A perfect mix of us both. Summer adores her little sister, who we named after Aiden's mother as he requested.

"They are so delicate and petite, I'm terrified of breaking them," I tell Lydia, who smiles down at me and her granddaughters.

"I know, they are almost four weeks old, and they are still little dots. I caught your father singing to them last night. They wouldn't settle and I was exhausted, so he told me to have a sleep and he would look after them. I found him about an hour later. The girls were looking at him like he was an alien and he just kept singing at them."

I smile at her. Although my father and stepmother are both

still heartbroken and grieving, Junior's little girls have given them both something to carry on for.

"We are all sorted, Shortie; we can go home when you're ready." Aiden tells me as he enters the room again.

"Did you burn the heart?" He nods his head at me and holds up a small glass vial.

"Yes, these are the ashes. I'm going to take them home and find a decent hiding place for them." The curse is broken, the only thing that could affect it is if the ashes are released. We have to do all we can to ensure that never happens. Nikki had become too weak, and too far gone mentally. Her babies were born prematurely when she began to die. We couldn't get her to break the curse for us before she died, so we had to perform the heart-burning ritual. Now, it is our lifelong job to keep these ashes safe and secure.

"It's over now. We can all go back to living our lives as we should," Aiden tells me as we travel back to our cottage and our own little girls. Everything worked out in one sense or another. Life is good.

~~~ The End ~~~

STAY IN TOUCH

Sign up for my Newsletter on my brand new website:

Emma Lee-Author: Up and Coming Indie Romance Author (emmalee-johnson.com)

The one-stop place for all my information.

Follow me on Amazon:

http://viewauthor.at/emmaleejohnson

Follow me on social media for exclusive content and updates.

Facebook: Emma Lee (Emma Lee-Johnson)
 Emma Lee-Johnson | Facebook (Profile)

 Emma Lee-Johnson | Facebook (Page)

Author Group: Emma's Angels with Attitude

(14) Emma's Angels with Attitude | Facebook

Instagram: author.emma.lee

TikTok: @emmaleejohnsonauthor

BOOKS BY THIS AUTHOR

The Alpha's Property

Book 1 in the Onyx River Series

Festive Flings

Keep a look out for my steamy christmas offering, coming soon.

** Disclaimer This book is of a seriously hot nature, reported side effects include involuntary kegels and spontaneous pantie-wetting incidents. Read at your own risk... and pleasure! **

A christmas book for all year round.

ACKNOWLEDGEMENT

There are many people I would like to thank for encouraging and supporting me. In the first instance, my husband and sons for putting up with me, for the copious amounts of tea (and cake!) and for always making me feel happy, loved and secure. You four are my reason and inspiration, love you all the world, and more

To my Broom Bitches- there are too many of you to name but you know who you are and I love each and every one of you. Thank you for the laughs and for keeping my spirits up and my feet firmly on the ground.

My books would be pointless without readers, and I have been fortunate enough to have plenty of readers who have positively challenged me and supported me in equal doses. I have my own posse now, in the form of : Emma's Angels with Attitude, my very own motley crue! To all my Angels with Attitude, you are amazing and I am very grateful for your support.

Last but by no means least I want to once again, send love and acknowledgement to my very dear friend and fellow author, **Melody Tyden**. I have no doubt that Melody is destined for big things. She is not only a talented writer, she has morality and tenacity in abundance. Thank you for everything you have done for me, Melody I will be forever in your debt. (You still owe me a muffin though!) Check out her romance novels on Amazon, you wont regret it.
Melody's link:
viewauthor.at/melodytyden

RECOMMENDED PLAYLIST

1. Physical- Dua Lipa
2. Need You Tonight- INXS
3. Sex on Fire- Kings of Leon
4. Adore You- Harry Styles
5. It Feels So Good- Sonique
6. I Shall Believe- Sheryl Crow
7. She Drives Me Crazy- Fine Young Criminals
8. Try- Pink
9. Let Me Love You- DJ Snake, Justin Bieber
10. Fighter- Christina Aguilera
11. You've Got The Love- Florence + The Machine

https://open.spotify.com/playlist/2qkU8sdJ5Oj7vtJStjAvfE?

Coming soon from Emma Lee Johnson:

~*~ The Smuttiest Christmas Story of the Year! ~*~

Festive Flings:

Jamie Knowles is facing a Christmas all alone after her childhood sweetheart dumped her for another woman. Until she realises for the first time in her adult life she is very single and ready to mingle. She may be ready to find something new but has the man of her dreams always been right in front of her?

Jamie's older sister Billie is married with children but both her and her husband can feel the spark fading. In order to save their marriage, they decide to spice things up both in and out of the bedroom as a Christmas present to one another.

Jamie's work colleague and friend Tim has a particular taste in women. In the past he has worried about his friends' reactions. But when he meets a woman, one who ticks all his boxes, can they both be brave enough to take what they want?

Are you ready for fun, fetishes and frolicking and a few Festive Flings?